He brushed a thumb over my cheek and across my lips as if memorizing the contours of my face before he kissed my forehead. "I'll be back as soon as I can."

Then he let me go, turned on his heel, and left the shop. The Consortiu   And I was left w   wasn't going awa   nt me to investigate, and an appointment who tripped ___ gh the door staring wide-eyed after Alexei and carrying—gods help me—another dog.

PRAISE FOR *THE RULE OF LUCK*

"Imaginative. Fans of romance in science fiction are going to love this!"

—Kim Harrison, #1 *New York Times* bestselling author

"Cerveny's debut blends steamy sci-fi with breathless intrigue and action, all set on a far-future Earth that's equal parts fascinating and terrifying."

—Beth Cato, author of *The Clockwork Dagger* and
Breath of Earth

"A compelling and intriguing read built on a fascinating premise. Cerveny's future world is richly drawn, and Felicia and Alexei's adventure is definitely an edge-of-your-seat ride."

—Linnea Sinclair, award-winning author of the Dock Five
Universe series

"A fresh heroine pairs with a dangerous hero to confront nuanced and compelling ethical dilemmas...fast-paced, tightly plotted."

—*RT Book Reviews*

"A novel with depth...a terrific story."

—*The Qwillery*

BY CATHERINE CERVENY

THE FELICIA SEVIGNY NOVELS
The Rule of Luck
The Chaos of Luck

THE
CHAOS
OF
LUCK

A FELICIA SEVIGNY NOVEL: BOOK 2

CATHERINE CERVENY

orbit

www.orbitbooks.net

Copyright © 2016 by Catherine Cerveny
Excerpt from *Six Wakes* © 2017 by Mary Lafferty
Excerpt from *The Immortals* copyright © 2016 by Jordanna Max Brodsky

Author photograph by Ash Nayler Photography
Cover design by Lisa Marie Pompilio
Cover photos by Trevillion, Shutterstock
Cover copyright © 2017 by Hachette Book Group, Inc.

Orbit
Hachette Book Group
1290 Avenue of the Americas
New York, NY 10104
orbitbooks.net

Originally published in ebook by Redhook in December 2016
First Trade Paperback Edition: December 2017

Orbit is an imprint of Hachette Book Group.
The Orbit name and logo are trademarks of Little, Brown Book Group Limited.

The publisher is not responsible for websites (or their content) that are not owned by the publisher.

The Hachette Speakers Bureau provides a wide range of authors for speaking events. To find out more, go to www.hachettespeakersbureau.com or call (866) 376-6591.

Library of Congress Control Number: 2017952542

ISBNs: 978-0-316-51055-4 (trade paperback), 978-0-316-35552-0 (ebook)

Printed in the United States of America

LSC-C

10 9 8 7 6 5 4 3 2 1

To my parents, who never really got what the fuss was all about in the first place and couldn't understand why anyone would want to go to Mars since there wasn't any Disney World there, but supported me anyway.

I

It used to be that you didn't often see dogs on Mars. With the strict quarantine laws bordering on the ridiculous, and the month-and-a-half-long voyage from Earth, it was easier to clone one from the pet you'd left behind. However, that tended to be expensive when you'd already spent your life savings trying to get to Mars in the first place.

When the Tsarist Consortium took over the transit routes, they'd lobbied hard to abolish the quarantine—a move applauded throughout the tri-system. One Gov relented under pressure from just about everyone and now all sorts of pets were appearing on the once red planet. But still, the fact that I was seated across from a woman with a teacup Yorkie was actually pretty amazing, given I hadn't known the breed even existed. That the woman wanted me to run my Tarot cards and tell the future of said Yorkie was not. It took a concerted effort on my part not to sigh out loud or reach over to throttle the woman. Besides, I'd hate to upset the dog, who, though I was loath to admit it, really was a cutie.

"I'm sorry, but I don't do readings for dogs," I said, not for the first time that week. "I know Sunbeam is a member of your family, but that's not how the cards work."

The woman on the other side of my card reading table, Lila Chandler, was a potential new client. Definitely older, though only her eyes gave it away. They had a hardness to them that came from decades of Renew treatments and a lifestyle that said been there, done that, and had all the T-shirts. I would have put her around ninety, or maybe even a hundred. Otherwise, she was flawless with pale porcelain skin, blond hair cascading down her back, and luminous blue eyes—and *luminous* wasn't a word I threw around just for fun. And she was absolutely filthy rich. The kind of rich that got whatever it wanted and could afford to indulge in frivolous things most people would never think about. Like Tarot card readings for dogs apparently. Mars had two social classes—the ultra-rich and everybody else. I was still working out which class I fell into.

About a third of my clients were of this sort—rich, curious women with nothing but time on their hands. In fact, she was the fourth client this week who'd come in requesting a pet reading.

"I'd heard you ran the cards for Mrs. Larken's dog Puddles and I want the same for Sunbeam," she insisted.

Puddles belonged to Mrs. Larken, whom I'd met on board the *Martian Princess* during the trip from Earth. She'd been old—like really old, maybe two hundred—and something about her charmed me. Maybe because she reminded me a little of Granny G, and gods knew I was a sucker for anything that put me in mind of family. Plus, I don't think my head was screwed on straight once I'd reunited with Alexei after having thought him dead for six months. When we'd come up for air, I'd met Mrs. Larken, taken a liking to her, and done a reading. Once on Mars, she'd opened doors for me I'd never dreamed of touching on my own. When she'd imported one of the first dogs allowed on Mars and asked me to do a reading for her mini schnauzer, I couldn't think of a polite way to refuse. The end result was I'd been tagged as some sort of psychic dog whisperer. And although Mrs. Larken had genuinely liked me and vice versa, Lila Chandler was something else entirely.

"Well, then perhaps Mr. Petriv might be here and you could introduce us? I'm told you're acquainted with him and he drops by quite frequently," Ms. Chandler said, meeting my gaze with a level one of her own.

Wonderful. Now the claws were out and we'd come to the real reason for her visit: Another portion of my clients came in the hopes of spotting, and presumable landing, Alexei Petriv.

"I'm sorry, but he isn't here at the moment. Unfortunately, I can't predict when he'll decide to drop in."

"Oh, that is too bad. In that case, perhaps I should rethink this entire appointment. Things don't seem to be going well for either of us today, do they?"

Fuck. And now I was being threatened over a dog card reading.

"Not necessarily. I can run a combined reading for you and Sunbeam," I said, and proceeded to shuffle the Tarot deck, making a mental note to tell Lotus to screen for dogs and their psycho owners beforehand. This would have never happened with Natty back on Earth.

Sorry, Granny G, I thought out to the universe. *A gold note is still a gold note and a girl needs to eat and keep the shoe industry afloat. I can't lose business on account of crazy.*

3

"Oh, how exciting!" Ms. Chandler exclaimed. Then she held her little dog to her face and proceeded to baby talk us to death. "Isn't that right, Sunbeam? Who's a good girl? You are! Mommy loves you. Yes, she does. You're going to get a card reading today! Yes, such a good girl," and on it went until I wanted to put all of us out of our collective misery. At least Sunbeam seemed happy, given how quickly she gulped down her doggy treats.

Like my shop back on Earth, I'd used the same décor scheme of exotic Old World meets space-age New World, yet somehow the look hadn't translated well to Mars. And the fact that I now essentially had a day job was depressing. On Earth, I'd only worked nights. On Mars, it just hadn't attracted the same clientele, so I had to open during the day instead. The only time evenings were profitable was on weekends during the Witching Time. Then, I could pretty much double my fee. People expected a show extravagant enough to blow their minds, so I gave it to them. A Martian day, or rather a sol, was thirty-nine minutes and thirty-five seconds longer than an Earth day. For some reason people went wild then, as if the extra time meant the rules didn't exist. They partied harder, committed more crimes—even wanted their babies born then. And if it helped my shop's month-end numbers, who was I to argue?

Half an hour later, I walked Ms. Chandler out of my reading room and to the front reception area. I made sure she transferred her three hundred gold notes to the shop's account and reassured her I'd already uploaded the reading transcript to her memory blocks on the Cerebral Neural Net. The CN-net linked every human mind in the tri-system of Earth, Mars, and Venus into a sort of electronic collective of information sharing via One Gov's t-mod implants. Implants I didn't have. Then I got her the hell out the door. I'd jacked up the price on the spur of the moment, tripling the rate to include an annoyance fee— Sunbeam had passed out in a treat-induced coma after making little tiny doggy poops on my reading table. Besides, we both knew she wouldn't become a regular client. No, all she wanted was a glimpse of the infamous Alexei Petriv, leader of the Tsarist Consortium who was too damn hot for his own good, and to see if she could get the current competition out of her way. Namely, me.

I stood in the middle of my small reception area, taking deep breaths in hopes of avoiding a meltdown. I turned to Lotus, who looked at me like having me explode might be entertaining to watch. That she was my fourth cousin and had been recommended to me by family back on Earth sometimes made me regret I was such a softy when it came to my relatives.

"No more dogs, Lotus. I don't care how rich the client is, if they have a dog, I don't want to see them."

"Sorry, Felicia." Lotus hung her head, her blunt-edged pixie cut doing nothing to hide her grin. Did I mention I come from a family of con artists? "But you have to admit, little Sunbeam was so cute! Did you see her little tiny doggy paws? I've never seen a teacup Yorkie before and I couldn't pass up the chance. Didn't they bring those back from extinction?"

"I don't care where they brought them back from. Screen the clients first. If you get the slightest whiff of dog, forget it."

"Fine, whatever. I'll have Buckley sift them on the CN-net and let you know what shakes out," she said, referring to her boyfriend, who was fully wired with t-mods, unlike me and Lotus, who relied on antiquated tech like charm-tex bracelets and flat-file avatars on the CN-net. I wasn't sure I liked the idea of

Buckley going through my potential clients, but decided to let it slide. "I thought you said you needed to increase the shop's revenue. You said—"

"I know what I said, but I changed my mind. I don't need that much money or the headaches that come from dealing with those women," I said, then ran a distracted hand through my hair and froze.

Ah hell. I'd forgotten I braided a thin chain-mesh weave through the nearly black waves that morning. Now my hand was stuck. I sighed as I tried to get free, pulling out a few strands in the process. Lotus watched me struggle before bursting out laughing and coming to rescue me from my own damned hair.

"You really should cut it off. It's so much less work," she said, gesturing to her own short hair.

Hers was just a shade lighter than mine, just like her eyes were a darker green, her skin a little more olive-toned—everything in keeping with the Romani looks she shared with most of the Sevigny family. I just happened to look more like my mother, which drove my father crazy. Literally. Me too actually, though not so literally. I'd gotten off easy in the crazy department, considering my mother had cloned me, then tried to kill me so many months ago. With family like that, it was a wonder I wasn't in therapy.

"I like it long," I said, even as I winced when she tried tugging at my two rings still caught in the mesh weave. "Ouch. Take it easy!"

"Sorry. And does *he* like it too?" she asked with seeming innocence. "I bet he does. I bet he wraps his fists in it and—"

"Just put whatever dirty thoughts you're thinking right out

of your mind. We're at work and I'm not discussing this with you now."

"Fine. Don't be any fun. See if I care," Lotus griped. A beat of silence, a little bit of tugging, and my hand was out. "There, you're free, Medusa. You shouldn't wear that mesh thing anymore."

"You're probably right," I agreed as I pulled a few long black hairs out of my rings, all of them elaborate costume jewelry I'd brought from Earth. Maybe it was time I did away with the props. It seemed like everything I used back home wasn't cutting it on Mars. Maybe I needed to rethink the whole business model. "And for the record, yes, he does like it. A lot. Now if you need me, I'll be sanitizing my reading table and spraying air freshener everywhere. Sunbeam shit on it in the middle of the reading."

"Oh, Felicia, I'm sorry!" Lotus laughed behind her hand, green eyes wide. "That's awful. You're right. No more dogs. Let me take care of that since I feel like it's my fault anyway. I'll get the cleaning stuff."

She headed to the supply closet, where we kept a few basic cleaning supplies since the shop was professionally cleaned every evening. Then she froze, caught like a baby rabbit in some big bad hunter's trap. I knew the exact reason for her reaction. It was written all over her face, plus it wasn't the first time I'd seen this particular behavior from a woman before.

"Good afternoon. Nice to see you," Lotus said in girlish tones. Her cheeks flushed and her tongue darted out to lick her lips as if tasting something sweet.

I turned and my heartbeat seemed to skid to a halt before resuming again, just as I suspected it did for all the women who met him. Except in my case, I knew the look he wore was solely for me.

Alexei Petriv stood in the open doorway of my shop, removed his sunshades, and slid them into the breast pocket of his charcoal gray suit jacket. Tall, broad-shouldered, well-muscled, and built like a rock, he seemed to fill every room he entered with his presence alone. He didn't have to do anything other than just stand there, and he was still overwhelming. His thick black hair fell nearly to his shoulders and his eyes were so intensely blue, sometimes I wondered if they could cut into me if he stared at me long enough. At the very least, they gave the disturbing illusion he could look into your soul. Saying he was gorgeous and sexy as hell was a ridiculous understatement. In fact, words failed me. His MH Factor was off the charts, up in some stratosphere no one could calculate. The same could be said for his t-mods, meaning his mind could manipulate the CN-net in ways few others could. Looking at him left me breathless and sometimes made me doubt what I saw was real because he was utterly perfect. So perfect, in fact, he might not be human anymore.

I'd secretly been cataloging the oddities I'd noticed during our time together. So far as I could tell, he never got sick—not even a cold. If he hurt himself, such as when he'd once sliced his palm with a paring knife, the wound healed in hours with no skin renewal patches required. He needed very little sleep, and some nights I wondered if he even slept at all. He was definitely stronger than average and had little trouble keeping in shape, though he worked out like a fiend—doing even more than was required by One Gov mandate. He could hold his breath for ridiculously long periods of time, something I'd learned when we'd gone on a day trip to Aeolian Beach. And one thing I'd discovered soon after the first time I'd slept with him—he needed almost zero recovery time before he was ready to go again. Sometimes it was thrilling to have that much attention. Other times, it was exhausting and made me wonder how I could ever be enough for him.

"Hello, Lotus. Glad to see you're doing well," he said in that deep voice of his, a slight hint of a Russian accent present. Sometimes it felt like that voice could slide around your mind, commanding you do to things you weren't entirely sure were a good idea. Or maybe I was the only one he had that effect on?

"I'm fine, Mr. Petriv. Thanks for asking." Lotus continued to stand there gaping, mouth slightly open. I rolled my eyes. Was it *always* going to be like this when other women had his attention?

"Dog shit, Lotus. Remember?" I reminded her, none too subtly.

Lotus shook herself and flushed a brilliant shade of red. "Oh, right. I forgot. I'll get that cleaned up right away. Excuse me."

In a flash, she was at the supply closet, gathering some rags and a spray bottle of cleaning solution. Then she disappeared into the back room, slamming the door so hard behind her, I winced.

"Sorry about that. It's been an interesting morning."

"Another dog card reading?" Alexei asked, arching an eyebrow. He left the door frame and crossed the shop to me, fighting to stop a grin from filling his face. "How many has it been this week? Three? Four?"

I shrugged. "Four, but who's counting?"

"You are."

"Lotus is enamored with dogs lately so she keeps booking pet readings whether I want them or not."

He laughed. "Maybe she thinks you need a dog."

"Not if they're going to get excited and shit on everything I own. At least this latest did it on my table, so that's something new." I looked around the shop—a shop that wasn't as successful as I'd hoped it would be. I was doing okay, but not like I had been back home, and I couldn't figure out why. I missed Charlie Zero and his business savvy.

"I assume you were able to convince the owner to stay for a reading of her own?"

"Of course, but you know they're only here because they're hoping to catch a glimpse of you. It's like I have to beat the women away with a stick and it's getting exhausting."

He'd reached me now and his hands were on me, sliding along my neck to tilt my face up. Even in my highest heels, my eyes were barely level with his shoulder. My gaze locked with his and my neck arched under his hands. "You have to stop doing this to yourself, Felicia. You're making yourself crazy and imagining things that don't exist. I have no interest in any other woman."

I swallowed. "I know, but it's hard when I have yet another Martian blueblood in here, judging me. I never cared about any of that before, and now it seems to be bothering me all the time."

His expression hardened. "I hate it when you do that, compare yourself to things I have no interest in, because there is no comparison." He looked like he wanted to say more. Instead he stopped and his mouth quirked at the corners. "Besides, you're the only one who can keep me from jumping off the deep end into megalomania—or so you keep reminding me."

"Very funny. Someone needs to keep you humble or you'll think you own the tri-system."

"Actually, I believe I only own half of it, or thereabouts," he said drily. His hands drifted down my body, coming to rest at the small of my back. "Tell me who was here and made you feel this way, and I'll deal with it. Then it's no longer a problem."

It sounded tempting, but Alexei's way of dealing with problems tended to be extreme, with no chance for the other party to recover. Depending on what he was after, such as securing ownership of most of the off-world asteroid mines, it ran the gamut from driving his opponents to financial ruin, undercutting prices on business rivals, or pitting family members against one another and taking advantage of the chaos. While none of it was technically illegal, it didn't sit well with me—and those were just the things I knew about. The Tsarist Consortium was considered a legitimate corporate and political entity with plans to revolutionize lives throughout the tri-system, but you could never forget how it started, or where its roots lay. They'd come a long way, but not far enough in some people's minds.

Long before me, I knew that as Alexei worked his way up the Consortium hierarchy, he'd seduced both wives and girlfriends, using his looks and his perfect body to gain whatever secrets they'd offer him regarding the men in their lives. Then he'd use those secrets to either buy or steal whatever it was he was after. I suspected that was why he didn't seem to care about how he looked or the things he was able to do. To him, his body was just another tool to be used.

"I'm a big girl. I'll get over it. It just puts me in a bad mood whenever I have to deal with one of them. What are you doing here anyway? Aren't you supposed to be holding secret closed-door meetings and can't be disturbed?"

"My plans changed and I needed to see you," he said, leaning in to brush a kiss along my throat.

It made me sigh and melt into him, my hands sliding over the ridges of well-muscled abdomen until my arms were around his waist under his jacket. My head dropped to his shoulder and the kiss at my throat turned into something more heated. Soon, he kissed along the line of my jaw and his tongue ran the outer edge of my ear. My hands fisted in his shirt as I wondered how fast I could get to his bare skin. Still, some measure of common sense clamped down on my lust-filled brain.

"This is really nice, but Lotus is in the other room and I have another appointment in about fifteen minutes." Weird how my voice had gone all breathy and I was barely holding my own weight as I leaned into him. How the hell had he gotten one of my legs hooked around his hip and my dress bunched at my waist so quickly?

He raised his head and the dark look he gave me made my toes curl and had me squirming against him. "We both know I don't need very long to get you exactly where I want you."

No, he didn't. Still... "Maybe, but it might get awkward if my next client sees you bending me over the reception desk. Come to my place tonight. I can have dinner ready for seven if I rush."

Was it weird we didn't live together? I wasn't sure. It was one of those things I tried not to think about too much. I'd never been so on edge in a relationship before. With Alexei Petriv, the highs were so high, they could be terrifying, but the lows were equally scary. How could I hold on to someone so frighteningly perfect and fundamentally dark when the only thing I had going for me was luck—another thing I filed under unresolved issues not to be examined too hard.

Alexei let me go, setting me on my feet and letting my dress settle around my hips. His expression became rueful. "That's why I'm here, and what I wanted to talk to you about. There's been a slight change in plans."

I frowned. "Slight change how exactly? Does this have anything to do with finishing up the big project you've been working on?"

"Or 'getting me out of the Consortium muck,' as you so elegantly put it." He grinned and I jabbed him lightly in the chest with my finger.

"Hey, that's not what I said! Just that sometimes the Consortium does things that scare me and I don't want to have to pick a side."

"I know what you meant." He caught my hand and kissed the knuckles. "I can't say I was thrilled with the Consortium's approach either, but at least now the mining unions are under unified leadership and we avoided an all-out revolt with the workers. There were issues with some of the mines collapsing, but production yield didn't drop, and no one in the tri-system was the wiser. The troublemakers were handled discreetly, and it showed both the unions and the Consortium in the best possible light. The union leadership would rather deal directly with me than any One Gov agents they send into the field. My being here on Mars has actually made things easier."

I rolled my eyes. "Isn't it lucky you were here then?"

"Yes, it was." He kissed the inside of my wrist before letting my hand go. "And now that it's almost done, I can focus on things closer to home and spend less time directly on-site. That means more time for us."

My breath caught in a tiny gasp. "Really?"

He grinned again. "Yes, really. Unfortunately"—and there the grin faded—"I'll need to be off-planet for a few weeks to ensure all the key players are in place before I step back. Konstantin specifically requested I attend negotiations, so I can't delegate to someone else."

Konstantin Belikov. The name made me shiver. At nearly five hundred years old, the man had seen things and lived through events that would have sent most people screaming. He'd survived the Dark Times on Earth at the end of the twenty-fifth century, when the polar ice caps melted, earthquakes ravaged continents, and billions had died. He watched as humanity terraformed Mars and turned it into a paradise, and laughed as they struggled to do the same with Venus, with less than spectacular results. He knew how to work every angle and drafted plots inside of plots. He was ruthlessness personified and lived his life to ensure the Tsarist Consortium would one day replace One Gov as the ruling power in the tri-system.

He'd all but raised Alexei and ensured Alexei took over as head of the Consortium. He also wasn't pleased I'd lured him away to Mars since wherever Alexei went, so went the Consortium's power. Frankly, I resented the accusations. When I left for Mars, I hadn't even known Alexei was alive. I wasn't in a position to lure him anywhere. I was just glad I was safely here on Mars, and Belikov was over a hundred million miles away on Earth. Sometimes, though, I wondered if it was far enough.

I ran my hands absently over his chest, enjoying the defined ridges as I looked up at him. "A few weeks? How long is a few?"

"Two, possibly three at most."

"*Three?* Where are you going? Is it to the mines on Vesta or Pallas? Are you sure someone else can't go in your place?" It was the only thing that made sense since it wasn't possible to travel to any of the asteroid belt mines and back in a few weeks. Vesta and Pallas both orbited Mars, so a three-week trip was doable. Didn't mean I liked it, though.

"I'm afraid not. I need to oversee this personally. The union leaders will only work with me and those collapses need to be fully investigated."

"But it's for so long. Will you at least shim me?"

He touched my hair, running his finger through the strands and toying with the mesh. I might have made a joke about how he was more handsy than usual, but right then, I needed the contact. "Konstantin requires a complete blackout on this. Closed-loop Consortium access only."

I frowned. A secret mission and that sneaky asshole Belikov was involved. Alexei would be gone for possibly three weeks and I couldn't contact him. It went without saying my gut kicked me hard enough to almost knock the breath out of me. That scared me too. I hadn't had a feeling this intense in months—not since I'd arrived on Mars. I thought everything had settled down. Apparently I was wrong.

"I know it's a long time to be out of contact," he murmured, brushing a hand along my cheek and tilting my face back to his. "I also know you don't trust him. Neither do I to some extent, but he has significant power in the Consortium."

"I don't have a good feeling about this. Are you sure you have to go?"

A kiss on each of my cheeks, then my hairline. "I'm doing it for us," he whispered. "When this is finished and I've secured the Consortium's power base on Mars, we can begin making inroads into One Gov's leadership. That's when I can pull back. I may be the head of the Consortium, but I'm not here to appoint myself king of Mars."

I knew there was something I was missing in his words, but my focus had turned inward, picking at my gut feeling like a tongue wiggling a loose tooth.

"And unfortunately, we're leaving tonight. They're waiting for me outside. I just couldn't go without seeing you first."

That brought me up short. I pulled back enough to look at him, my roaming hands going still. "You're leaving me *right now*, for three weeks?"

"I know. I'm sorry, Felicia. I was just informed of the change in plans today. You know I would never tell you like this if I could avoid it." Alexei's hands were on my forearms, his thumbs stroking the insides of my wrists. And he looked genuinely sorry too, sorry enough that I had a moment where I wondered if I could pull him into my card reading room and convince him to stay. But no, Lotus was back there, and my gut was kicking me hard enough that I needed to pay attention. Unfortunately the feeling was so vague, I didn't know what to focus on.

So I said what, to me, was the most logical thing in the world: "I need to run my cards."

His hands tightened, stopping me when I would have pulled away. "No."

"Why not? It won't take long."

"No," he said, more firmly this time.

"But…" I looked up into at his face, bewildered. "Something isn't right and I want to check into it."

"No, Felicia. Don't." His voice had gone very soft. "I don't want you to run a spread for me. Not now. Not ever."

Stunned, I'm sure my jaw dropped open. This wasn't anything we'd ever talked about before. Actually now that I thought about it, he'd never really asked me to run the cards for him except for when we'd first met. There was a seriousness to his tone that made me wary. "But it's what I do. I'm good at it. Why wouldn't I run them for you if something feels off?"

"Because I don't ever want you to think I'm with you because your luck gene twisted events in your favor, or I'm using you for some advantage you'll give me over everyone else. I'm with you because I want to be. Because you're the only woman I want."

Then he leaned down to kiss me, just a brushing of his lips over mine before he pulled away. It was the kind of kiss he gave me when he was trying hard to be gentle but in reality wanted to throw me down on the nearest flat surface and bury himself inside me for hours. I knew it and he knew it, and I think I may have swooned a little because he reached out to steady me and chuckled softly.

"As you say, there's no time for that, or you know I would," he murmured.

"But... I guess if you don't want a reading, I can't force you," I sputtered out.

Behind him, the door to my shop opened and two Consortium bodyguards stepped inside, tall, overly developed muscle with close-cropped hair, the ubiquitous sunshades, and wearing identical black suits so it was impossible to tell one from another. Though I had my suspicions, I'd never been able to get Alexei to confirm if the Consortium grew all their muscle out of the same vat of genetic goo or what their Modified Human Factor might be.

"Looks like your ride's getting anxious," I said, peeking around his shoulder.

He threw a negligent look behind him before refocusing on me. "So it would seem. We'll table the rest of this for later." He brushed a thumb over my cheek and across my lips as if memorizing the contours of my face before he kissed my forehead. "I'll be back as soon as I can."

Then he let me go, turned on his heel, and left the shop. The Consortium chain-breakers fell into step behind him. And I was left with nothing but a sharp ache of loneliness that wasn't going away anytime soon, a gut feeling Alexei didn't want me to investigate, and an appointment who tripped through the door staring wide-eyed after Alexei and carrying—gods help me—another dog.

2

Two weeks later found me at my shop, counting the minutes until Witching Time ended and hoping for walk-ins. Venusol was the only night I kept to anything resembling my old Earth hours, often staying open until the wee hours of the morning. But if no one came in after Witching Time when the clocks restarted, then I'd close up and call it a night. Weekends in Elysium City during Witching Time were crazy, with Venusol—or rather Saturday—being the wildest. Even after four months, I had trouble remembering the Martian names for the days of the week. Sorry—sols.

It was a warm autumn evening for February—no wait: Leo, the Martian name for February. With the Martian year being twenty-four months long, every month was twenty-eight sols, and every other year a leap year. I'm sure the calendar made sense to whoever designed it, but using it gave me brain cramps.

Most of the populated areas on Mars lay on or slightly south of the equator, making the year-round weather patterns in Elysium City similar to those back in Nairobi—warm days, cool evenings, and, thankfully, no snow. Also, no rainy seasons either. Nope, didn't miss those or the frizzy hair I sported most of the year.

I stood in the doorway looking up at the sky, watching the fireworks and trying not to cringe. Venusol Witching Time always had fireworks. Once, I used to love them. However, that was before the horrific night in Brazil when my mother had tried to kill me and I thought Alexei had died. Now, fireworks upset me. I was trying to build up a tolerance since it was difficult to escape something that went off once a week like clockwork. Unless I had a client, I forced myself to watch the display. Usually, Alexei watched with me or was nearby if I panicked. Now it was just me, although Lotus was somewhere in the shop as well—probably getting ready for a night out with Buckley or her girlfriends once we closed up. Sometimes I went with her if Alexei was away on Consortium business. Providing I didn't have any last-minute customers, tonight was one of those nights. I needed to distract myself from the jittery feeling in my gut—a feeling that hadn't settled since Alexei had gone off-world.

He may not have wanted me to run the cards for him but I hadn't let that stop me. It just meant I wouldn't tell him the result. In fact, I shuffled the deck at the first opportunity. What I saw, I hadn't liked. Too many swords meant strategy and conflict. I also had the Devil—fear, deception, and trickery—along with the King of Swords, which I'd always associated with Belikov. The King was reversed, meaning an abuse of power. I also had the Knight of Cups, which focused on love, romance, and emotion. That should have been a good thing. Instead, the spread showed it as an outside force, coming in as something new rather than something that already existed. Was someone from Alexei's past about to blow our relationship apart—someone Belikov approved of since I knew he barely tolerated me?

I checked my c-tex, then watched as the last of the fireworks faded in the night sky. Looked like tonight was another bust. No clients, so I may as well lock up. I let the door close behind me. From the corner of my eye, I saw one of the Consortium's chain-breakers moving in the shadows of the buildings lining the street. Yes, I had my own security detail. Since the incident where my ex-boyfriend had tried to kill me, Alexei wanted me protected at all times. It was annoying, but I couldn't stop him. Besides, I could see his point; I wasn't in a hurry to die anytime soon.

I glanced about the shop, looking for anything out of order before I locked up. The reception desk was tidy. Beyond it, the small waiting area containing a sofa and a few chairs looked the same as it always did. On the walls were prints of various Old World Earth city scenes from before the Dark Times. One of them was crooked so I crossed the room to straighten it. The walls themselves were set to a soft blue so as not to compete with the prints. I could smell lavender in the air and checked my c-tex to make sure the AI still knew to shut off the scent diffuser before we left for the evening.

Lotus emerged from the washroom that was tucked into the shop's back corner wearing what looked like two neon blue scraps of fabric—one over her breasts, the other her groin. Both covered her with strategic precision and laced up in back into a complicated knot. It made her look like a pornographic present waiting to be unwrapped for porn Christmas.

I blinked. "I haven't been out of the club scene that long. What are you wearing?"

Lotus modeled her ribbons for me, twirling in her matching slippers. "It's fresh off the runway from the Olympus Fashion Blitz. Total knockoff, but still amazing, right? It blew Buckley's mind when he saw it. What do you think the Russian would say if he saw you in this?"

The Russian was her nickname for Alexei. It had taken Lotus a while to feel anything other than disapproval toward him. Oh, she could appreciate how he filled out a suit, the chiseled cheekbones, and the hair you ached to run your fingers through, but I knew he was still "other" to her. With whatever t-mods he carried and his off-the-scale MH Factor, his abilities stretched far beyond what most people could do. If Lotus was any indication, he might never be accepted by my family of tech-averse holdouts. It annoyed me, and it hurt. Family mattered and I'd gone out of my way to meet the members of the Martian branch of the Sevigny clan when I moved to Mars. I knew I didn't need their approval to be with Alexei, but deep down, part of me wanted it regardless.

"I think he'd like it, but I also think he wouldn't let me leave his sight," I said finally. Lotus took fashion risks even I wasn't willing to take.

"Mmmm...You're probably right. The way he looks at you is so hot, it's scorching. It's like he's dying of thirst and you're the only water around. I wish Buckley looked at me that way," she said, her expression dreamy. "I barely rate above a ham sandwich."

I probably should have said something to reassure her about Buckley's feelings but I wanted to talk about Alexei. I needed a female perspective to drive away the doubts the Tarot reading had left behind. "Does he really look at me that way?"

"The man can't keep his eyes off you," she assured me. "And don't think I haven't heard you two in the back room when business is slow and he happens to drop in. Sometimes I have to walk around the block just to cool down because *I* can't take it. It'd be nice if he could bottle some of that stamina and give it to Buckley."

Okay, not quite the reassurance I'd expected as I felt a blush heat my cheeks. "I guess the walls aren't as thick as I thought."

Lotus smirked. "Guess not."

If Alexei felt that way, how could Konstantin possibly come between us? Then again, it wasn't like I had a stellar track record when it came to relationships. I either got dumped or didn't care enough to fully commit. It was no wonder I kept second-guessing myself with Alexei. I hadn't even told the man I loved him and we'd been together for months. Maybe the problem wasn't him always getting dragged away on Consortium business. Maybe it was me.

"You still going with Buckley and me tonight?" Lotus asked, breaking into my thoughts.

"Sure. It beats sitting at home by myself." I gestured down to my outfit—a haltered, shimmering lime green dress that hit mid-thigh paired with a beaded pink belt slung low on my hips. I wore matching ankle boots, the heels studded with emerald flecks. I knew they were ridiculously expensive, but since Alexei had bought them, I tried not to worry about the cost. If he was determined to keep me in designer shoes, it wasn't my place to stop him. "Is this okay, or do I need to change into fabric scraps?"

"Ha-ha, so funny. You're dressed a little too conservatively for the Red Dust scene, but it's not like you're trying to pick up anyone."

I ran my fingers though my hair, shaking out the loose waves flowing to the small of my back. My hair would be fine and I could fix my makeup on the way. "What do you mean? I thought you and Buckley were good."

"We are, but sometimes we like to add variety."

"Variety?" I stared at her, eyes widening. "You mean, there are three of you?"

"Or more," she said, matter-of-factly. "It's not like it means anything and it's fun. We're not married or have a kid to worry about, so what's the harm?" Then her look turned speculative. "You've never tried it?"

I shook my head. Either Lotus was more adventurous than I thought or I was woefully naïve. I suspected it was probably a mix of both. "It's not something I was ever interested in."

"The Russian hasn't suggested a threesome?" Lotus asked, her tone clearly disbelieving. "I was positive he'd be into that. I bet he's done things I can't even imagine."

"No, he's never said anything," I answered faintly.

"Well, you're still a new couple. Give him time and he'll probably want more than vanilla sex."

My mouth opened and closed. Gods, could she be right? Was that why my gut was reacting this way? Was that really what he wanted, but he hadn't said anything? Was I *boring* him?

"Wow, you should see your face," Lotus marveled. "You look like you might throw up. Are things that bad between you?"

"Of course not. Everything is fine," I choked out.

"Well, what works for one couple doesn't work for another.

He's too possessive anyway. I don't think bringing in another person would satisfy him. He'd probably just break up with you," she said philosophically, brushing it away with a wave of her hand.

What? My stomach took a nosedive into my shoes. "Gods, Lotus! Enough! We're not breaking up."

Lotus put her hands over her mouth, covering her laughter. "You are *so* easy to rile! I had no idea you were this sensitive about him."

"Look, are we going out or not?" I interrupted before we went down this ridiculous road any further.

"Of course we're going! You seriously need to relax, Felicia. I was going to suggest you get laid, but I guess that's not an option tonight. We're going to try that new club in the Vibe District, Red Dust. The place is hot right now. They have a Euphoria bar that brews a fugue cocktail so strong, Buckley says it makes his t-mods feel like they've upgraded to the next level. It's only temporary, though. One Gov would be all over it if anyone really scrambled their lids. They've also done something to mess with the gravity so you actually float on the dance floor. Wild, huh?"

"I think Alexei said the Consortium owns it. Supposed to be themed, showing old Mars back before the terraforming days."

Lotus looked intrigued by this nugget of information. "Figures the Russian would have his hands in it. That means you'll be our ticket to avoiding the line. Maybe they'll even let us drink for free."

If there was an angle anywhere, my family could work it. I sighed, not my first of the night. "Let me get the lights and we'll go."

I was about to call out to the shop AI and have it power

down the reading room lights and sound system when the front door opened. We both turned to see a young woman huddled in the doorway.

She was young enough that it looked like she hadn't started her Renew treatments yet. Her dark blond hair was pulled into a messy knot at the base of her neck and her clothing was shabby. The fabric was muted colors of gray and brown, with her skirt hitting her legs at an odd angle that was neither fashionable nor bohemian. In comparison, I looked like a tropical bird in my shimmering dress. And Lotus... Well, I didn't know what to say about her outfit other than at least she'd put some effort into it.

It wasn't until she was inside that I noticed the sleeping baby on her back. I couldn't tell if it was a boy or a girl, catching only a tuft of dark hair and closed eyes. It was strapped into one of those synth-leather slings people used when they wanted to keep their hands free. Like everything about the woman, the sling looked shabby. I had the feeling it was all secondhand—the clothes, the sling, everything the woman carried.

The pang I felt seeing the baby took my breath away. Once, I'd been obsessed with having a child because I couldn't; I'd been blacklisted by One Gov from participating in the Shared Hope program that legally allowed every couple to conceive a child. Once my blacklisted status was revoked, I'd pushed baby thoughts to the back burner. A year ago, I hadn't been emotionally ready. And now... Well, thanks to my horrible bitch of a mother, the thought of having a child terrified me.

Luck will always work to preserve itself, forever putting itself in a situation to its best advantage.

Those were her exact words and they still haunted me. She'd

been obsessed with my luck gene and combining mine and Alexei's DNA. I'd avoided thinking about all the things I used to want because it was easier than having to deal with the potential reality.

However, seeing this sleeping baby brought everything back. It wasn't that I hadn't been around babies lately; it was just part of a growing realization that maybe I wasn't doing this right. The jittery feeling that had taken up residence in my gut made me wonder if something needed to change. Maybe fear had made me give up too much of what it meant to be me, and I needed to find myself again.

"Excuse me, but we're closed," Lotus said, approaching the woman the way you might a wild animal—cautiously, trying to hide all fear. "If you want a reading, you'll need to come back on Jovisol. Or you can book an appointment over the CN-net."

The woman looked panicked. "I know it's late. I just hoped I could have a quick reading. I'm worried about my husband. I think he's in a bad situation and I need help. This was the only time I could get away. I have money, if that's what you're worried about. Please."

She was clearly desperate and out of options. I couldn't turn her away.

"It's no problem. I can do a reading right now," I said, gesturing to the back room. I shot Lotus a look. She sighed in response, but sat back at the reception desk.

"I'll start the payment transfer process," Lotus muttered, tapping her own c-tex bracelet, probably sending Buckley a shim telling him we'd be late. Then she dug around inside the desk, before locating the blue chip wafer we used to transfer gold notes on the CN-net. "I just need your avatar reference data."

The woman looked about nervously. "Novi Pazidor. Mars. Davis District, Elysium City. R4-6B1."

Now that Lotus could track the woman's avatar, she tapped on the wafer, waited a second, then nodded to me. The transfer had begun. A hundred gold notes. Back on Earth, I would have done this woman's reading for free—that's how desperate she seemed. On Mars, I didn't have that luxury. Every gold note counted if I didn't want to rely on a stream of Lila Chandler–like clients. Never mind that Alexei had bankrolled my shop and didn't care if I repaid him; I didn't plan on falling behind on my payments.

"Come back to my reading room," I said, directing her to follow me. "I'll see what I can do to help. My name's Felicia, by the way."

"Oh, I know who you are. I just never thought I'd be here," she said, gawking as she followed.

"Why's that?"

"Too fancy. You can just tell by looking this place isn't for people like me."

Too fancy? "What do you mean, *people like you?*"

"Miners. Driller Dive—yeah, I know what people call it and it isn't in the best part of the city. It's fine. I barely notice anymore. But like I said, I need help and everybody knows you're good."

I swore under my breath. There was a lot of wealth on Mars thanks to the raw materials out in the asteroid belt and the fuel resources of hydrogen and helium that humanity was just beginning to syphon from Jupiter. And if you could harvest them, you could gather diamonds as big as your head bobbing along the Jupiter fuel stream. But it took ingenuity and *someone* had to get dirty and do the hard work. AI drones couldn't do everything. Unfortunately, it created a class divide on Mars almost impossible to cross. I thought I'd be able to bridge the gap the way I had on Earth—everyone wanted to know what their future held, after all. But no, I'd been lumped in with the rich bitches. All those women strolling in and out of my shop, trolling for Alexei, probably gave the impression they were the only sort of people I did readings for. Gods, I was probably missing all sorts of opportunities because of those dog-toting man-eaters.

I schooled my expression into a friendly smile. "Just because the shop looks fancy doesn't mean you're not welcome. My door's open to anyone curious about their future."

I'd set up my reading room similarly to how I'd had it on Earth, with two chairs situated around a low marble clawfoot table for my readings. The overhead lights were muted shades of pastels, casting a gauzy and delicate light throughout the room. I'd always thought it was comfortable, but if Novi thought it was too much, maybe I needed to rethink my approach.

The music volume was set low and sounds of cascading water played in the background. "I can turn the sound off so it won't disturb your baby."

"No, it's okay. She'll sleep through anything."

"She's adorable. How old is she?"

"Six months. First of the family born on Mars," she said proudly, and then her face fell. "I had to bring her with me tonight. I had no one else to look after her. Sometimes being here is harder than I thought it would be. Her daddy works off-planet in one of the asteroid mines. I only see him every couple of months."

Was it a coincidence Novi had come in while Alexei was off-planet investigating the mine collapses? Maybe, but I didn't believe in coincidences. Did that mean her husband was involved? Only one way to find out.

I held up my hand to stop Novi from speaking. "Rather than tell me more, how about we let the cards do their work? Please have a seat."

She nodded uncertainly, taking the chair I led her toward. I watched her remove the sling from her back with jerky movements until she had the baby on her knee. The baby looked startled and opened blue eyes as if checking to see if she should start crying, but resettled quickly. I felt that pang again and it scared me. Was that really what I wanted? A baby?

I removed my c-tex bracelet, setting it on the table. Novi eyed me curiously.

"It's true you don't have t-mods? Nothing up here to log on to the CN-net?" She tapped the back of her head when she said it. That was where the One Gov–sanctioned implants went in just before puberty. Then they grew along with your body, radiating around the spine and throughout the brain, wiring everyone directly into the CN-net and to the rest of the tri-system's population. Everyone except me, my family, and any others who shared a similar tech-phobia. Turns out there weren't many.

"It's true. No t-mods. No MH Factor. Not even chipped. Not much keeping me connected except this"—I tapped my bracelet—"and luck."

Novi gave a bitter laugh. "I used to believe in luck. Now, not so much."

I left it at that and shuffled the cards, half watching as she

THE CHAOS OF LUCK

held the sleeping baby stiffly in her arms. She didn't look very comfortable. Maybe I should offer to hold the baby. Maybe I could—

Absolutely not. Ruthlessly, I squelched all baby-related thoughts and shuffled Granny G's cards with extra vigor. It was a wonder the oversized deck didn't go flying from my hands. Even so, their ebony and star-patterned backs flashed by quickly and I saw Novi's eyes drooping as she watched. It always happened. The cards were mesmerizing, with a display of a spinning void on their backs. Once, a client had been so enthralled by the cards, she'd fallen out of her chair.

Since I had no desire to see Novi pass out or drop her baby, I stopped shuffling and offered her the deck to cut in half. Then I reassembled the halves and laid a traditional Celtic Cross spread, placing ten cards faceup on the table.

"Keep your question in mind," I advised. "That will help focus the reading."

"I am," she said grimly, her eyes narrowing on the cards as I turned them up.

The cards really were lovely. The nano-dip treatment I had done annually kept the centuries-old deck looking as if they'd been painted yesterday. The people looked almost lifelike, and the objects seemed as if you could reach in and pluck them out from the cards themselves.

I took a moment to look over the spread, letting my mind sift through the potential meanings and how they might apply to Novi's husband. She was clearly upset, so I didn't want to say anything to make it worse. Still, it was all I could do not to let out a low whistle. Whatever her husband was into, it looked like trouble.

"What does it say?" she asked, looking at the cards.

I pointed to the first card: the Page of Wands. "This is your husband. People respect and follow him. He's always looking forward to the future, but gets impatient when something's in his way. And hovering over him is the King of Swords. This could be someone he reports to at work, or has authority over his life. The King is preventing him from getting what he wants, or creating a hostile situation where he feels like he can't get ahead. There are a lot of pentacles in this reading, meaning your husband is concerned with money or material status."

"That's why we came to Mars," Novi said, eyes tearing. "There was nothing for us on Earth. We thought starting over was the only way to get ahead."

I pointed to another card: the Four of Pentacles, reversed. "He wants to protect what he has and provide for his family, but there are conflicts with those closest to him. It's causing delays and he hates the obstacles. He's been off-planet longer than he intended and he doesn't want to come home because he doesn't feel like he's doing enough to make you happy."

"But I'd never do anything to make him feel like that!"

"Maybe you haven't, but that's what he believes," I said gently. I tapped another card. "The Four of Cups means he's dissatisfied when he shouldn't be. Everything is good in his life, but he can't see that. He's lived so long with this idea of needing more, he's missing out on the good things coming his way. It's making him suspicious, and putting him in situations where he thinks his friends are against him." I pointed to the eighth card: Justice. "He believes he's right, and whatever actions he's taking are justified. But your final card here is the Tower. He's going to lose everything if he continues on this path. If it's wealth he craves, he'll realize it isn't the important thing he once thought. His whole view of the world will change, but the upheaval may be too much for him."

I looked up to see a pale, terrified expression on Novi's face. She held her baby so tightly, she started to squirm in her mother's arms. I reached out and touched Novi's hand.

"This is the future," I said gently. "If you tell him you're worried, you can change this. I've been doing this a long time and I know this outcome doesn't have to happen if you work at it."

"Really?" she asked, sniffing and swiping at tears.

I handed her a disposable wipe from a drawer in my reading table. I always kept a supply on hand for moments like this. In my experience, when people felt you were telling them something personal or you seemed to understand their problems in a way no one else could, they cried like babies. I didn't mind. I understood how cathartic the whole card reading experience could be.

"If he loves you, he'll listen. You say he works in the mines, so maybe the next time he's on leave, bring him here. I'll do a reading and see what can be done to get this situation resolved."

"Yes," she said, drying her tears quickly. It was like her own outburst surprised her, making her angry because it was so unexpected. "He says there's been a lot of upheaval recently. Things aren't like they used to be. I don't know... I'll tell him what you said."

"I always send my clients a copy of the reading transcript they can upload to their memory blocks. You can send it to him, if you want. That might help," I suggested gently.

"Yes, I'll do that. Thank you, Felicia. I'm so glad I came to talk to you. Bless you."

33

I slipped my c-tex bracelet back on and got up. Novi followed suit. Her gushing praise was a little over the top, but it felt nice to help someone who needed it instead of creating a star chart for someone's dog, or predicting when and why such-and-such a man didn't ask so-and-so's daughter to a party.

"I'm happy to help," I said as I walked Novi to the front of the store.

Lotus was already there with the door open as if she couldn't wait to usher Novi outside. I arched an eyebrow when Novi wasn't looking. Lotus merely gave me a half shrug. Obviously, someone was in a rush to see her boyfriend.

On the doorstop, Novi turned to me, grabbing my hand and pumping my arm vigorously. The move jostled the baby, but the girl showed no signs of waking up.

"Thank you!" she babbled. "You've really made me feel so much better about this. I'm going to tell my friends. They've wanted to see you, but they always found this part of town too intimidating. I'm going to let them know otherwise and how much you helped. Thanks again."

Before I could say anything, she released my hand and hustled down the well-lit street. A few skips later, she was gone. Lotus and I stood there looking after her, both of us open-mouthed. Lotus recovered first.

"That was a lot of love," she said drily.

I shrugged. "I'd like to hope I really helped her."

"Maybe, but it was *too* much love, like she was forcing it. Something tells me not to trust her," Lotus murmured, watching the street, trying to follow where Novi had disappeared. Then she turned to me. "You're too naïve sometimes, wanting to help everyone and always getting taken in by a sob story.

You're reading cards, not doling out life advice. I'd never use Granny G's cards like that. I'd use them for the good of the family."

Great, this again. How many times would I have to endure this before my family gave it a rest? Besides, I was hardly naïve after what I'd been through with my mother, Roy, and even Alexei. It amazed me I'd come through with my ability to trust still intact.

"This is what I want to do with my life and *my* cards, so get over it," I retorted. "And I do use them to help the family. You all get readings for free whenever you want. Besides, everyone knows I'm better at this than the whole lot of you so suck it up." Then because I was feeling mature, I stuck my tongue out at her. "Now tell me why you don't trust her because I'm not feeling it."

Like me and almost everyone in the family, Lotus experienced the same gut reactions I did, all courtesy of the luck gene—another thing I hadn't told my family about. No one else needed to carry the weight of that knowledge around. They didn't need the burden of second-guessing their actions or trying so damned hard not to question whether people's feelings were genuine.

"I can't put my finger on it yet. Maybe it was the way she kept gushing, or how her story went on and on. You're the card reader. You're getting paid to figure that stuff out, not have her drop the answer in your lap and regurgitate the words back to her. And did you see how she handled her baby? It was like she'd never held one in her life."

I frowned. Why hadn't I felt anything? Was it because my own reactions had been haywire since Alexei had left? Maybe my gut couldn't process the finer details. "You don't think her story was true?"

"Hard to say. I just know it had too many details."

Spoken like a true Sevigny, brought up in a family of con artists. Still, "How do you even know what we were talking about?"

Lotus shrugged. "I wanted to know how much longer you'd be, so I listened at the door. Thin walls, remember?"

"Yes, I remember."

Lotus snickered. "Speaking of the Russian, you going to tell him there's a troublemaker in the mines?"

I shrugged. "I don't talk about things clients tell me in confidence, but if I think it could be a problem, I might. I'll see what the cards suggest."

Lotus nodded and left it at that. One thing I had to say about my cousin and made me glad she was there even if she annoyed me sometimes—she got me. No one understood like family did.

"You heard from him at all?"

"No, but it's barely been two weeks. He said it might be three before he got back."

"If I couldn't see Buckley for that long, my girl parts would dry up," she sympathized. Then she brightened. "Well, if we're done here, Buckley says he's at the club. I told him no need to wait because you were our secret line-skipping weapon. Ready to party?"

I looked dubiously at Lotus and her ribbons, and wished Alexei were with me instead of wherever the hell he was. "Okay, let's party."

3

One handy thing about my chain-breaker watchdogs: I always had a flight-limo available without ever having to ask. Sometimes their level of attentiveness made me wonder if Alexei had chipped me without my knowledge. Or was I so boring, my routines were easy to predict? When I thought about complaining, I'd remember I never had to walk anywhere or fight over public air-hacks, so I kept my mouth shut. Besides, it meant Alexei cared, which made me feel all gushy inside thinking about him.

On Mars, energy was cheap. The HE-3 shortage hadn't impacted here as it had Earth, where the fuel was eked out of the Moon and shuttled back. Mars was the gateway to the riches of the outer solar system with everything funneled through it first before shipping out to the rest of the tri-system. And like a corrupt One Gov official, Mars skimmed a portion off the top. Many people had their own personal vehicles, though mass transit was also popular. You could hire an air-hack to whisk you wherever you wanted to go, so the air byways were always jammed.

And the stories I'd heard about water being rationed on Mars—urban legends. I had all the hot showers a girl could want, with and without Alexei. When they'd terraformed Mars, the water-rich dwarf planet Ceres was tapped. I didn't understand the planning involved to prevent Mars from shattering like an egg on impact; only that Ceres was harvested from the asteroid belt to increase the planet's mass and give Mars a gravity boost more in line with Earth's. Also, more water.

Mars was given two extra moons—Vesta and Pallas, also culled from the asteroid belt. Their combined gravitational pull was enough to heat the iron core of Mars, thus magnetizing the planet and protecting it from solar radiation. Mars was also nudged closer to the Sun, shifting its position farther into the habitable zone. Hey, I guess if you were going to terraform a planet, you may as well go all out.

Lotus fidgeted beside me on the bench seat while I applied more eyeshadow until my eyes shimmered like my dress. I touched up the rest of my face, then threw the cosmetics into my makeup bag and stashed it in a compartment under the seat. Though the trip wasn't long—fifteen minutes to the Vibe District—Lotus had already knocked back two shots of tequila from the minibar.

"Don't like flying?" I asked.

"Just anxious. You took longer with that reading than normal."

Though she might tease me about Alexei and act blasé about threesomes, I knew Lotus worried Buckley might hook up with another woman. If so, that would be the end of them and I knew she wasn't ready to give him up. While I'd never interfere unless she asked, I couldn't see them lasting much longer.

Tonight could end with me either having to watch them fight or make out. Neither would be entertaining.

The twinge in my stomach warned me the flight-limo was descending to street level. I peered out the window. There was more than enough light to see the Vibe District in all its vibrant splendor. It encompassed three square blocks and catered to anyone with a mind to party, with some sort of entertainment always available at any time.

Originally, I'd wanted to locate my shop there. Alexei had flat-out vetoed me, claiming it wasn't the safest part of Elysium City, no matter how low the overall crime rate. The buildings were a riot of colors and shapes, lit up with glaring neon outlines that chased away the darkness. It was so bright, you couldn't even see the stars—not that anyone was looking given how intent they were on having a good time. The only objects you could really see in the sky were two of the four moons, Vesta and Phobos. Vesta was full as it made its way across the sky, while Phobos was a blip of light as it zoomed around Mars pretty much doing its own thing. It orbited the planet three times a sol, its presence in the sky so common a sight, you forgot it housed the harshest penal colony in the tri-system. After all, One Gov had to put its criminals somewhere. I guess outer space was as good a place as any.

Though we still hadn't landed—there must have been a line out front causing a delay—music from the club assaulted us. The thud of a heavy bass line made the armored flight-limo rattle. I could even feel the pounding on my body, thudding against my chest. It had been a while since I'd been to a club like Red Dust—big, loud, lots of dancing, too much drinking, and so many drugs. I tried to psyche myself into the right mind-set. I used to love hitting the clubs back in Nairobi. Of course this would be fun. I was going to have a good time. I would enjoy myself and not pine for Alexei and wish I was with him. "It sounds wild inside. Maybe I should be wearing ribbons too."

Lotus grinned. "Maybe you should."

"Think we'll find Buckley?"

"We'd better or I'll kill him."

So much for true love.

Our c-tex bracelets both shimmered and vibrated at the same time, which was weird and a little freaky. Lotus got to hers first, then groaned.

"It's Celeste. Family chain-shim time. It's one thirty in the freaking morning. Why isn't that crazy broad asleep?" Lotus complained while tapping the screen.

"She told me she has anxiety issues so she has trouble sleeping. She keeps her mind busy until she passes out from sheer exhaustion."

"Huh, I didn't know. There's drugs for that," Lotus said, not sounding the least bit interested. Then her tone turned disgusted. "Ugh! Another reminder about the fucking picnic in a couple of weeks. She's really set on being queen bee, isn't she?"

"I guess someone needs to herd the cats," I answered, tapping my own bracelet and releasing the shim. "She's been really welcoming since I arrived on Mars. She gets my vote if she wants to be queen."

"So you're going to the picnic?"

"Not this time. Celeste is great, but for once it'd be nice if the family was excited to see me rather than Granny G's deck."

Celeste was yet another distant cousin on Mars. She was forever making announcements and hosting parties, pulling together whatever family was available and turning ordinary gatherings into "events" that bordered on ostentatious. While I'd met most of the family on Mars thanks to her, at times it felt like she was taking advantage of me and that made everything a lot less fun.

"I don't know if you can skip out. I think it's going to be a big deal. She's after everyone. Hell, she's sending shims at one thirty in the morning, for fuck's sake. It'll be your chance to introduce everyone to the Russian."

"Oh, hell no then! I don't need a baptism by fire."

"You have to bring him around sometime. You can't keep the family in the dark forever."

I sighed. "I know. I'm just not ready for my two worlds to collide yet."

"Let me know when you are. I want to make sure I'm there to enjoy the show."

"Geez, thanks for the support."

Lotus grinned. "Isn't that what family's for?"

The debate on family politics came to a halt as the flight limo door slid open. Music blasted us, with the ground seeming to shake beneath me. A hand reached in and we were helped out by one of my chain-breakers. Looked like I had an army of four on babysitting duty tonight—a big step up from the usual one or two.

The evening was warm and people milled about. After the Witching Time and with the fireworks over, people were either on their way home or deciding what to do next. Finding Buckley would be a chore in this crowd.

A giant red neon sign in front of us boldly displayed the club's name—Red Dust. In halting Russian, I asked the closest chain-breaker if we'd be able to get inside. He gestured for me to wait before cocking his head to the side, obviously in touch with someone via the CN-net.

"Do you see Buckley?" Lotus asked, standing on tiptoe and scanning all directions. "He said he'd be by the door." Then she was tapping her c-tex before scoping out the area again, grinding her teeth in frustration. "If he's not here, he's a dead man."

A few more minutes of Lotus tapping and cursing until I heard a voice vying for our attention. Following the sound, I saw Buckley frantically waving at us while another chain-breaker detained him a few dozen feet away. Rolling my eyes, I told the closest chain-breaker to let Buckley through. Seconds later, he bounded up like a frisky dog—I'd seen enough dogs lately to know—and threw an arm around Lotus.

Buckley was average height with a long swath of dirty blond hair that swept to the side and covered his right eye. The rest of his head was shaved clean. He was cute, but not particularly memorable—the way most people were when their parents couldn't afford MH Factor upgrades beyond the basics. His internal t-mods were base model too, so he actually didn't rate much higher than either me or Lotus with our c-tex bracelets. He worked in the booming Martian construction business, and spent his off time at the gym though he wasn't as dedicated as Alexei. Compared to Earth, it was difficult to build muscle mass on Mars with its slightly lower gravity though I suspected Alexei's MH Factor allowed him to maintain muscle more easily than most.

"Get off me! You're all sweaty," Lotus complained, smacking him. "Where were you?"

"I was here the whole time! I just couldn't get by them," he said, jerking his thumb at the chain-breakers.

"Sorry. My fault," I apologized.

"Hey, Felicia," Buckley said, throwing his other arm around my shoulders. "No worries. Just glad I'm not having my ass handed to me." Then as if remembering himself, he removed his arm and glanced about. "Is the Russian here?"

"No, he's out of town. He'll be back next weekend or the week after."

I couldn't help but be amused at the relief on his face or how he allowed his arm to drop back over my shoulders. "So it's just the three of us? Should be fun."

"That's if we can get inside," I cautioned.

"Oh, I think I know how to get inside," Buckley answered, shooting us both a look that said he meant getting inside more than the club.

Um...gross. Buckley may have been the perfect guy for Lotus given his low-tech status, but I felt she could do better. If my boyfriend had creepily implied a three-way with my cousin, we would have had serious words about it. I definitely wouldn't be engaging in the tonsil-licking session they'd abruptly started. Thankfully, it didn't last long as a chain-breaker approached and gestured for us to follow. I got out from under Buckley's arm and pulled Lotus after me.

"Come on, kids. You can save that for when I want the retinas burned out of my head."

One chain-breaker led us past the line of club-goers waiting to get inside. Another prevented people from getting too close, deflecting anyone reaching out to stop our progress. Lotus grinned, and I returned it. I couldn't help but get a kick out of the whole "being connected" thing and made a mental note to thank Alexei later.

Many in the crowd wore outfits tinged with neon fringes. It was the latest fad in the Elysium City club scene, something even a person like me could try. You lined your clothing with a thin, flexible tubing of tiny filaments that dangled and swayed when you danced. The color variations were endless, though green, pink, and blue were the most popular. I'd heard that when you took a Euphoria hit, the neon created color waves that tripped the mind into a state of consciousness you couldn't achieve anywhere else—not even on the CN-net. Though I hadn't tried Euphoria myself, I was curious. It caused intense hallucinations, heightened sexual arousal, and even dulled pain. Maybe I'd give it a whirl if Alexei was with me, but not when the only person looking out for me was myself. What if the Euphoria state went bad, which had been known to occur. I didn't have any stabilizing t-mods to save me. What might happen to me during a Euphoria trip was anyone's guess.

Instead of heading to the main entrance, we were taken to a side door around the corner. Our chain-breaker sized up the club bouncers, some words were exchanged—Russian, though it was too fast and the music inside too loud for me to follow. However, I heard Alexei's name, then a gesture toward me. Abruptly the side door opened and we were whisked inside.

"Remind me to go places with you more often," Lotus noted with approval.

I laughed. "It isn't always like this."

Lotus linked her arm through mine while pulling Buckley after her. "Come on, let's ditch the watchdogs and have some fun!"

We were in a back hallway behind the main part of the club. In front of us were a series of doors that likely went to staff offices. With Lotus urging us, we abandoned our chaperones, Buckley whooping excitedly behind us. The thudding music grew louder until we rounded a corner and cleared the hall. There, we stood on a balcony overlooking the whole club, blasted with sound and light.

"Wow."

I wasn't sure who said it. Maybe it was all three of us. I felt Lotus clutch my hand as we looked down at the writhing mass of bodies and sea of neon. It just seemed to go down into forever as if the floor had been dug out and descended another several stories. On the walls were abstract red-hued projections that moved and twisted in time with the music, looking like an actual dust storm swirled around us. Up above on the blackened ceiling was an array of lights that twinkled like pulsating stars. I saw three separate bar areas serving drinks with colorful liquor bottles lined up in pyramid formations, backlit in a way to entice patrons to drink. The bartenders looked sexy and chic, dressed in skintight black catsuits with neon red piping. Somewhere down there was the Euphoria bar, where patrons could take a hit of the latest designer vapor and scramble their neurons for the night.

In the center of it all was the dance floor—although I wasn't sure it could technically be called that since no one was on the floor. Everyone floated in midair in a caged-off area that prevented people from drifting back to normal gravity. To get in and out, people stepped onto the floor and immediately started rising, then used the caged sides to climb up and down. It made me wonder what the liability might be if people started dropping to the floor like flies. Still it looked amazing, like the true zero-g of outer space.

While we took in the view, chain-breakers surrounded us again. I shrugged when Lotus scrunched her face in irritation. She leaned in, her mouth next to my ear. "How can you stand them around all the time?"

I shrugged. "You get used to it."

"Are they going to follow us all night?"

"Me, yes. You, don't worry. They can be discreet. Plus, they'll get us VIP access and you'll live your dream of drinking for free. After a while you won't even notice them. You can make out with Buckley in some dark corner to your heart's content."

Lotus beamed. "You had me at free drinks."

A chain-breaker took us down a set of stairs and to the main level. I didn't think it was possible for the music to be louder. I was wrong. It actually felt like a physical thing bouncing off the top of my head. Thank the gods the shop was closed tomorrow, because I was pretty sure I would need the whole day...uh, sol, to recover from tonight.

Lotus made the universal "I need a drink" gesture, and the three of us headed to the bar. We were stopped halfway by an intimidating-looking bouncer, all flexing muscle and shaved head, who directed us to a roped-off platform near the dance floor. There, plush velvet couches and elegant tables waited. I sat on one of the couches and it felt like sinking into a dream—even better than what I had at home. Lotus and Buckley took the couch across from me, equally dazzled.

We'd barely made ourselves comfortable when a server appeared and took our drink orders. Moments later, she was back; I don't think I'd ever been served so quickly in my life. Lotus and I both had a Cassini Swirl—three layers of vodkas, each with a different mixing point, with a layer of chocolate between each vodka. Buckley went for the more traditional gin and tonic.

Lotus clinked glasses with me. "I could get used to this. Any other clubs the Russian owns we can enjoy?"

"Don't know. I never asked," I admitted.

"Well, ask! Hook us up," Buckley said. "The crew is never going to believe we're here. I'd shim them and tell them to meet us, but they'd never get in."

"I could probably leave word at the door and say we had more people coming," I suggested. Generally, I liked hanging out with Lotus and Buckley's friends. Also, it wouldn't hurt having more people around. I'd feel like less of a third wheel that way.

"Excellent!" Buckley grinned, then downed the rest of his drink before signaling for another. "Let's see who I can round up."

I sipped my Swirl while Buckley scanned the CN-net. The first sip burned before the sweetness hit. Next came the warm glow and I relaxed into the couch. I could feel my gut unwinding, the tension giving way under the alcohol's influence. It was still there, but the uneasiness wasn't so sharp.

"Looks like something interesting is going on," Lotus commented, pointing to a commotion on the other side of the VIP lounge.

I turned, rising from my couch for a better look. A crowd of people were clustered around one of the table groupings. They were loud and boisterous, dressed in outfits more outrageous and revealing than even Lotus and her ribbons. There seemed to be some excitement in the middle, focused on a single person. I could feel my face break into a grin as I turned back.

"It's Mannette Bleu."

Lotus bounced in her seat and clapped her hands, screeching with excitement. "Mannette Bleu? *Here?* Could this night be more awesome? Come on, let's go see her!"

The three of us were out of our seats before Lotus even finished speaking.

By all rights, I should have hated Mannette given how she'd screwed me over when I first arrived on Mars. If Alexei hadn't walked back into my life and swept me off my feet, maybe I would have. Instead, Mannette Bleu was far and away the most interesting person I knew.

An old friend of Charlie Zero's from Earth, she was to be my planet-side contact on Mars. Unfortunately, she was highly unreliable when not properly motivated. She'd forgotten I was coming or that Charlie had even contacted her. In fact, I think she was on a two-week Acidalian cruise when the *Martian Princess* docked at the space elevator. When Martian Immigration Services couldn't reach her, I was placed under arrest, spent two nights in jail, and endured a week of hell as I tried to prove I had the right to be on Mars. You'd think I would have seen that one coming, but no. It went without saying that Alexei had a meltdown of epic proportions and dragged Mannette off her cruise. Between the two of them, they cleared up my problems with both Immigration and Martian Planetary Law Enforcement.

She was a pseudo-celebrity with her own reality show on the CN-net where she put every minute of her life on display for the tri-system to watch. She had a staff of eight, who trailed her, recording and uploading her exploits to the CN-net, running simulcast experiences so a moment was never missed. Whenever she visited my shop, my clientele actually increased for a few sols afterward thanks to some weird celebrity halo effect.

She was fun, smart, and had more business savvy than I ever would. She was also vain and extremely selfish, so I'd learned to take the good with the bad.

Tonight Mannette was in her element as she whooped it up with her entourage. She was gorgeous with mocha-colored skin, a cascading mane of white-blond hair, and blue eyes that looked like the Caribbean back on Earth. She wore a sleek white dress that barely covered her butt or breasts, trimmed with enough hot pink neon it almost hurt to look at her. White knee-high platform boots completed the outfit, making her taller than everyone as she pranced around, the drink in her hand perilously close to spilling.

With her were two of her live-feed streamers—PVRs—recording everything with their optic implants, running it through their memory blocks, then spooling it to the CN-net for the tri-system to consume. She had four others with her—two men and two women—who encouraged her antics as they alternated between drinking and taking hits of Euphoria from the clear glass bowl on the table.

It was easy to get by the crowd of onlookers—people from other VIP tables who wanted in on the stir Mannette created. She always traveled with her own bodyguards, who recognized me and let us pass. Plus, with Lotus and I both pushing our way through, who was really going to stand in the way of a double dose of the luck gene?

"Felicia! Lotus Flower!" Mannette shrieked. She slammed her glass on the table, breaking its fragile stem. She tottered over to capture first Lotus, then me, in hugs bordering on strangulation. "It's been too long! What are you doing here?"

"We needed a night out." Lotus jerked her thumb toward

Buckley. Then a gesture to me. "And Felicia is on the loose because the Russian is out of town."

Mannette grinned down at me. This close, she smelled of some exotic perfume that actually made me want to lick her. "Still with him, huh? The man may be every woman's wet dream, but he will seriously fuck up your life."

This was *exactly* the conversation I didn't want spread all over the CN-net. "Yes, we're still together and everything is perfect. But what about you? Where have you been? I haven't seen you in ages."

"Para-skiing at Olympus Mons. Can you believe it? It's phenomenal! That's where I met Glitch."

She pointed to one of the men on the sofa, who got up to shake our hands. Glitch? As in, a mistake? Talk about irony, because that was all he would be on Mannette's radar—another relationship mistake. I didn't even bother to remember him because he wouldn't be around long. Mannette went through men like they were an all-you-can-eat buffet and she wanted her money's worth.

"Sit!" she cried, pushing people aside to make room. She held my hand now, pulling me to her. "I need another reading! The last one you did was unbelievable, it was so dead-on accurate. But I need to know more about this man you saw. Was it Glitch, because if it wasn't, I don't want to waste my time."

This was said while Glitch sat beside her, obliviously sucking back a hit of Euphoria.

"Sure. Come by my shop whenever you want."

"Wonderful! Let me tell you about what happened while I was in Olympia!"

And she was off, describing her trip in vivid detail until we all howled with laughter. Drinks were refilled and I could feel myself unwinding more. Gods, it felt so good to have a sliver of peace after being on edge for weeks. I sighed and sank back, letting myself enjoy the alcohol, the music, and the laughter.

Lotus leaned in close to me. "Don't make it weird, but there's a guy over there checking you out."

I sat up abruptly. "Really? Where?"

"I told you not to make it weird! He's by the bar where we came in. Blond. Black suit. He's just standing there, not doing anything. Just looking at you. It's kind of hot, in a creepy, stalker-y way."

"Is someone checking out our little Felicia?" Mannette asked, catching the last bit of our conversation. "Where is he? I wanna see! The Russian isn't gonna like this."

She stood up, making a spectacle of herself as she searched in all directions. I groaned and covered my face, hoping whoever he was didn't take Mannette's display as an invitation to approach. When I looked up again, the entire group scoured the club for my admirer, laughing as if it was the funniest event of the evening.

"I don't see anyone. Where is he?" I asked, scanning the club for myself.

Lotus huffed with annoyance. "Well, he's gone now. These idiots here scared him away!"

"He probably saw my place holder flat-file avatar on the CN-net and lost interest," I consoled. "Besides, I'm not the one who's looking to pick up, remember?"

"I can help with that," Mannette volunteered, plunking down between us. "Just show me who you want and we'll see if he's interested. You too, Buck. See anything good out there?"

Buckley looked like he'd just been set loose in a candy store, and Lotus punched his shoulder. "If we're picking up, I'm doing the picking," she informed him.

"I'd pick both of you girls, if you were into it," Mannette said to both me and Lotus, grinning. Then she laughed. "Come on, we have to dance. I want to see how those ribbons hold up, Lotus. Everyone take a Euphoria hit and let's go." She gestured to the clear bowl. Attached to its top was a long thin tube that fed into the bowl. Inside I saw thick, swirling mist—Euphoria. It writhed into sinuous shapes, beckoning me.

"Me first," Glitch said, picking up the tube and inhaling deeply. Then he slumped back, a blissed-out look on his face— that was how fast it hit, between one breath and the next. He handed it to the woman beside him and so it went around the table until it came to me.

I'd never been a casual substance taker. Most of the drugs were so powerful, they knocked someone like me right on her ass—someone without any tech implants and no MH Factor. Everything was designed with an extra kick to get around the One Gov gene modifications, so I knew I couldn't handle what was in the bowl. Even my gut knew it, warning me against taking the tube Lotus held out. But in that moment, I was so sick of the jangling, roiling feeling inside me, I wanted to shut it down if only for a little while.

So I took the tube and inhaled while the group cheered their approval.

I felt the Euphoria fill my lungs and everything in me narrowed down to a single breath. I held it a beat, and when I exhaled the thick haze of smoke, everything changed. My gut fell silent for the first time in my life. The calm I experienced was like nothing I'd ever known. I exchanged a look with Lotus, who gave me a lazy grin before her head rolled onto Buckley's chest.

In my next breath, the music felt more intense, the velvet couches more luxurious, the zero-g dance floor more inviting. All outside stimuli were more vibrant and the internal ones were just...off. When I looked to Lotus again, she and Buckley were heading to the zero-g dance floor. Mannette got up and pulled Glitch after her, giving him a "come hither" look. In fact, it seemed they were moving the party to the dance floor, where they could bump and grind against each other. I waved away the hands that tried to pull me with them. I had the most spectacular feeling of calm invincibility and all I wanted to do was be alone to enjoy it.

That feeling lasted all of five seconds—about the amount of time it took me to realize I wasn't really alone. I still had Consortium chain-breakers watching me, didn't I? How could I be by myself when they were always there? It followed then that to be alone, I actually needed to *be* alone. The idea intrigued me and took up all the available space in my brain. Did I have what it took to ditch them? Time to find out.

"I have to go," I said aloud to absolutely no one.

Standing, I walked to the edge of the VIP platform, where the roped-off entrance separated me from the rest of the club patrons. The Euphoria gave me the sensation I could do anything, even disappear in a puff of smoke.

I made eye contact with one of my chain-breakers posted nearby, standing in traditional bodyguard stance—massive arms crossed over a deep chest, looking like his suit jacket could barely contain his shoulders. I smirked a little, and then like I was diving into a pool, I let myself fall into the crowd.

I was swallowed in an instant. It was as if the people parted then closed behind me like ripples of water. I felt like a fish, swimming with the current. I laughed, then clamped a hand over my mouth to hold in the laughter, afraid to let it get away. Then I removed my hand because obviously I had more laughter. It wasn't like I was storing it up, which was just as hilarious as thinking I might be a fish.

I swam through the crowd. It seemed wonderfully simple and everyone moved exactly the way I needed. If I was jostled, I didn't feel it, though it was difficult to judge how hard the jostling might be. Probably not too badly or it would hurt more, I reasoned.

The crowd carried me until I was splayed against one of the red wall projections, looking up with awe as dust swirled above me. I'm not sure how long I stared at it, mesmerized. I think someone groped me, but I wasn't sure. It was difficult to pay attention as I stared up at the dust. Maybe hands were on my ribs, then my breasts. Maybe they weren't. It hurt a little, but not much. Someone pressed against me and I didn't care until I realized I didn't like it. I elbowed them in the ribs and they let go. Then I remembered I was sneaking away from my chain-breakers so I crept along the wall until I ran across a door.

It opened at my touch, which was perfectly sensible. Doors always opened for me. I wanted it open, so it was. Easy. I was in a dark hallway. Not the least bit surprising. I ran as far as the hall would take me. My shoes cut into my feet so I took them off. I tried carrying them since I was sure I liked shoes but holding them exasperated me. I probably had more at home anyway so I could just leave these.

When I got to the end of the hall, I found another door. Another hall. Another door. Then another hall-door combination until the cycle got annoying and all I wanted was to get to the end. At the last door, I was outside. Wow. I looked around. I was in a back alley with very little light. But no chain-breakers. I, Felicia Sevigny, had finally given them the slip! I fist-punched the air, cheering for myself. Then I fell down, but that was okay since it didn't hurt.

If the air was cool, I couldn't tell. All I wanted was some light, so I ran toward the street. It was farther away than I thought and I may have fallen, but I didn't think so. If I didn't feel it, how could it have happened?

Once I made it to the street, I looked up at the sky, pleased with myself. I was on Mars and I was doing okay. The moons weren't the same as on Earth though, which bugged me. Mars had too many. I could see three now. There was Vesta, full and pale. Then Pallas, low in the sky but almost identical in size. Then Phobos, rocketing past everything. I held up a hand as if I could catch it. I couldn't, but I liked to think I could if I put in the effort.

"Hello, Felicia. It's a pleasure to finally meet you."

I whirled at the voice. I was supposed to be alone! Not fair!

Male. Young, but everybody looked young. The only immediate tell that gave away age was the eyes, but I couldn't see his in the dimly lit alley. Blond hair cut short. Above average height. Probably blue eyes since those just sort of went with blond hair, didn't they? He looked familiar and I felt I should know him, but didn't. I'd never met him before and yet...

"I don't know you," I announced.

"I know, but I know you, and for now, that's enough. Though the circumstances aren't ideal, I've looked forward to this meeting." His voice was mildly accented. I couldn't place it, but it sounded like something I'd heard before... Something about the way he rolled his *r*'s.

"It's good that we're alone. I'm sure the Consortium wouldn't be pleased we were meeting, certainly not Alexei Petriv after the trouble he's taken to hide you from the rest of the family."

The family? I already had all the damn family I could handle. This man wasn't any family of mine. He didn't look like me at all. No wait... He looked like... What had Alexei done? What was going on?

Suddenly I was very aware of how alone I was.

"Your grandmother wanted to meet you, but it wasn't possible for both of us to make the trip to Mars."

Grandmother? She still hated me because I got the Tarot cards when Granny G died. That old bat wouldn't cross the street to help me if I was dying, and I would have told him that if I could get the words out.

I backed away. He advanced. "I know you're nervous. I am too. But family is important, and we've waited a lifetime to meet you. Your mother demanded we stay away, but... I suppose that's in the past now."

And then I had it as that slip of something I couldn't quite grasp fell into place. Monique. Somehow this man was connected to Monique Vallaincourt.

I backpedaled away in horror. Monique—the nightmare I couldn't ever forget was now in front of me. I turned and ran down the street, fighting to move in the murky Martian gravity. Sprinting was almost impossible and I fell, skidding across the concrete. I barely felt the pain. Instead, I forced myself up, searching the sky to get my bearings.

That was when I saw the explosion—a dot of light high in the sky that I could reach out and catch in the palm of my hand. In an instant, it brightened the entire night sky and turned it into day before everything faded back to darkness again.

Phobos, it seemed, was falling out of the sky.

4

I must have had a Euphoria crash, the shock of events eroding my buzz. Without t-mods stabilizing me, I blacked out. All I knew was one minute I ran down the street in my bare feet, the next I lay in bed fully clothed with sunlight streaming through the window. I had flashes where I remembered running and possibly hiring an air-hack, but little else.

I rolled over, groaning. Everything hurt. My head. My body. Gods, even my hair. Every nerve felt raw and exposed. With agonizing slowness, I eased out of bed. Standing took incredible effort as my feet protested any weight on them.

When I'd first moved into the condo, I decorated my bedroom in creams, pale pinks, and soft lavenders. The furniture was bleached wood—synth, not real—and the bed linens were patterned with delicate florals. I wanted something that didn't reflect anyone's taste but mine. Everything was meant to be light and airy as if it might float away on a cloud. Now the colors were glaring and I couldn't open my eyes without wincing.

"Blinds," I croaked out. The window covering snapped shut,

plunging the room into semidarkness. That eased some of my agony. I'd need stronger stuff to handle the rest.

The walk to the kitchen was the longest of my life. Along the way, I called out to the unit AI to shade every window. I'd kept the condo's color palette light and delicate throughout, and right then, I needed sunshades to walk from one end to the other.

A fumble through the cupboards turned up the aerosol vial pain meds. I took several puffs, breathing them into my system. That was when I noticed my palms were scraped raw. Most of my nails were broken and the polish chipped. Assessing myself, I saw my knees were bruised and scratched, and my feet...well, not good. Bloody and embedded with gravel. I could apply skin renewal patches and regrow the skin in about a sol, but I needed a shower first. Otherwise, I'd heal in all the dirt, which led to infection.

It took a few more minutes to realize the cramp in my stomach was hunger and I was overwhelmed by thirst. When had I eaten last? I had no idea.

I drank water straight from a pitcher in the cold unit. Next, cold take-out pizza—a surprise since the cold unit was usually bare. I rarely ate at home, and when I did cook, Alexei ate everything in sight. He could shovel down a surprising amount of food, but then he burned more calories than I did.

The hike to the shower took forever and I peeled off my dress as I walked. Somewhere along the way I realized my c-tex bracelet was missing. Fuck. If it wasn't in the condo, I was screwed. Aside from connecting me to the CN-net, it contained my One Gov citizenship chip. Most people's chips were implanted in their palms once they became full citizens at eighteen. Naturally my family hadn't gone for that, so mine was in my bracelet. Without it, I could say good-bye to any full citizenship rights like the Renew treatments and the Shared Hope program. My calorie consumption allotment would be halved and I wouldn't be allowed to own a business or property. I'd become a ward of the state unless I could prove my identity and secure a new chip.

Even without the chip problem, finding another c-tex bracelet would be nearly impossible, and if I did, it would cost a fortune to replace. Gods, it *had* to be somewhere. I couldn't have gotten into my condo without it since it held all my access codes. I'd find it eventually.

The glaring light in the bathroom was not pleasant. As for what the opaque window mirror reflected back at me...Ugh. Everything was black-and-blue, even my breasts. I recalled being groped at Red Dust. At the time, I hadn't felt anything but amazing and invincible. Now I just felt violated and stupid. I should *never* have tried the Euphoria.

The shower felt like needles digging into my skin, and every scrape stung like tiny knives as I lathered with soap. Eventually it became bearable as the pain meds kicked in, but it took forever to clean myself. Washing my hair was sheer misery. My broken nails snagged in the strands so I used clippers to clean up the ragged mess.

It was only as I dried myself that I remembered the encounter that had sent me spiraling out of control. Who the hell was that man? Someone connected with my mother's family obviously. Someone who wanted to reach out to me and...what? I had no idea and my terror had been enough to trigger a Euphoria crash. That, and Phobos exploding. No, I couldn't be remembering that right. My gut...No, I'd effectively turned it off.

But as I towel-dried my hair and started feeling human again, I couldn't help but wonder if I'd hallucinated the whole thing. Maybe the explosion hadn't even been real and I'd been blinded by an overhead light at the same time Phobos passed by. I poked at the idea, uncertain. I could have imagined the explosion. Or maybe I hadn't and these feelings existed because something really wrong was coming. Something I wasn't prepared to handle and the Phobos incident was a wake-up call. What if... Gods, I didn't even want to think about it, but what if something had happened to Alexei? Why, I had no idea, but what if it was so awful, I couldn't deal with it? What if he'd been hurt... or... I had to find my c-tex immediately!

I threw on the bathrobe I kept on the back of the bathroom door and hobbled to my bedroom. I tore through the room, finding nothing. Then I searched the condo, looking into everything because gods only knew what my frame of mind had been while I'd crashed.

Ultimately, I found it between the couch cushions. When I powered it on, the charge was low. I slapped it on my wrist, where it began charging as it tapped into my bio-energy. I had over a hundred unchecked shims, which was kind of insane. How was that even possible when...

Holy shit, it was Tuesday—Sunsol afternoon. I'd been out cold for two and a half sols?

I scanned the messages. Nothing there that I really cared about, though I did see a few from Lotus, which was good news. That meant she wasn't in the same mess I was. Then I flipped to the CN-net news feed, gasping as I read and flicked through the imagery.

The night I'd been at Red Dust, there had been an explosion

at the Phobos penal colony, the result of a prison break. Dozens of inmates had escaped. All were recaptured though several were dead. No names had been released. Phobos, which was porous, had actually cracked and splintered from the force of the explosion and there were concerns as to whether the penal colony should remain on the moon after the damage it sustained. Fuck. I'd witnessed a prison break.

Logically, I knew Alexei wasn't connected. I knew he was out there somewhere dealing with the tunnel collapses in the off-world mines and speaking to the union leaders. I was overreacting because of the Euphoria crash. Yet at the same time, I didn't really know what sort of situation he was in. The last Tarot reading I'd done hadn't left me feeling warm and fuzzy. I had no way to confirm where he was. No way to talk to him or see if he was okay. Alexei frequently went away on Consortium business but this was the first time I'd ever felt so disconnected from him. Seeing the explosion on Phobos brought up memories I thought I'd buried since Brazil.

My knees gave and I sank down on the couch. No, I couldn't let my thoughts drift in that direction. This wasn't Brazil. History wasn't repeating itself. Alexei was fine and there was no reason to believe otherwise. But what about this anxiety I couldn't shut off? What if something *had* happened—maybe not on Phobos but in one of the off-world mines? What if I lost him again, only this time, it was permanent?

A little over five months ago, that's what I'd believed—that he was dead and I'd lost him forever. I hadn't even realized I'd found something worth having until he was gone. And then he'd walked back into my life, determined to prove himself to me. I'd lived with the fear that I could lose him. Something else could take him from me. So I'd held myself back, terrified to go all in with him. I know I had. If I didn't fully commit, it wouldn't hurt so much if he disappeared again. Except I could see now I'd been lying to myself. If being without Alexei was my new reality...

I couldn't go through that a second time. I didn't want to imagine a future without him in it. I needed my cards. Even if he didn't want me using the Tarot for him, I needed to run a spread now. I had to see if he was okay. I couldn't settle until I checked, his feelings on the matter be damned. Yes, once I ran the cards, everything would feel better.

I pushed up from the couch on unsteady legs, about to hobble to my office, when explosive pounding smashed against the door. Stunned, I yelped and froze in the entrance hallway. Then the door opened and thumped hard into the wall. I think the plaster behind it may have cracked on impact.

Alexei stood in the doorway, looking more disheveled than I'd ever seen him. His thick black hair stuck up in all directions as if he'd shoved it impatiently out of the way and he hadn't shaved in at least a week. He was dressed like he'd just gotten off a shift at a construction site, wearing a dark T-shirt of some indecipherable color stretched over his broad shoulders and chest, canvas pants full of pockets, and work boots. Speechless, I watched him enter and slam the door behind him. He dropped something that looked like it might be shoes, but I immediately lost track as I found myself backed up and pinned to the wall by his body.

His lips crashed down hard on mine as he kissed me with enough force and heat, it seemed he might devour me. His tongue plunged into my open mouth and a hand fisted in my damp hair. His other hand slid down my back to cup my butt then lift me up on my tiptoes to grind against him.

It was a kiss that should have had me tearing at his clothes, desperate to get him naked. Except after the Euphoria crash and my crawl through the back alleys of Elysium City, the kiss hurt. He was too rough, too demanding, and my body was in a hurry to remind me how much I'd abused it.

"Alexei, don't. It hurts," I whimpered against his lips.

Immediately he stopped and set me back on my feet. Then he frowned as both hands came up to caress my face, my shoulders, and down my arms, examining me. The frown deepened as he inspected my skinned palms and broken nails.

"Your poor hands," he said, kissing one then the other. "I've always loved watching them move when you talk or you run your cards and how soft they feel against me. Seeing them like this feels like it might actually kill me."

Of all the things he could have said, that was the most unexpected and made me cry at my own stupidity. I never imagined he might notice a thing like that. He wiped away my tears and pulled back enough to take in my entire sorry state: bruised, cut, and practically falling apart in front of him.

"My people found your shoes in a deserted hallway at the Red Dust nightclub," he said, drawing my attention to what he'd dropped earlier. The shoes I thought I'd imagined were real, making me feel like I was in some twisted fairy tale. "They lost track of you for over an hour. Then your bracelet powered off. And now I see you like this...Do you know what this does to me? How much it terrifies me? The Euphoria you took isn't the same as what's available elsewhere. It's enhanced military-grade pain management mixed with opiates to increase the pleasure response. The Consortium was using Red Dust as a test market before releasing the product on a wider scale. You could have…I don't even want to contemplate what could have happened."

"I'm sorry. I shouldn't have done it."

"No, you shouldn't have," he agreed, voice hardening. "What the fuck were you thinking?"

I shrugged weakly, not looking at him. "I just wanted to feel something besides this edginess that's been eating at me for weeks. I thought it would calm me. Believe me, I won't do it again."

"Good, because I've shut down the club. As far as I'm concerned, testing is over."

He'd done *what?* "But…But what about the people working there?"

"Do you think I'd care about any of them if you died?"

I ducked my head, utterly humiliated. I should have known he'd react like this. Still, "They shouldn't lose their jobs because I made a bad decision."

He took a deep breath, letting it out slowly. In a calmer voice, he said, "They're all Consortium people. They'll be redeployed elsewhere."

"Oh. Okay," I said, letting it go.

He waited a moment, then said, "The fact that you're not arguing about this actually worries me. Why aren't you asking about the enhanced Euphoria and demanding to know what it's for?"

"I would, but I don't think I can spare the brain cells to ask the right questions." I looked up and met his amused expression. "Besides, I'm just so glad you're here."

The amusement faded. "I've spent the past two sols out of my mind. Even though I'd been assured you were home, I needed to know for myself you were safe."

I groaned. "You shouldn't have to waste your time babysitting me. I know you're busy with projects that cost billions of gold notes and you don't have time for this."

His thumbs stroked the insides of my wrists, moving in unhurried circles. "You are never a waste of my time. If you need me, I'm here. It doesn't matter what it is. Just don't make me relive this nightmare where I thought I'd lost you. Don't ever do that to me again."

"I really am sorry. I haven't been thinking straight," I admitted. "You've been off-planet for the Consortium before, but I never worried like I did this time. It felt different. Everything in me has been so unsettled, and the feeling won't stop. I just wanted to shut it off."

"Different how?" he asked softly.

I shrugged, not sure I could explain. "I saw what happened to Phobos. I was looking right at it when the explosion happened, then my Euphoria crash hit. You weren't involved, were you? The Consortium didn't have anything to do with what happened on Phobos, right?"

"Why would you even think that?" he asked instead.

"I don't know. It's just..." I shrugged again. "Maybe it's all mixed up in my head because everything happened at once. You were off-world, I took the Euphoria, and I've had this awful feeling of doom hanging over me. Plus when I ran the cards—"

"I asked you not to run the cards for me. That's not why I'm with you," he said patiently.

"I know, but it's like asking me not to breathe," I confessed. "Regardless, when I got up this morning, I realized how much the explosion on Phobos felt like Brazil all over again. I thought maybe that's why I'd been feeling so unsettled. Maybe Phobos was a warning you were gone and I would never see you—"

"No," he said urgently, interrupting me, hands stilling on my wrists. "I allowed foolish decisions to come between us and made mistakes I don't intend to repeat. I don't regret my actions in stopping your mother, but I regret putting us in a situation where that was the outcome. I regret the time we lost."

"I know. Or I thought I did. It wasn't until this morning that I realized how scared I am. It made me see how much I've been holding back because deep down I thought you would hurt me and disappear again. I thought if I acted like this didn't matter, it wouldn't hurt if you were gone." I swallowed around the lump in my throat, knowing he was the only thing in the world truly holding me up. If I lost him a second time and never told him all the things I'd been afraid to say, I couldn't live with myself. "I love you. I was a coward not to tell you before. I should have let you know how I felt and how much you mean to me."

He went utterly still. There was a look on his face I'd never seen before, a kind of amazed wonder that shocked me. "I didn't think you would ever say it."

My eyes widened, outraged. "What's that supposed to mean?"

Careful of my hands, he lifted my arms until my wrists rested on his shoulders. His lips curved into a smile and his hands settled around my waist. "I knew you were afraid, but I worried that if I said anything, you would run. I wasn't entirely certain you trusted me enough to let me in. And the thought of losing you was so paralyzing, I didn't want to risk what you'd already given me. You needed time and space to decide how you felt, and I tried to give it to you."

"What if I'd wanted to go?"

"I would have let you. Or I'd like to think I would. I'm not certain since I've waited too long for you to let you go. I love you. I've loved you since Brazil. I just haven't said the words because I knew you weren't ready to hear them, *moya lyubov.*"

My mouth opened and closed like a fish's. "*Brazil?* That was a year ago!"

"I know, but as I said, you weren't ready," he whispered. "Now you are."

"Alexei—"

"Say it," he murmured. His hands went to the sash of my robe, tugging gently on the knot. "Please, I need to hear you say it."

The awe in his voice made my stomach flutter. "I love you."

He sighed and bent until his forehead rested against mine. In that moment I knew he belonged completely to me. The Consortium may have created him, but only I owned him.

"Again. I need to hear it again."

"I love you."

"I adore you, Felicia," he murmured. "I will love you for as long as this life will let me. I don't know how to stop loving you."

I felt tears threatening again as I reached up to run my fingers through his hair. Nothing in my life had felt like this. Absolutely nothing. This man knew me better than anyone did or ever could, and to think he loved me this much while I ignorantly bumbled about, trying to sort out my life...

"I'm sorry I never told you before."

His hands slid under my robe and pushed it off my shoulders. "Then you'll need to make it up to me."

My breathing hitched. Any lingering aches and pains from Red Dust were forgotten. "How?"

Whatever he'd been about to say or do next, it all stopped as he pulled away, his eyes trained on my bruises. He pushed aside my robe until it was on the floor, swearing viciously under his breath in both English and Russian when he saw the extent of the bruises covering my ribs and breasts.

"What happened to you?" he ground out, raising a hand to my breast, his fingers skimming the bruises. "Who did this?"

"It happened at the club after I took the Euphoria," I said in a small voice. "Someone grabbed me from behind."

"Did he do anything else? Touch you anywhere else?" His voice was deceptively calm but rage poured off him in waves like it was a physical thing.

I knew what he was asking and I shook my head, shivering. "No. Just this. It was my own fault. I shouldn't have—"

"This was not your fault. It was mine for not being here and taking better care of you. Mine for always being pulled away on Consortium business and leaving you alone. Mine for not keeping you safe."

"It's bad enough you have a security detail following me everywhere except the bathroom. You can't expect to watch me every minute. It's creepy and it's weird," I shot back, suddenly nervous. "Besides, sometimes things just…happen."

"Not to things that belong to me."

"I'm not a thing you can own," I retorted.

I may as well have been talking to myself at that point because, just like that, he was gone. His mind had flown to the

CN-net and all I had left was a shell. He was still alive, but for all intents and purposes, he was no longer with me. His mind could travel the CN-net faster than anyone's, sniping information, searching down leads, gathering data. It was one of many things I'd never be able to do. I didn't have the t-mods. I couldn't load my thoughts into the CN-net and participate in that online world the way most of the population could. It hadn't really bothered me until now—moments like this when he was completely gone from me.

I didn't know what to do when he got like this—especially not when he had one hand on my breast and loomed over me. Disturbing, and it freaked me out. When I tried to wriggle away, he was back, his blue eyes focusing on me with laserlike intensity. Then he bent and lifted me until my legs were wrapped around his waist.

"Alexei, what happened? What did you do?"

"It's been dealt with" was all he said as he carried me to my bedroom.

"How?" I had an idea of what he'd done—gone through the club's security AI, analyzed all the CN-net avatars whose citizenship chips had been scanned that night, broke into memory blocks to search for anything involving me until he found who'd attacked me. No doubt he'd already located the responsible party and sent chain-breakers to deal with him.

Alexei said nothing, setting me on the edge of the bed instead. He disappeared, and when he came back, he carried a handful of skin-renewal patches.

"Alexei, please. Tell me what you did."

He knelt before me, tearing off pieces from of the first patch and smoothing them over the cuts and abraded skin on my knees. Seconds later, I could feel the tingle of new skin graphing over the damaged areas.

"You already know," he said, looking at my hands and applying patches there as well. Then my elbows because apparently I'd spent my evening falling over every single pebble on Mars. "You're mine to protect. Mine to keep safe. You were assaulted. You could have been raped. If you hadn't gotten away, he would have done just that and thought nothing of it. Just blamed the Euphoria. Claimed you were willing because you didn't say no. If I could, I would rebuild this world so nothing could ever hurt you. Since I can't, I deal with the threats the only way I know how." He examined the bottoms of my feet now, smoothing skin patches there as well.

"Is he still alive?"

He finished with my feet and his blue eyes met mine. "Not for much longer."

My eyes widened. "You can't kill a man because he touched me!"

"He wanted to do much more than touch, Felicia." He set the unused skin renewal patches on the floor. "I'm perfectly aware of how unhinged I sound. I would fail a One Gov rationalization test were I to take one now. Unfortunately for both of us, you make me irrational. I lose all common sense where you're concerned. A threat to you existed. I dealt with it."

"Even if he intended something worse, it didn't happen. You can't kill him for that."

"I disagree. To protect you, I would do that and more. This is what the Consortium created and turning off that conditioning is difficult." He paused, caressing my cheek. "I won't kill him, but I will destroy his life. Ultimately, he will end

71

up killing himself, which is the desired outcome so it doesn't really matter."

My mouth opened, but I was speechless. What kind of comeback was I supposed to have for that? How had we gotten so far away from normal?

"I'm sorry I'm scaring you," he said, and he looked sorry too as he knelt on the floor in front of me, his head bowed and hands at his sides. "If you want me to leave, I will."

"I just want you to be a regular guy and for us to not have conversations like this."

"I'm trying, but I may still do things you won't like because, for the Consortium, that is who I have to be. It's difficult to be one thing for you and something else for them. I'll make mistakes. You're not my conscience, but I need you to help me. I need you so much I would destroy this world if I lost you."

He looked so miserable and pained, I had to reach out to him. I may not like what he'd done, but I also couldn't let him go because of it either. My fingers brushed his hair from his face and tilted his head so I could see his eyes. I knew I should be angry and afraid, but seeing him like this undid me. He was undoubtedly one of the most powerful men in the tri-system yet he needed me. Only me.

"I need you too," I whispered. "I don't want to go back to that part of my life where you weren't in it. Just...ease up on the death threats. Notify One Gov instead of whatever it is you planned. Don't kill anyone for me. Don't do anything that might drive us apart."

"Never. I would never do that." He paused, slipping away from me again and back to the CN-net. A moment later, he murmured, "One Gov is on their way to apprehend him."

I let out the breath I'd been holding. "Thank you."

"*Pazhalsta*, but I'll be watching him and will deal with him as I see fit if I think it necessary. That's the best I can promise you."

What could I say to change his mind? Probably nothing. "Okay. I guess that's fair."

He rose up from where he knelt and his lips met mine. Slow, soft, and gentle, the kiss was little more than a brushing of lips. No part of his body touched me other than his mouth, the kiss a caress on its own.

To my surprise, he pulled back. "Would it be best if I left?"

I had to salvage this situation, afraid it might become a hurdle we couldn't overcome. In answer to his question, I leaned back on my elbows, spreading my legs in invitation, putting myself on display. I couldn't imagine behaving like this for anyone but him. His eyes went where I intended and stayed there. "I haven't seen you in over two weeks. What do you think?"

The hesitancy turned into something else. He said something softly under his breath in Russian I didn't catch. "I think we'll be ordering dinner in tonight," he said.

He stood and stripped off his clothing faster than I'd ever seen anyone move, throwing his T-shirt on the floor and somehow pushing off his pants and boots all at once. As always, I couldn't help but admire his body. He was perfect, all sculpted and defined muscle that felt like warm granite under my hands. His broad shoulders and deep chest tapered down to a lean waist and a set of abs I could probably do my laundry on. His arms and legs were also heavy with a chiseled muscle that begged my touch—hands, mouth, with whatever part of me that could reach him. Lastly, my eyes were drawn down to his penis, fully erect and swaying slightly under its own weight. It was beautiful yet daunting, unnerving me with worries that, just like everything about him, it would be too much for me.

However, what really caught the eye were his tattoos. Done in blue-black ink, they might be considered works of art if you didn't know how he'd earned them. The Madonna and child over his heart said he'd been born into the Consortium. The spider on his neck marked him as a thief. The crucifix on his chest signified he would never betray the Consortium and loyalty to death. High up on his right bicep, I'd once thought it a rose, but in reality it was dozens of tiny skulls shaped in the outline of a rose, meaning time in prison and also murder. He'd killed many times, and it was likely a number that would horrify me. The dragon around his waist and coiled down most of his left leg meant he was in the Consortium's grip for life. Last were the stars on his knees and both shoulders proclaiming him *vory v zakone*: thief in law and a ruler of the criminal underworld. He was the pinnacle of organized crime. And while the Tsarist Consortium took pains to show One Gov and the tri-system it had shed its ancient roots, the tattoos proclaimed some of the original element remained.

Before I could finish looking, Alexei tumbled me into the bedsheets. I found myself on my back, repositioned up the bed, him over me. Rather than kiss my lips, he ran his mouth over my body. My throat, my shoulders, along my arms and hands, then my breasts and stomach, to my thighs and lower—every part of me was kissed and licked and caressed with his mouth until I was an aching ball of need. His touch was worshipful as he whispered how much he needed me, how important I was to him, that I was the only thing in his world that mattered.

He'd never been so gentle before, never so reverent. I was on fire from those kisses, lost in him and begging him to take me because I needed him too. I couldn't live without him. Didn't want to live if he wasn't in my life.

An infinite amount of time later, he took pity on me. His body was poised over me and he held himself up on his elbows. He kissed me deeply, groaning into my mouth while his tongue danced with mine. Then with torturously slow movements, he pushed into me. I felt stretched and filled, crying out with relief after having been so long without him. My legs went around his waist and I dug my heels into him, trying to get him closer, faster. He wouldn't be rushed. Instead he continued his excruciating glide, making me feel all of him as he settled deep inside me. My eyelids fluttered closed at the sensation and I arched against him, begging him with my body, letting him know what I needed.

When he went utterly still, I opened my eyes to find him looking down at me, his blue eyes dark with want. The muscles in his neck were tightly corded as he strained to hold back rather than give in to what our bodies demanded.

"Say it," he whispered hoarsely, bracing himself on one forearm and fisting my hair. His other hand gripped my left hip hard enough to bruise as he fought to keep me from bucking against him and snapping his control. "I want to hear it. Please, Felicia."

"I love you. I don't know how to do anything else but love you. All I want is you. Oh gods, Alexei, no one but you!"

The hand on my hip moved, changing the angle until my hips canted up against his. He finally began to thrust in the powerful, fluid strokes I wanted that stole my breath away. My awareness of the world disappeared under the speed and urgency of his movements. In and out he went, the friction wonderful and overwhelming, pushing me past anything I'd felt with him before. His lips were on mine again, his tongue thrusting in a rhythm that matched his hips.

The orgasm hit so hard, I thought I was dying. I screamed into his mouth and clung to him. Felt his body jerk in response, and his hold tighten on me as his hips slammed into me. A heartbeat later, I felt him coming, his body convulsing with savage force. He roared his climax, greedily using my body and wringing every last bit of pleasure from both of us.

He rolled to the side then, moving so his weight didn't crush me. I found myself sprawled on his chest, my face against his throat. Both our hearts were racing, each of us breathless. I felt him twist my hair in his hands, using it to lift my head so our eyes met. For a long time, we simply looked at each other. I'd never experienced a moment with another person that felt so intense or weighted with potential.

"Move in with me," he said. "I don't want us separated any longer. I never wanted it, but you needed time and now I don't want another sol apart from you."

And because it seemed that easy and I wasn't sure why I'd resisted in the first place, I nodded. "Okay."

He smiled, making my heart swell. He eased me aside and climbed out of bed. Then he cleaned us up, and resettled the sheets around me. Before I realized it, he pulled on his clothes and crouched by the bed.

"I was in such a hurry to get to you, I left some things dangling," he murmured, kissing my forehead.

"Did everything go okay with the mines? Did you find out why they're collapsing?"

"That's not something I want to bore you with. Certainly not right now," he said, drifting in for another kiss.

Somehow that didn't seem like the right answer, so I tried again. "But it went okay?"

"There were some unexpected issues, but it's fine."

"You don't make it sound fine."

"It will be," he assured me. "For now I want you to rest and let the renewal patches do their work. I'll be back shortly with takeout."

I nodded. "Okay. I'll be here."

"I would hope so," he teased, brushing fingers through my hair. "I could get used to this agreeable Felicia."

"Don't worry. It won't last. We'll be fighting again soon enough."

"Until that happens, I plan on enjoying this immensely." He pressed a kiss to my lips before standing. "I love you. I'll be back soon."

It wasn't until he'd left that I realized he never said if he'd been on Phobos. And even though he was safe and I'd told him I loved him, nothing had changed. The unease in my gut that said something big and life-altering was heading my way hadn't disappeared. If anything, it was worse.

5

My brush with Euphoria took more out of me than I realized, so Alexei convinced me to close up shop for the rest of the week. While he was right, the idea hadn't thrilled me since it meant I might fall behind in my payments to him. When I mentioned that, he looked at me like I'd lost my mind before gazing at me thoughtfully.

"I suppose you could make it up in other ways," he suggested. It was later that evening after he'd returned and he was pulling my thigh up higher on his hip so he could thrust leisurely into me.

I stalled him with, "I still have to pay Lotus. She's rescheduling all my appointments and she feels just as awful as I do."

"Pay her? I'd like to strangle her for taking you to Red Dust. Mannette Bleu as well."

"If you're not here and I want to go out, I will. You're away a lot and I'm not a shut-in."

"That changes as of tomorrow."

I wanted to ask what he meant by that, but he drove into me

forcefully and refocused my attention until my train of thought was utterly derailed.

I slept most of the next sol with Alexei there when I needed him, be it to feed me or something more. I wasn't sure what he did while I slept. Worked via the CN-net probably, since I don't think he left my condo. Having him there was nice, although I wished I was awake enough to enjoy it.

By Thursday, or Deimosol, I felt more like myself so I agreed when he suggested checking out a resort in Apolli. I could have gone back to work, but playing hooky with him was more fun. We hadn't been together like this since the *Martian Princess*. I'd heard great things about Apolli, the resort town located at the base of Apollinaris Mons—one of the midrange mountains on Mars. There was skiing, or you could lie by the pool, which was definitely more my speed. Alexei mentioned he had Consortium business there that would take a few hours so we were killing two birds with one stone. The Consortium had invested heavily in the area, building Apolli into a tourist destination to rival Olympia. Presumably he'd be looking into that, though I didn't ask. When your boyfriend headed what many believed was a multiplanet crime syndicate with aspirations to replace One Gov, you tended to ask questions only when you really wanted answers.

I knew Alexei believed One Gov was corrupt and bloated, no longer focused on the interests of its citizens. He felt it held the human race back instead of letting us leap forward and some of the current programs constrained humanity. Though I agreed things needed to improve, did I want him to overthrow One Gov? If I was honest with myself, not really.

Sometimes I wondered how much we changed each other.

Was he toning down his more radical views because he knew I couldn't support them? Was I altering my stance on technology and genetic modifications because of who he was? And how did my luck gene play into events? Was it modifying things to...To what? To have its own advantage, whatever that was? I shuddered, afraid of the implications.

Since Mars only had one space elevator docked to Space Station *Destiny* and no high-orbit flights, it was about a six-hour flight-limo ride from Elysium City to Apolli. I mostly slept when I wasn't catching up on my shims. I ended up either deleting them or forwarding any work-related ones to Lotus. A couple had to do with the family picnic with a special reminder to bring the cards and my potato salad. Also, Celeste wanted to know if I had a "plus one" because she needed numbers. Ah, the joys of dealing with family.

Fuck. Family. I sat up with a start. Gods, how could it have slipped my mind?

Alexei was alert beside me. "What's wrong?"

"I forgot to tell you what else happened at Red Dust."

"That can happen with Euphoria. Short-term memory loss is one of the side effects we want to eliminate," he said, reaching out to stroke my hair and pull me back against him. I settled into his chest, my head on his shoulder, his arm slipping around me. I squirmed as I tried to get comfortable. He chuckled, amused as I struggled.

"Problems?"

I poked him in the stomach, meeting a solid wall of hard muscle. "Sometimes snuggling with you is like trying to cuddle a rock."

He laughed at that. "I believe that's the first time I've heard this particular complaint. Would you like me to do something different to accommodate you?"

"Um...no. What you're doing is fine." My poke became a caress. I could feel the ridges of his defined abdominals through his shirt and had to admit I was becoming increasingly sidetracked the more I touched him. My hand started to wander lower.

"Don't. That's too distracting." He plucked my hand away, lacing my fingers through his. "Tell me what happened."

"Oh, right. There was a man at the club. Lotus said he was watching me the whole night, but I didn't see him until afterward, once I was outside in the back alley."

"Did he hurt you?"

His voice had gone flat and I knew him well enough to know he was fighting for calm. He was trying to be the caring boyfriend I wanted, not the ruthless Consortium leader who crushed his enemies.

"No, nothing like that. He said he'd wanted to meet me for a while, but you'd been hiding me. He talked about my mother's family and how they wanted to know me but Monique wouldn't allow it. He mentioned a grandmother and how she wanted to meet me too, but couldn't travel to Mars. I had the Euphoria crash right after that."

I felt Alexei tense and I looked up at him. Beneath his stubble, I saw a muscle twitch in his jaw. "Stay away from him. He's dangerous."

"Why do you sound like you already know him?"

"Because I do." His tone was frightening. "He's Monique's father, Felipe Vieira."

I sat up, my gut doing this terrible thing where it kicked me so hard, I thought I might throw up.

"I hope that isn't the Felipe Vieira I think you're referring to." His eyes met mine. "Unfortunately, it is."

"The Under-Secretary of One Gov? How is that even possible? He's second only to Secretary Arkell, but everybody knows Vieira's the real power running things. He's..." I swore and felt a wave of disbelief. "You can't be serious. He can't be my grandfather."

"I assure you, he is."

I pulled away so I could face him head-on. "Felipe Vieira. Gods, was I named after him too? Was it some warped tribute on Monique's part? How long have you known? No, that's a dumb question. You've probably always known."

His expression was inscrutable, telling me everything I needed.

"Why didn't you say something? The file you gave me said my mother's family was connected with One Gov, but it never referenced anything like this! I never imagined I'd be related to the power running the damned tri-system! Don't you think this is something you should have told me?"

"At the time, my own plans were in motion and I couldn't let you jeopardize them. I knew it would either scare you away from me or you would do something reckless, such as confront Vieira."

"That was pretty damn selfish of you," I ground out.

"Perhaps, but I also wanted to protect you. Now, that's all I want. I don't want anything drawing his attention to you because I honestly don't know what he might do."

"But you still should have told me!"

He shrugged. "And I thought it best to keep it to myself rather than worry you. You've already been through enough at One Gov's hands."

I guess I could see his logic, as twisted as it might be, but it didn't make me any happier. Did he think he had to shield me from everything? "Looks like it doesn't matter anymore. He already knows. Why is he here on Mars? What if he knows about Brazil and what happened with Monique? Or if he knows about the clones?"

"Felicia, calm down. You're going to make yourself sick," he said, grasping my shoulders and holding me still when it seemed like all I wanted to do was hurl myself out of the moving flight-limo—which even I agreed would have been incredibly stupid.

"But what does he want? Do you think he knows about the luck gene? What if he's here to exploit it? Or what if he just wants good old-fashioned revenge?"

Alexei ran his hands up and down my arms. "I know he arrived a few weeks ago but his visit to Mars has been very low profile. It barely made the CN-news feed. The Consortium has always had eyes on him, just as he has eyes on us. I suspected he might make a move in your direction, but until he approached you, I couldn't be sure. As for what he wants, I'll find out. It would be difficult, but if I have to, I'll access his memory blocks. One Gov's queenmind is challenging to snipe for someone at Vieira's security level, but I'll make the attempt regardless of how many avatar aliases I burn through."

I bit my lip. "But won't you get caught?"

"Maybe. Maybe not. There are other things I can try first. He may have let something slip to one of his aides. Them, I can snipe. In the meantime, stay away from him. I'm serious, Felicia. Even if you think he wants something harmless, he will draw you in until it's a trap you can't escape. The man is known for his ruthlessness. He wouldn't be where he is today if the case were otherwise."

I met his gaze and tapped him lightly on the chest. "Sounds like someone else I know."

"The difference is, I'm in love with you. Not the same at all." He grinned slightly before sobering. "You said you felt unsettled. Could Vieira be the cause?"

"Are you saying you think my luck gene wanted me to meet him?"

He shrugged. "I've no idea. How you do whatever it is you do is beyond my ability to process."

"Gods, my family is a write-off on both sides! Why would I even entertain the idea of us having a baby with all this hanging over me?"

As soon as I said the words, I wished time travel actually existed so I could go back and shoot myself. Alexei had gone so still, it was like he wasn't even there anymore. Suddenly the space on the seat between us felt wide enough to swallow the universe.

"Sorry. I didn't mean to say that," I mumbled, looking out the window, examining the scenery as we flew by it. "Ignore me."

"Do you want a baby?" he asked softly. "Is it something you've been thinking about?"

"I was just talking rhetorically." I concentrated on the view outside the window, looking at the trees and rolling hills. We'd come a long way since the first humans walked on Mars. Not so long ago, this was nothing more than dirt under a red sky. No water. No air. Totally barren.

"Felicia, look at me."

"I'm not sure I can right now. I feel a bit stupid. We haven't even officially been together that long."

"Five and a half months, since the *Martian Princess*," he said. No doubt he could tell me the time right down to the second if I asked.

"See, not long. This isn't even a subject worth discussing. Forget I mentioned it," I said, playing with the hem of my dress and smoothing the chiffon material with its lilac floral pattern.

For long moments, the only sound was the hum of the flight-limo's engine. Panic flared and I felt sick. I was giving an offhand comment too much significance when it shouldn't have any. I should just pretend it hadn't happen and move on. Yes, moving on. Perfect. I should really get back to looking at my shims anyway.

"Before the Dark Times, the *vory v zakone* didn't have children or long-term relationships. I never really understood the reasoning behind it," Alexei said finally, because I was still sitting there rigid in my seat like a fool instead of trying to make the moment go away. "For the first time, I understand why we had such rules."

"I'm not exactly sure what you're trying to tell me," I said, because really, that was not a promising way to start a conversation about kids and marriage. "Maybe you should start over, but with less negativity."

"It wouldn't be safe for us to have a child. I have too many enemies and they would see our child as a tool to use against me. I'd worry I wouldn't be able to protect both it and you. We'd live in constant fear that something might happen. I already live with that fear and I don't want you to know how that feels."

"What are you afraid of?" I asked, not really sure I was getting it.

"I haven't hidden how important you are to me. People see

85

us together and think you make me vulnerable, and if they can get to you, they'll hurt me. And they're right. If something happened to you, I'm not sure what I'd do, so I do what I can to keep you safe. A baby would make it that much worse."

All this was news to me and I was completely blown away by his revelation. "Have people tried to hurt me?"

He sighed. "It's not anything you need to worry about."

"I guess that's a yes then."

"There have been attempts, but nothing you need to concern yourself with."

"If something's going on, you have to tell me. I can't live in a bubble where you try to protect me from everything."

"So far, I've done a fairly respectable job."

"Until the other night when I got ambushed by the Under-Secretary of One Gov in a back alley, you mean."

"Yes, until then," he conceded, looking angry. "I just think it best not to bring a child into that. It isn't the right time."

I nodded, dazed, because it awed me that he'd even thought about it at all. At the same time, I couldn't help but wonder if that meant there might never be a right time, and said so.

"Yes, there will, but you said it yourself—we haven't been together long. Let's enjoy this time now before we rush to the next stage. I know a child is important to you and I'm not downplaying that, just... I intend for us to last and I want us to take our time."

"Okay," I said, letting him pull me back into his arms. "When you put it like that, you're right. It's not like I'm blacklisted anymore. I can have a baby when we're ready."

"Exactly," he said, kissing my exposed throat and running his hand along my stomach, fingers caressing idly.

"Besides, we need to figure out all the other shit first, like why Felipe Vieira wants to see me."

"We will," he agreed, using his nose to nudge aside the silk scarf I'd slung around my neck. Once he bared my skin, he added his tongue to the kisses along my throat. The caressing fingers crept lower and raised my dress hemline until one finger found its way into my panties to make me squirm against him. "We'll just do it later."

"Later is fine," I agreed, giving myself up to his hands and lips until I was sprawled exactly how he wanted me. "Later is perfect."

<hr />

We reached the resort by midafternoon. Apollinaris Mons loomed in the distance, seeming to overshadow the entire town. The mountain was actually an ancient shield volcano from the early sols of Mars. While it was tall, it was nothing compared to Olympus Mons, which lured extreme sports junkies like flies to shit, enticing many to their deaths. Apollinaris Mons was the perfect height to challenge skiers but not outright terrify them. And with its base being almost two hundred miles in diameter, that meant there was plenty of variety for everyone once you ascended to the correct elevation. The area also boasted a fabulous hot springs, discovered when the terraforming was finished. Plus, with it being close to the equator, the weather was perfect all year round.

The flight-limo set down and I got out to stretch my legs. Immediately I found myself flanked by chain-breakers. Alexei got out behind me, handing me the sunshades I'd forgotten on the seat.

"Is it going to be like this the whole time?" I asked, gesturing to the chain-breakers.

He threw an arm around my shoulders, kissed the top of my head, and pulled me after him. "Only until we're inside. Come on."

Construction on Mars wasn't like it had been on Earth. After all, the terraformers hadn't seeded Mars with rain forests and vegetation just so future generations could cut them down. Almost everything on Mars was built from synthetic material created by recombining raw asteroid resources, pressurized gases and fuels from Jupiter, rocky material from Mars, and rejigging a few molecules. So while it wasn't technically wood, synthetic wood was close enough that no one could tell the difference. Fewer still cared. As we strolled along the pathway of large stone slabs to the resort's reception center, I knew that what looked like an exotic retreat made up of palm leaves and bamboo really wasn't.

Around the buildings were thick green foliage and bright exotic flowers, all things once native to Earth and re-created on a new world. It made the resort look wild and untamed, like we trekked through some lush jungle and were about to go on safari. Overlooking it all was snow-covered Apollinaris Mons, piercing the brilliant blue sky overhead. I had to stop for a minute, overwhelmed. My chest felt tight. I rubbed a hand against it as if that might loosen the knot.

"What's wrong?" Alexei asked, noticing my hesitation.

"This feels like I'm back in Kenya again. It reminds me of home," I whispered, looking up at him.

"I know it does," he said, grazing his knuckles along my cheek. "Why do you think I bought the resort?"

He bought a resort because he thought I might be homesick? What could I possibly say to that? I hugged him fiercely. "Thank you."

He grinned and took my hand, pulling me after him. "You're welcome. I'll let you thank me properly later."

"Why does it sound so dirty when you say it like that?"

"Because it's meant to be. The sooner we're in our room, the sooner you can start thanking me."

I laughed, suddenly excited. Our hands swung between us and I knew we were grinning at each other like idiots. It hadn't really been just us since we'd arrived on Mars, and I wanted more times like this—time where we could enjoy ourselves and not be consumed by other, pointless things that wasted our energy.

Inside looked exactly as I imagined. I took in the bamboo and stone walls set with large floor-to-ceiling windows that let you view the majesty of Apollinaris Mons. The ceiling beams were overlaid with more palms and the floor was worn-looking stone. The walls were decorated with shields, spears, and enormous wildlife paintings showcasing the big African five: lion, elephant, Cape buffalo, leopard, and rhinoceros. Though they were long extinct, their holos mesmerized me. Also intriguing were the huge orchids kept in protective glass domes throughout the lobby, their colors so bright, I wondered if they were real. Lastly, in the center of it all was an enormous baobab tree that grew right through the roof, as if the resort had been built around it.

I pulled my attention back to Alexei. We stood at the concierge's desk and he spoke in Russian to a handful of men— Consortium members dressed in expensive suits and all young thanks to the Renew treatments. Though I could make out only about every fourth or fifth word, he sounded downright pissed.

I gave Alexei a resigned look. "Guess there's been a change in plans?"

"Unfortunately," he said, annoyed. "Apparently word has spread about Under-Secretary Vieira's presence on Mars. I need to hold hands and calm fears."

I sighed. So I'd be alone tonight. I fought to wrestle up a smile. "That's okay. Do what you need to do. I'll just order room service, have a bath, and go to bed. I'm pretty tired anyway."

"Do you even know what you're doing to me? Now you have me imagining you naked in bed, waiting for me," he whispered so only I could hear. "I could fuck you right here and no one would raise a hand to stop me. Is that what you want?"

When Alexei turned on the dirty talk, I was a goner. I let out a shuddering breath, leaning into him, rubbing my palms over his chest. "Only if you want them seeing me naked too, and we both know how terrible you are at sharing."

"Touché." He chuckled softly and kissed me, using the gentle kiss that always left me breathless. Then he said something to the chain-breakers, who nodded and gathered up our luggage, most of it mine, naturally. "They'll take you to our room and see you settled. I'll be there as soon as I can."

"I'll be waiting."

I grinned up at him. Why had I been so afraid to commit to him? I couldn't remember my reasoning now. He was everything, and the only thing, I wanted.

And that's when I felt it. That horrible, awful, terrible kick in the gut that made me step back from him as if I'd been burned. One hand flew to my mouth on an intake of breath, the other to my stomach to press against the phantom ache. It was so powerful, I actually winced under the burden of so much—gods, *portent* was the only word for it—weighing down on me. All these weeks of unsettled feelings and vague warnings coalesced into one big tremor that rocked and reset my world.

"Felicia, what's wrong?"

Alexei. He tried to brush his fingers along my cheek. I pulled away farther, turning, not wanting him to touch me. Nothing was clear to me in that moment, not even my own feelings.

A man approached, casually dressed as if he'd just finished a round of golf—which on Mars could yield some impressive results. Tall. Broad-shouldered. Nicely muscled. Brown hair short on the sides and a little longer on top, full of golden highlights only a certain type of brown could get. Green eyes lighter than my own.

"Alexei," the man called as he crossed the lobby to us. "I thought it would be easier for us to meet here away from prying eyes rather than in the city. I should have realized you wouldn't be alone. I apologize."

His voice faded when he saw me. I wanted to back away but couldn't—not with Alexei behind me. Hell, I wanted to run from the lobby and pretend this moment had never happened. Instead I stood rooted to the spot, my eyes widening.

"Hello, Felicia," the man said, gazing down at me. "I have to say I never thought you'd make it to Mars, or that I'd see you again. It's nice to realize I was wrong on both accounts."

"Hi," I said, because I couldn't just stand there and not say something. "Yeah, I guess you were. Good thing we didn't bet on it."

"It's a bet I wouldn't have minded losing. Funny how things work out sometimes," he said, before shifting his gaze to Alexei then back to me.

It was too bad we weren't all born with an instruction manual for life warning us of impending danger, I decided. Then I remembered mine did in the form of the luck gene, and that still didn't make things easier, because there standing in front of me was Brody Williams. The last time I'd seen him was four years ago when he'd asked me to go to Mars with him and I said no. He then gave me a deck of Tarot cards as a gift, told me to think of him whenever I used them, and disappeared from my life forever. Oh, and we'd also both been naked too since it was the last time we'd slept together before he left for good.

People always wondered about the one who got away. Hell, half the questions people asked me were about lost loves and previous relationships. Everybody had one—that one person they'd let slip through their fingers for whatever reason. They would speculate on what might have been if circumstances had been different, or if they'd met at another point in their lives. If I hadn't liked shoes so much, I could have gotten rich just from answering that question alone.

Well, standing in front of me was mine. Brody Williams was my "one who got away." And now, the universe had dropped him right into my lap.

Fuck.

6

assume you know each other?"

Alexei's voice came from behind me. The words may have formed a question, but it didn't sound like one. His tone was unlike anything I'd heard from him before—surprise mingled with suspicion—and that in itself was scary. Alexei wasn't stupid nor did he startle easily. He could piece things together more quickly than I could, and the tone said he'd understood more than our brief exchange implied.

Usually I could come up with something, *anything*, to turn a situation around, but my mind was blank. Thought was beyond me. He made it sound as if I'd gone out of my way to hide something from him when nothing could be further from the truth. Alexei had researched every facet of my life, so I assumed there was nothing left to tell. Besides, who wanted to rehash details of an old relationship with a new one? Everyone had exes. Brody and I had been together for several months about a year after my first serious boyfriend, Dante, dumped me. Why didn't Alexei know about him, and why was he acting so stunned, it stopped me in my tracks?

I looked at Brody—no help there. He watched me like I was a ghost he fully expected to disappear if he so much as blinked. He seemed torn between hugging me and wondering why the hell I was there in the first place. Hugging appeared like it might be winning out. This didn't bode well at all. I turned to Alexei because I couldn't just stand there, none of us speaking, locked in this frozen tableau.

"How do you know Felicia?" Alexei asked with deceptive casualness.

Brody shrugged. "It's been years. I had a few readings done at her shop in Nairobi." Then to me, "If I recall correctly, you had a cute receptionist working for you."

I laughed because it was the easiest option available. "That's right. Next time I talk to Natty, I'll be sure to tell her you said that."

"Natty. Yes, that was her name. I doubt she'd remember me."

"You'd be surprised. If memory serves, you two spent a lot of time flirting with each other. She never seemed to work very hard when you were around. I think she was actually upset when she found out you were bound for Mars."

He looked pleased. "I hope she wasn't the only one upset."

"Well, so was Charlie Zero. He hates to lose gold notes after all," I said, sidestepping that potential minefield. "And now it looks like you're doing well on Mars, working for the Consortium."

"It's mostly consulting. It might be long-term, if all goes well. It's difficult to say until we hammer out the details." Brody shot a look to Alexei, mute at my side. "I didn't get it at first, but I see now why Alexei would want to free up his time to concentrate on other things."

It shouldn't have, but the comment made me blush. Brody saw it and grinned. Not good. I needed to get out of there before I did or said something to make things worse. I looked back to Alexei, whose expression was unreadable. Maybe he wasn't even there anymore. Maybe he was on the CN-net doing…I couldn't even imagine what. I touched his hand, and when he looked down at me, I felt something chill inside me. The look said he wasn't seeing me, distracted by whatever else went on in his head while plugged into the internal world of the CN-net. I would rather have had his smoldering rage instead of this nothingness where I didn't exist for him.

"I'm pretty tired, so I'll head to the room," I said, plastering a smile on my face.

"Of course," he said flatly. "I'll join you when I can."

"I'll wait up."

"That's unnecessary. I may not see you until tomorrow afternoon, depending on how this goes."

Tomorrow? Two sols ago, he'd told me he loved me and we were closer than we'd ever been, and now…Gods, what the hell was going on with him? How had the world suddenly gone sideways?

I cleared my throat over the lump I felt forming. "Well, whenever you have time." I turned to Brody because it would be rude not to. "It was nice to see you again. Hopefully we'll have a chance to catch up—if Alexei isn't working you too hard."

His grin turned into a smile that was just for me. "I'll make time. It was good to see you, Felicia."

I hadn't meant for it to happen, but somehow Brody caught me in a hug and it wasn't the friendly, quick one between acquaintances. It was a hug like he was sinking and I was the only thing keeping him afloat. It completely enveloped me and I was pressed hard against his chest, drowning in his scent and his warmth. I couldn't help but note it was a pretty nice chest and he smelled really good, and he felt...familiar.

"Do you still have the cards I gave you?" he asked, looking down at me.

"Yes. I don't know why, but they always smell like cinnamon when I use them."

"Then it was worth the expense. You're a hard girl to impress."

I rolled my eyes. "You are the biggest flirt in the tri-system."

"So you've said in the past," he said before letting me go.

I didn't dare look at Alexei, afraid of what I'd see. I ran to the waiting chain-breakers instead and let them whisk me away.

And my gut? It didn't care in the least about what was happening. In fact, it seemed to have settled. No more jangling, edginess, or kicks. Apparently now that my life had become a marvelous fucking disaster in the span of a few minutes, my luck gene was finally happy.

⟫•◆•⟪

Naturally, I didn't rest. That would have been impossible. I couldn't enjoy the room. I couldn't eat. I couldn't even think. All I could do was shuffle my Tarot cards, scattering them onto the bed because my hands shook so much. When I did lay a spread, I didn't know what the hell I was looking at. Even a

single card with a simple yes-no answer wasn't making sense because I didn't know what question to ask.

Why did I feel like I had this convergence of disaster around
me? Had Brody known I was with Alexei when he'd hired
out his services to the Consortium? And I couldn't imagine
Alexei would have approached Brody if he'd known about us. I
thought of the reading I'd done all those weeks ago when this
feeling had first hit. I recalled the Knight of Cups as an outside
influence, and because it was a court card, that meant it could
manifest as an event or a person. I'd assumed it was a woman
from Alexei's past because gods knew that roadside was littered
with enough jilted lovers to start multiple support groups. In
comparison, I could count my old boyfriends on one hand and
still have a thumb left over. I never imagined it might be someone from my past getting in the way.

Abandoning my cards, I flitted around the room, feeling
helpless. The cards were obviously wrong. My gut had to be
wrong too. I was missing something, and as soon as I calmed
down, I'd figure it out.

So I unpacked my suitcase and put everything away as if I'd
planned on doing nothing more than enjoying myself the next
few sols. I had a bath. I ordered room service. I even had an appointment with a resort staff esthetician for a mani-pedi to deal
with the mess I'd made of my nails during my big night out in
Elysium City.

I sorted through the last of my shims, noticing an interesting
one from Lotus with regards to Novi Pazidor, the wife of the
disgruntled off-world miner. Novi wanted to book a Tarot
reading party at her home and hoped to invite half a dozen of
her friends. Lotus wanted to know if she should book it. On

Earth, I'd done numerous reading parties. They were fun and I enjoyed them. This would be my first on Mars, and if it went well and word got out, more might follow. Novi was the type of client I wanted as opposed to the Lila Chandlers of the world—someone I felt I could actually help. I shimmed Lotus and told her to book the party for whenever it fit in my schedule.

I opened the balcony doors and wandered out into the cool evening air. Before me loomed Apollinaris Mons, the fading sunlight turning its rocky, snow-covered face blush pink. It was so pretty and there I was looking at it, alone—which dragged my thoughts back to Alexei.

What had he been thinking when he'd seen Brody and me together? What direction had his thoughts gone when he'd stood silently beside me, his expression blank? What if... No, I just needed to talk to him. Everything would be fine. It had to be.

I did something then I hadn't done in a long time—I found an inhaler of sleeping gas I'd packed in one of my bags and took several puffs before I changed my mind. I peered at the dosage label, wincing when I realized I'd inhaled more than I'd intended. Well, it probably wouldn't hurt me. I'd relied on it heavily back when I'd thought Alexei was dead and sleep had been impossible. Actually, being awake hadn't been a picnic either. I always traveled with it, whether I needed it or not, and the fact that I thought I needed it now didn't say much for my mental state. If only for a few hours, I wanted to turn off this reality and not have to think.

I set the inhaler on the bedside table, feeling its effects almost immediately. I barely made it under the sheets before collapsing in my ridiculously inappropriate pink satin negligée I'd bought specifically for Alexei to see. Turns out I could have saved my gold notes and gone neck-to-ankle flannels for all the attention he showed me. Maybe that would be something to remember for next time. My last thought was I wished I'd gathered up my cards because in about two seconds I wasn't going to be able to manage it. Once the meds hit, I wouldn't even be able to dream, and right then, that didn't seem like such a bad thing.

I woke to hands shaking me, which is just as unpleasant as it sounds. I heard someone shouting my name, also annoying. I tried swatting at the hands in the hopes I could go back to sleep, but they wouldn't go away. Then blissfully, the shaking stopped and I sank back into wonderful oblivion.

Sleep was interrupted again by pellets of ice raining down my back. I shrieked from the cold and bolted awake so quickly, I nearly fell when my feet slipped from under me.

I wasn't in bed anymore. I was standing on tile. Tile in an ice-cold shower in the bathroom—completely naked, I might add. Alexei was with me, fully clothed in a suit for fuck's sake, his expression grim as he held me under the frigid downpour.

"What the hell?" I screamed, slapping at him, fighting to loosen his hold.

All that earned me was a mouthful of water and a precarious moment where I thought I might crack my head open on the tile when my feet slipped again. He hauled me upright and thrust me back under the water until my teeth were chattering and I was shrieking at him to stop. Only then did he turn off the water and wrap me in a towel. When my legs weren't interested in supporting me, he picked me up and carried me back to the bed. He shoved a mug of hot black coffee in my hands.

"Drink it," he ordered, the grim expression still on his face.

I noticed dimly that my fingers were blue with cold as I brought the mug to my lips. It was so strong and bitter, I started to cough and tried to set it down. Alexei caught my wrist, holding the mug to my mouth.

Having no choice, I choked down the terrible stuff. He was only satisfied once he could see the bottom, taking the mug and placing it on a nearby table. Then he handed me an inhaler—the wake-up jolt to nullify the sleeping gas. Mixed with caffeine, I'd be ready to jump out of my skin in about ten minutes. Still, I inhaled one puff, which seemed to appease him.

"I'm not sure where this urge to harm yourself came from, but this stops now. First the Euphoria, now this. For me to come in here and see you in bed like that, not waking up... Don't ever do that to me again," he said.

As he spoke, he stripped off his wet clothing—which was when I realized he'd changed from yesterday. He'd shaved as well. Off came the jacket, the shirt and pants, all thrown on the floor in a soaking heap and probably ruined. No underwear, though. I don't think he'd ever worn any in all the time I'd known him. There was something to be said for going commando and I watched as he went back to the bathroom for a towel; he really did have a very fine ass. Definitely worth checking out. Above it, spread out over his entire back, was a cathedral tattoo with several distinct towers. I often traced its outline with my finger and knew it had something to do with time spent in prison, but Alexei wouldn't elaborate on the details.

"I just misjudged the dose," I called. "I don't have the tolerance I had before."

Alexei came back to crouch in front of me, studying me intently. "That kind of tolerance is dangerous. It's nearly three in the afternoon."

I said nothing, just huddled in my towel. He knew why I'd once relied so heavily on sleeping meds. There was no need to lecture me. The silence stretched and I had to look down at the floor. I heard him shift and drop his towel before he leaned closer. "What's going on here? Who is he to you?" he asked, sounding confused. I didn't need to ask who "he" was.

"He's an old boyfriend, but I haven't heard from him in years."

I heard something that sounded like a growl rumble out of him. "I thought I knew everything there was to know about you, but not this. There was nothing on the CN-net. I can't access his memory blocks and you have none. There is literally no evidence anywhere in the tri-system to indicate you were together and yet the way he looked at you yesterday is all the proof I need."

"Proof of what? It's been years," I repeated, in case he'd missed it. "You know about my relationships with Dante, and Roy, and even Charlie. None of those bothered you. This isn't any different."

But Alexei didn't seem inclined to let it go. His hands fisted on the bed beside my thighs, close but not touching me.

"To know he's touched you, that he's wanted you the same way I do, that he's been inside you and made you scream his name...It's all I can think about. I feel like I might snap and do something I regret."

"Stop it. You can't think about it that way. All you did was shut me out and made me feel like I meant nothing to you, or like you didn't even see me." I let out a shuddering sigh, almost afraid to admit it aloud because that made it more real. "I've never felt like that with you before, and it hurt."

I felt his hand touch my hair, then turn my face toward his. "You are the only thing I *do* see. I didn't know how to handle my feelings yesterday."

"You have to know what I felt for him is nothing compared to what I feel for you. It isn't even close."

"What are the odds that the man I need to crack open One Gov's queenmind also happens to be your former lover?" he asked instead. "Konstantin recommended him, so I assume he already knew this."

"And you don't think that's weird? If Konstantin had a tool he thought would drive us apart, he'd use it."

"Of course I'm suspicious. How could he have known this about you when I didn't? But I suppose all I really want to know is will his gambit be successful? Will you react the way he hopes?"

"Don't, Alexei," I begged. "Don't let anyone plant doubts about us."

"Then tell me what it was like between you. What makes me different from him?" It sounded like he was challenging me to prove myself. The hand touching me dropped away. "You say I treated you like you meant nothing. In reality, we both know you pulled away from me. I could see you were drawn to him. Did you love him when you were together? Do you still want him?"

"No, of course not!"

"Then explain what I saw yesterday."

I shrugged helplessly. "I was just shocked. We were together a few months, about a year after I broke up with Dante. I was depressed about my blacklisted status. Charlie Zero and I were under pressure with starting up the shop on Night Alley. My great-grandmother had died and the whole family hated me because I got her cards. Everything was against me. Then Brody came along and he was...fun."

"Fun?" Alexei looked skeptical.

How could I tell him Brody helped me through one of the worst times in my life—when I felt less than worthless and getting out of bed was a struggle? How could I say he made me feel like living again? The truth was, I couldn't.

"We hung out and did things together, but when he told me he was leaving for Mars, it ended."

"He asked you to go with him."

"And I said no."

"Yet you're here now."

My eyes flew to his. "I wasn't in the right headspace to love anyone then. Now, I love you and it's stupid for you to be jealous. Don't give that relationship power to cause a rift between us."

"How can it not when I see you've wondered about him, even if only in passing?"

Panicked, I reached out to touch his face, running my fingers over the strong line of his jaw. "I don't want him. I don't want anyone the way I want you. Please believe me."

"If the Consortium didn't need him, I would dump him back where I found him. If I could, I would change events so you'd never laid eyes on him." He turned his head, kissing my palm where it rested on his cheek.

I tried to think about what my life would have been like without Brody in it, and how things might have been different. I had to be honest with myself—I wasn't even sure I'd still be around. "He's my past," I whispered instead. "You're my future."

He stared at me a long moment as if deciding what to do with me, and I felt another hit of panic. I needed to reassure him how important he was to me.

"I want to touch you," I said, sliding to the edge of the bed. "Let me show you how much I want you."

Down to the floor I went, dropping my towel. I knelt with him, running my hands up his chest. Compared to my chill, his skin seemed like it was on fire. His muscles, always so hard and formidable to the touch, felt like stone under my fingers as I caressed his shoulders, chest, and abdomen. He sighed as my hands danced along his skin, followed by my lips and tongue. I traced the tattoos and kneaded the sculpted ridges of muscle, loving the way he felt against my body. I felt him relax as I touched him, as if only I could drain away his tension.

With gentle prodding from me, he stood, towering over me as I knelt on the floor. My fingers dragged over his skin as he moved, my hands stroking his hips, skimming his ass, and coming to rest on his thighs, heavy with muscle. I tipped my head back to look up at him, my damp hair tumbling down to brush my bare feet as I admired his absolute perfection. Even his scent got to me, musky and so male, making me weak with wanting him. Though I'd never admit it to anyone but him, I loved looking at him like this. There was some tiny part of me that got off on knowing how easily he could dominate me. At the same time, I couldn't help but feel a euphoric giddiness knowing he was mine. Mine to look at. Mine to touch. And for the moment, I could do anything with him I wanted.

He'd been half aroused before. Now his erection grew and lengthened until he was rock hard and thick. His hands went to my head, his fingers threading through my hair, clasping my skull. He tipped my head back farther, looking down at me, his expression half glazed yet anticipatory. I smiled to myself. I knew exactly what he wanted, but took my time giving it to him. I'd never been a big fan of oral sex. Before, I only doled it out grudgingly on birthdays and special occasions, and even then, under protest. That was until Alexei.

I rose up on my knees, my hands lightly running along his thighs until I reached up to cup him. My fingers grazed his shaft. I kept the touch gentle and felt him twitch restlessly in my hands. When I increased the pressure and stroked along the length of him, his breath came out in a hiss. Then I took him into my mouth, opening to take as much of him as I could. He was so large, I couldn't go as deeply as we both wanted without gagging. Instead, I flicked my tongue over him and cupped his balls, massaging with one hand while I rubbed his shaft with the other. Sucking and licking, his grunts of approval spurred me on to increase the tempo and the pressure. I tasted his pre-cum, salty on my tongue. He wouldn't last much longer, not when he was this worked up.

His hands tightened in my hair and his hips began to thrust in and out of my mouth, making me pull back so I wouldn't gag. Above me, he groaned harshly and I watched as his abs flexed with every thrust as he picked up his pace. I sucked harder, feeling my own arousal grow in response as I worked my tongue over him. Then a final glide and he was coming, the hot jets shooting down my throat as I swallowed.

I pulled away, pleased with myself. I was getting better at

reading his body's cues. He continued to look down at me, panting, his chest glistening with a light sheen of sweat. His hands stroked my face, keeping my head tilted back to meet his gaze. I could see even after what we'd just done, he was still aroused and wanted more. But the look on his face said something else and kept me from reaching for him.

"What's wrong?"

His expression was stricken, an emotion I rarely saw from him. "Why can I never get enough of you? Even when I'm in you, the wanting never stops."

His admission should have thrilled me. Instead it left me feeling raw and exposed.

"You don't have to make it sound like wanting me is so horrible. It's normal to want someone this much. Sometimes I spend all day thinking about getting you out of your suits." When I tried to stand, he wouldn't let me. "Alexei?"

"I would come back to you for anything you had to give, whatever it was, because I just can't stay away," he said, now stroking my hair. "When I saw you that first time in Nairobi, I never imagined I would feel the way I do now. I didn't think I was capable of feeling so intensely, and part of me hates this crippling need I have for you."

"I'm not holding you against your will," I said, a sob rising in my chest. "You could go whenever you wanted."

"No I couldn't. You are the only thing that makes this world real to me. Without you, I wouldn't remain in this reality anymore. I would do anything to keep you, but when I saw you with him, I understood I could lose you anyway. It kills me to know for all that I am, I'm not enough."

I tried to stand and still he wouldn't let me. Frustrated, because this wasn't a conversation I wanted to have on my knees, I ground out, "You're the only man I want to be with. Why can't you believe that?"

"Because your cards say otherwise. I see them behind you and I know they haven't given you the answer you want. They are one of the ways your luck gene manifests and they're telling you to go. If that's what you believe, how can I stop you?"

He released me then and headed to the bathroom, closing the door behind him. When I heard him turn on the shower, I realized he wasn't coming back. Getting up, I took in the scene behind me, finally seeing what he'd been looking at this whole time. My cards were scattered all over the bed, as if I'd been doing readings in my sleep. They were jumbled and chaotic, saying nothing and everything, and betraying me as obviously as if I'd spoken aloud. I may have said and done all the right things to Alexei, but the cards were saying something else, and that left me cold and scared in a way I hadn't felt in a very long time.

7

Alexei was called away on Consortium business soon after that. I suspected it was minor stuff he could have delegated, but his leaving was actually a relief. I sat outside on the balcony for the rest of the afternoon and early evening, first sunning myself, then looking up at the sky and listening to the other resort guests enjoy themselves. He hated that he wanted me. What was I supposed to do with that little nugget of pain? What did that mean for us going forward?

When I got up the next morning, Alexei was still gone. However, I found evidence he'd returned to the room at some point. I also found a shim telling me he'd gone to work out in the resort's fitness center and would find me later. I'd moved past feeling hurt and sorry for myself, to pissed off and annoyed. He'd wanted me to close my shop and brought me to Apolli for this romantic getaway. And now I was supposed to feel guilty over a relationship from years ago he didn't know about? Enough was enough. I was seeing the sights if it killed me, pissed-off boyfriend or not.

I passed on ordering room service since I still didn't feel like eating. Stress and anxiety could do that to a girl. I consoled myself by imagining how I would waste the extra calorie consumption points later. I took the time to curl my hair and pull it into a high, loose ponytail that cascaded down my back in waves—a look I knew Alexei liked given how he'd wrap the curls around his fingers whenever I wore it this way. Then I selected a pink halter dress with a shimmering pink overlay. It did wonderful things to support my breasts, yet still flowed loosely to midthigh and covered all my bruises. Lastly, a pair of cute matching sandals for walking and I was ready to go. I couldn't say why I went through all this extra effort when he wasn't even there to see it, but I was mad and throwing a temper tantrum seemed childish. If Alexei was going to leave me to my own devices, fine. His loss.

I sent him a shim saying I'd gone to explore the town. Usually, his replies were instantaneous. He could think out a detailed response in no time whereas I had to tap laboriously on my bracelet for a few lousy sentences. Quicker if I did a voice record shim. No face-chats, though. That only worked c-tex to c-tex, and as wired as he was, not even Alexei could manage that. His implants were too advanced to work with my antiquated tech. Now was no exception: My bracelet vibrated almost immediately. I ignored it. I had a feeling I might not like what he'd sent back.

I decided to walk to the center of town. What I'd originally thought was a street was actually a glamorous pedestrian walkway that glittered with what looked like gemstones. They were crushed under a layer of a clear, flexible material that sprang back when stepped on. It created a cushiony effect, making me feel like I could walk for hours and never have sore feet.

The street was lined with baskets of vibrantly colored flowers.

As I watched, tiny drones flew between them, ensuring the plants were watered and pest-free. The sun felt warm on my skin and I hadn't bothered with sun protection. The sun wasn't as damaging on Mars as it was on Earth with its ravaged ozone layer One Gov still had yet to fully repair. Pretty shops and cafés lined both sides of the pedestrian walkway. I noticed a few sporting-goods stores for those interested in skiing opportunities offered at Apollinaris Mons. Or you could book helicon tours that took you to the top of the caldera, some fifty miles across. Though it was less than half the height of Mount Everest on Earth, it was still impressive to see an ancient shield volcano rising out of the ground and soaring overhead.

I window-shopped and bypassed most of the stores without dropping a single gold note. I was obviously more upset than I realized if I couldn't shop my way to happiness. That was when I saw the All People's Temple past a small park at the end of the walkway. Wow, talk about a kick in the ass from karma. Visiting a temple was exactly what I needed.

Before the Dark Times, organized religion had been waning on Earth. After, it had rebounded like wildfire as people clutched desperately at any straw to save themselves. Faiths got blurred and rules became less rigid as global disasters decimated the population and billions died. It wasn't that the old faiths no longer existed. They'd just sort of fused into a stew of beliefs as people took what they wanted, which was how the All People's Temple sprang into existence.

They were everywhere on Earth, but not so much on Mars. I'd noticed Mars, founded on science and reason, was more secularized than Earth had ever been. Compared to Earth, it was a paradise, making it understandable why people wouldn't cling to any log in the ocean. Perhaps that explained why I didn't find running my shop as fulfilling now. People weren't desperate for the same reassurance they would be okay. Maybe my skills were lumped in with the same religious hodge-podge as everything else and I just hadn't realized it.

Even if religion wasn't popular on Mars, it didn't look like this temple was suffering from a lack of donations. Its roof was a series of golden steeples leading to an arching dome overhead, and its walls were rounded, smooth, and glistening with crystals. The gardens along the walkway were lush, full, and colorful. It was so pretty, I had to go in. And it had been so long since I'd been to any sort of religious service, I felt residual guilt. My father's family believed in everything and anything. Alexei believe in nothing. It was safe to say I fell somewhere in the middle.

It was cool and quiet inside the temple. I was the only one there. Figured. It smelled of incense and candle wax thanks to the votive candles in the temple's center. It was also dark, but the numerous crystal statues along the rounded walls were lit up by overhead lights, all symbols of the many gods the temple encompassed.

Since this was sacred ground, I took off my sandals and set them by the door. The floor was warm under my bare feet, which was nice. I was a big fan of heated floors. Approaching the votive candles in their vast array of colors housed in clear glass holders, I scanned my c-tex against the reader and offered a donation to the temple. I lit two candles—green for hope and yellow for optimism, though I supposed that was like asking for the same thing twice. Then I knelt on a nearby pillow, closing my eyes and trying to lose myself in the prayers I'd learned from Granny G as a kid.

I'm not sure how long I prayed—tough when I had so much

whirling around in my head—when the door opened. Someone else had come in to pray. It was too dark to see who it was, and I closed my eyes and tried to get back to my prayers. My c-tex vibrated on my wrist. I hit "ignore" because it didn't seem appropriate to read my shims while praying. I had about two seconds of peace when it vibrated again. I almost hit "ignore" a second time before it occurred to me that it might be important. I didn't often get back-to-back shims.

I glanced at the new person, stunned to find a One Gov hooah approaching. I think my stomach dropped to the floor and I almost fell off my pillow as the black-clad soldier stopped in front of me. He was dressed in head-to-toe body armor as if expecting an all-out assault, wearing everything except a faceshield. Shock warred with horror as he stood a scant few feet away. My last run-in with a hooah had left me paralyzed from nerve gas and my ass thrown in jail. It wasn't an experience I wanted to repeat and it took everything in me to stifle a scream. My bracelet vibrated, stopped, then started again, but I couldn't look it. I didn't dare take my eyes off the hooah.

Except instead of arresting me, the hooah held out a tiny blue-jeweled disk—a holo-adapter that could be used to communicate and transmit near life-sized holographic images. It was also old tech and something I could plug directly into my c-tex bracelet. I looked from it to him, then back to the holo-adapter. I couldn't help but note the One Gov symbol emblazoned on its face—a yellow sun and three white dots representing Mars, Earth, and Venus.

"Please take it, Ms. Sevigny. The Under-Secretary would like to meet with you. He knows of your tech limitations. This will allow you to contact him directly."

I blinked, relief hitting hard when I realized I wasn't being arrested. It was followed by a fresh squirt of panic. The Under-Secretary, my *grandfather*, still wanted to see me. "What if I don't want to contact him?"

"He said he thought you might say that. I was told to tell you, he knows your heritage will make you curious."

It wasn't the answer I expected. Then again, none of it was. "Did he happen to mention which side of my heritage would be curious?"

"If you want more answers, you'll need to speak to him personally."

Wow. You couldn't argue with that level of inscrutability. "I get to pick the time?"

"And the place."

So what else could I do? I held out my hand and let him drop the holo-adapter into my waiting palm.

Task completed, the hooah marched briskly down the aisle, past the altar, and disappeared into the shadows between the crystal statues. What the hell? Was there a secret door back there? I tried rising to follow, more curious than scared. Apparently I wasn't as unmoved as I thought since my legs didn't seem interested in cooperating. Getting up from the kneeling pillow felt like the most impossible thing in the world.

Which was about the same time the main door of the temple crashed open, filling the room with light. In seconds, Alexei knelt in front of me, his hands running over my face, shoulders, arms, back, as if checking for wounds. His expression was a combination of worry and anger.

"I came as soon as I was notified. Are you all right? Were you hurt?"

"I'm fine."

"What the fuck does Vieira want?" How he'd guessed what happened so quickly, I had no idea, but he'd always been fast that way. Worry was giving way to anger.

"I don't know, but he wants to meet with me."

Alexei swore softly. "Where did the hooah go?"

"Out the back, behind the altar."

Immediately two of the chain-breakers with him peeled off, heading in the direction I indicated. Alexei stood, pulling me with him and swinging me up in his arms. I gasped and threw my arms around his neck, thrown off balance by the suddenness. Then he strode down the aisle, carrying me the whole way.

"Put me down," I protested. "I'm not some suitcase you need to haul across town."

He ignored that, instead asking, "Why didn't you answer my shims?"

"I was in the temple. I thought it would be rude to check them when I was supposed to be praying."

He made a noise that might have been a laugh if the look on his face wasn't so disgusted.

"Besides, I hate to admit it, but I was scared. Lately it seems like every time I see a hooah, I end up behind bars."

There, his arms tightened around me and he pressed a kiss to my temple. "That will never happen again; not so long as I'm alive to prevent it."

I experienced one of those weak-kneed, girly moments knowing he'd do whatever he could to keep me safe. I wanted to burrow into him and sigh into his neck until it suddenly occurred to me: "Don't you have people watching me? How did the hooah get past your security?"

Another disgusted noise. "Two of my people failed to report in. They were found unconscious back at the resort, stuffed into a utility closet."

One Gov had taken out his security. Not good. Now I could see the reason behind his irritation.

"Then how did you find me? Wait...Do you have spyware installed in my c-tex?"

"Of course," he said as if it should have been obvious. "If I thought I could get away with it, I'd put tracking nanos in you as well."

That squashed the girly feelings. "Over my dead body are you tracking me with nanos! If that happens, I hope you're ready for a lot of alone time because I will *never* have sex with you again."

His expression said that clearly wasn't happening. "Which is why I haven't done it. Not yet anyway."

Soon we were outside, and I found myself bundled inside a cool, darkened flight-limo.

"Now what?" I snapped, slapping away his hands when he tried to smooth my dress over my thighs. "Don't tell me I have to go into lockdown at the resort."

"You're going to the room, and once I determine it's safe, we're heading back to Elysium City."

"We just got here! I didn't get to try the hot springs! I haven't even bought any tacky souvenirs yet. What the hell kind of vacation is this?"

"You were just contacted by a representative for one of the most powerful and dangerous men in the tri-system. A man who is an enemy of the Consortium, and whose daughter tried to kill you, in case you need reminding. Do you think I want you in a place where I can't be confident you're safe?" The look on his face said there was no arguing with him. "Where are your shoes?" he asked abruptly.

I looked at my feet. Crap. No sandals. "Still in the temple."

He ran a distracted hand through his dark hair, leaving it a wonderful, sexy mess I wanted to touch no matter how upset with him I might be. I must have been doing just that because he caught my hand, and put it back in my lap. Then he sighed and shook his head. "For someone who claims to love shoes, how is it you keep losing them?"

I shrugged. "Does it matter so long as you keep finding them and bringing them back to me?"

He gave me a long look that made me squirm. It felt like a caress along my body, as much as if he'd run his hands over my skin. "Yes, I will keep bringing them back. Always," he said, and I knew we were talking about more than just shoes.

"Alexei, I'm sorry you think being with me makes you weak or if I've dragged you into some mess with One Gov," I whispered. "I wish I could—"

"Don't," he cut in harshly before I could blurt out any half-formed thoughts. "Do you think I want to turn off these feelings? I don't, so don't wish for things to be different between us. Don't tell me you want anything to change."

"I...Okay."

"I know this trip didn't turn out as planned, and for that, I'm sorry," he murmured, brushing his lips over mine. "I promise once I determine what Vieira wants and we deal with this, we'll come back and you can soak up all the hot springs you can handle."

How could I stay mad when he looked at me like I was

the most important person in his world? "I assume you'll be at these hot springs with me?"

"Where else would I be?"

The grin he gave me was enough to make me want to tear his clothes off and straddle his hips. I sighed, annoyed I could be so shamelessly and easily cajoled. "Fine. Just don't forget to bring back my shoes before you head off to intimidate your next victim."

I caught his fleeting smile. "I'll have someone locate them, and see you back at the resort."

He slipped from the flight-limo and the door closed behind him. I found myself whisked back to the resort with little more than a pretty apology. I couldn't tell if things were better with Alexei or not, and I had a worried feeling I was about to make things worse. In my hand, hidden under my dress so Alexei wouldn't see, was the holo-adapter the hooah had given me.

I held it up, looking at it carefully. What Vieira really wanted, I didn't know, but the hooah had been right: I was curious. Curious enough I hadn't told Alexei because I knew he would stop me. He said he wanted to protect me, but I suspected this was one thing he couldn't save me from, nor did I want him to. I only hoped my curiosity didn't ruin us in the process.

8

An hour later found me packing, which mainly consisted of me hurling belongings into luggage, annoyed with everything and nothing. When I heard the knock on the door, I whipped it open in mindless irritation rather than have the room AI confirm the visitor's identity. I was in the mood to vent and didn't care who heard me. Except...

Brody lounged in the doorway, dangling my sandals from his fingers. "Seems you forgot something in your travels."

"I...Thanks." Definitely not the deliveryman I'd been expecting.

This close, it was easy to remember why I'd been attracted to him. The first time I met him, he was far and away the hottest guy I'd ever seen. His hair had been longer then, the brown full of golden highlights. He'd been wearing a dark suit and looked like he'd just gotten off work—something in business where he sat at a desk and ran the CN-net all day. Yet I could tell by the way he carried himself, there was something worth seeing under the clothes.

I'd been food shopping at the local market near where I lived in Nairobi. I'd wanted strawberries and we both found the last basket at the same time. We had argued until we noticed they were rotten. I stalked off in a huff because I didn't get my strawberries, oddly intrigued by this stranger. He'd argued so passionately for that damned fruit, it made me laugh when I thought about it later. When he appeared at my shop the next day—with a basket of strawberries—and asked me out, I'd agreed. He was the first man I'd been remotely interested in since Dante. I wasn't sure the relationship would go anywhere, but decided to give it a chance. Dante had left me convinced no man could possibly want me—after all, who would want someone blacklisted by One Gov? Being with Brody had taken away the agony of both rejections.

"Why do you have my shoes?"

"Seems you're not an easy one to keep secure. Alexei has terrorized his people for not doing their jobs and now everyone's avoiding you."

"So Alexei gave you my shoes?"

"Well, I mostly helped myself," he admitted. "However, the rest is true. You're making their lives hell."

"Seems to be my MO lately. It's not like I go out of my way to be difficult."

"I know. I remember what you're like. Drama has a tendency to follow you around." With a grin, he held out my sandals.

"I don't get off on drama."

"I never said that. Just that being around you was never boring." He shook my sandals at me. "Now that I've made my delivery, I need to get back."

Amused, I took them. "Did you want to come in?"

Brody leaned against the door and shook his head, laughing a little and rubbing the bridge of his nose. "I'd like to, but you look busy demolishing the room. Plus, you're not really dressed for company. Maybe we can rehash old times when you're wearing something a little less shiny." The last part was said as he waved a hand in my general direction, taking in my glittery blue boy shorts and matching tank.

Shit. I was standing in the doorway, talking to my ex-boyfriend, wearing little more than my underwear. Maybe Lotus could wear ribbons in public, but I couldn't. I blushed, and to my complete and utter horror, my nipples decided *now* was the perfect time to perk up. I could feel them tighten under his gaze and hurriedly I crossed my arms over my chest.

Dashing back into the room, I dropped the sandals, found a resort bathrobe in the closet, and threw it on. Behind me, I heard Brody laughing.

"Not funny!" I shouted at him.

"I'm not the one who opened the door without checking," he called from the doorway. "Still, it's nice to know the real thing still holds up against my memories."

I think I blushed harder and I willed myself to calm down before heading back to him. "Are you coming in or not?" I demanded, sounding bitchy even to me.

"Only if you promise not to jump me."

"You're hilarious," I muttered as I slammed the door behind him. "Gods, you're in rare form today."

"All part of my charm. You'd be surprised how far you can coast. I never go anywhere without it."

I laughed despite myself, then had another brilliant moment as I realized I probably shouldn't have invited him inside. Well, it was too late to kick him out now. He looked around with interest. Gods, were any of my panties in sight? That'd be all I needed. And what if Alexei came back and saw the two of us? Not that I should have to explain, but still…

"Nice to see what you can afford with unlimited gold notes," he said mildly. "Leading the Consortium is a better gig than I imagined. I wouldn't want the headaches or have to deal with the bullshit, but the perks look pretty good."

"This doesn't happen as often as you might think," I said, gesturing around the room. "Alexei is away on business a lot, which is why I'm annoyed we're leaving. I guess this isn't really the trip I'd hoped it would be."

I regretted the words the instant they were out of my mouth. I shouldn't be complaining about Alexei to Brody, of all people. He didn't need to know about any issues we might have.

"That's why the Consortium hired me. I'm here to pick up the slack," Brody said. "At least he knows he can't do everything himself. Some in his position wouldn't dream of bringing in a consultant."

Which reminded me—Alexei had hired Brody on Konstantin Belikov's recommendation. Why did Belikov want Brody in a role so potentially important? Not only was Brody my ex, but he was an outsider to the Consortium, and gods knew the Consortium wasn't big on involving strangers in its business. Had Belikov really wanted to cause trouble between Alexei and me, or was there more going on than I knew?

"Does the name *Konstantin Belikov* ring any bells?" I asked.

That made him pause. "Everyone knows Konstantin Belikov. The man's a terrifying legend in certain circles."

"Have you ever spoken with him? Did you know I was with Alexei when you took this job?"

"What are you getting at, Felicia?" he asked, studying me.

"I don't know. Nothing, maybe." I shrugged. "I guess it's just weird seeing you like this after all these years."

"I could say the same. I never pictured you with the leader of the Tsarist Consortium."

"What did you picture?"

He shook his head, smiling ruefully. "I don't really know what I expected if I ever saw you again. I didn't think you would be with someone like Alexei, though."

"Why not? We have more in common than you might think. Besides, he gets who I am."

"And can you say the same about him?"

I gave him a level look. "I know exactly who he is and what I've gotten myself into. We've been through things that forced us to accept who the other person is, and right now, I'm comfortable with that."

"Doesn't sound like you're thinking long-term with him. What happens tomorrow? Or six months from now? I'd say you have more work on your hands than it's worth. You know there's something to be said for easy."

His meaning couldn't be any clearer, so I decided to ignore it. "Are you seeing anyone?" I asked instead.

"Me? No one. No wife. No kid either, just in case that was your next question. These last few years, well...Let's just say relationships had to sit on the back burner."

"What have you been up to then? Working on your consulting business?"

"Mostly. It's hard starting from scratch, especially on a new world. It feels like I'm always hustling, trying to make a name for myself and looking to land the next big contract. Seems like it's either feast or famine."

I nodded, understanding perfectly. "Yeah, I know what that's like. It sucks."

"Yes, it does. So when the Consortium approached me, I jumped at the chance. This opportunity could lead to more."

It sounded harmless enough. If Belikov was working an angle aside from driving Alexei and me apart, I couldn't see it. "What are you doing for the Consortium?"

"I manage their assets and workload by handling negotiations with One Gov's queenmind. The Consortium are smart enough to know when they need help. The One Gov issues they're having on Mars are fairly complex, such as the Phobos problem."

Phobos? I was instantly alert. "What problem?"

Brody gave me a look. "Honestly, it isn't that exciting. With the best geologists all employed by the Consortium through the off-world mines, One Gov is asking if they could look into the stability of the chasm created by the penal colony explosion. That's a bit of a red-tape nightmare to maneuver through, what with getting the correct permits and permissions from the AI queenmind. It's a wonder One Gov manages to function and doesn't choke on its own bureaucracy."

"Oh, I never thought of that, but I guess it makes sense," I said.

"You almost sound disappointed," Brody teased. "Were you expecting something more cloak-and-dagger?"

"No. I don't know. Never mind. It's stupid."

"Well, if there is something more, you'll have to ask Alexei. I'm not sure what's supposed to be kept confidential from you and what isn't."

Suddenly I was annoyed, not liking the implication that Alexei might be keeping secrets from me. That may have been the case once, but we'd learned from our mistakes. I also didn't like that an ex-boyfriend was pointing out the flaws of the current boyfriend, especially when said boyfriend was irrationally jealous. I needed this conversation to end—earlier gut feeling be damned.

"Well, I guess we're done here. You've brought my sandals, so thanks. I've got them now and you can go back to your consulting. See you later."

Brody looked hurt. "Look, I'm sorry if that's not what you want to hear, but I don't know what the rules are between us. I work for the Consortium and we...I don't know what we are, but I assumed we could be friends."

"Yes, we can be friends. I just don't like you implying Alexei and I are temporary or I don't really know him."

"I'm sorry," he said again, then he looked pained. "I know I'm not entitled to an opinion, but Alexei Petriv? Of all the men in the tri-system, he's the one you end up with?"

"You're going too far, Brody," I warned.

"It's only because I care what happens to you. I always regretted pushing you for more when you obviously weren't ready. Except now that you're ready, it's with him—someone who could hurt you worse than I ever could."

"You're wrong. Alexei knows better."

"Then he's smarter than I am. I guess I was afraid I'd left you worse off than when I found you. I wanted you to come with me to Mars, you turned me down, so I got angry and walked out. Time passed, I realized I was an idiot, and I told myself if I ever saw you again, I'd make it up to you. Do you think if I hadn't rushed you, it could have been different?"

I hadn't expected this outpouring from him. "I don't know.

I still had to get my life together. I probably would have driven you away with how irrational I became later."

"Or maybe I could have helped."

"I became obsessed with my blacklisted status until it took over my life. I did some pretty stupid things thinking I could get around the system."

"And did you?"

"Eventually, but it gave me some emotional scars I'm not sure I'll ever get over."

"Then I'm sorry I wasn't there for you. I'm guessing Alexei was and now you're committed to him."

"Yes. Completely."

I expected some reply from him, but he wasn't looking at me anymore. His eyes had landed on something I'd meant to put away but forgot in the midst of packing and the emotional upheaval of the past few sols. The holo-adapter from Vieira. Shit.

Brody strode over to the dresser as if the room was his, and scooped up the adapter. "Felicia, what's going on?" he asked, One Gov's emblem clearly visible. His tone sounded like he hoped a reasonable explanation was forthcoming but didn't expect it. "What are you doing with this?"

"It's kind of a long story."

"I'm sure it is. Does Alexei know?"

"I haven't mentioned it yet."

Brody frowned. "Are you feeding Consortium secrets to One Gov?"

"Of course not! I'm not a spy and I certainly wouldn't help One Gov after it almost ruined my life."

"Then get rid of it. Having this is dangerous."

Just what I wanted to hear. Why couldn't I have simple conversations about easy things like the weather? "I can't. It's more complicated than flushing the adaptor down the toilet. I don't think I can avoid him. Even if I get rid of that, he'll just find another way."

"Avoid who? Are you in some kind of trouble with One Gov? Do you need help?"

I choked back a laugh, stopping it before it could get out. Help? I doubted there was enough help in the tri-system. "Felipe Vieira wants to see me."

"Why? What are you to the Under-Secretary?"

I swallowed. "I think I might be his granddaughter."

He froze, his green eyes widening. "What does he want?"

"I don't know. I'm supposed to contact him through the holo-adapter."

"You know you can't do that. Alexei wouldn't let you. Hell, *I* wouldn't let you. Felipe Vieira is dangerous and makes Alexei look like a choirboy. Whatever he wants, even if it's just a fireside chat with tea and cookies, forget it."

He began listing the reasons why seeing Vieira was a horrible idea until I stopped listening. My gut started in, a silent counterargument to every statement Brody made. And that was weird because I hadn't even realized how much I wanted to talk to Vieira until Brody tried to convince me I shouldn't.

"You know I'm going, right?" I said when he paused for breath.

"Then you're delusional. Alexei would physically lock you in a cage if he thought it would keep you safe."

"That's ridiculous. He's protective, but he won't lock me up," I scoffed.

"No? I was with him five sols ago when he learned his girl-friend was missing. For one hour no one could locate her. He. Lost. It. Even when she'd been found and he'd been assured she was all right, there was no dealing with him. Of course, now that I see you're involved, I'm not surprised. If I were in his position, I could justify that behavior too."

"What did he do?" I asked, both mesmerized and worried.

Brody shook his head, indicating the topic was off-limits. "Just know he'd do whatever he thought necessary to protect you."

"I'm still going to see Vieira."

He sighed. "I know you are. No one can stop you when your mind is made up. I'd advise you not to say anything until after you meet with him then."

"That was kind of the plan," I said, not even realizing I had a plan until now. Brody was right. Obviously I couldn't tell Alexei, and subconsciously I think I knew that. I wouldn't have hidden the adapter otherwise.

"Someone should know what you're up to in case it all goes wrong. Care to fill in the unenlightened?"

I thought fast, letting my gut lead me and fill in the gaps. "You're going with me as backup."

His eyebrows seemed to rise to his hairline. "I am?"

"Of course. We're going back to Elysium City today. I'll contact Vieira in a few sols to arrange a meeting, and you can join us. You can step in if you think things are veering out of control or I'm over my head. Where will you be if I need you?"

I could tell he was still reeling. More so when I held out my hand for the holo-adapter and he gave it back without protest.

"Just shim me. I'll be there wherever, whenever." A pause, then, "I've just sent you my contact info."

I felt my c-tex vibrate and I checked the new shim, verifying it was from him. I would have liked to say I was surprised he could so easily access my flat-file avatar after four years, but it didn't seem appropriate.

"Great. Now if you'll excuse me, I need to pack and you need to leave."

I waved at the clothing I'd strewn about the bed to illustrate my point. Then I grabbed the first thing I could lay my hands on, waded it up into a ball, and hurled it into my suitcase. Gods knew I needed to do something with my hands, and I didn't want to have to face Brody and explain my actions. To be honest, I wasn't sure if I could even explain them to myself. All I knew for certain was, now that I'd seen Brody again, my gut didn't want me to lose the connection.

"Felicia, are you sure this is a good idea?" He stepped so close, I felt his warmth through my robe. "I don't want to make things complicated for you with Alexei. I just want you safe."

"I know," I assured him, folding more clothes. "This is how you're going to do it."

He was silent for a long time. I knew he wanted me to look at him so I resolutely focused on packing. Finally I heard him sigh. "If this is what you want, I'll do it. I was always terrible at saying no to you. Besides, maybe this will be fun. It'll be like the old days. There's been no woman in my life quite like you."

I wasn't sure how to reply. Did I say I was glad to see him too? Or tell him I wondered about him sometimes? Should I admit there were times when I imagined what a life with him might have been like? No, probably not a good idea. "I'll shim you when I have the details," I said instead.

Nervous energy kept me moving, knowing he watched as I

made a mess of everything on the bed. *I should tell him to get out*, I decided. *He needs to leave and I need to stop behaving like a hormonal teenager with her first crush.*

When I felt I could finally risk looking at him, there was an amused expression on his face.

"What's so damned funny?" I demanded.

"Are you aware you're packing all the hotel's towels in your luggage? Does Alexei know you steal from his hotels?"

I followed to where he pointed. In with my clothes, I'd thrown in most of the towels from the suite, even the wet ones. I swore under my breath, feeling stupid and like I'd been caught with all my feelings and thoughts out on display.

"The towels here are very nice," I said lamely. "I was thinking of getting some for my bathroom back home."

"I'm sure you were" was all he said. "I need to get back to whatever it is I need to be doing. I'll see you around, Felicia."

I watched him leave, waiting until I heard the echo of his footsteps outside the door fade before I let out the shuddering breath I'd been holding. Looked like I had a good news–bad news story on my hands. The good news: I had handled Brody and the conversation hadn't been overly weird. Well, it was weird, but I'd managed. The bad news: I now had a date with him that he seemed to be looking forward to.

But the worst news? As I pulled the wet towels out of my suitcase, I knew that deep down, I was looking forward to seeing him again too. I wouldn't be dealing with a waded-up ball of wrinkled and soggy clothing otherwise. If I wanted proof I was in for trouble, apparently all I needed to do was look at my laundry.

9

The trip back to Elysium City was quiet. Though I'd spent much of the past few sols asleep, I slept on the ride home too, lulled by the hum of the flight-limo engine and the growing darkness as night fell.

I woke to the sensation of being carried and the noise of fireworks exploding. When I lifted my head, arms tightened around me. I burrowed deeper into a hard chest and a cologne scent I recognized.

"Where are we?"

"We're home. It's Witching Time, hence the fireworks."

"I hate fireworks," I murmured, pressing my face against his shoulder to block out the brightness.

Alexei chuckled softly. "I know. Just sleep. I've got you."

Which may have been the most reassuring thing I'd ever heard because I knew it was true—whatever happened, he would look after me. How stupid could I be to jeopardize that? Why would I ever want anyone else?

My clothes and shoes were removed before I was tucked into

a bed that didn't really feel or smell like mine. The room was in shadow, lit only by light from the hallway, making it difficult to tell where I was. Still, it felt nice. I had this vague worry that I hadn't brushed my teeth, and must have said something because I heard more soft laughter.

"I think you'll be fine if you skip this one time," he said, kissing the top of my head before pulling away.

"Stay until I fall back to sleep."

I felt the bed dip as he slipped in behind me. I rolled over, turning in to him, pressing my face to the curve of his neck and shoulder and tucking my arms so my hands rested on his chest. His arms went around me and brought me flush against him. Then he threw a leg over mine until I was completely surrounded. It wouldn't be long before I overheated, but for right then, it was perfect. I'd fallen asleep in this position on more than one occasion, and it felt so normal to settle in like this, I sighed.

"Are we okay?" I whispered. "The cards...What you saw...It doesn't mean anything."

A beat of silence before he answered. "I'm sorry for yesterday. It scared me to realize anything could come between us. I don't want to lose this."

"You won't." Then, in Russian, "*Ya lyublyu tebya.*"

"Were you practicing?" He pressed a kiss to my forehead.

"A little."

"It was perfect. I love you too."

Naturally, he was naked as we had this conversation but I was too tired to react as I normally might. Still, I couldn't help but note his erection pressing insistently against my stomach.

"Can I deal with that in the morning?" I murmured into his skin, my eyes drifting closed.

Again, the soft laughter. "Ignore it. It will go away."

It didn't, but I fell asleep anyway. In that moment I knew with certainty I wanted to be with him forever. I would do anything to keep things like this as long as I could, gut feeling be damned.

———◆———

I woke alone, though that wasn't surprising. Alexei didn't need much sleep and was always up hours before me. When I discovered I was in his bed, that wasn't surprising either. However, what blew me away was opening the closet, asking the AI for a robe from among the few items I kept at Alexei's, and finding my entire wardrobe on offer. All of it—every single stitch of clothing I owned—was there. What the hell?

I crossed the bedroom with its enormous bed and ornate headboard, oversized furniture, thick carpeting, all done in dark, rich colors that made me feel like I'd wandered into some medieval lord's sexual playroom—which wasn't far off the mark. My next stop was the bathroom, which continued the same decorating theme with dark marble floors, heavy gold hardware, a claw-foot tub you could swim in, and the most elaborate, decadent shower I'd ever experienced. I opened a few drawers and found them full of my toiletries. I stared at the contents, wondering how I should feel as I floated simultaneously between surprise, panic, and anger.

Since I was there, I brushed my teeth and washed my face, all the while counting to one hundred in my head to avoid a complete and utter meltdown. Once finished, I padded barefoot down the tiled hall, opening doors along the way. When I reached the room at the end near the staircase, I found something worth seeing.

In the center of the room was my card table Eleat. Against one wall, the cabinet where I kept my Tarot decks. Another wall, my desk. All were from my condo, set up and ready to use. The walls were set to the muted lavender color of a sky at sunset I liked so much. There were also a couple of plush chairs, more comfortable than anything I'd had before. Sliding doors led to a balcony with a breathtaking view of the Utopian Ocean. I could even see the space elevator in the distance.

The room was perfect. Too perfect. I had a sinking feeling that if I went through the house—because of course he had a house palatial in size with a sprawling property requiring an army of staff to see to its upkeep—I would find my things scattered throughout, waiting for me.

That...fucker! While we were away, he'd moved everything into his house! I'd only just agreed to live with him and now all my things were there! Gods, he'd probably made arrangements to move me the minute I'd said yes. Never mind if I got cold feet or wanted to do it myself. And maybe I didn't want to live in his house. Maybe I wanted some place we could pick together, although gods knew I hated moving. As a child, my family was always moving from one place to the next. And it was nice to have a house with a yard where I could go outside rather than a tiny strip of condo balcony that overlooked someone else's bathroom.

No, I was getting sidetracked. Maybe this was exactly what I wanted and maybe it seemed like he knew me better than I did myself, but he could at least talk to me first. I wasn't a child for him to coddle. Or was I getting mad for the sake of getting mad? I had agreed to live with him, and this did make things easier, but...

I couldn't decide whether I was pleased by his thoughtfulness, pissed at his arrogant high-handedness, or terrified because it happened so fast. Or maybe what really bothered me was it seemed too good to be true and I was terrified it would fall apart. As much as I fought it, my gut was pushing me, but it wasn't in this direction.

"I see you've noticed the changes."

I yelped in surprise as Alexei materialized behind me. I whirled on him, swiping my hair out of my eyes so nothing could get in the way of my furious glare.

"You moved me in while we were in Apolli!" I accused.

"Seems that way," he agreed, looking from the room back to me, unconcerned.

He held out a mug of coffee that smelled like heaven, and I suspected was made just the way I liked. I took it from him and had a sip. It was perfect. Gods, he was using my need for caffeine to manipulate me. I started counting to one hundred in my head again.

He merely gazed down at me, wearing loose pants and a fitted black T-shirt that clearly showed the definition in his shoulders and chest, and left his chiseled biceps bare so I could admire them while he drank from his own mug. I bet I could even touch them if I wanted—which felt like more manipulation. He knew how much I loved running my hands over him and feeling the hard swell of muscle. His black hair was damp and slicked back from his face, just skimming his shoulders. He looked so damn hot, his blue eyes glittering and his expression smug, knowing I liked the coffee and couldn't come up with a legitimately good reason to argue with what he'd done that didn't make me sound like a crazy bitch. Worse, I felt like I might spontaneously combust from looking at him, and he probably knew that too.

"I'm really mad at you right now," I told him between sips of coffee.

"I see that."

"And we're going to fight later."

"Probably," he agreed.

"And if I'm not happy with where my things are, you're going to move everything wherever I want it."

"I have nothing else planned for today except taking care of what you need."

"Good. I'm glad we sorted that out." Then I eyed him up and down, because really I just couldn't help myself. I was starting to feel flushed and turned on as I ogled my own boyfriend.

"Anything else you wanted?"

"Nope. Can't think of a thing."

"You're certain?" The cocky bastard was grinning into his mug.

"All right, fine," I groused. "You know I'm dying to get my hands on you."

He took my coffee and set both our mugs on the desk. "You know I'm always happy to take care of whatever urges you have, whenever you have them."

Then he grabbed me around the waist, hoisted me over his shoulder, and carried me to the bedroom. My gasp became a shriek when he had the nerve to slap my ass like some damn Neanderthal. A few seconds later, I found myself tossed on a bed with a very large and very aroused Russian on top of me.

Needless to say, the furniture didn't get moved—well, not the furniture I wanted moved. Still, by the time we were done, I'd worked out my initial irritation. I decided moving in with him had more benefits than I'd originally anticipated. For now, I could live with that.

———◆———

I was in my new office, sorting through the endless array of card decks I collected the way other women did knickknacks and tchotchkes, when I felt my bracelet flutter on my wrist. It was late, almost ten in the evening. First glance showed it was a face-chat shim, meaning family. Yup—Celeste's avatar appeared on the display. I hit the jewels and up popped the face-chat shim.

There was Celeste, looking relieved. "Finally! You are the absolute *worst* at returning shims."

"I am not the worst. I've just been busy. Hey, Celeste, it's good to see you," I answered, settling into one of my new chairs. I propped my wrist on my knee so I wouldn't have to hold up my arm to see her image.

"You too," she said, before launching into a one-woman gossip-fest where she proceeded to give me the rundown on everything family.

Unlike most of the Sevigny clan, her shoulder-length hair was blond rather than black or dark brown. Her eyes were hazel, also unusual. Still she looked fantastic at sixty-one thanks to her Renew treatments. That was the one thing I'd always found hypocritical about my family—they were anti-tech, but I couldn't name a single one who'd skipped a Renew treatment.

It made me curious about what else they protested yet indulged in on the down-low.

I also suspected Celeste hadn't inherited the luck gene since she never talked about gut feelings the way most of us did. She had a pretty good life regardless. Happily married for over thirty years, she had a son, Kacey, who had turned out well enough—I mean, he had a steady job for the most part, and she got along with everyone. She was vying for the position of matriarch, the same way Granny G had once been the center of the clan. Granny G's death had left a void we were all trying to fill. Grandmother, Granny G's daughter and only child, just couldn't cut it—too cold, too aloof, too positive we should be crawling to her. Even Granny G's siblings, and she'd come from a family of ten, couldn't pass muster. Yes, ten—three boys, seven girls—but that was before the Shared Hope program and explained why I had so many third, fourth, and even fifth cousins underfoot.

"You haven't replied to my invite. I'm saying it's a picnic potluck, but it's really an engagement party for Kacey and his fiancée. I need to confirm numbers for registration with the local One Gov bureau," she said.

"Sorry, but I can't make it."

"Everyone will be there! We need your potato salad, and the cards. Didn't Lotus tell you how important this was? Having you there will be like having Granny G in spirit."

Oh boy, that was a new angle. "See that's the thing, Celeste. Sometimes it seems like the only reason I'm there is because of the cards."

"Well, no one can read them like you and this *is* for the new couple. We want to know they'll have a happy future together.

Or if it's bad news, how they can get around it. It's a family tradition. And you know you're the only one with Granny G's potato salad recipe."

"That's bullshit. She shimmed it to everyone before she died."

"But yours has something extra. Everyone knows that," Celeste wheedled.

I laughed despite myself. "Must be because it's made with so much damn love."

"You're coming then?"

I groaned. If I said no, I'd be dead woman walking to the rest of the family. "I don't know. It's just—"

"Lotus says you're seeing someone. This would be the perfect opportunity to introduce him," Celeste continued, plowing forward. "Unless you don't want us to meet him. Are you ashamed of us?"

"Of course not! It's not like that at all."

"Is there something wrong with him? Does he come from a bad family? Too hopped up on t-mods? Although I'm not sure that matters. Look at Helena's boyfriend. He's a complete techhead, but he seems nice."

I rolled my eyes. "That's because he's the only one who likes your cabbage casserole. He was so zoned out last time, I don't think he knew he was eating."

"It would still be nice for us all to be together. We could meet your mystery man, and there would be less pressure on you with the cards. I'm expecting fifty-eight. You and your boyfriend would make sixty."

Just the thought of Alexei and my family together had me cringing. They would so not approve of him with his obvious amped-up MH Factor, never mind that he was head of the

Tsarist Consortium. They'd probably ask him to invest in at least a dozen half-baked schemes before dinner. Someone that powerful with that much wealth, suspected of being a criminal by half the tri-system—they wouldn't be able to resist.

"He works a lot. I don't know if he'd be available."

"Felicia Sevigny, what would Granny G say about avoiding family?"

"I'm not avoiding family. He's just busy."

"How about this: We'll start slow. You could come for dinner some night, and Hamilton and I could suss him out."

"You live in a trailer that's never in the same place for more than a few weeks. We can't just come over for dinner."

"Sure you can. Shim me next week and we'll arrange something."

"I'm not sure this is a good idea. I mean—"

"Felicia, if family is as important as you claim and this man matters, he needs to meet us. And by bringing him, you're showing him he means something to you. You may not like it, but that's how it works."

Damn it, I hated when people used my own logic against me. "Fine, put me down for two."

"Wonderful! I can't wait to see you both!" She made kiss motions in the air. "Gotta go. More people to shim, engagements to plan. Don't forget the cards. And the potato salad. Love ya!"

She disconnected. I'd been hosed by my family yet again.

I'm not sure how long I sat there bemoaning my fate when I felt strong hands on my shoulders. I jerked in surprise, then relaxed once they began massaging. My shoulders sagged and I leaned into the hands, my head lolling to the side because it felt so good.

"I could get used to this," I said, pretty sure I had drool on my cheek. "If you ever leave the Consortium, you could do this professionally."

"Sorry, but there's only one person I want to touch like this and she keeps me very busy," Alexei said, his fingers working on a knot in my right shoulder. "I heard part of the conversation. What does your family want?"

I stretched languidly under his hands. "Did you know I make the best potato salad in my family?"

He laughed. "No, I didn't. You've never made it for me."

"Probably because it annoys me every time I peel a potato. Apparently mine has something special no one else can replicate."

"Now that sounds like something I'd very much like to try."

"My family are professionals when it comes to taking advantage of a situation. You could probably learn something from them." My back arched as he ran his hands down my spine. I could feel my body melting into warm, sticky goo as he touched me. "Then again, you already know enough without their help."

He laughed again, but softer this time. "What does your family want?" he repeated.

"There's a thing next weekend, on Saturday."

"Venusol," he corrected.

"Right, Venusol," I said. I would have agreed to anything so long as he kept massaging. "It's an engagement party for one of my cousins. I forgot about it, plus I was kind of hoping it would go away. I told Celeste we'd go, but you don't have to. I know you're busy."

His hands stilled on my shoulders, their heat seeping into

my body, and I felt myself tensing. Logically, I knew mixing Alexei and my family was a bad idea. It would be simpler if I went alone.

Yet if he didn't go, I had this ridiculous feeling I wouldn't get over it. I'd never asked him to do anything like this—never really let him see how much I needed him. I hated looking weak and needy. But Celeste was right. Meeting each other's family was important. It was declaring ourselves a couple in front of everyone who mattered. It was also so completely normal, it freaked me out. Alexei wasn't normal. He was so far beyond normal, he might not even be human. Knowing that fed my insecurities that said maybe we shouldn't be together.

"Do you want me to go with you?" he asked, his hands still unmoving on my shoulders.

"Not if you're busy. I know you don't have a lot of spare time."

"Next week will be demanding. It may not be easy to get away, but if you need me, I'll be there."

"Why? What's happening?"

He hesitated and I had the feeling he was struggling to come up with the right words. "The *Martian Princess* is docking midweek. I'm meeting with several high-ranking Consortium members coming from Earth."

What? That was news. "You didn't tell me this before."

"It isn't anything you need to worry about."

Which naturally made it seem like I *did* need to worry. My gut thought so too. "Is there trouble?"

"I invited them. Our base of operations here is weaker than on Earth. If I want to solidify the Consortium's hold on Mars, I'll need their expertise."

"I thought you only needed Brody."

"I need him to handle any One Gov concerns. For now, it's still necessary to work within One Gov's framework. He's more skilled at manipulating the AI queenmind."

"Aren't you the best at everything?"

He laughed softly. "I am. I just wasn't made to be a One Gov lackey."

And because I couldn't let it go, I asked, "Is this what you've been working toward all these months? You're finally going to implement your big project—whatever it is."

"Yes, that's my hope."

For some reason, a shiver of fear raced down my spine. "Whatever you're working on, it's not going to get you arrested, is it?"

There was a long moment of silence, then, "Not if it succeeds."

I had no response to that. The sheer vagueness in his words told me more than enough.

His hands tightened on my shoulders, which in turn kicked my tension up another notch. "It's nothing to concern you," he murmured. "The groundwork has been laid for years. It isn't going to fail, and I won't be arrested. Everything will be fine."

"But there's no guarantee."

"Nothing in life comes with guarantees." The silence stretched, until he asked a second time, "Do you want me to go with you?"

"It sounds like you might have other things to deal with."

"You know I'm yours, Felicia," he murmured against my skin as he crouched behind me. "If you want me to go with you, just ask."

"Why didn't you tell me about the Consortium coming to Mars?"

"Because that's irrelevant to what's between us." He swiveled my chair so I faced him. His kiss caught me off guard, slow and sweet, gently coaxing. "Ask me."

My hands went to his shoulders, pushing him away. It felt like he was manipulating me with a kiss designed to distract me, and I didn't like it. "Don't try to kiss me into not worrying about what's coming at us next."

"There's no need to worry because nothing's coming at us. I want you to ask me to your family's engagement party, so ask."

"Fine. Will you come with me?"

"Yes."

I should have been thrilled. I wasn't.

He kissed me again, shifting my body closer to his. His tongue boldly stroked mine, the kiss growing more urgent as he showed me with his mouth what he wanted to do with my body. I could feel myself melting for him, but I was also upset. He was keeping secrets when he knew better. Or so I'd told Brody yesterday. What if I was wrong about that? I broke off the kiss.

"I still have a lot of unpacking to do," I said, shoving the chair back so I could stand. "I'd better get to it if I want to finish tonight."

"I thought you were done." He knelt on the floor, looking up at me.

I turned to my cabinet, deliberately putting my back to him. "Not yet. Plus I'm going back to work tomorrow, so I need to get organized."

I started piling decks of cards on top of one another, not sure how long I could stack them while he knelt there, watching me. I heard him sigh and get up. "I'll leave you to it then."

"Great." I stacked more decks. "And thanks for agreeing to go to the engagement party. Sorry I didn't tell you sooner."

I winced at the bitchiness in my tone. That, along with the suspicion, the anger, and if I was being honest, the fear. I wanted to get back at him, I realized. I wanted to get in a dig at him for not telling me about the Consortium and anything else he was keeping from me.

"The Consortium's arrival doesn't affect how we feel about each other or our future together," he said finally.

"Of course it does. You're moving forward with the Consortium's plans for Mars and One Gov. It means things will change for the whole tri-system. I understand you wanting to protect me, but you can't keep me separate from everything else in your life. When does protecting me become lying to me?"

"What do you think will happen with more Consortium on Mars? Do you think it will be a bloody red revolution with casualties in the billions? Or I'll plunge us all into another Dark Times when One Gov topples?"

I whirled to face him in time to see his expression close down, his blue eyes narrowing. I felt fear rumble through me, cold and unsettling. Was that what I'd always secretly believed? Did I really think he would destroy everything? Or maybe that he would change things so radically, us being together would be even more improbable?

"No, of course not," I said. "I've never thought that. You just shouldn't keep things from me."

"Because that's what I do, isn't it? Keep secrets and withhold the truth."

"I didn't say that. I just want you to be open with me. If

we're in this together, you have to see me as an equal and not someone you need to protect or cage or lie to."

"Felicia, you know what I am and what I've done for the Consortium. I want to be what you need, but I'm not certain either of us knows what that is. If I gave you all the answers you were looking for, would they make you happy? Or would they destroy everything between us so there would be no way to put us back together?"

"Why would you say that? What else aren't you telling me?"

He ran a hand over his face as if he was tired. "It's nothing. I'm a fool and…I apologize. I should have told you about the Consortium arriving. Finish unpacking. Just don't stay up too late. Good night and I'll see you in the morning."

"Alexei, what's going on? Is there something happening with the off-world mines? Or maybe with Phobos and One Gov and the penal colony?"

"Are you looking for conspiracies everywhere now? Do you think there's an ulterior motive in everything I do?"

Gods, was that how I seemed to him? Hysterical? Suspicious? Crazy? "No. I never…I wouldn't…I'm sorry," I said meekly, hanging my head. "I just don't want you to shut me out."

"I haven't. I love you, and that is one thing that is never going to change. But until you stop comparing me to those who've betrayed you in the past, you're setting us up to fail. I'm trying to do this right for you but…" He shook his head as if words were beyond him, then he left.

Instead of going after him, I sank into a chair. The worry and anxiety bubbling up inside me gelled into a crippling fear like nothing I'd ever experienced. Everything I believed I could count on suddenly felt in question and I didn't know what to do. I should run my cards, but the thought of what they might say petrified me. Worse, my gut was pushing me in a direction I wasn't even sure I wanted to go.

I always wanted the truth, which was why I'd been drawn to the Tarot with its ability to give answers. Except now I'd accused him of hiding things when I had secrets of my own. After all, I hadn't told him about Vieira's holo-adapter or the pseudo-date with Brody. Maybe Alexei was right. Maybe deep down, I'd always expected us to fail. I expected betrayal and disappointment, so I got it. Why did I do this to myself? What was the point of having a luck gene if it didn't make things better?

I looked down at my stomach, as if I could physically see an answer explaining my determination to ruin things. If my gut had anything to say on the subject, it kept its opinions to itself. All I had were my fears, my unfounded suspicious, and a boyfriend I'd upset but didn't know how to apologize to. I'd started this week off with a Euphoria crash that could have killed me. If I'd known that was going to be the high point of things, I would have found a way to skip everything else altogether.

10

The next sol found me back at my shop. I couldn't claim to be rested, but Lotus looked tan so at least one of us had a good time.

She and Buckley were happy again, having worked through their latest round of issues. She also lamented Red Dust's demise—the club was there one minute and gone the next, like it had never existed. I made noncommittal noises, deciding not to mention my role in Alexei's decision to close it. She'd managed to reschedule all my appointments, meaning this week would be busy—even after canceling the dog readings. Seriously, still with the dogs! Sometimes I wondered if Lotus actually listened to me.

"Don't forget about the reading party tomorrow evening," she reminded me. "I transferred it to your schedule this morning."

"Oh, shit! It's tomorrow?"

"You told me to fit it in where you had room."

I swore again. "I forgot to tell Alexei about it." Great, another secret apparently.

"Why does he need to know? It's your shop. You can do whatever you want."

"I know, but things are complicated. We moved in together, there are Consortium issues cropping up, the bodyguard thing is starting to get out of control, and—"

"You moved in with him?" Lotus looked dumbfounded. "When were you going to tell me this piece of news?"

I shrugged. "It happened on the weekend. We're still adjusting."

"Wow. Can't say I saw that coming. He's out of town so often, I assumed he had some action on the side."

"Could you please not make me feel more insecure than I already do?"

"Actually, I'm impressed. At this rate, he'll be going to Celeste's party and wanting to marry you by the end of the week. You told her you're not going, right?"

I squirmed uncomfortably. "Well, she talked me into it then pressured me to bring Alexei, so we'll both be there."

Lotus looked at me, jaw dropping. "Holy shit, do you have a magic vagina? How are you getting him to agree to all this? What kind of voodoo hold do you have over that guy? Nothing against you, cousin. But you're you and he's...Well, he's Alexei Petriv. He could have anyone."

It probably wasn't a good thing her thoughts so closely mirrored my own, so I said, "Gods, Lotus, don't make it seem like it's so impossible he wants to be with me."

"Know what? Let's just be happy things are moving forward for you," Lotus said, banging her hand on the desk as if that might somehow clear the air. Then she bent over her c-tex bracelet. "I'm looking at your schedule now. I can try rebooking the party with Novi Pazidor, but since I've moved your appointments from last week, I don't know where to put it. You could always cancel. I don't trust her anyway."

"Keep it where it is. I'll think of something."

"You need a backup plan," Lotus advised. "Just in case the Russian starts thinking protecting you also means trying to run your life and won't let you go. I mean, it's Driller Dive after all. It isn't the safest part of town, even with the muscle he has following you around. He still might try to kibosh you. Men are always screwing women over."

"Screwing me over? This sounds like something you'd normally say when there's trouble with Buckley."

"I just think it doesn't hurt to have the upper hand in the relationship," Lotus said with a regal sniff. "Buckley and I are perfect. In fact, we were talking about having a baby."

I stopped everything and whirled on her. "What?"

"Yeah, we're thinking we should both get our fertility inhibitors removed and finally do this. Take the next step. Become functioning adults."

"But two weeks ago you hated him."

Lotus waved it away. "That was then. Now it's different. Besides, we've been talking about it for a while and we're ready."

I slapped a smile on my face because what else could I do? "Just remember, it's going to tie you to him for a long time. You may like him now, but he could be an asshole again next week."

"Believe me, I know it. But I think we can do this," she assured me. Then she gave me a speculative look. "You think you and the Russian might do it one day?"

I think my jaw dropped a little and I honestly had no good

reply. Not one I wanted to get into with her at any rate. "I don't think we're ready for that."

"Okay, but just don't waste your time with him if he can't give you what you want," Lotus advised, examining her nails.

I frowned. According to Alexei, I didn't know what I wanted. "I'll be sure to take that under advisement."

"You could always use your cards to find a new guy if you don't think he's the one. True love is just a shuffle of the deck away. Isn't that what you tell people?"

"I've never said anything so ridiculous in my life. The day I start spouting gimmicky clichés is the day I give up card reading," I told her, outraged. "Besides, finding true love has nothing to do with shuffling the cards. They show what's going to happen, not make it happen."

"Better not say that too loud," Lotus said, her voice dropping to a conspiratorial whisper as she glanced at the door. "Looks like your next appointment is here. You might chase them off if you can't guarantee results."

I followed her gaze to see three teenage girls enter the shop. They all looked nervous, as if they'd made their appointment on a dare. Based on the cut of their clothes, the accessories they carried, and their matching bird-inspired cheek tattoos that rippled with a rainbow of colors, all came from money. I'd need to be "on" until my head ached—charming, sympathetic, bubbly—while I counseled them through a variety of adolescent woes. Not a bad way to spend a few hours, but not particularly satisfying either. It actually made me look forward to tomorrow night's card reading party with Novi Pazidor.

"Looks like true love might only be a shuffle away after all,"

Lotus continued in a stage whisper, before getting up to greet the girls.

I rolled my eyes and stifled a laugh. With these girls, she was probably right. I'd most likely be picking out new boyfriends for everyone. Well, at least they weren't dogs, I consoled myself. Plus, they wouldn't shit on the floor. Depending on how you looked at it, everything had a bright side.

<hr>

I was in my reading room working on an assignment from my Russian language class when I heard soft male laughter and lots of giggling from the reception desk. For a while, I ignored it as I worked through the exercises then listened to the spoken language translation on my c-tex. For the millionth time, I wished I had t-mods to download the language all at once instead of doing things the hard way. Alexei was supportive when my pronunciation was off or I mixed up the word order, but that was the extent of his help. Asking him to tutor me had been a waste of time. To be fair, he'd tried. Unfortunately, he was more intrigued with getting me stretched out under him than he was in teaching me Russian. It was better if I did the work myself or saved my questions for the evening class I took twice a week. Since I'd missed both classes last week, I was trying to catch up by working through the assignments posted on the CN-net between appointments.

When the laughter became too much, I got up to close the door before realizing Buckley and Lotus usually fought more than laughed. Time to investigate. I hadn't gone far when Lotus giggled again, followed by male laughter I recognized. I froze in the doorway, caught by a wave of déjà vu so potent, it staggered me.

It was like I was back on Earth, watching Natty giggle at her desk over something Brody had said—because of course it was Brody. She would touch his arm or his chest, he would grin and say something funny, and the laughter would start again.

Taking the scenario further, after he'd finished flirting with Natty, Brody would turn his attention to me, I'd close up the shop, and we'd go back to his place. Since I worked nights, I would often sleep there in the morning, he would leave work early, and we'd spend the afternoon together. Or some days, he didn't go to work at all. On those days, I didn't get any sleep, despite an entire day spent in bed. Brody had always worked to accommodate my unusual schedule, fitting in to wherever I could make space for him in my life, even if it was just a lull between appointments in the middle of the night. My stomach gave a lurch and I just stood there, dismayed at the direction of my thoughts.

Just seeing him bent over Lotus like that...I didn't know what it was. The déjà vu, the lurch in my stomach, the way my gut had been reacting for weeks now—I suddenly remembered all those long-forgotten Brody-centered feelings. They were as familiar and uncomplicated as the sun in the sky. I didn't have to think, worry about where I stood with him, or negotiate every aspect of our relationship.

He wore a dark gray suit with a green shirt that brought out the green in his eyes. The cut was perfect, emphasizing his shoulders and lean figure. He wasn't as big as Alexei, but there was still some bulk underneath that suit.

He really was attractive. I'd forgotten that. I'd forgotten how tall he was too. Again, not as tall as Alexei, but still a height that made me tip my head back to look up at him. And his hands… They had done things to me that had to be illegal somewhere in the tri-system. And he'd always been amusing and fun—the perfect boyfriend I hadn't even realized I'd had.

Brody looked up and caught me standing in the doorway. His grin faded, and became something more private—a look just for me. I knew he could tell exactly what I was thinking because he was thinking it too.

Lotus spotted me. "This guy claims you know him. He wanted to see you, but I'm pretty sure he doesn't have an appointment. Where do you find all these men anyway? 'Hot Guys "R" Us'?"

I had to put a lid on it and make this stop. I couldn't be feeling like this. "Yes, I know him, and no, he doesn't have an appointment. You booked me solid for the rest of the week, so tell him he'll have to come back later."

"He tried to bribe me with strawberries. Amateur," Lotus scoffed, shooting Brody a flirtatious glance. "You should try them, though. They're amazing. Says he got them at the market, but I didn't think they were in season this time of year."

She gestured to the small wicker basket on her desk, filled to the rim with the plump, red fruit. Then she bit into one, yelping in surprise when berry juice dribbled down her chin. She wiped at it hastily with a napkin before it could travel too far.

I looked from the basket to Brody, saw him watching me. Again the déjà vu hit, walloping so hard, it was a wonder I didn't crumble under the force of it. Strawberries? He'd brought me strawberries in Nairobi the first time he'd come to my shop. Then he asked me out. I'd said yes, and then…

I did the supremely mature thing of striding back into my reading room and slamming the door. I felt like my heart would beat its way out of my chest and my gut was roiling until I thought I might be sick because everything was too intense and familiar and *this should not be happening to me!*

There was a knock on the door, and before I could say anything, Brody was inside, an eyebrow arched in question. "Looks like someone might be jealous she isn't getting any attention."

"I'm not jealous! Why are you even here, and don't say you were in the neighborhood." My voice came out shrill and I felt brittle and anxious. He needed to leave and I needed this feeling to go away. "Aren't you supposed to be occupied with Consortium business?"

"Would it make you feel better if I said I'm specifically here to see you?"

Gods, no, it wouldn't. He closed the door behind him and leaned against it, as if he thought I would bolt. Hell, maybe I would. It trapped us in the windowless room and suddenly the space I'd always thought intimate and cozy was too small. He was just too *there*, invading everything.

"I said I'd be in touch once I contacted the Under-Secretary. I haven't done that yet. Why are you here and why the hell are you bringing me strawberries?"

"Felicia, calm down. I just wanted to make sure you were okay. No hidden agenda. No secret plans. Just old-fashioned concern."

I shook my head. "It's not your job to be concerned."

He gave me a long, considering look. "Actually, I thought that was normal behavior between friends. They check up on each other. See how the other person is doing. Drop in to visit occasionally. Plus, I was curious about your shop. I wanted to see what it looked like." He looked around the room, studying the space. "It's nice. Charlie Zero would like it. Reminds me of your place in Nairobi."

"That was the goal," I said, following his gaze around the room.

"I can see I'm upsetting you," he said eventually. "I guess having an ex suddenly drop back into your life would shock anyone. I can see now how this might seem stalkerlike, especially with the strawberries."

He looked so apologetic, it made me wonder if I was the one overreacting and not the other way round. "A little," I agreed, softening my tone. "Maybe give me some warning before you stop by, or add a few sols been visits."

"I'll remember that for next time."

Great. And now I had a potential "next time" lined up with him.

"I still haven't contacted Vieira yet," I reminded him. "I'm not sure I'm ready to meet with him. Plus I'm busy."

"Yes, I see that. Lotus is filing her nails out front and you're"—he looked at the paperwork on my card reading table—"doing your homework. If you're nervous, you're nervous. Believe me, I understand. I'd need to get myself into the right mind-set before I contacted him too. And I'd definitely find ways to procrastinate before I did it."

I made to scoop up my homework before I stopped myself. I didn't have to explain anything to him. "If I say I'm not ready, I'm not ready. Besides, I can't just shim one of the most powerful people in the tri-system and expect him to jump to my schedule."

"If he's really here to see you, then that's exactly what you do and he'll make himself available," Brody reasoned. "I know Alexei would. And if you needed me, I would too."

At his comment, my stomach did a swooping, excited lurch that wasn't at all appropriate. It was only supposed to do that for Alexei.

"When I walked in today, it felt like old times, didn't it?"

Oh shit, was I blushing? Did he know what my stomach was doing? I could feel something coiling tightly within me, begging to be released. Maybe it was even worse after last night's confrontation with Alexei that left everything feeling at loose ends. "I have no idea what you're talking about."

"Sure you do. It was like we were back in Nairobi, on Night Alley. I saw the look on your face. You felt it too. The pull's still there."

"There's no pull."

"Of course not. No pull at all." He laughed softly, considering me. "Sorry if I made things awkward again. I just wanted to say how I felt." He looked around the office as if casting about for something else to say. He spotted my books on the table. "You're still into languages? Russian now?"

"Yes," I said cautiously. "It's a bit trickier than I thought."

He glanced through the pages. "Does Alexei help with your homework?"

"Sometimes, but I won't learn if someone hands it to me."

He paused on a page, frowning before pushing it aside. I looked at it, wondering what was up before noticing I'd made a mistake in verb tenses. Was that what Brody had caught— my page full of mistakes? Which made me pause. Did he speak Russian? If so, I hadn't known that. Before I could ask, he sat down and stretched out his long legs.

He grinned expansively. "I thought maybe you could try contacting the Under-Secretary while I'm here."

Oh, did he? "Ever think I might have a client coming in?"

"I already checked with Lotus. She said you had free time now."

I wanted to get angry at his presumptuousness, but he was right. I did have free time, and since he was already there, it would certainly make things easier to do this now. Still, it should be my decision when I contacted Vieira, not his.

"I assume you haven't told Alexei yet?" he continued.

"I thought we agreed that was a bad idea. Remember the whole 'locking me in a cage' thing?"

"True, but if things go sideways, Alexei can bring the whole Consortium down on Vieira's ass."

I frowned at that. "I don't want to start something between them. I just want to hear what Vieira has to say."

"Hopefully, it's that easy and he just wants to talk," Brody said, though it didn't sound like he believed it.

I didn't either. "I don't want to make this about One Gov and the Consortium. Why does it even need to be like that?"

"It doesn't. Or it shouldn't. You shouldn't be in the middle of a conflict that's been building behind the scenes for decades, if not longer. For that at least, I'm sorry."

"That's not..." My voice trailed off. Fucking stupid luck gene. Was that why I was in this position? Because luck wanted me there? "I shouldn't even be telling you this stuff. Gods, I don't need a war for the fate of the tri-system on top of everything else."

"Fate of the tri-system? That's a bit much, even for you. You know I only want the best for you, right? If Alexei is putting pressure on you because of Vieira and making you miserable—"

"I never said that."

"All right then," he said, continuing the ruse we were having a perfectly normal conversation. "If that isn't the problem, then something else must be causing you grief."

"You mean besides you suddenly showing up out of nowhere?"

"Yes, besides me. Maybe your business isn't going well—I don't remember you ever having enough free time to do homework between appointments. And I know you loved working nights rather than being tied to a day job. If I recall, you once called me a mindless drone tied to the corporate clock of capitalism, dancing to the fake idealism of One Gov's promise to the tri-system of equality for all."

I laughed because I couldn't help myself. "I never said anything like that, and if I did, I was probably drunk."

"Well, I may have been paraphrasing. My point is—then and now, I just wanted you to be happy and I don't think you are."

We both fell silent, looking at each other. My cheeks felt unaccountably flushed so I gathered all the papers on my reading table—anything to keep myself from thinking about whatever he wanted to imply. Brody merely watched my pointless busywork, and the silence felt weighted with expectation.

Finally I'd cleared the table and because I couldn't think of anything else to do and he didn't seem inclined to go anywhere, I pulled out the holo-adapter I'd kept hidden from Alexei for the past two sols. Brody arched an eyebrow, knowing he'd cracked me.

I sniffed regally, refusing to acknowledge his grin. "If we're going to do this, we need to hurry. I've got an appointment in about half an hour."

"Maybe you should reschedule."

"I can't afford to. Any regular clients I have are going to dump me."

"So I was right about the business part not going well."

"No, it's fine, but..." I sighed, shrugging. What was the point of trying to hide anything when he could read me so easily? Had he always been able to do that? "It's not Nairobi. I don't feel like I'm helping anyone. I miss Earth sometimes. Don't get me wrong, I love being here, but it's like I'm missing the one key ingredient that makes it all work the way I want. I know once I have it, everything will click. Unfortunately, I don't know what that ingredient is."

"And does Alexei know you feel like this?"

My eyes narrowed as I studied him. "Don't try to analyze our relationship."

His grin widened. "Wouldn't dream of it." He nudged the holo-adapter with his finger. "Ready?"

In response, I removed my c-tex and set it on the table. Then I snapped the adapter into one of its removable jewel ports. Immediately, a blue-toned holo-bubble appeared over the bracelet's display, about the size of the bathroom mirror at home. Or rather, former home. Wow, this was really old-school tech—definitely before my time. There was a single item on the drop menu: the Connect prompt. Brody got up to stand behind me so he could look into the bubble the same way I could; it was unidirectional so anyone facing me couldn't view it.

My finger hesitated over the prompt. Even my gut fell silent.

I looked over my shoulder at Brody. "I know it doesn't seem like it, but I'm actually really glad you're here."

He placed his hand on mine. His swamped mine and his skin felt warm compared to my icy chill. I fought not to shiver at the intimacy of the contact.

"So am I."

Then I moved both our hands forward until my finger swiped Connect.

II

The holo-shim launched immediately, the image undulating like ripples across a pond. I could hear the old-school auto-dial and we listened a good ten seconds before anything more happened. A series of connecting clicks followed, as if the shim were being rerouted and reconnected.

"Maybe he's bending his mistress over the desk and can't get to it right now," Brody suggested in a stage whisper. "Or maybe you caught him on the crapper."

I elbowed him lightly, connecting somewhere around his thigh. Uh-oh, not a place where I'd want to hit an unintended target. "Is that supposed to be funny?" Then, "Do you think he has a mistress?"

"I know for a fact he has three."

I digested that bit of information. "But he's married," I protested, maybe too naïvely.

"I doubt he lets that worry him."

"But that's not fair to his wife. If I were in her shoes, I'd be gone so fast, you'd hear the sonic boom when I left."

"Plenty of women would look the other way in exchange for being connected to a powerful man."

"If you knew how many women I've seen cry at this table because their husbands or boyfriends cheated on them, you wouldn't be so flippant. I know what it's like and I never want to go through it again."

"*Again?*" he questioned, his tone sharp. "Was it Alexei?"

I frowned, realizing I'd given something away I hadn't intended. "No. Another ex, before Alexei."

"And he cheated on you? Where is he now?"

"He's dead actually."

Brody made a noise as if he agreed with Roy's ultimate fate. Before I could pursue it, the clicks ended. I squeezed my hands together in my lap, trying to focus myself. I could feel Brody standing close, a brooding presence behind me. I wanted to suggest that maybe he get out of sight but the bubble went opaque, and abruptly, Under-Secretary Vieira was there. He wore a pleasant, inviting smile, making him look all the more handsome. Without the Euphoria in my system, I clearly saw the family resemblance between him and my mother. And I could see now, despite my nearly black hair and olive skin tone, I looked more like my mother's side of the family than I realized. Whatever One Gov genetics modifications I'd gotten from Monique must have been potent if they could dilute the Sevigny gene pool.

"Felicia, it's so good to finally have this chance to talk. I realize now I made a mistake approaching you as I did and I want to apologize. I was eager to see you and took the first opportunity available. Mr. Petriv has made meeting you something of a challenge," he said warmly. Then his eyes strayed over my shoulder. "Ah, I see you aren't alone. Mr. Williams, it's always a pleasure."

Brody and the Under-Secretary knew each other? What the hell? I felt Brody lay his hand between my shoulder blades, either instructing me not to acknowledge the comment or letting me know he would answer my questions later. I wasn't sure which.

"And you as well," Brody answered.

"Will Mr. Petriv be joining us?" Vieira asked, the smile never leaving his face.

"No, it's just us," I said. "I wanted to talk to you myself first."

"Of course. This is a family matter, after all. Although will Mr. Williams be remaining?"

"I . . . Yes, he will." It was better to keep it simple rather than explain why I wanted Brody there. I wasn't even sure I could.

"I'll send a flight-limo for you and we can meet—"

"No flight-limo," I interrupted. "Why can't we just talk now, like this?"

"I can't guarantee the reliability or security of this connection. Also I had hoped we could meet in person." To my surprise, the man looked disappointed at my suggestion. It was actually a point in his favor until he added: "There is also the concern regarding Consortium listening devices."

I glared at him, outraged. "My shop isn't tapped, if that's what you're implying. Alexei would never do that to me." Well, I hoped he wouldn't.

"I'm sure it's as you say. Still, if we could meet and discuss matters face-to-face, I would prefer it. If it isn't too much to ask, I'd like to meet with you now," Vieira continued. "Somewhere open and where you'll feel comfortable, of course."

"You're really pushing it here," I warned.

"I know, and again, I apologize. I'm just afraid you won't allow me another opportunity, and I don't want to waste this moment. I've come all this way from Earth and all I ask is for a few minutes of your time. Please, Felicia."

And gods help me, I actually believed him. I reached over to the deck of Tarot cards beside me, cut the deck, and flipped over the top card. Justice, upright. Fairness, and searching for the truth. A decision needed to be made, and as long as all parties played fair, it would be the best decision possible given the circumstances. I returned the card, reshuffled the deck, and pulled another. Again Justice, upright. My gut kicked me as if to say I was an idiot for questioning the universe's plans.

"All right," I said finally. "There's a coffee bar and garden near my shop. We can meet there in half an hour."

Vieira smiled at me. "I'm looking forward to it."

I disconnected first and pulled the holo-adapter from my bracelet before slapping it back on my wrist. I sighed and put my head down, resting it on my forearms. Suddenly, I felt tired and overwhelmed. This was too much converging on me at once.

I heard rather than saw Brody sit opposite me. "That must have been one hell of a card to make you agree to see him."

"Justice," I said, my head still on my arms. "And I drew it twice. He's here to do right by me. Or do what he thinks is right." I raised my head, then stood. Time to get on with the rest of this fiasco.

Brody stood with me. It seemed like he was too close, gazing down at me with an expression I didn't know how to read— probably because Vieira had just fried my brain. "I'm almost afraid to know what he thinks he can do to make amends."

"Do you think I should tell Alexei now?" I asked. "He has his security following me and they'll report back. It could get messy if he finds out about this from them instead of me."

"It's up to you. You know I'll support whatever you decide. But I will say this: You should get to hear what Vieira wants without anyone else influencing you. Alexei is biased when it comes to the Under-Secretary."

I frowned. "Alexei can be stubborn but he isn't stupid."

Brody gave me a rueful smile and chucked me lightly under the chin as if I were a silly little kid. "That's not what I meant. The man is so in love with you, he views anything coming near you as a potential threat he needs to neutralize. If I had to make an educated guess, I'd say this is the first time he's ever been in love. When it comes to you, his objectivity is shot to shit so he overreacts to everything."

My mouth opened, but no sound came out. Never been in love? That couldn't be right, but it was staggering to think it might be true. While I had no idea how many women Alexei had been with, I'd venture it was a quantity that would probably horrify me. And to have never loved anyone? Had he even cared? Or had he slept with them simply because his body had urges that needed to be addressed? "I wish you hadn't said that. Now you have me doubting myself and feeling like I need to walk on eggshells around Alexei."

Brody shrugged. "Until he learns to control himself when it comes to you, maybe it's what you have to do."

I thought about Alexei's behavior lately and how it seemed like everything either of us did was wrong. I didn't want Brody to be right, but what if he was? I couldn't live my life like that, always on guard and careful of everything I did. And if Alexei and I couldn't be for each other what the other person needed, then what? I shook my head. I couldn't worry about this now. Not when I had to be ready to face my long-lost grandfather.

As an afterthought, I asked, "If he's so out of control that he'd risk everything just to protect me, what makes you think you're safe from Alexei? Maybe you're the one who should go into hiding."

Brody grinned. "Where's the fun in that? You know I like to live dangerously. Now let's go see what exciting offer Vieira has waiting for you."

And he took my hand and pulled me out the door.

<hr />

"Felicia, you beautiful creature! You told me to drop in anytime I needed a reading. Well, here I am. Help me because I need someone to sort out my mess!" a voice cried.

Mannette Bleu was standing in the middle of my shop as if she owned the place. Hell, as if she owned the entire block.

I found myself swallowed up in a hug that nearly knocked me off my feet and suffocated me all at once. As soon as I escaped her strangulating hold, I started grinning. For all I knew, Mannette had sprayed herself with pheromones that messed with my senses and made everyone nearby fall in love with her. Frankly, I wouldn't have been surprised to learn she had her own luck gene.

Even though it was the middle of the afternoon, Mannette wore a hot pink skintight cat-suit with a plunging neckline that pretty much demanded everyone check out her spectacular cleavage. Platform thigh-high black boots completed her ensemble, which was why her hug ended with me nearly smothered by her breasts. With her were a man and a woman, dressed in less flamboyant outfits, watching the proceedings and recording her every move. Glitch, the latest boyfriend, was nowhere to be seen. At the same time, I noticed my basket of strawberries had been pillaged shamelessly until it was almost empty.

"Who is this?" Mannette proceeded to sashay over to Brody, examining him from head to toe as if he were a piece of meat she wanted to purchase. With her boots on, she was nearly as tall as Brody. I exchanged grins with Lotus, still seated at her desk. Mannette threw a look to me. "Is he yours or is he free to a good home?"

"You'll have to ask him. Mannette, this is Brody Williams. He's an old friend from Earth. And this is—"

"Mannette Bleu," she purred, holding out a hand with hot pink nails, tipped with diamonds, for him to take. "If you don't belong to Felicia, I'll happily add you to my collection."

Brody took it all in stride, clasping her hand and actually kissing it. There was a playful look on his face. "Watching you on the CN-net isn't half as fascinating as meeting you in person. Felicia, I didn't know you ran in such interesting circles."

Mannette preened. It was all I could do not to roll my eyes as I watched the show unfold. Mannette was clearly intrigued. "Felicia is my go-to girl when I want to see what my future holds. Girl, is this the one you saw in the cards for me?"

"Unfortunately, Mannette, my time isn't my own," Brody said, sounding regretful. "For the time being, I'm at Felicia's beck and call, but when that's done, maybe we can discuss how I can be of service."

Mannette shot me a look out of the corner of her eye. "I like this one, Felicia. Let me know when you're done because I'll happily take him off your hands."

"What happened to the guy you were with at Red Dust? I thought he was the one," Lotus said.

Mannette waved a dismissive hand. "I kicked his ass out of my bed ages ago. I don't need those kind of crumbs littering up my life. That's why I'm here. You need to use those magic cards to show me where I went wrong."

"I'd love to, and I'd do it in a heartbeat, but we're sort of in the middle of something," I admitted. "It's fabulous to see you, but could we try tomorrow instead?"

Mannette's eyes narrowed suspiciously. "I thought you said I could come by anytime."

"Well, you can, usually. Just not right now."

Mannette might have been self-centered and outrageous, but she was also smart as hell. She tapped her lips thoughtfully with one of those long hot pink, diamond-tipped nails as she regarded me. "From the look of you, I'd say you have something interesting in the works."

I looked at Mannette's two personal video recorders, watching us from different angles, knowing everything we said and did was being uploaded to the CN-net. Normally I didn't care if feed of me went up on the CN-net, but this bit of information wasn't something I wanted the tri-system to consume.

"It's just private family stuff," I said blandly. "Nothing to get excited about."

"Really? Is that why you look like you might jump out of your own skin right now?"

I hoped watching me squirm on the CN-net brought her oodles of ratings because it certainly wasn't doing me any good.

For the millionth time, I wondered why the hell I liked being around her so much. Maybe because she was so comfortable being herself—apparently something I had trouble doing.

Brody eased her away from me. "As much as we all love being the center of attention here, we need to get going."

"Oh no, Felicia doesn't get to wiggle out of this so easily," Mannette replied, putting her hand in the center of Brody's chest and pushing lightly. Then she looked intrigued. "I think I like what I feel under here. Where do you find these treats, Felicia? I have to say, girl, you've been holding out on me."

I groaned, knowing I was about to get pulled further into the constant circus that surrounded Mannette, whether I wanted to or not. "I'm not holding out on anything. If you two want to scratch each other's backs, don't let me stop you. It just has to be sometime other than now."

"Hear that, Mr. Williams? She says you're all mine."

I caught the anticipatory look on Mannette's face, but I didn't see Brody's reaction. Not that it worried me. Brody had charm enough for ten people. He could handle whatever Mannette threw at him. Instead I leaned down to Lotus, dropping my voice when I spoke.

"Can you reschedule any clients for the next couple of hours? I've got an appointment this afternoon and I don't know when I'll be back."

"But I already moved everyone last week and you have a client in twenty minutes!" Lotus protested.

"I know, I know. Just tell them I'm very sorry and I'll do their reading for free next time. Do the same with everyone I have lined up for today."

"Do you know how annoying it is to be your appointment

keeper?" Lotus griped, conveniently forgetting that was the reason I'd hired her in the first place. "I'm going to schedule a flock of birds next time, pet whisperer. I'm not even going to help clean up when they shit on everything!"

"Seriously? You're threatening me with more pets?"

"It's always 'reschedule this, reschedule that' with you, and then I get stuck having to deal with people yelling at me. Who needs that kind of crap in their lives?"

"Is there a problem, ladies?" Mannette asked, watching the two of us with interest.

"No problem," I assured her. "Just some scheduling conflicts I need Lotus to resolve."

"Conflicts, my ass," Lotus said, looking mutinous, but said nothing more. It made me incredibly glad I'd once sat Lotus down and told her to think twice about what she said in front of Mannette. While I loved spending time with Mannette, if you didn't want your business out there for all the tri-system to watch, you learned to keep your mouth shut.

I grabbed Brody's arm, pulling him in the direction of the door. "Okay, we're heading out. Lotus, see what you can do for Mannette."

Apparently I didn't have enough hustle in my step because Mannette followed us instead of focusing on Lotus. "Where you off to next? Want some company?"

"No, but thanks. Like I said, see you later."

Mannette raised an eyebrow. "I could always tag along," she said, eyeing me speculatively. "It could make for great ratings and any publicity is good publicity, right? Come on, spill it."

"And you say she's supposed to be your friend?" Brody asked me, voice low.

Funny how much he sounded like Alexei just then, and I shrugged. To Mannette: "Thanks, but I'd rather not be fodder for the CN-net today."

"Now you've got me intrigued. Let me have a taste," she wheedled. "I can give you a full minute blackout before I start losing viewers. You can float me a few details, and if it looks promising, I can give you more airtime."

Normally, I'd have gotten a kick out of spending time with Mannette, but not when I was about to lock horns with my potential new grandfather. "I don't really want more airtime."

Mannette made a disbelieving noise. "Everybody wants more airtime, and here I am, practically giving it away. How can you be so ungrateful after everything we've been through together? Besides, once you leave, I can always follow behind you if things look promising."

Brody rounded on Mannette. "If Felicia doesn't want to tell you anything, that's her prerogative. I'd advise not going against her wishes." While the tone was mild, I could sense the steel in those words. I had the feeling that if I asked him to, he'd find a way to put Mannette and her two PVRs out of business.

Mannette seemed to think so too. She eyed him, her head tilting to the side and a half smile playing on her lips. Then she looked at me from the corner of her eye. "Must be nice having all these knights in shining armor around to save you, girl."

She met my gaze, all hint of pretense gone. The coy minx who lived in front of the cameras had been replaced by the savvy businesswoman. "The other reason I'm here is because of what happened that night at Red Dust. Lotus told me about your Euphoria crash and I felt badly about any part I played in it. It seems you always run into trouble when you rely on me.

It's probably just as well we aren't business partners, though you do wonders for my ratings whenever we're together." She held up a finger, stopping me before I could speak. "She also told me about your card reading party. If you like, I can clear my schedule and go with you. Who knows? Maybe it'll help with future bookings. Consider it payback for any issues we've had in the past."

Having Mannette Bleu in my life was probably better than any fairy godmother I could have wished for—even if Alexei loathed her. "Thanks, Mannette. That would be wonderful. I'd love it if you could come with me."

She nodded and returned my grin. "Of course, this means I want an inside scoop on what you're up to. This is my show and you're messing with it. Even if I think the man in your life is a top-notch asshole, the two of you are good for ratings."

Oh crap. Again not something I needed broadcast all over the CN-net. "Okay, give me my minute blackout."

"Done. Now spill it, Sevigny."

Okay, so my fairy godmother had bite. "I'm meeting my grandfather. It's kind of a long, lost thing, so I'm nervous."

"Family reunions are great for ratings. People love that shit!" Mannette said. "This will look great on my show."

"Felicia, this isn't a good idea," Brody warned.

I gave him a "do you think I'm stupid" look. No kidding. It was a terrible idea.

"A grandfather?" Lotus burst out, looking offended. "You never told me!"

"That's because I didn't know I had one. You heard the 'long, lost' part, right?"

"So he's from the crazy side then? He's the father of the

172

mother who tried to kill you?" To Lotus, any side of the family not related to her was the crazy side. She failed to realize I had it coming at me from both directions.

Mannette looked fascinated. "Your mother tried to kill you? Why does no one keep me in the loop about these things?"

"Felicia, we need to go or we'll be late. I'm not sure your grandfather would appreciate it," Brody said pointedly.

"Who exactly is your grandfather and why do I get the feeling seeing this reunion would be worth the price of admission?" Mannette asked, practically salivating at the thought of higher ratings at my expense.

"I just need to work through this first and figure it all out."

"And then what? By the way, you've had your minute. I'll need to go back to live feed in the next blink. Unless, of course, you have something you'd like to add. Then I could probably afford another minute of dead air. Your choice."

Fuck. She was actually threatening me. If I didn't have this silly fan-girl crush on her, I would have hated her then. "It's Felipe Vieira, One Gov's Under-Secretary. He's my grandfather. That's who I'm going to meet."

It was like I'd dropped a bomb on Mannette, so big and so explosive, she didn't know what to do with it. She gasped and just looked at me so stunned, she dropped her cool-girl act. I was disappointed and felt a little ripped off—where was her snappy comeback? And then she smiled, the grin growing slowly but steadily, encompassing most of her face and almost stretching to her ears. It put me in mind of the Cheshire cat.

"Hold off on that, kids," she barked out, waving to her two PVRs. "Give me a five-minute delay. Go with a bar montage and a boyfriend flashback to keep the viewers happy."

I breathed a sigh. "Thanks, Mannette. I appreciate it. I'm not ready for this to get out yet. I haven't decided what to do about it."

"Not a problem," she said, nodding and still grinning wide enough to make me nervous. "I'll hold on to this secret for you until you're ready. But when you are, I hope you'll be in touch."

"Is she connected to Charlie Zero?" Brody asked, jerking a thumb toward Mannette. "I could have sworn I heard a round-about reference to gold notes and trying to cash in at your expense."

"I like this one," Mannette said to me. "He has a sense of humor, unlike some of the other men in your life. You really should hold on to this one. Maybe consider a trade-in."

"He's just a friend."

"Of course he is." Mannette nodded to her two PVRs, who began rotating around her, and us, again. Apparently live streaming to the CN-net had resumed. "Lotus, put me down for an appointment with Felicia in the first available slot. I really need to sort out this man problem I keep having. You"—a nod to Brody—"watch out for the Russian. He'll kick your ass if he thinks you're too close to his woman. And you"—a finger under my chin to tip my head back so I gazed up at her—"good luck with the grandfather thing. Keep me in the loop, because you know I'll want the juicy details. This is going to be good. I can just feel it. See you soon."

And with that, Mannette Bleu left my shop as abruptly as she'd appeared in it. Wow. If I wasn't the one embroiled in her latest manufactured drama, I'd be waiting breathlessly to see what happened next.

Brody looked at me like I'd made a deal with the devil. "Is she always like that?"

I shrugged. "You get used to how she does things when

you're around her long enough. She was supposed to be my planet-side contact when I got to Mars. Instead, she got me arrested. To this day, I'm still not sure if she legitimately forgot about my arrival or if she hung me out to dry for ratings."

"Sounds like she's a better enemy than a friend," Brody observed.

"Maybe, but I can count on her knowing when to keep something to herself, especially if it works to her benefit."

"It's still early," Lotus said darkly. She popped a strawberry in her mouth before going back to filing her nails. "I have a gut feeling anything could happen."

Great. If Lotus was getting gut feelings on my behalf, the universe had it in for me indeed.

It felt even more the case when it looked like the basket of strawberries was empty. I had a stupid surge of disappointment. Brody had brought them for me and I didn't even get one. It must have shown on my face because Brody reached inside and held up a berry.

"Last one," he said, looking at me. "Want it?"

I sighed, knowing I'd been caught. "You know I do," I said, plucking it from his fingers.

I bit into it, hit immediately by its sweetness. And it was fresh too, as if it had just been picked. Without caring how many calorie consumption points I may have wasted, I ate everything but the stem. It had been so juicy, I had to lick the stickiness from my fingers. When I looked up again, Brody was watching me, mesmerized, making me self-conscious and all too aware of him beside me.

It was even worse when he said, "You have some juice on your...No, let me get it."

175

And before I knew what either of us was really doing, he wiped his thumb over the corner of my mouth, brushing away whatever bits of strawberry he found. The hand lingered, moving slowly from my mouth to my cheek, and all I could do was stand there and let it happen.

"Thanks," I said, blushing and unable to do a thing to stop it.

He grinned. "My pleasure."

Lotus looked at me like she'd never seen me before and couldn't believe what she'd witnessed. That, more than anything, made me realize I'd temporarily lost my mind. I needed to back away from Brody and whatever was happening between us.

"Don't you have an appointment you need to get to?" she asked.

"Yes, right," I said, maybe a little too brusquely. "I'll see you later. Brody, let's go. My grandfather's waiting."

And before I could drown in guilt as the ocean of feelings I'd once carried for Brody started trickling in—ones I'd forced myself to shut off because going to Mars with him back then was out of the question—I turned on my heel and stepped outside into the warm Martian-afternoon sunshine.

12

Garden Variety was the only shop in the whole district where I could happily spend my time doing nothing but people-watch while I sipped my coffee. They served coffee varieties from all over Mars, under a huge glass solarium filled with exotic plants from Earth. What I loved most was the fountain in the middle and the tiny little wrought-iron tables and chairs spread out around it. It was what I imagined the Old World of Earth had looked like before it disappeared under the rising waters after the polar ice caps melted centuries ago.

I sat at a table, an untouched latte in front of me. I'd selected a spot away from the rest, surrounded by colorful orchids and ferns. Giving my chain-breaker security the slip had proved impossible, but at least I'd gotten them to wait outside rather than follow me into the shop. I trusted Vieira to have a way to work around them as he had in Apolli. Otherwise, the meeting might be over before it started. Brody had offered to sit with me, but once we'd actually reached the coffee shop, I found I wanted to be alone with Vieira. This was about me. My family. My history. My decision. I wanted to hear what Vieira said before anyone else could jump in with their opinions or try to influence me.

I didn't wait long. One minute, I tapped my nails anxiously on the tabletop, staring into the fountain. The next, Vieira stood a few feet away. He was alone, which surprised me. I expected he might have bodyguards. Maybe he did for all I knew.

He took the empty chair across from me. In the filtered sunlight coming through the glass overhead, I noticed his eyes weren't blue as I'd originally thought. They were green, like mine. For a long time, we just looked at each other. Then I had to look down into my mug because I wasn't sure what to do next, and noticed the heart design on my latte had disappeared. I found that upsetting. Finally I sighed. I was better than this, damn it.

"Thank you for agreeing to see me," he said quietly.

"It was hard not to, considering how you've been chasing me all over Mars the past few sols."

He laughed at that, and despite the rumors I'd heard about him, I found his laugh charming. No wonder the man had three mistresses on the go.

"I can be persistent. I'm told it's one of my best traits. Quite useful in getting things done."

"And in no way creepy."

"You're a difficult woman to pin down."

"I assume you got around the security detail Alexei has watching me whenever I leave the house?"

He shrugged modestly. "I've played this game for nearly sixty years. Petriv made things challenging, but not impossible. Unfortunately, I had to resort to sordid when I would have preferred straightforward. I apologize, but I was uncertain how to reach you otherwise."

"You make it sound like he's holding me prisoner."

"No, nothing like that. He merely wants the things he cares about to be left undisturbed. You are his sanctuary from the rest of the world, so he goes to great lengths to protect you. Believe me, I understand that better than most. However, you are my granddaughter, and after all this time, I thought it only fair that I be allowed to see you."

"Well, here I am. Not sure if I'm what you expected, but this is me. Sorry if you're disappointed."

He smiled kindly. "I'm not. I really do wish your grandmother could be here, but we couldn't both be off-world. One Gov doesn't run itself."

"But Secretary Arkell's the one in charge. He makes the final decisions, right?" I asked before realizing I didn't honestly know how One Gov conducted business. I just knew it was a huge bureaucracy that monitored and regulated all aspects of society from birth until death, and everything in between. It told us how to live our lives, what sort of employment we could have, whether we could have children, and if so, how many. We had to report in via the CN-net how much we exercised, what we ate and how much per our calorie consumption allotment. One Gov even decided on our physical appearance for the most part—all to ensure a healthy, happy citizenship that would be the greatest society in the history of the human race. However, as for how all those controls worked and what went on behind the scenes, I was as in the dark as the rest of the tri-system.

"Yes, I suppose nominally he does. But I've been through six such Secretaries and sometimes all the hand-holding and information channeling become exhausting," he said. "Perhaps it explains how the Consortium gained the foothold it did. However, that's not something I want to talk about with you."

"But you will eventually," I pressed, eyes narrowing. "If I'm just a means to getting information on the Consortium, I'm leaving."

"No, Felicia. Never. I suppose it's impossible for it not to seem like that, but..." He looked at me, his expression troubled. "Your grandmother and I never thought things would turn out as they did. We were so careful with Monique, giving her the best of everything. She was smart, ambitious, and beautiful. We were so proud. But somehow, it all went wrong. She had this idea that she needed to prove herself on her own or it didn't count. Perhaps I encouraged that independence, demanding perfection and success above everything. That's why she changed her name to Vallaincourt—so it wouldn't be associated with me or anything One Gov. Her successes would be on her own merit and no one could say she traded on her family's power and reputation.

"She'd no sooner finished her education than she disappeared. We discovered she'd gotten married and had a child, and she wouldn't let us be part of that. You can't imagine what it's like to have your own child run from you and not want you to be part of her life. We didn't know what we'd done wrong or how we'd driven her away. All we wanted was for her to succeed, yet everything we did was somehow wrong. We took whatever scraps she would give us. The irony turns my stomach sometimes. I control the lives on three planets, but couldn't control my own daughter."

"And did you know what was going on?" I asked harshly,

leaning forward, daring him to take her side. "Did you know what she was doing and how she used me?"

"I knew," he admitted, looking upset. "She needed One Gov's permission to conduct her research, and I gave it to her. It was the only way she would let us see her. And even then, she wouldn't let your grandmother or myself visit with you. She said we would contaminate the sample, though we didn't truly understand what she meant. It wasn't until after her death we realized the full extent of what she'd done. We were horrified. She was a genius, even as a child, and we thought she would perform miracles someday. We had no idea that she'd made full-body clones of you and experimented on those clones. If we had, we never would have allowed it."

"I was just an experiment to her and she would have killed me in the end. You know that, right?" I railed, just in case he wasn't clear on that detail. "Your crazy daughter would have murdered me if I'd gotten in her way. If it wasn't for Alexei, she would have made my life a living hell."

Vieira looked stricken. "You have no idea how much we regret what our inaction caused you. It was only later that we became aware of her psychopathic tendencies. Perhaps our geneticists aren't as careful at screening as we'd thought. You can't imagine how it tore our family apart once we learned the truth."

"And you know how it ended and what happened?" I pressed, because even though I was angry, I was scared too. How much did he know?

"We have…accounts and been able to reconstruct what happened. We don't blame you, if that's what you think. I'm not here for vengeance. We just wish things had gone differently. If it's anyone's fault, perhaps it's mine for pushing her to be the best. Then we wouldn't have lost you in the process."

I couldn't decide if I wanted to cry because I could see how much regret he harbored, or be pissed because it was too little, too late. "Don't feel like you need to beat yourself up. My life wasn't so bad."

"Perhaps not, but it could have been so much more. We could have given you everything."

His words so echoed what Alexei had said earlier, I couldn't help but shiver. Vieira truly believed he could give me the world, which made me wonder what more could I want that I didn't already have.

He fell silent then, as if he'd said more than he intended and needed a moment to recover. I looked down at my mug because his eyes were overly bright and it didn't seem fair to watch his struggle. I sipped my latte, then put it down since it was cold.

Finally he asked, "Did you ever wonder about us? Who we were or why we weren't there?"

"I know this sounds awful, but I assumed you were dead. I didn't really think about you. I'm sorry."

"That was never how it was supposed to be. We always wanted you in our lives. Maybe things might have been different if Monique hadn't... It doesn't matter now. It's the past. We want something different for our future, and we're hoping you could be part of it."

Uh-oh. And here came the pitch. "I'm not really sure what that means."

"We'd like to have a relationship with you, if you'll let us. We'd hoped we could give you the family you didn't have; well, I suppose I mean the other side of your heritage, since I'm aware you have more than enough family on your father's side. I'm afraid you might find us terribly disappointing. On Earth, there are just three of us—your grandmother, myself, and my mother. Tanith's parents live on Luna Prime, so it's rare we see them. My father has passed but my mother still roams the family estate in Brasília, terrorizing the servants—truly a force of nature. If you have a temper, you get it from her."

"I don't think I have a temper," I said, just to have something to say when he looked at me expectantly. "At least, I don't think so, but maybe other people feel differently. I do seem to be surrounded by drama on a regular basis." *Kind of like this situation now*, I added to myself.

"I know this may seem overwhelming, but I want you to know how serious we are. We want you in our lives, and for you to feel like you're part of something more. Your grandmother very much wanted to be here, but as I said, Arkell can't be left on his own. Tanith is very good at keeping him in line, most of the time. Perhaps someday you'll come to Earth and meet her in person. I know she would love to see who you've become."

Go back to Earth? Was he serious? This had to be the most bizarre, surreal conversation I'd ever had in my life. And yet at the same time, as weird as it might be, I could see he was sincere. He was also lonely.

"We wouldn't get in the way of your relationship with Petriv," he rushed on. "I know it might be awkward at first, given who he is. We have no wish for him to view us as a threat to him or anything involving the Consortium. Perhaps in time, he and I could come to some sort of terms with regards to balancing our personal and public lives for you, if that would make you feel more comfortable. And if you were to have a child, if it wouldn't be too much to ask, perhaps we could have a relationship with him, or her. We would love to be a part of that future."

Gods, a child? A child I didn't even have a father lined up for yet, and there he was, already making playdates?

"You do realize I was blacklisted from the Shared Hope program for most of my life."

"Yes, and that's been corrected. You have a standing appointment for both you and whomever you choose as the father-elect to have your fertility inhibitors removed at any fertility clinic in the tri-system. Although if Petriv is your choice, he'll have his own methods of working around the Shared Hope program restrictions."

"I...You've given me a lot to think about," I said because it seemed like I had to keep talking or I'd shatter the illusion this was a normal conversation. Going back to Earth, a great-grandchild, getting along with Alexei like one happy family and the past hadn't happened...Did he have any idea how impossible it all sounded?

"I can see I've overwhelmed you. I knew better than to lay everything out in such a manner but I was uncertain I'd have another opportunity. Just tell me you won't dismiss what I've said out of hand. At least consider what your life could be like before you decide. That's all I ask."

He reached out to take my hand. I jerked away, my movements sending my mug flying to the ground, where it smashed on the cobblestones. I stood up quickly, my chair legs scraping roughly on the cobblestones. I felt like maybe if I moved fast enough, I could get away from this moment and forget it had happened. I'd always thought I faced everything head-on, but after last night with Alexei and now this... This was too much.

As if I'd conjured him up, Brody appeared. He caught my hand and pulled me into his chest. "I believe this conversation is over. Felicia has heard everything she needs to hear," he said, his arm around my shoulders.

"Felicia, please. Just tell me you'll think about what I've said," Vieira begged, rising from his seat. "Promise at least that much."

"Ignore him," Brody murmured, a hand now rubbing my back. "We're leaving."

For a moment, I considered letting Brody whisk me away. The expression on Vieira's face stopped me. The supposedly most dangerous man in the tri-system looked like I was about to stomp all over his heart. He wasn't angry and didn't seem like he'd burst into a tirade of fury. He just appeared defeated and hopeless. How could I leave him like that? I couldn't.

Stepping away from Brody, I hugged the Under-Secretary of One Gov, who also happened to be my grandfather. He smelled like some kind of sweet spice and his jacket was scratchy under my cheek. It was a quick, almost blink-and-you-miss-it moment, but at least I'd done it. He certainly hadn't expected it at any rate, because his arms were motionless at his sides, only moving to catch me after I'd already gone.

"It was nice to meet you. I promise I'll think about what you said."

Just as hurriedly, I brushed past Brody and the other coffee shop patrons, until I was out on the street. I took huge, gasping breaths of air, finally feeling like I had space and everything wasn't crowding around me. I hugged myself, as if I could stop my heart from beating like it wanted to get out from behind my ribs. Was this what a panic attack felt like? Was that what was happening to me?

"Felicia?" I heard Brody somewhere nearby, asking questions that seemed to have impossible answers.

I said the only thing that made sense to me. "I want to go home."

Disregarding my chain-breaker security and the waiting flight-limo, Brody hailed an air-hack. One arrived in seconds. It spoke to my state of mind that I didn't think to question him. I just climbed in, making room for Brody when he slid in next to me and slammed the door. The air-hack smelled like body odor and leather, the cushioned seat was lumpy, and the floor stained from countless shoes. It was nowhere near as smooth as a flight-limo and it darted into the stream of low street traffic with a jerk that made my stomach roil. When the auto-drone asked for address input, Brody told it to just drive, which left us coasting along in midafternoon traffic.

"Felicia, are you okay?" Brody asked gently. When I didn't answer, he shook me. "Felicia? Tell me you're okay."

"I don't know. I'm not sure what reaction I'm supposed to have."

"Remember, the Justice card. Maybe he thought this would make you happy."

"It makes me scared, not happy." I sat back, rubbing my temples. I could feel a crippling headache coming on. "He wants me to go back to Earth. He wants a great-grandchild. He's planning tea parties with Alexei and the Consortium. What the hell? It's going to change everything. It's going to change every part of my life."

"Nothing needs to change," he murmured, an arm going around my shoulder. I could feel the calluses on his palm as he rubbed gently. I had the oddest thought in the middle of all this chaos—that I didn't recall his hands ever being this rough. "You tell him thanks but no thanks. Not interested."

"I can't do that. He's the Under-Secretary. He's my grandfather. It's not that simple."

"Yes, it is. If he wants to see you, you make the rules. Take what you want. Throw the rest back," he said, pulling me into his chest, his voice going quiet as he rubbed small circles into my skin.

I relaxed under his fingers and let him soothe me. The feeling was as familiar as looking at the back of Granny G's Tarot cards and the spinning hypnotic void. Well, not exactly. Something about his touch had changed. I picked up his hand on my shoulder, examining it and running my fingers over the roughened skin. It looked like he'd done hard labor, though I couldn't imagine what. Any work that physically demanding would typically be done by drones, guided by AI units. You didn't get hands like that riding the CN-net, running a consulting company.

"What happened to your hands?" I asked, smoothing my fingers over his palm. "What have you been doing the past few years? Digging ditches?"

"A little of this, some of that. You'd be surprised what you have to do to survive sometimes."

He sounded sad then. It reminded me of Vieira and the despairing look on his face when I left. It upset me to think I could be responsible for making anyone that sad. I laced my fingers through Brody's, holding our hands up together and noting how much larger his was than mine.

"What kind of things did you have to do? What were you trying to survive?" I wanted to know, still looking at our joined hands.

"Someday I'll tell you about it. Just not right now."

"Okay." I unlaced our fingers and looked at his palm again. "These will go away eventually. Why don't you use a skin renewal patch and speed up the process?"

"Because I don't want to forget the reason why I have them or where they came from." The words were said close to my ear.

"Doesn't sound like it's a pleasant story," I guessed.

He slid his fingers back through mine. "It isn't, but it doesn't seem important right now."

"I'm sorry anything bad ever happened to you. I'd always hoped that wherever you ended up after you left Earth, you'd at least be happy. But I can see that probably wasn't the case."

I'd settled in against him, lulled by the gentleness in his voice and something as innocent as studying the palm of his hand. His scent enveloped me, and it suddenly threw me back in time. Funny how scent could do that, triggering memories I thought I'd forgotten. He smelled like whatever soap he'd used and something that was unique to him I couldn't even name but had grown to love. Something elusive I'd catch whenever we lay naked together, after we'd made love. Alexei wasn't like this. He wore a subtle cologne whose smell I'd come to associate with him—dark, decadent, and so sinfully good, I had to have him whatever the cost. Brody's scent was uncomplicated, simple, and so achingly familiar, it had me turning in toward him so I could smell more.

As I turned, my eyes seemed to be even with his mouth, my

forehead on his cheek. He'd gone very still and his breathing was shallow as I rested against him, looking at his lips.

"Felicia, tell me what you want. Tell me what you need me to be and I'll be it," he said quietly.

"I don't know what I want," I answered, just as softly. "Why did you have to come back and make this complicated?"

"I'm sorry," he said, though he didn't sound sorry. His head lowered an inch. "Just tell me you're glad I'm here. At least say you wanted to see me again."

I felt the light scratching of stubble along his jaw and my nose brushed against his. "I am. I did. You know, I really did want to go with you to Mars back then, but I couldn't."

"I know. Maybe that's why it feels like we never really let each other go."

We hovered there, skirting the edge, lips close but not touching, breathing each other's breath. My hand rose up to brush against his chest, not sure what it was supposed to be doing— pushing him away or reaching up to bring him in closer. Uncertain, I rested it there and felt his heart beating wildly under my hand.

"Do you ever wish for something so badly, it consumes your every thought, and when you're finally lucky enough to get it, you're not sure what to do with it?" he asked, his lips brushing my skin with every other word. I shook my head, not sure how to answer. "Because that's what this feels like. You're here and now I don't even know what I'm supposed to do. All I know for certain is I don't want to ruin this moment."

"Do you think you will?"

"I know I will, so whatever you want from me, I'm leaving it up to you."

What did I want from him? I had no idea, but I was curious enough to find out. So I plunged in for both of us and kissed him.

Slowly, carefully, our lips brushed. It was so tentative, it was like we each thought the other person would break. Or rather, the kind of kiss you might give if you weren't sure what you were doing or if the one you were kissing even wanted it in the first place. But it only took a moment for my body to remember what it was supposed to do and how it used to move with his. Only a second before I pressed into him. My hand slid up his chest and over his shoulder until my fingers rested lightly along the back of his neck.

It was as if I'd finally given Brody the sign he'd been waiting for. Instantly the kiss deepened. His mouth descended swiftly on mine, opening my lips with his tongue in a kiss that suddenly felt as familiar as it did wrong. It was like I could actually taste the pent-up desire and fierce longing he'd carried with him all this time. Everything spoke to how much he wanted me, how badly he'd wanted to do this from the first moment he saw me. I could sense it in how he held me, how his mouth slanted over mine, and the force in his lips, the glide of his tongue. He wanted this so desperately, he no longer cared who knew, who saw, or what it might do to the rest of his life.

The kiss made me remember how much I'd once wanted this, wanted him. How I'd spent hours kissing him until my lips were swollen and raw. He would kiss me dizzy and breathless while his hands did things that left me aching for him. Things Alexei could do as well, but Alexei swallowed me whole, consuming and commanding until I ecstatically went where he demanded. With Brody, it was never about one person dominating another. There was always laughter, fun, and an openness between us where I never had to worry I might say or do the wrong thing. I could do or be anything I wanted, and he'd be right there at my side, willing to give it a try.

I could feel myself weakening and sinking into him. My head tipped back against the seat, and my tongue stroked his. It was enough for him to groan into my mouth, to slide his hands over me until I felt the brush of his fingertips against my breast. At the touch, my nipples instantly contracted. I could feel a restlessness stirring in my gut as his hand drifted to my thigh, then to the hem of my dress, then under it. It was like my body already knew what was about to happen and couldn't wait to make itself ready for him. The only thing it wanted was for us to hurry up and get to where we needed to be because it would feel so good when we did.

No. This was *not* happening! I pulled away, pushing hard against Brody's chest. The moment I did, his grip loosened, and I broke free. I slid as far away as the air-hack seat would allow, my back pressed to the door. Gods, what was I doing? What the hell was I even thinking?

"I shouldn't have done that. I'm sorry. This was a mistake," I blurted.

The disappointment on his face stabbed straight at my heart. "You know that isn't true. We both wanted this. The only mistake was when I left you in Nairobi without looking back. When I discovered you were here on Mars, I knew this was the universe letting us have a second chance."

The words so closely mirrored the feeling in my gut, it was terrifying. "This isn't a second chance. This is me being stupid and confused. I couldn't commit to you the way you wanted then, and I can't now."

"You know he'll never make you happy. He can't give you what you want. I can."

"How do you even know what I want anymore? It's been four years. I'm not the same person."

"Some things don't change, Felicia. You think they do, but they don't. Alexei isn't right for you, and if you opened your eyes, you'd see that."

"What's that supposed to mean? That I can't handle Alexei or put up with the Consortium's demands?"

"You said it yourself: Something is missing in your life. A family. A baby. Someone who cares enough to put you first before everything, or where you'll never have to worry about what sort of bullshit he's involved in or where he's been. I can give you that. You know I can."

This was crazy! I shouldn't even be listening to him. But was he right? Could he give me those things? Suddenly, I could picture us together in a way I couldn't with Alexei. Even after almost six months together and the Tarot at my disposal, I still had trouble imagining what a future with him might be like. Yet with Brody, I could practically see it stretching out in front of me, and it would be nice. In fact, it would probably be damn near perfect. Knowing that potential existed in a place I wasn't even looking was as scary as hell.

"You don't know what you're talking about. I love Alexei and you need to forget this ever happened." I said it as much to convince myself as to convince him.

"I can't." He slid across the seat, closing in on me. "Admit you never once wondered what we could have been, and I'll go away and never look back."

I couldn't, because I had wondered. Once, I'd wondered

about it more than was probably good for me—not that I could tell him that. Not now, like this.

He seemed to take my silence for the assent it was.

"Felicia, I've been dying for you all this time. Nothing and no one compares to you. If you didn't feel anything for me, we wouldn't be here like this. You would have confided to Alexei about Vieira, not me. If he was really the one you thought could give you everything, you wouldn't so much as look in my direction. But you did, and all I can do is hope this means something to you." He reached up to tuck a strand of hair behind my ear. "Tell me this means something."

Suddenly I felt doubly trapped. By my new grandfather. By my old boyfriend. By all these doors opening up that weren't supposed to exist because my life was with Alexei. Because I loved him. Didn't I? *Didn't I love him?*

When I said nothing, he asked, "What does your gut tell you?"

And there came the shot of reality I needed. Brody knew about my gut feelings but not the luck gene. Not even I had known about it back then. Right now, my gut urged me in Brody's direction with the same fierce intensity I'd once felt pushing me toward Alexei. It was doing the thing I'd once confessed to Alexei I'd been afraid might happen—that I would turn away from what I thought I wanted most because something better had come along. Simple question: How could I trust a feeling like that? Simple answer: I couldn't.

I banged on the autopilot override panel, accessing the air-hack through the CN-net interface. "We're stopping here!" I yelled into the microphone. "Pull over now!"

The air-hack dropped curbside, the descent rapid enough to

turn my stomach. I tore open the door before we'd fully landed, stumbling when I jumped out.

"Felicia, stop!" Brody yelled, following me. "Do you even know where the hell you are?"

"Don't come near me, Brody. Don't touch me or kiss me, or do whatever else you're thinking. We are over and we're staying over."

He looked at me, standing half a dozen steps away from the air-hack, his hands curled into fists at his sides. "It's not safe here. Get back in the air-hack."

"I'm not going anywhere with you."

Brody let out a breath, angry and clearly frustrated. He gave me a wide berth, circling me until I now stood between him and the air-hack.

"Then you go and I'll make my own way back. I'm not leaving you out here alone. I've already paid for the air-hack. It'll take you wherever you want."

I shot him a hard look, mad at him, myself, and this whole sordid chain of events. "I'm going home."

"And when you get there, what will you tell Alexei?" he asked. "Will you tell him we kissed and how much you wanted it?"

I said nothing, merely got into the air-hack and slammed the door behind me. I gave the autopilot Alexei's address and didn't bother looking back. I couldn't because that would be admitting Brody was right.

Besides, there was nothing to tell. If my chain-breaker security detail reported back the way I suspected they did, Alexei already knew.

13

I ended up going back to my shop instead. I wasn't in the right frame of mind to go home. I needed to calm down and regroup before I faced Alexei. If I showed up distraught and overwrought like some weepy Old World heroine suffering the vapors, gods only knew how he would react.

Though it wasn't technically closing time, Lotus had closed up shop, obviously deciding to give herself the rest of the sol off. Frankly, I didn't blame her. Who would, given how unreliable I'd become—taking a week off without notifying anyone, closing the shop in the middle of the afternoon, rescheduling appointments multiple times. What did it say about the state of things if Lotus was suddenly the responsible one? If I got any flakier, I'd qualify as a breakfast pastry.

I let myself in and went to my reading room, locking the door and turning the lighting on to its lowest setting—just enough so I wasn't sitting in the dark. I think I was stunned by the entire chain of events. How had my life had gone so sideways in such a short amount of time? How had I not seen this coming? When I felt my c-tex flutter on my wrist with a shim, I was tempted to ignore it. Gods knew I didn't need anything more coming at me. The universe had already filled up my plate with a heaping portion of confusion; I didn't need another scoop.

To my surprise, it was a shim from Novi Pazidor. Not what I expected, especially considering I'd see her tomorrow at the card reading party. Crap. She didn't want to cancel, did she? I hoped not—not after I'd gone through all the hassle with Mannette and Lotus earlier.

Novi's message was...*gushing* was the only word that came to mind. Gushing with excitement about tomorrow night, how she'd invited all her friends, and how things were so much better with her husband after she'd shared my advice with him. He'd gone to get help from his union rep and didn't feel such resentment toward the new mine owners. He'd actually be home in a few weeks so he and Novi could work out the rest of their concerns.

I sent a quick reply letting her know how pleased I was for her and how I was looking forward to tomorrow night. But was I? I sat back in my chair, thinking about it. I couldn't remember the exact details of the reading I'd done for her; I'd have to look up the transcript Lotus uploaded to her memory blocks for the specifics. But it was nice knowing I'd helped her and made a real difference in her life.

Still, Lotus didn't trust Novi and I respected her feeling. Gods knew she was more together than I was lately. It almost made me want to cancel the party and reschedule for when I felt more like myself. But I couldn't. How could I walk away if I was really helping Novi and her husband? She was counting on me. And if there were serious issues with the mines, I should try to find out what I could and let Alexei know. Maybe he didn't want me to read the cards for him, but it would be irresponsible of me to overlook a legitimate concern. If I did nothing and something awful happened, I'd feel that much worse. For that reason alone, I'd go to Novi's tomorrow regardless of how out of sorts I felt.

Just to be safe, I grabbed a random deck of cards from those I kept stashed in the drawer of my reading table. I shuffled, my hands going through the motions without me being consciously aware of what I was doing. Instead, I thought about what I wanted to know. It wouldn't hurt to take a peek at what I could expect tomorrow night. A quick spread might help settle me.

A glance down showed me I'd grabbed my fairy deck. I stopped shuffling, chilled. Not good. The cards were cute and colorful, covered with adorable little winged creatures that danced from flower to flower. Each card was cuter than the last, the faces so glittery and vibrant, the deck practically dazzled my clients. It wasn't a deck I used often, not because of the glitter but because it always predicted the darkest readings I'd ever seen come to pass. So dark, I often thought about throwing the deck away. But I figured that would be like a medic throwing away her tools. So I'd held on to it, and used it with caution. Apparently, today, caution was required.

Depending on what I wanted to know, there were endless variations on how I could lay a spread and the number of cards I'd use. If I was concerned about a relationship, I would use a different spread than I would for business questions. If I wanted a quick answer, I could use three, five, or seven cards.

The more cards, the deeper the meaning, and depending on their placement, they gave hints of the past, present, or future.

I stopped after I'd dealt out nine cards, using a "should I or shouldn't I?" spread. I lined them up carefully, feeling nothing but dread and foreboding with each card I'd set down. The four cards on the right showed what would happen if I stayed in the same situation. The four on the left showed what would happen if I changed the situation. The last card showed the hidden piece of information I needed to know in order to make the right decision—to do it, or not do it.

My gut was roiling and I felt sick to my stomach as I looked over my selection. It was as bad as I feared. I was looking at too many thorns and not enough daisies. Thorns meant conflict and strife; daisies meant love and friendship. Also absent were acorns. Those represented wealth, meaning I shouldn't expect to make any lasting contacts tomorrow and there would be no future business from Novi's friends. However, there were a few wings, which stood for hope and the potential to overcome. But there were wings on both sides and not enough of them to change the final outcome. Essentially, whatever choice I made, I failed. But the kicker was the final card: the Eight of Thorns, reversed. Treachery and opposition from an unexpected source. Someone I trusted would betray me. There would be a potentially fatal accident, coming from a direction I didn't expect.

The hell? How could I prevent what the cards showed if no matter what I did, it was still coming? I couldn't even tell what the cards were reacting to. Was it Novi and Lotus's gut feeling? Was there an issue with the mines that could affect Alexei? Or was this in reaction to my meeting with Vieira? Or was it all because of Brody and that stupid, reckless kiss? I didn't know, and the cards wouldn't, or couldn't, tell me. I was still locked in the same cycle of confusion, with the same unspecified gut feeling, with nothing any clearer. The only difference was instead of feeling vaguely worried, I could be definitely worried. I sighed, sinking back in my chair as I stared at the spread I'd laid. There was nothing to do but keep trudging forward. Bad things were on the move—end of story. And like fate, whatever was coming was inevitable. Nothing could get me out of its way. All I could do was hope to survive it.

⟫◆⟪

I took an air-hack home, completely forgetting I had a flight-limo on standby. I think I may have even walked by my chain-breaker security without seeing them, such was the fog cluttering my head. Or at least, I didn't recall seeing them. Ironically, even after it felt like I'd faced enough drama and activity for three different sols, I got home at around six in the evening—roughly the same time I would have reached my old condo after a normal workday.

My threatening headache had arrived as anticipated, bringing friends. I felt both sick to my stomach and sick at heart with what had happened. I hadn't just committed one betrayal, I'd committed two. If Alexei knew what I'd been up to today, which I suspected he might, what would he do? What kind of scene could I expect at home because of my utter stupidity and the poor decisions I'd made? Maybe the Eight of Thorns was the fallout that came from betraying Alexei's trust by throwing myself at Brody. If so, maybe I deserved whatever I got.

It was with utter humiliation that I went through the automated security check at the front gate of the house to confirm who I was, scanning my c-tex bracelet countless times so my damn citizenship chip would beep. Then I had to walk up the long drive to the house and let myself in with another swipe of my bracelet, which seemed to take another seventeen sols. By the time I made it into the house, I was carrying my shoes because they pinched my feet, my hair was unbraided because Brody had made a mess of it, and I was feeling pretty sorry for myself.

The house was dark. I trudged to the front staircase, instructing the AI to turn on the minimal amount of lights. All I wanted to do was shower, take something for my headache, and go to bed. I paused at one of the rooms off the main hallway—a sitting room that didn't get much use. A faint light shone from inside.

Alexei sat in a high-backed chair, head back, an empty glass in his hand. On the table beside him were a single lamp and a crystal decanter, nearly empty. He opened his eyes when he heard me, his face unreadable in the low light from the lamp.

"You didn't take the flight-limo home," he said. "I was worried."

"Sorry. I forgot. I took an air-hack instead. It wasn't a good day," I said from the doorway, afraid to come closer. He didn't look worried. He looked controlled and icily calm.

"Are you all right?"

I cringed. The way he said it made it sound like he merely asked out of courtesy because he already knew. "Not really," I admitted. "Things happened today. Things I wish would go away and leave me alone."

"Did you want to talk about it?"

Oh hell, no. "I don't feel very well. I just want to lie down."

He nodded. "We can talk when you're feeling better."

"Okay." I turned, about to walked away, then paused. "Do you ever think about going back to Earth?"

He was silent so long, I gave up nonchalantly examining the door frame to look at him. He was watching me, his expression so inscrutable, it scared me. I toyed nervously with a strand of hair.

"Why are you asking me that?" He sounded puzzled, as if it had broken through the chill.

I shrugged. What did it matter what I did when everything was inevitable and couldn't be changed? "It's nothing. Forget I asked."

"The Consortium is looking toward Jupiter and its moons," he said, stopping me when I would have turned away again. "It's easier to manage from Mars. I don't think returning to Earth is an option in the foreseeable future."

"Oh." I think something wilted in me a little then, something I hadn't analyzed yet. It felt like it may have been the tiny shred of hope I'd harbored that maybe this wasn't all unraveling as I watched. "That makes sense. Why would you leave when everything you want is here?"

We both fell silent then, as if each of us waited for the other person to say something. When I couldn't take it anymore, I stepped out into the hallway, feeling like I was dying and everything was broken and wrong.

"Speaking of Earth," he said so I had to pause yet again, "I wanted to let you know we'll have guests staying with us. Konstantin will be arriving with the other members of the Consortium in two sols. I want you with me to meet him when the *Martian Princess* docks."

My breath caught and I felt chilled. There it was—my Eight

of Thorns, blindsiding me senseless. Forget everything else; this was the event I'd been dreading and had never thought would happen. Konstantin Belikov was coming to Mars. "Why didn't you tell me earlier?"

"I'm telling you now. Isn't that enough?" The way he said it made me flinch, like he purposely wanted to inflict the deepest cut. "He's always wanted to visit Mars. Now's his chance."

So I nodded like this was actually good news, which was just another lie on top of the others. "How long will he be on Mars?"

"As long as he needs," he said.

My hand went to my stomach, rubbing absently as if that would make all the bad feelings go away. I stopped when I saw him watching me, his eyes narrowing. What did he know? Should I confess to everything and tell him all his fears about me were justified, in addition to new ones he didn't even know about yet? Would he even hear me if I tried to explain?

"I can't wait," I said instead. "Good night, if I don't see you later."

I'd almost reached the main staircase when I heard glass shattering. Not the sound of a dropped glass hitting the tile floor, but of a heavy crystal decanter being hurled into the wall and smashing into a million pieces on impact.

I froze, swallowing the sob in my throat. Once I'd mastered it, I called out because I couldn't go to him. "Are you all right? Do you need help?"

"I'm fine. Just...go."

And because I didn't know how to handle the mess I'd made of everything, I went.

The next morning, all I had from Alexei was a shim saying he'd be unavailable for the next twenty-four to thirty-six hours, and it was unlikely I'd see him before we met Belikov at the space elevator. He then indicated I was never to use a public air-hack again and a flight-limo was available whenever I needed it. I could almost hear the chilling command in his voice. I bristled at that, annoyed he thought he could order me around like some Consortium lackey and I would jump to do his bidding.

If he knew about Brody, he wasn't saying, though his actions made it clear he at least suspected. Was he waiting for me to come clean? If so, the longer I took, the worse things would be. And if I did say something, I was afraid of what might happen to us. Even if things were rocky between us, at least we were still together. Losing Alexei might be the most crippling blow of all. At some point, I knew I'd have to tell him about Vieira too. Funny how between Vieira and the kiss, telling him about my grandfather felt like the lesser of two evils. For now, I decided to focus on the card reading party and push everything else out of my mind.

At the shop, it was one of those sols where everything was unremarkable, and I wondered how long the calm before the storm would last. I had several appointments, but wasn't invested in the clients. I had a feeling Lotus wanted to grill me about what she saw yesterday with Brody, but I managed to dodge her in between clients and finishing up my Russian homework for tomorrow night's class. Of course, that was assuming I'd still be going to class after Belikov and the rest of the Consortium arrived. If not, that would make three in a row I'd missed. At this rate, I'd have to re-enroll next semester.

Eventually, it was closing time and Lotus went home. Mannette and company would meet me at my shop in an hour so I killed time by grabbing a bite to eat from the deli on the corner before getting ready back at the shop.

I debated how flamboyant I should be. I didn't want to overwhelm these women. On the other hand, Mannette would expect a show for her CN-net series. In the end, I decided not to go overboard with the whole exotic Tarot card reader experience. I'd be entertaining, but not make anyone feel uncomfortable about participating. Plus Mannette had one of the most successful shows on the CN-net. These women would be broadcast as part of her series, and there were few people in the tri-system who wouldn't get a kick out of being included.

I tied my hair back with a turquoise scarf and threw another one around my neck. I also wore a modest dress that reached my ankles and was supported by thin shoulder straps. It was aqua colored and patterned with what resembled gray storm clouds. It might have seemed dowdy to some, but I felt the dress was saved by the fact that the clouds perfectly accentuated all my curves. That, and the slit up the back that stopped short of baring my butt to the world. Then big earrings, lots of jingly bracelets, and a pair of lace-up sandals. Lastly, Granny G's cards because no show was complete without them. The bracelets were a bit annoying because they kept tangling around my c-tex bracelet but I could make do for one night, provided I didn't have to shim anyone.

A few minutes after I was ready, I heard tapping at the door. Outside were Mannette, two of her PVRs recording her every move as usual—different from the ones from yesterday—three other women I assumed were show-friends, and two bodyguards. Dark-skinned with hair in long dreadlocks, both were built like old-school battle cruisers going off to war. They gave off the same "don't fuck with me" vibe that was universal to bodyguards.

Mannette didn't disappoint. She wore a skintight black dress accented with large vertical rows of red diamonds. Her hair was tall enough that it added another foot in height, making her tower over me. The dress was slit almost to her waist and she wore shiny black crotch-brushing boots. She'd dressed her entourage to match her outfit, with even her bodyguards wearing suits covered in tiny red diamonds.

For a second, I just stared at her, not sure which of us was the Tarot card reader. "Wow," I said finally. "You look... Wow."

She bowed with false modesty. "We want to make it a night these ladies won't forget, am I right?"

"No, you're right," I agreed, returning her grin and feeling something a little like excitement. Tonight would be fun. With Mannette there, how could it not?

"What about them?" she asked, gesturing to my waiting flight-limo and the security detail stationed behind her own crew.

When I saw the chain-breakers, annoyance speared me. It was the same burst I'd felt when Alexei ordered me to stay away from public air-hacks. Gods, did he think he controlled everything now that we lived together? Was he looking for incriminating evidence to see if I spent more time with Brody? "Ignore them. That's what I plan on doing."

"Your new friend isn't going to join us?" she asked coyly after we'd arranged ourselves in our seats—one of the security detail with us, one up front, one of her PVRs with me and one with Mannette to record everything, and her show-friends spread between us. The flight-limo took off into low-street orbit, merging into the rest of the traffic.

"No," I said firmly. I had to be careful. Everything I said and did would be broadcast over the CN-net. I would be scrutinized by the entire tri-system, who consumed gossip with an endless appetite. "He will most definitely not be joining us."

She pouted. "Such a shame. We were just starting to get acquainted yesterday."

"You could probably get in touch with him yourself."

"I would, but he made it clear his interests lie elsewhere. Not sure I'd be able to turn his head, even if I used all of this." She gestured to her body from breast to thigh.

I couldn't help but laugh. "Maybe you didn't put in enough effort."

"Oh, believe me, there was effort. The boy just didn't seem into me, but I think I can wear him down." Then she gave me a calculating look. "And did things go well with your grandfather?"

Oh shit. I wondered if Alexei was watching the broadcast. Even if he was up to his neck in alligators, he could still split his attention to see what I was doing.

"It went well enough."

"Too bad I didn't get a chance to meet him. Maybe some other time," she said, arching an eyebrow. "Felicia Sevigny, no one surrounds themselves with as many fascinating people as you. It must be a gift."

"Yeah, I'm lucky that way." Time to steer this conversation in a less horrific direction. I whipped out my cards from their case and started to shuffle. Then I looked over Mannette and her crew, beaming at all of them because gods knew I wanted to look pretty for the whole damn CN-net to see. "Okay, who wants a demonstration on how this works?"

The rest of the ride passed with me reading cards for Mannette and friends. All made the appropriate noises in the appropriate places with one of the women squealing in delight when I told her she'd meet the love of her life within the next six to twelve months. The male PVR looked a little glum at that, making me wonder what unrequited feelings he harbored. Well, it wasn't my job to ferret that out. I just read the cards, kept the people entertained, and tried to head off any awkward questions before anyone could ask them.

It didn't take long before we were on the other side of Elysium City, in Davis District, aka Driller Dive. It was a poorer, dirtier section of the city, but I'd seen worse on Earth, so it barely fazed me. Growing up in near poverty and living on the edge of the largest slum in Africa could give you a different perspective on things. However, my companions gave horrified gasps and made snide comments about the sketchy-looking buildings. There was still enough daylight to see the graffiti, the piles of refuse, the homes that needed repair, and overgrown weed beds that passed as gardens.

One thing I did like, however, was that everyone lived in individual homes instead of apartments piled up on top of one another or trailers that never stayed in one place. These people had permanence. They had yards where kids could play and parks where people could gather. Even if it wasn't in the best repair, it was nice, and I told them so.

Mannette laughed while her show-friends looked at me in horror. "Would you give up what you have now with the Russian and take all this instead?" she teased.

"I didn't say that. Just that it would have been nice to grow up in a place where you actually had something to show for your efforts, and you belonged to a community. We moved around a lot when I was growing up, probably because someone was being chased out of town by the local One Gov officials."

"Must be that gypsy blood," one of the show-friends said, making me want to punch her for her thoughtless racial slur.

I smiled at her, though she probably had no idea of the less-than-friendly thoughts behind it. It made me wish I could predict something bad for her like she was about to fall off a cliff. "Yes, must be." I turned away, pointedly cutting her out of the conversation. "Are we almost there yet?"

As soon as I asked the question, I felt the flight-limo descend, my stomach jerking in response. The door slid open and I climbed out to investigate my surroundings. I'd looked at the aerial-nav CN-net maps ahead of time so I could be familiar with the area, but the house I saw now wasn't like the one on the maps.

While the single-family dwelling was the same, it was rundown and the yard overgrown. I would have said the house was abandoned, but the lights were on. Miners spent nine months on-site, with one month traveling back and forth, and two months' paid leave to spend with their families. It wasn't an ideal life, but I always thought the pay made up for its shortcomings. Apparently I was wrong, although who knew how many gold notes Novi's husband transferred home each pay cycle and how many he kept.

I was also wrong about something else. As I gazed at the broken-down house in this shabbier-than-usual area of Driller Dive, my gut woke up, prodding at me in a way that demanded I pay attention or suffer the consequences. I frowned, studying the house, hearing Mannette come up beside me.

"Doesn't look good," she said softly.

"No, it doesn't," I agreed, agitation stirring in me. "I have this feeling... Maybe we shouldn't be here."

Mannette had this way of looking at you that made it seem like she was staring into your soul, probably because she was recording everything she saw so she wanted as much detail as possible. Even if that's all it was, her gaze was penetrating and disturbing.

"You think we should leave?" she asked in that same soft tone. All hint of the party girl had vanished.

Had I misread events and this was my Eight of Thorns? Was I wrong about Belikov? Hard to say. I was so off course, it seemed not even my gut knew which direction to lead me. I had no idea if it was telling me the right thing to do now, but I'd made a commitment to Novi and I didn't go back on my word. "You don't have to, but I'm going in," I answered, looking from her back to the house.

As if my words had summoned her, Novi appeared on the front porch, waving. There was a bright smile on her face as she gestured for us to come closer.

"Glad you made it. Everyone is waiting inside, excited to get started. Come on in!"

I pasted on a smile and made my way down the front sidewalk to the porch. Even as I walked, my gut protested each footstep, demanding I turn around and walk the other way. As I got closer, Novi slipped inside the house, disappearing behind the front door, leaving it slightly ajar. My footsteps slowed to a stop. Mannette kept walking with her show-friends, her PVRs in front of her, one facing her, one facing the house. Her security team was playing catch-up for some reason, taking up the rear when they should have been in front. Although maybe that was what Mannette demanded of her crew.

Suddenly, I wanted my own security detail to check every room in that house before I set one foot inside. I had zero desire to go into that building, commitment or not, but now Mannette's people were on the front porch, almost to the door, and I wasn't sure what to do. I felt my c-tex bracelet flutter on my wrist, but I couldn't check it—not with all the other bracelets halfway up my arm.

"Maybe we should wait," I called out, even as Mannette's male PVR entered the brightly lit house. "Let's have security check it out first."

My gut jumped up another notch. I couldn't just let them go in there. I needed to stop this. Swearing under my breath, I hurried up the sidewalk, the last to enter.

Inside looked just as neglected as outside, and I couldn't help but wonder why anyone would want to live in such conditions. It was dirty and squalid, with no pictures on the walls and no decorations of any kind.

"What a rattrap," one of Mannette's friends said, wrinkling her nose as she looked around. "Haven't they ever heard of soap and water?"

I frowned. "Where's Novi?" Not only that, where was everybody else, because it seemed like not only was there no party, we were the only people in the house.

I heard a door slam in back. Ignoring my gut, I raced down the hall on the warped floorboards, trying to keep up with the source. Had Novi just run out the back, ditching us? My c-tex vibrated again. Again, I ignored it. I couldn't get to it—not now at any rate.

There were footsteps behind me. Mannette's male PVR, keeping up with me as if I might be onto something interesting.

"You hear the door slam too?" I threw over my shoulder.

"Yup."

Steps from the back door, I skidded to a halt in front of an open doorway, again ablaze with light. Weird. Nothing in the house, yet all the lights were on.

Well, that wasn't entirely true. This room had one piece of furniture in it. A cheap-looking baby crib, heaped with blankets. I stopped because I couldn't help myself, paralyzed at the sight. Why had Novi left her child behind? Who the hell could leave their baby?

I took a step toward the crib, drawn like a moth to a flame. Had Novi known that? Had she noted my fascination with her baby and known I wouldn't be able to stay away? My gut wanted me to get the fuck out, but the baby...I couldn't leave a baby behind regardless of how messed up the situation might be.

Mannette's PVR muscled past me, anxious to see what was in the crib, getting to it first. My c-tex was fluttering on my arm nonstop. Whoever wanted to get through was so desperate to reach me, my arm started to itch. I scratched at it absently through the layers of bracelets, watching the PVR approach the crib. I let him go, not sure what I was supposed to do. I was in full-blown panic mode now, my knees threatening to buckle in their desperation to run away, rebelling against the part of me wanting to stay.

I had the oddest sense of déjà vu, of other cribs and other babies back on Earth—of little clones rigged to explode if anyone so much as tried to leave the building with them. And I realized then there was no way in the world Novi would leave her child behind under a heap of blankets. Whatever was under those blankets wasn't a baby.

I lurched into the room, smacking my hip against the door frame and knocking the travel case with my Tarot cards off my shoulder and to the floor. As the same time, the male PVR was lifting the blanket.

"What am I looking at?" the PVR asked, sounding confused as he gestured at the metallic cylinder with the flashing red lights in the crib.

Gods, how many damn disasters was a girl supposed to deal with in one lifetime? A year ago, I would have said my quota should be none. Now, I couldn't even tally the list of nonsense and bullshit I'd had to wade through.

"Get out! It's a fucking bomb!" I screamed, yanking him from the crib.

My momentum hurled him back against me. I collided into Mannette, who'd come in behind. And behind her was a virtual conga-line of idiots, all of us watching the cylinder's lights flashing faster and faster.

"What's happening?" Mannette demanded.

Then her security detail came in so we were all trapped and looking at the bomb like it was the most interesting object on Mars.

"Back up! Get out! Move!" I screamed, fighting my way through the horde and trying to bodily push everyone out by myself.

At that point, common sense and panic kicked in. Everyone made for the door, each trying to get through it first. The male PVR shoved me aside, knocking me over in his haste. I saw my travel case get kicked to the side, out of reach and impossible to nab as everyone fled. I felt arms snatch me around the waist and jerk me upright with enough force to knock the breath out of me. Then we were all moving as a group, down the hall, and to the back door. After that, I really wasn't sure what happened because that was when the bomb exploded and sent us all reeling out of control, deaf and blind to the world.

14

Somehow, I made it home. Dirty, bruised, my ears ringing from the explosion, with both shoes intact, but no Tarot cards. Granny G's cards were gone, destroyed in the explosion that also demolished the house and part of the one beside it. My chain-breakers had stepped up, plucked me out of the backyard, where I lay sprawled on the ground, then whisked me away before I was fully aware of what was happening. I'd lived through this disaster, but was it the one the Eight of Thorns had predicted? Or was there another event looming on the horizon even worse than this?

In Alexei's house now, I wandered around, shell-shocked, not entirely sure where anything was, or where I needed to go. My c-tex bracelet vibrated crazily on my arm. I turned it off, unable to deal with whatever shims were coming through. I coasted on autopilot, my brain unable to stop long enough to dwell on any particular thought as the night's events played on in an endless loop inside my head.

I'd lost Granny G's cards. Someone had tried to kill me.

I wasn't sure if Mannette or any of her entourage was okay. What would I tell the family about the cards? I'd be shunned by everyone now. What I'd done was unforgivable. No one would understand. Was Alexei's life in danger? Had someone been trying to kill me to get to him? Was Novi working on her own, or had the miners used her to strike out at the Consortium? Why hadn't I seen this coming more clearly? I was better than this. Things didn't normally catch me so off guard. Not something this significant. Maybe it was too much for my luck gene. Maybe it couldn't handle how it had lined up events so dramatically. No wonder I couldn't handle Granny G's cards anymore.

The thought made me laugh, but the sound that came out of my mouth was downright manic. I slapped both hands over my mouth and ran through the empty house, trying to find a place where I could hide, somewhere I felt less exposed with doors that locked. The house AI turned on lights as I entered each room until I found myself in the master bathroom. I slammed the door behind me, locked it, then slumped to the floor.

The master bathroom had a magnificent shower. With multiple showerheads and nozzles, water could potentially come at you from every direction with varying pressures and speeds. It also had seats, which I'd thought strange at first until I realized it doubled as a stream room and sauna. Also, I'd been shown there were other, more interesting things you could do besides sit.

Even though sonic cleansers were growing in popularity, I'd grown up poor, so this was the ultimate sign of luxury. Not the shower itself, but the fact that you had enough gold notes to afford all the different products that went with it, like soap, lotions, or fluffy towels on heated towel racks. And if you had enough gold notes for such unnecessary things, it meant you didn't have to worry about food, clothing, and whatever else came with growing up in a family of con artists who didn't hold normal jobs like everyone else.

It occurred to me I wanted a shower, so I proceeded to strip. Dress, scarves, jewelry, shoes—all of it went to the floor in a heap. I felt better as soon as I stepped inside the shower stall with its glass walls textured to look like waterfalls, cocooning me in safety.

I had no idea how long I just stood there under the hot water when I felt Alexei behind me. Of course I hadn't heard him come in and so what if I'd locked the door? If he wanted in, a tiny thing like a lock on a bathroom door wasn't going to stop him in his own house. I couldn't even say I was startled. Even if things were unsettled between us, I knew if I really needed him, he'd be there. And right then, I needed him more than I needed air.

I didn't turn to face him—just sank into his chest when his arms went around me. I felt something tightly wound inside me start to loosen as he held me and my head went back against his shoulder. Water rained down on both of us as we stood there, him holding me, me leaning on him. I didn't want to say anything to break the moment. Neither, it seemed, did he. He reached past me and picked up my shampoo. Then he proceeded to wash my hair, which had to be the most luxurious feeling I'd ever experienced. By the time he was done, I felt so boneless, I was amazed I hadn't washed down the drain.

Eventually, he pulled me from the shower. He proceeded to dry me, wrapping a towel around my body before seeing to my hair. I let him treat me like a doll, moving me where he wanted me, feeling too fragile to protest.

We ended up sitting on the edge of the bed—me in a towel between his legs, my back to him while he brushed my damp hair. All this was done without speaking, as if he knew I'd talk when I was ready. While I still wasn't myself, just having him there made me feel better.

He'd worked his way through most of my hair when I finally said, "She was a client who came to see me the night of the Euphoria disaster. She said her husband worked in one of the off-world mines and had issues with the Consortium ownership. I had no idea she had this in mind when she booked her appointment."

"I have people looking for her." From his tone, it sounded like it wasn't going to be pretty when he found her.

"I thought all the problems with the mines were resolved."

"For the most part they are, but some are still not happy with the changes made when the Consortium took over. My guess is this woman and her husband belong to a larger group with enough resources to put behind their agenda. They saw you as the easiest way to strike at me, so they took advantage. I don't know who they are yet, but I will."

It surprised me he would admit something like that. I knew how much he hated not being in control. "You can't be expected to see everything coming at you. If they have spooks in their group and stay off the CN-net, you wouldn't be able to see them at all."

"Even still, it should never have touched you."

"I should have been more on the ball too," I confessed. "I've felt off ever since you went away. I can't seem to tell up from down. I'm not reading people right. I'm messing up everywhere."

"This isn't your fault. It's mine for bringing this chaos to our door. They think hurting you will cripple me. They don't realize you're the only thing preventing me from crushing them out of existence. Now I think it's the only approach they understand."

I had no response to that, so I remained silent and let him brush my hair.

"The MPLE asked to be allowed to question you," he continued. "I told them no, and I would send a statement when you were ready."

"Can you do that?"

"Do you think I'd let the fools they call a police force anywhere near you given what happened last time?" he asked, sounding disgusted. "Since no one was technically hurt and the property damage was restricted to abandoned buildings, no charges are being laid. They agreed an interview was unnecessary."

"Mannette and her people are all right?"

"They're fine. Ms. Bleu is already spinning this into gold notes. Her viewership has quadrupled in the past few hours. She's no doubt wishing she'd blown something up years ago."

"You don't think she blames me for putting her in a bad situation, do you?"

His laugh was short and derisive. "Unlikely. As soon as she comes down from her CN-net media high, I'm sure she'll be shimming to thank you."

"Don't say that. Mannette is my friend."

"A friend I wish was out of your life given how she's taken advantage of you."

I had nothing to say to that because as much as I adored Mannette, in some ways, he was right. He set the brush down on the bedside table and pushed my hair over my right shoulder until it was off my neck. He wrapped his arms around me and pulled me against him. Then I felt his lips at the base of my neck. I sighed, shivering at the contact.

"Don't you know how important you are to me? Why are you going out of your way to make me insane with worry?"

"I'm sorry," I whispered, squeezing my eyes shut, bringing my hands up to lay over his. His words reminded me of something Vieira had said. I was Alexei's sanctuary from the rest of the world, to be protected at all costs. It was a pretty sentiment, but I was beginning to wonder if it was stifling as well. "You know I don't go out of my way to look for trouble."

"I know. It just seems to happen." With his lips brushing my skin, he said softly, "I want to propose something to you and I want you to consider it logically before you get angry."

"You make it sound like I have a temper," I complained— another thing I'd heard from Vieira. How bizarre it was all coming back to me now.

"I never said you did, though you do have a tendency to re-state your points with greater intensity if you don't think I'm listening."

"Alexei—"

"I asked you to consider what I have to say first. I haven't even told you yet and you're already upset."

Ouch. That shut me up. "Then say it."

"I think it might be best if you closed your shop."

I stiffened. "Alexei, no! You can't ask me to do that."

"You almost died tonight. How many times does your life need to be in danger before you take precautions? Being with me makes you a target. With the Consortium's arrival tomorrow, things will become worse."

"I agree it was scary, but I don't see how closing the shop makes a difference."

"Then think about this: What if Lotus had been hurt? Or Mannette? What if tonight had ended differently and she'd died in the explosion? How would you feel knowing your actions put her in danger when you could have prevented it?"

Damn it, he was right and I was just being stubborn for stubborn's sake. If something truly awful had happened to Mannette tonight, I wouldn't be able to live with myself. The guilt would have eaten me alive. Still, it hurt that this was even happening. I sighed and sagged in his arms. "I don't disagree with you. I just don't like it. This is what I'm good at. If I can't do this, what am I supposed to do with myself?"

"I know the shop isn't making you happy. Take this time to think about what you might want to do instead."

"But I don't know anything else," I ground out, frustrated.

"It will come to you. For now, this is the way things need to be. It won't be forever," he said, lips still against my neck. "Let me take care of you."

When he put it like that, what could I say? How could I complain when he was being sweet like this? "All right, but only until you find the people responsible and turn them over to the MPLE."

"Of course," he agreed too easily, which made me think he was just humoring me.

I felt him lift up my left hand, and before I could register what he was doing, he slipped a ring on my finger. I looked down at the diamond, which had to be as big as a robin's egg, sparkling so brightly, it seemed lit with an inner fire. It was circled with two rings of smaller diamonds in what was probably a white gold, diamond-dipped setting. Though the fit was perfect, it looked ridiculously enormous on the third finger of my left hand.

I stared at it, not really getting it, because I honestly wasn't sure what he intended. Then because absolutely nothing was going as expected, I blurted out, "What the fuck is this?"

"I wanted to give this to you in Apolli, but that was a disaster. Then I thought after you settled in here. And now tonight has happened and you were nearly killed. Apparently making the perfect moment happen is beyond my ability to control, and I can't let this go any longer."

I couldn't decide if I was thrilled or upset. Trust me to settle on upset because, damn it, I was sick of being blindsided. "And what exactly does this mean? Are you asking me to marry you, or are you telling the Consortium I'm more than your fuck-toy? Or is it a consolation prize since you're taking everything else away from me?"

He sighed gustily against my neck, exasperated. "If you want to lash out because you're angry, I accept that. However, I assumed we were doing more than fucking, and being together meant something."

He sounded so hurt, I winced. How had I ruined what should have been a perfect moment? Worse, how could I let my stupid gut feeling pull me in a direction I didn't want to go?

"I thought we were happy with the way things are. You said we should enjoy this time together before we rush into something else, and I just moved in with you a few sols ago. Why are we suddenly moving at light speed?"

"This was always what I intended. I just don't want to wait any longer. I can't lose you," he said, his arms tightening, the words spoken between kisses. "I want the entire tri-system to know how important you are to me."

"Considering someone just tried to kill me, I think it knows."

"That isn't very funny."

"I know. Sorry. I promise you won't lose me. There's honestly nowhere else I want to be other than wherever you are." I looked at my left hand again. It was time to spill the secrets I'd been keeping, secrets I never should have kept in the first place—not from someone I claimed to love. "I need to tell you what happened yesterday before this goes further."

He pressed another kiss to the base of my neck, making me shiver. "I already know who you were with and that you met the Under-Secretary. I pay attention because I want to keep you safe. I have no idea what you discussed. I was angry because I told you not to see him, but I also knew you would go regardless. I'd just hoped you would tell me and let me help you in whatever way I could."

In that moment, I hated myself, the luck gene, and the mess I seemed to be making of my life. Alexei had accused me of not knowing what I wanted from him or our relationship and what had I done in return? Thrown myself at my old boyfriend at the first opportunity. Did he know about the kiss, I wondered again. I knew I should tell him, but what if he reacted as he had when he learned about the incident at Red Dust? What if his reaction was worse? I'd initiated the kiss—stupid, thoughtless me, and while I couldn't imagine Alexei hurting me, what would he do to Brody? I might feel guilty, but I also couldn't let anything happen to either of them. This was one secret I'd need to live with.

"I'm sorry I was so thoughtless and didn't tell you about Vieira. I should have handled it differently," I said instead. "I was curious and I think all he wanted was to meet me. He apologized for Monique and everything she'd done to me. He didn't know about the full-body clones or the experiments. Then he told me about his family, and his wife. I get the feeling that whatever they went through with Monique tore them apart. I think he'd like me to go back to Earth someday and meet my grandmother."

Alexei was silent for so long, I wondered if he'd slipped off to the CN-net to investigate if what I'd said was true. The idea unnerved me, and made me want to see his face so I could gauge his thoughts. I turned in his arms until I stood between his thighs. Then I touched his cheek with my fingertips, bringing his gaze to mine. My other hand, my left hand, rested over the eight-pointed star tattooed on his shoulder. I tried not to look at the ring, pretending it wasn't there.

"What are you thinking?" I asked.

His hand came up to cover mine, the one resting on his shoulder that wore the ring. "You would go back to Earth with him?"

"Of course not. Honestly, my first thought was he might try to pump me for information about the Consortium, but he didn't."

"It's likely he already knows. After all, we each have our spies, watching one another."

"What you're working on—is it something that might worry One Gov enough, Vieira felt compelled to contact me and just used Monique as an excuse?"

"Unlikely. His approach wouldn't be this obvious or direct. He'd use other methods to discover Consortium secrets."

"Okay." I nodded, accepting it. "Besides, it isn't like I know any Consortium secrets I could leak."

He met my eyes. "We'll be launching a neural system to rival the current CN-net. The CN-net is what allows One Gov to both modify and monitor the tri-system population via the t-mod implants. The Consortium's system will do away with that. We would no longer be hampered with the restrictions or controls One Gov inflicts through the AI queenmind. But first, we need to untether everyone from their control and prepare the linkups for the new system."

I blinked and it took me a moment to absorb the enormity of what he'd just said. Without One Gov monitoring us, it would change everything from what we ate, to our careers, the number of children we had, how we decided to modify them, to how much time we spent on the CN-net. Everything was measured and portioned out carefully by One Gov, but if we no longer had someone watching our every move, how would the human race behave? How would we survive without that hand guiding us? "How long have you been working on this?"

"Years," he admitted. "Long before I took over the Consortium."

"You'll cripple the entire tri-system if you do that. Some people are so wired in, they'll lose everything. People will die."

"Not if it's handled properly. That's why more Consortium are arriving tomorrow—to ensure no loss of life and the transition is seamless. I handpicked them myself."

"Could you have done it without them?"

He nodded. "Yes, but the transfer wouldn't have been as clean. Before, a slight margin of error was acceptable if the ultimate goal was achieved. However, I knew you would never forgive me if something went wrong. That was the risk I couldn't take. I would never implement anything if I thought it would jeopardize the two of us."

Holy shit. I stared at him, overwhelmed. "But you can't know how the future will play out. It could still jeopardize us anyway."

His eyes met mine, the gaze steady. "It won't," he promised. "We won't allow it."

I nodded, letting it go rather than arguing about something I wasn't sure I believed. "All right. We won't." I ran my fingers through his hair because I couldn't help myself and I knew he liked it. "Despite what you're telling me, I don't think that's why Vieira is here on Mars. I think he's lonely and he wants a real relationship with me."

He frowned. "I know and that makes him all the more dangerous. He wants a piece of your life, and your time. He wants to create the relationship he couldn't have with his daughter, and right his past mistakes."

"Is that such a bad thing? People deserve second chances."

His hand tightened over mine. "And what happens when he decides I'm not appropriate for you? What might he offer you to lure you away? If I were in his position, I wouldn't want my granddaughter involved with someone like me. I would do whatever I could to end the relationship."

It was in me to deny it. After all, Vieira had said he wouldn't interfere with us. Still, maybe Alexei was right. Or at least, right enough that I couldn't immediately disagree. I considered it, trying to work through the possible implications, and suddenly had a terrible thought. "He told me I had a standing appointment at any fertility clinic in the tri-system to remove the inhibitor whenever I wanted. Could he take that away? Could I be blacklisted again if I don't do what he wants?"

Alexei swore. His hands went to my waist, pulling me closer to him. "No. No one will hold that over your head again. He does not get to dictate how this works. He has no control over what we do or the decisions we make. We decide what happens in our lives, not him."

I nodded, riveted by his vehemence. "Only us."

"Yes, us."

With a quick tug, he yanked my towel away until it pooled at my feet. Then he leaned closer, his lips hovering over my breast, so close I could feel his breath against my already erect nipple. His right hand slid along my thigh and between my legs until he was almost covering me, teasing with a touch that wasn't quite there.

"Will you marry me, Felicia?" he said, his lips almost on my breast.

I caught his wrist with my hand, preventing him from touching me. Not that I could truly stop him if that was what he wanted, but the point was he understood what *I* wanted.

"Do you think we're ready? You said you wanted us to last. I want that too. But with the way things are now, are we going to make it through to next week, never mind the next hundred years?"

"Nothing will come between us," he said simply, his hand now resting on my thigh, caressing lightly. "Not One Gov. Not the Consortium. Not the Under-Secretary. Nothing."

He didn't mention Brody, but I could plainly hear what he'd left unsaid. "But these past few sols, things haven't been good. We've had a lot of changes hurled at us and it's been hard. You asking me to marry you won't magically make the other things go away."

His hand dropped and he pulled back. "So you're saying no?" He sounded frustrated.

Gods, talk about a slippery slope awash with bad ideas. Why couldn't I just say yes and stop poking at every problem with a giant stick?

"I'm saying let's not rush into anything. I want to be with you for however long we have, but I won't do this if you think this is the way to make everything better and you're trying to distract me with something shiny. We need to be open and honest if we're going to make this work."

His blue eyes met mine, locking on me with an intensity that made me shiver. "Can you do the same or does it all fall on me?"

I absolutely refused to think about Brody. Rather, I shook my head and brought my hand to his cheek. "We're in this together. It falls on both of us."

"Then let's start with something simple. I have never asked anyone what I'm asking you. I've never wanted to. Now all I want is to be with you. Everything I do is measured against whether or not it will make you happy. Sometimes I'm successful. Sometimes not. All I know for certain is I don't want this life to go on without you in it. Please, Felicia, say it. Say you want to marry me."

I'd never seen his expression more earnest. Had rarely experienced a moment with him where he seemed so open that the smallest mistake on my part might wound him forever. How could I question our love like this? How could I ever doubt him when I saw how much he wanted to change for me?

I let out a shaky breath and brushed a damp strand of hair from his forehead. "Even if I'm scared this is happening too fast, yes, I want to marry you. The answer was always going to be yes."

That seemed to decide something for him because his hand drifted back up my thigh to cup me, his fingers running over me in a way that made me squirm. I fell into him, my knees buckling as he manipulated me with his hands and his lips. His mouth went to my breast, sucking so hard I felt the pull all the way to my groin. At the same time, I felt a finger, then two, dip inside me to stroke deeply. I moaned softly, my hands going behind his head and my fingers tangling in his hair as I pulled him closer. I felt heat pooling in me and my breath coming in little pants as I arched into him.

His lips found mine and he moved me with ridiculous ease until I was stretched out on the bed. He angled my hips to his liking and then he urgently pushed his way inside me. As always, I was already wet and dying for him to take me. I cried out because it just felt so good to be so filled and wanted.

My orgasm came fast, rushing out of nowhere and tearing through me, the pleasure barely having time to build before it crested. Still he plunged in and out, and I had to brace both hands against the headboard as the force of his thrusts threatened to shove me up the bed. The ring on my left hand bit into my skin with each drive of his hips into mine, a constant reminder of his need for me.

I felt his thumb press down on my clit, circling in time with his thrusts, making me cry out again, my need for him consuming me. I couldn't resist him and would take anything he wanted to give, my hunger for him more powerful than any drug. My legs went around his waist, my heels digging into his backside as I tried to bring him closer than we already were.

"Look at me," he ordered.

His blue eyes locked with mine, making the moment intimate as he pushed me into another orgasm so powerful, I couldn't even scream. I felt him come with me, my shuddering climax bringing his. He dipped his head and I felt his teeth sink into my shoulder, marking me as he growled into my skin with a sound of pure ownership. Then his weight fell heavy on me as he collapsed into my arms and he stopped shaking.

When the world had calmed and he'd eased off me, I said, "I am *never* telling anyone the story of how you proposed to me."

He ducked his head to chuckle breathlessly into my neck. "I'd like to think the two orgasms you had worked in my favor."

"They were both very nice," I assured him.

He propped himself up on his elbows, meeting my eyes. "I want it to always be like this. Promise me nothing will come between us."

I shivered at the intensity in his voice and his expression. "Okay," I said, pulling him down so he could kiss me again. "I promise."

I wanted to believe those words. Really I did. But how could I when my gut was utterly silent, as if it didn't, or couldn't, agree?

15

The next morning, Alexei dealt with my shop by sniping into the CN-net and posting an announcement that it was closed until further notice. He took care of any rental property issues and arranged to have everything moved into storage until I needed it again. Items like card decks or clothing would be delivered to the house for me to sort later. When he tried to cut off Lotus's salary, I insisted he pay her for however long she needed since it was his fault she was unemployed. That earned me a few choice comments about her work ethic, but he did it anyway. He also prepared a statement for the MPLE with my input, then sent it to their AI for processing. He did in a few minutes what would have taken me weeks, which once again made me wish I had t-mods and didn't have to do everything the hard way. Then he left—after we'd spent time rolling around in bed—telling me to be ready by 3:00 p.m. The flight-limo would pick me up at home for the trip to the space elevator landing platform, and we'd meet whichever Consortium members were rolling into town.

After he left, I sorted through my shims, which had exploded out of control during the night. Mannette's CN-net feed was even more popular than I thought and I had concerned messages from all over the tri-system. While there was some time-lag between the planets, I was surprised to see shims from as far away as Venus. There was even one from my father, which made my breath catch. When I tried reaching out to him, I received no response. Still, I left a message and told him I was okay, asked how he was doing, where he was, and as an afterthought, said I was getting married. Everyone else got a generic shim saying I was fine. Then I spoke personally to Lotus via face-chat and informed her of her new unemployed status.

She was philosophical. "It wasn't my dream job though our midday shopping trips were fun and some of the clients were entertaining. I was thinking about quitting, but didn't want to leave you in the lurch. Once my fertility inhibitor is removed next week, I'll be implanted the week after and busy with baby stuff."

"You're okay with getting implanted?" I asked.

"Buckley wants a boy instead of a fate-baby, but I'm happy with either."

Though most continued to use One Gov's predesigned embryo plans, fate-babies were what happened when a couple left things to chance and conceived naturally. Right after the Dark Times, predesigned embryos were the only option. Every couple selected their baby's characteristics using the gene specifications chart created from their DNA, plus the base model One Gov upgrades, then whatever MH Factor boosts they could afford. However, some couples were now opting for fate-babies, believing the overall gene pool had been modified sufficiently enough that any DNA misfires were eliminated. That's what had happened in my case: My conception had been pure, random chance. Any MH Factor boosts I might have were inherited down through my mother's side. With my father, it was all luck—pun intended.

"Aren't you worried you're moving too quickly?" I asked, thinking about my own conversation with Alexei.

"We wanted to do this before we changed our minds. I know that makes us sound crazy, but I have a feeling it's going to be okay. What I can't believe is you're marrying the Russian. I mean I know I called it, but I was kidding. I never thought it would actually happen. Maybe you'll have little shitty baby pants in your future too. Maybe we'll have little shitters together."

"It's so weird how what you said sounds so unappealing."

"Hey, you never know what the universe might send your way," she said sagely. Then her eyes narrowed. "I saw Mannette's feed. I don't know if anyone else noticed, but you had Granny G's cards when you went into that death house. You didn't when you came out."

And there it was, the moment I'd been dreading. "I sort of…lost them in the explosion. I asked Alexei to check, but his people couldn't find them."

Lotus whistled. "You know the whole clan's going to lose it, right? What are you going to do about Celeste's party?"

"I don't know. Part of me wants to bolt, but that's being a coward. I'm just going to tell the truth, and the family will have to get over it."

"Brave words. At least you'll make the party livelier than it would have been otherwise. See you Venusol," she said before disconnecting. Great. Nothing like having the feelings of dread and impending doom more tangible instead of less.

I also had a shim from Under-Secretary Vieira. I sent a brief reply telling him I was fine and still thinking about what we'd discussed, because what else could I do? He wanted an answer, but I didn't have one.

And lastly were the shims from Brody. There were two more from him in addition to those from last night. I deleted them without reading any, and sent a simple shim stating that I was okay. I received an immediate reply: He needed to see me. I ignored it. It'd be a smarter move to set myself on fire than spend time alone with Brody. Sadly, my gut disagreed.

Two hours later, I was sweating my ass off at the high-end fitness center where Alexei had purchased our memberships. Fitness centers were free of charge to all One Gov full citizens since everyone had to log a mandated number of fitness hours per month, but you could pay for more upscale facilities if you could afford it—so much for equality for all.

Apparently jumping back in after a week's break wasn't my brightest idea, and I struggled through my workout. Working out on Mars was different from Earth. With the lower gravity on Mars, pure weight training was impractical. Though weights were modified to suit the environment, in some instances you could potentially end up with a bar holding so many weights, it was awkward to lift. Out of curiosity, I'd once asked Alexei how much he could bench-press on Mars and he honestly didn't know; he'd run out of space on the bar to add more weight.

On Earth, I'd done the absolute minimum needed to meet One Gov's mandated requirements. Unfortunately, I couldn't do that on Mars and expect the same results. Also, since I'd started seeing Alexei, working out was something we could do together. I hated the monotony of it, but gods, I enjoyed watching that man sweat. I alternated between machine resistance band training, weighted running, and yoga. Yoga was also boring, but I liked my improved flexibility— something Alexei appreciated too. I'd never been more bendy in my life, and he took full advantage of it.

Now, however, I had a stitch in my side and thought I might throw up as I fought with the resistance elliptical. I probably shouldn't have pushed myself, but it beat sitting at home, worrying. Being unemployed meant I had more time to devote to my list of things to fret about. When I finished agonizing over one problem, I could move to the next, then repeat as needed. At least at the gym I was too exhausted to give the list my full attention.

Once I'd inflicted enough pain and suffering on myself to cover some of my fitness shortfall, I hopped off the elliptical and hit the sanitize setting. I had just enough time for a quick blast of the sonic cleaner in the change room before heading home to prepare for Belikov's arrival.

As I wandered through the rows of machines, something familiar caught my eye. On the last row of resistance runners, sprinting full-out like a madman and barely winded, was Brody. Didn't he have things to do with the Consortium members arriving today? I wondered if Alexei knew he was there, then stopped wondering about anything as I watched Brody on the machine.

He wore one of those zero resistance thermal suits popular with runners. It cut down on wind shear, vented excess heat, allowed the body to reabsorb moisture lost during sweating, and prevented muscle fatigue. It also left nothing to the imagination as the light blue suit hugged his body like a second skin. I could clearly see the muscle definition as he ran, his arms pumping back and forth, his legs working against the pushback of the resistance bands.

He was leaner than Alexei, lacking the bulk through his shoulders and chest. Then again, Alexei was built like someone's idea of what a god should look like, so it was hard to make a comparison. Even so, Brody was nice eye candy on his own. I could see his muscles work and the strength in his body. Watching him now helped me remember other things I'd forgotten about him. Not just physically, but as a person. He had a sense of humor and playfulness Alexei lacked, or rather, rarely showed to others. He knew how to enjoy himself and how to have fun. Yes, he was driven or he wouldn't have started his own business, but he didn't let it define him or overwhelm the rest of his life. Case in point, he was at the gym when he should have been at work. I couldn't help but be amused by that, even if him being there felt a little too coincidental.

I sighed inwardly and made my way over to his machine. I had to see him sometime. It may as well be now.

"Hey, stalker. Get out much?"

"Before you say anything else, I swear this isn't how it looks."

I looked at him dubiously. "Really, because it looks like you're stalking me."

"Well, I took a chance in the hopes you might be here, but I wasn't sure. I went by your shop first but it was closed, and it's not like I can barge into Alexei's house. The Consortium has memberships here so I thought I'd log some time before checking back in with work." He turned off his machine and let it slow to a stop. "I just wanted to make sure you were okay."

"Didn't you get my shim? I'm fine."

"I know, but I wanted to see for myself. I'm glad I made the effort," he said, his eyes roaming over me in much the same way mine had him a few minutes ago. "I have to admit part of me enjoyed watching you sweating and panting for breath."

Ah hell. I blushed like a stupid teenager. Annoyed, I bit the inside of my cheek as if the pain might help me focus. "Shouldn't you be working on whatever Alexei hired you to do? The *Martian Princess* is docking at the space elevator as we speak. Why aren't you dealing with that?"

Brody waved it away. "Not part of the job description. I'm only here to worry about interactions with One Gov's queen-mind. If your boyfriend has a posse of pissed-off Consortium coming down on him, that's his issue."

I frowned. Pissed-off Consortium? That wasn't how Alexei had described it. "Is he in trouble?"

Brody looked uncomfortable. "I don't confess to knowing all the ins and outs but not everyone's happy with the new agenda he's pushing. He may have a power struggle on his hands."

New agenda? I knew he'd canceled some projects I hadn't been comfortable with, but hadn't really thought anything more about them. If Alexei was in trouble, why hadn't he said anything? Or maybe he didn't know. Was this the Eight of Thorns repeating itself? That wasn't supposed to happen. Or had I misread the cards entirely? No, impossible. I couldn't be that wrong.

"Do you think that's why Belikov is coming to Mars? Does he want to remove Alexei from power?" I asked aloud.

"I have no idea. Understanding Consortium politics is beyond my pay grade. Belikov would have been en route to Mars long before I appeared on the scene, so who knows what the man is thinking," he said with a shrug. "Honestly, I'm not really interested in talking about this with you."

That brought me up short. "I didn't realize I was boring you. Sorry for wasting your time. I guess I'll see you around and let you get back to something more exciting."

Annoyed, I was about to whirl away when he stepped off the machine and stopped me.

"Felicia, don't. I'm sorry. You know that's not what I meant. I don't want to talk about Consortium plots with you or speculate on Alexei's future. I want to talk about us." He sounded frustrated, miserable, and like he wasn't even sure where to begin. "What happened between us the other sol...I can't forget it. It meant something. You know it did."

"It doesn't matter what it meant. It was a mistake and it shouldn't have happened."

"You know that isn't true. You know how much I wanted it. How much we both wanted it."

And there it was again, that future with Brody where everything could be perfectly laid out and I never needed to be worried or afraid if only I just listened to my gut. Instead I backed away from him. "Stop pushing me to admit to wanting something that ended four years ago. You need to back off. I can't deal with you on top of everything else."

"You kissed me first, if you'll recall. Did you tell Alexei that part, or did you tell him anything at all? Are you being honest with either of us?" he asked. The words were as harsh as his tone. I winced because he was right and that hurt—I was lying to everyone, including myself. We both did. "Nice ring, by the way," he threw in as if it was an afterthought. "He certainly knows how to send a message, doesn't he? Mind if I asked when he proposed?"

I felt my anger threaten to boil over. "That's it!" I hurled the words as I stomped to the change room. "I'm not getting into this with you." I felt like throwing my water bottle across the gym. I slammed open the change room door instead and nearly hit a woman in the face, much to my embarrassment. Guess I had a temper after all.

I hurriedly used the sonic cleanser, changed clothing in a flash, and barely swiped at the hair escaping from my sloppy ponytail in my rush to leave. This was bullshit and the more I thought about it, the madder I got. I wasn't supposed to have doubts or be confused about who or what I wanted. And I certainly wasn't supposed to want someone other than Alexei. How the hell had I allowed this to happen? Why was I being pushed in a direction I shouldn't want to go?

I hurried from the fitness center, focusing only on the Consortium flight-limo parked curbside. The sooner I was inside, the sooner I could put this messed-up situation behind me.

When I saw Brody waiting, I quickened my pace, trying to breeze past him even as he moved to intercept me.

"Felicia, calm down. Let me apologize. I never wanted it to be like this."

I whirled on him. "Gods, you're ruining everything! This has to stop. I'm not your damn girlfriend anymore!"

Then I froze when I saw what he held in his free hand. My gym bag fell to the sidewalk, unheeded.

"Is that what I think it is?" I whispered.

He held a black metallic box. It was scuffed and dented, the closing latch was gone and the carrying strap was missing, but it looked enough like my case that I had to question it. He opened the lid, showing me the contents. I stepped closer. Inside were my cards—Granny G's deck—looking none the worse for wear.

I gasped softly and reached to touch them. Brody held the case as I scooped them out. Then I counted them, looking over their backs with the hypnotic spinning void and their faces with pictures of knights, wizards, and princesses. I even smelled them. They smelled a little charred actually, but a nano-dip could easily clean them up. The relief I felt was so staggering, I needed to sit. Brody must have sensed as much because he took my arm and led me to a nearby bench.

Just like that, my anger disappeared. "Where did you find them?" I breathed.

"I saw Mannette's live-feed and went over the explosion site before the MPLE arrived. I wanted to see if I could find any evidence as to who did it."

"And did you?"

He shrugged. "Your cards were under a pile of debris that escaped the fire. It's amazing they survived. I know you have plenty of decks, but I also know these are special."

I fanned out the cards, turning them this way and that. "I didn't know what I was going to tell the family," I confessed. "No one thinks I deserve them. And if I'd lost them..." I shivered, feeling a touch of panic again.

"When I watched you walk into that disaster last night, I thought my heart would stop. I thought you were going to die, and in all honesty, I don't think I've ever been that scared before. To see you enter that nightmare and know there was nothing I could do to stop it from happening...Please don't ever do that to me again. You're more important than any deck of cards." He reached up to stroke my cheek, a touch I didn't flinch from.

"I'm fine," I said, looking from the cards up to him. "Thank you, for this. I... Just thank you."

He grinned at me, his thumb still stroking my cheek. "Don't mention it."

I put the cards back in their case and took it from him. His fingers lingered on mine, tightening and holding my hands when I tried to pull away.

"Why aren't you at your shop? There weren't any lights on when I stopped by," he said.

"Alexei suggested I close it for now. He's worried people are targeting me to get to him."

Brody nodded. "That's probably one of the smartest things he's done, though I'm guessing it made you pretty mad."

It had, but I wasn't going to tell him that. It wasn't appropriate to bash the current boyfriend to the ex. *No, not just my boyfriend. My fiancé*, I reminded myself even if the word felt foreign as I turned it over in my brain.

"I have to go," I said softly. "Alexei wants me with him when the Consortium arrive. I need to get ready."

In response, he helped me rise from the bench, bent down to retrieve my gym bag, and walked me to the waiting flight-limo. A chain-breaker stood by impassively, with the flight-limo door already open for me to climb inside. Brody looked him up and down, shaking his head ruefully. Then he put my bag inside on the bench seat.

He leaned in close, his lips near my ear. "Be careful, Felicia. I don't know what I'd do if anything happened to you."

"You don't need to worry. I'll be fine. Thank you again for the cards," I murmured.

He caught me by the shoulders before I could pull away. "Sorry, but I don't think I can stop worrying about you."

His lips brushed my cheek then and he paused, his cheek resting against mine. I stiffened, not sure what to do or what I wanted to happen. Yet all he did was stand there with his cheek on mine, so close, all I could see, feel, and smell was him. Every time I breathed in, I could taste him. It made me remember how I'd once thought I'd never be able to get enough of him. My gut kicked me, urging me to reach out and taste him again. I didn't, but gods, I was tempted.

"I don't think I can stop wanting you either," he whispered.

"Brody...I can't do this. I'm engaged to Alexei."

"I've tried to forget you, but I can't. Tell me you want me too. Anything, Felicia. You wouldn't have kissed me like that if you felt nothing."

"I...Damn it, yes. I feel something. I don't want to, but I do."

His sigh ruffled my hair. "I hate that I walked away from you on Earth or that I let you go even for a second." He pulled back enough to look down at me, brushing loose strands of hair from my face. "You should consult your cards. Would they say I should have stayed and fought harder for you? Have you ever checked?"

"Yes," I answered honestly. "I've checked."

"And what did they say?"

It was like he could see into my thoughts and knew what we could have had together. Could still have, actually. Did he know how much everything in me was pushing me toward him? Well, almost everything. I looked up at him, wordless.

"I guess that's an answer, isn't it?" he said, and brushed his lips along my hairline.

I stepped away. "I have to go. Alexei will be waiting for me."

Like a coward, I dashed into the flight-limo. The door closed behind me and I slouched in my seat, taking a shuddering breath of Brody-free air. Wistfully, I watched him through the tinted windows. He did the same, staring into the window as if he could see me. Maybe he could. He continued to watch as we ascended into low-street orbit. Even when we were halfway down the street, I looked back and saw him still watching. How did I keep this thing with Brody from overtaking me? How did I turn off the part of me that wanted to go back to him?

I had no idea.

16

Since I didn't know what one wore to a crime lord reunion, I decided to err on the side of more formal versus less. I also figured black was the way to go since it helped with blending into the background. Unfortunately, I owned all of two items in black. I had an annoying tendency to want to stand out— too much time spent playing over-the-top Tarot card reader probably. One was an evening gown with a plunging neckline—no. Absolutely not. The other was a long-sleeved lace dress. The last time I'd worn that had been Granny G's funeral, so it wasn't exactly the most stylish thing I owned.

I felt like I was going to a funeral anyway so I went with the lace dress after I had the wardrobe AI run it through a refresh cycle. It hit mid-thigh and was a little big on me, but not so much it was noticeable. I added a pair of strappy black heels with the double advantage of being comfortable and making my legs look amazing, and kept my jewelry to a minimum. Except for the engagement ring, of course. That was enough jewelry by itself. I styled my hair poker-straight and went for dark, dramatic makeup. By the time I was done, I would have passed muster for attendance at any memorial service in the city.

I'd pulled Granny G's cards from the travel case, frowning at their smell. There wasn't time to send them for a nano-dip before the weekend. Hopefully no one noticed the stink. Still, I spread them over Eleat, hoping they'd air out.

With the few minutes I had to spare, I grabbed a random Tarot deck from my cabinet and laid a quick spread—what did the arrival of the Consortium mean for Alexei and me? I pretty much got what I expected from my final card, Nine of Pentacles, reversed: Plans gone astray. Deals made in bad faith, trickery, and deception. And there was the King of Swords again, my calling card for Konstantin Belikov, sitting in the center of things, spinning lies and spreading deceit. Not quite the Eight of Thorns from yesterday, but not much topped that card.

What I didn't expect was the Knight of Cups, showing up as an outside influence, *again*. I'd always associated that card with Alexei, probably because the Knight represented a lover who wouldn't hurt me even if things ended badly. Now I suspected it was Brody. I would have liked to do another reading for clarity, but there wasn't time. I hurried to meet the waiting flight-limo. A short ride later, I was dropped off at the unloading platform at the elevator's base—a floating construct in the middle of the Utopian Ocean.

I paused to gaze at the nanotube cable that ran from the platform up into space, and felt a rush of vertigo. Even though the sky looked ominous with the threat of rain, I could still see the cable stretching upward and disappearing into the darkening clouds. I'd come to realize I didn't like heights. Living in a sky-scraping condo hadn't bothered me, but looking at a cable reaching into infinity unnerved me.

I could still see the odd patch of blue sky through the clouds. In one of those patches, I saw a blip of light streaking its way across the blue. I followed with my eyes until the clouds blocked it from sight. Phobos was making one of its three daily trips around the planet. I shivered, unsettled. Then again, I'd felt unsettled about Phobos ever since my Euphoria crash. More so when Brody told me about One Gov's requests for the Consortium's geologists. It had gotten to the point where I avoided looking for it in the sky. Why did that tiny moon bother me so much? Was it possible to run a Tarot spread about the moon to figure out why? It couldn't hurt. Maybe it would even help.

An impersonal hand took my arm and hustled me onward with a businesslike stride before I could consider it further. A minute later, I was brought inside to a small waiting area and promptly deposited in front of Alexei.

He wore a black suit that nicely emphasized his broad shoulders and a black shirt open at the collar. I could see the spider tattoo on his neck and the top of the crucifix on his chest. We looked like a matching set, all dressed in black. Apparently we were going to the same funeral.

"What's the rush? Am I late?" I asked, looking around at the group of Consortium members. They averted their eyes in that unnerving way they used whenever Alexei was around, as if they didn't have permission to look at me.

And Alexei... He was staring at my legs. It took a good while before his eyes made it to my face. When they did, I recognized the look, the one that said he needed me alone, all to himself. If he knew about the morning I'd spent with Brody, he wasn't saying, and I pushed aside any guilt I felt. I belonged with Alexei. There was no place in my life for anyone but him.

"No, you're right on time," he said, pulling me into his arms before bending to kiss my cheek. Another kiss behind my ear. A third to my throat. "Do you know what I'm thinking right now?"

"I can guess."

"Then you'll know I wish we were doing that instead of this," he said, before pulling away enough to look down at me. "I'd hoped to escape the political drama when we left Earth, but it seems to have followed us here."

"I know you don't want me to, but can I say I ran the cards and I'm worried?"

"It would surprise me if they said anything else, but it's nothing that can't be handled."

"Is everything okay?" I asked, thinking of Brody's earlier comments. I ran my hands over his chest the way I did sometimes, just needing to feel his reassuring presence. "If something was really wrong, you'd tell me, right?"

He caught my hands and brought them to his mouth, brushing his lips against the insides of my wrists, the way he sometimes did. "Yes, I would tell you."

There was no opportunity to say more. The quiet drone of the elevator's engine picked up, growing louder. That meant the carrier would be arriving soon and, with it, its Consortium passengers.

With a final touch of my hair, Alexei let me go. I stood beside him, my arm brushing his as we watched the carrier descend and finally stop. It was a large metal rectangle, and from where we stood, all I could see were thick, windowless doors. The locking mechanism clicked into place, followed by a whoosh of displaced air that had me blinking back tears. I could feel the other Consortium members crowding behind, all vying for positions to greet those arriving. Frankly, I'd have traded spots with any of them, especially if it got me away from Belikov. But if Alexei wanted me there, I would endure this. I felt him take my right hand, squeezing it, though I wasn't sure if it was for my benefit or his.

The carrier's outer metal doors opened and chain-breakers exited. Hardly surprising given we were overrun by at least a dozen of our own, as if they were the ultimate Red Mafia accessory no one could leave home without. Then they cleared and we moved to the main event.

My experience with the Consortium on Earth had been limited, so I wasn't sure what to expect of the parade of men and women that followed. Most were young, some with true youth and some with that hard look of "seen too much, done too much" around the eyes. However, some looked older, which I'd come to learn meant they were well into their second century.

Even with the most basic Renew treatments, the average person could live to one hundred and fifty or so. With more money and access to better treatments, living beyond two hundred wasn't out of the question, though age started to show in lines around the eyes and mouth, less malleable skin, and a host of minor physical ailments. The Consortium had managed to surpass even that. If a person looked like they might be middle age—what once might have been fifty-five or sixty—that meant they were well into their third century. And if they looked older, it meant scary things indeed.

The first to approach was a blond-haired giant of a man. He barreled down the walkway with a grin, catching Alexei in a bear hug. Since Alexei hadn't let me go, I got swept up in the crushing hug whether I wanted it or not. He bellowed something in Russian that made absolutely no sense when I translated it literally in my head, before Alexei asked him to speak English for my benefit.

"English, of course!" he boomed with a thick Russian accent after clapping him on the back. Then he gave Alexei a once-over with a critical eye. "Mars seems to agree with you. And is this the woman who caused such an uproar?"

I'd caused an uproar? I hadn't known that. And the way he said "the woman" made it sound like it had extra significance, like I was *The Woman*, and there were no others. My free hand was plucked up in his beefy paws and brought to his lips. Eyebrows shot up at the ring.

"Stanis, it's good to see you too," Alexei said. Then he meaningfully pulled my hand from the big man's. "Yes, this is Felicia."

"Felicia, it is an honor to meet you. I look forward to making your acquaintance."

"I wish I could say Alexei's told me all about you, but I have a feeling he's deliberately kept me in the dark."

"Alexei, I'm crushed! How could you not tell her of our misspent youth? I'm sure Felicia would find it highly entertaining." Stanis looked offended.

I grinned at Alexei. "I'm sure I would. I can't wait to hear all about it."

"It would bore you to sleep. Perhaps another time," he said before turning back to Stanis. "I think you'll find that once you're settled, Mars is everything I promised."

Stanis gave him a smug grin, and they exchanged a look I could only guess at. No doubt growing up together in the Consortium would give them experiences I would never understand.

Then Stanis moved off and I was treated to a dozen or so more introductions—some as enthusiastic as Stanis's and some much cooler. I'd have to quiz Alexei later; I was usually great with names and faces, but rarely so many at once.

I was beginning to wonder where Belikov was when I was unexpectedly faced with a sandy-haired male with dark brown eyes, bowing stiffly over my hand. I frowned, recognizing him. Dr. Karol Rogov, the Consortium's tech-med, was rising from his bow and watching me with an anxious expression.

The last time I'd seen Karol, he was begging me to save his life. He'd been afraid Alexei would kill him because he'd let slip information about a Consortium project I was never to know about. When I'd learned the truth, it had caused such a rift between Alexei and me, I wouldn't have cared then or now if Alexei had killed him.

"It's good to see you, Ms. Sevigny."

"I don't know, Karol. Is it?" I answered coldly. I turned to Alexei. "Why didn't you tell me you invited him?" My tone was surprisingly even, all things considered.

"He understands the scope of the Consortium's neural interface. He will monitor the connections as we overwrite the CN-net's coding" was the answer.

"And he's the only Consortium tech-med you have on the payroll?"

In a quieter voice, Alexei said, "He made me. I need him to monitor me as well."

I snapped my mouth shut, eyeing Karol with barely concealed loathing. "I'm glad you're taking precautions, but it doesn't mean I like this."

The man actually flinched. "I apologize again, Ms. Sevigny. Our history together may have been rocky, but that shouldn't influence our future."

Oh really? We'd see about that. I shot Alexei a look that said we would discuss this later. His said maybe we would, maybe we wouldn't, and I let it go because I had to.

A hush settled over the group as everyone turned to see Konstantin Belikov make his way toward us. Or rather, be propelled toward us, because he was in a floating mobile-assist chair. I tried to remember when I'd last seen Belikov. It had been nine months ago, in Nairobi. Then, he'd had a nursemaid and his feet shuffled along the floor when he walked. His hair was pure white and flowed over his shoulders and his green eyes were milky with cataracts, which in itself was unusual. Then again, the man was nearly five hundred years old, and despite the Renew treatments, nobody lived forever.

He'd aged significantly since Nairobi. His shoulders and back were stooped and his skin looked translucent and paper-thin. His fingers were curled with signs of joint deterioration, and his hair was dull and limp though still as long as I remembered. I assumed his legs had failed him since he used a mobile-assist chair. They were covered with a dark gray blanket. He looked smaller now, thinner, shrunken, and frail. He had two nursemaids rather than one, and I might have felt some sympathy if they weren't both busty, doe-eyed blondes.

Beside me, I felt Alexei stiffen. This new Belikov had caught him unawares. Seeing such drastic changes in someone he'd most likely thought would live forever was a shock I don't think he was prepared to handle. He hadn't seen death up close before. Not like this, at any rate. I supposed it was one thing to kill people and quite another to watch death slowly overtake them.

Belikov stopped his chair at the end of the ramp, eyeing the both of us. I knew the assembled crowd wanted to see what would happen. So far, everyone had come to Alexei and more or less kissed his ring—symbolically speaking—as if they were all swearing fealty. Would Alexei go to Belikov or would he make the old man come to him? Even I could see the power play at work, though I didn't know what it meant in the Consortium hierarchy and who bowed to whom. All I knew was I wasn't moving one sweet inch closer to Belikov than necessary.

After an amount of time that felt like a second shy of forever, Belikov powered his chair over to us. The nursemaids and a few chain-breakers followed in his wake. Alexei's grip on my hand was just this side of painful. I tugged on his arm, letting him know he needed to either let go or ease up unless he wanted me writhing on the ground with a broken hand. Immediately, he released me. At the same time, Belikov stopped in front of us and held out a frail-looking hand for Alexei to take, which he did, grasping it in both of his.

"How are you?" he asked, bending down to him. "Are you well?"

"As well as can be expected," Belikov replied, his voice as frail as his body. Though he didn't have an accent, the words were mumbled. You had to bend closer to listen whether you wanted to or not. "It's been difficult since you left, but I didn't come all this way just to say such things to your face. I know everything you do furthers the Consortium's aims."

The way he said it sounded like a dig, but Alexei merely replied, "Moving to Mars has put us years ahead of the original timeline, but you will see that soon enough. We should have done this earlier rather than bogging ourselves down in Earth's failings."

"Perhaps. Perhaps not. I look forward to seeing your progress." Then Belikov turned his milky green eyes in my direction. "Hello, Felicia. I see you're doing well on Mars."

"Thank you, yes," I said, fighting to keep the smile on my face. I leaned down to kiss his cheek in greeting, though gods help me, it took everything in me to make the gesture he seemed to expect. He smelled of smoke and some musty, drug-like odor I vaguely recognized. I fought not to wrinkle my nose. "Hello, Konstantin. I hope you didn't find the trip too difficult."

"I would have preferred not to make it at all, but there's nothing for it. I'm here now, and I suppose that's all that matters."

His tone had me cringing inside, as if implying that now that he was there, he had no intention of leaving. Ever. I kept on smiling because, gods help me, what else could I do? He would be staying with us—him, his nursemaids, and gods knew who else. I'd have to see this man every sol, a man who barely tolerated my existence, ass-gnat that I was. Yeah, it was hard to forget that particular insult.

His eyes narrowed as I pulled away, focusing on my hand when he caught sight of the ring. He reached out and grabbed my wrist with surprising strength, pulling me back in. I would have fallen if Alexei hadn't slung an arm around my waist.

"What is this?" Belikov asked, looking from the ring, to me, up to Alexei. His tone was accusatory, as if someone had done something without his permission.

"I've asked Felicia to marry me. She's agreed."

The answer was matter-of-fact and to the point, and while I have to say I didn't expect hearty congratulations, I certainly didn't expect the gasps of outrage and horror around us.

"Of course she did," Belikov said dismissively. "I would be surprised to learn otherwise since I'm sure she's been angling for this since you first arrived."

The fuck? Angling? *Angling?* I yanked my hand away from Belikov, furious. So furious I didn't trust myself to speak. How dare he imply I'd manipulated Alexei into asking me to marry him! That it was a ploy on my part! *How dare he!*

Before I could blurt anything out, Alexei leaned in, his voice low when he spoke. "Don't, Konstantin. I am marrying Felicia. I would have married her on Earth had you not interfered. If you speak against her in any way, you will discover what regret truly means."

When he eased back, he pulled me with him until my back was pressed hard against his chest. When I risked a glance up at him, his expression was so cold, even I had chills, afraid of whatever threat he implied. At the same time, having him tell Belikov off was so hot, I wanted to get him out of his suit and do very bad things with him.

"I see. Then let me be among the first to offer my congratulations. I look forward to the nuptials," Belikov said, glancing between us. Then his gaze drifted away, dismissing us like servants. "Tell me, where is the newest acquisition you've decided to exploit? I'm curious to know if he can perform as advertised and the benefits he'll provide."

"Exploit at your recommendation, I think you meant to say. He was not invited," Alexei said, the words clipped. "He may work for us, but he is not Consortium."

"Of course. You're right. I wasn't thinking," Belikov replied, his gaze darting around the group. For a moment he looked anxious. It made me wonder what he hoped to see from those assembled.

I wasn't sure how long the glad-handing might have continued if the sky hadn't decided to rain. Though it was only a light misting, it had the potential to get worse. So much for my straight hair. Gods, if we could live on Mars, why couldn't science come up with a hair product that could permanently combat frizz?

The rain got everyone scurrying to the waiting fleet of flight-limos. Alexei let go of me as he began ordering chain-breakers about and got everyone where they needed to be. Belikov's mobile-assist chair led the way, and the rest followed behind.

I wasn't sure why, because gods knew my hair was no fan of the rain, but I hung back. Something felt off. My gut was kicking me, urging me to stay where I was rather than follow Alexei and rush madly into the Consortium chaos. It didn't care about rain or great hair or if I wore impractical high heels while standing in the middle of a growing storm. It only wanted the truth—whatever that was.

And that was when I saw *it* being unloaded. It had been stowed in back, out of sight so those of us waiting on the platform wouldn't see it.

Two chain-breakers carried a box. It was rectangular-shaped, quite large, and black so I couldn't see inside. In fact, it looked like a coffin, easily big enough to transport a human body. Dr.

Karol Rogov was with the chain-breakers, watching anxiously as if afraid they might drop some precious cargo. He looked up and saw me watching. Then he nodded imperceptibly. Once, twice—barely a movement of his head really, before he looked away. But it was enough. I knew what he was telling me just as I knew what was in that box.

I took a shaky breath and walked to the flight-limo where Alexei waited. The rain changed from sprinkle to downpour, soaking me to the skin. It felt oddly appropriate, washing away what was false to leave only the truth behind. And with that truth came a horrible, terrible dread.

Mr. Pennyworth was back.

——✦——

I was quiet during the ride, thinking, probably traumatized too. Did Alexei know? Had he seen the box? He said he'd personally invited Karol to Mars. He had to know. Then why hadn't he told me? Because he'd known it would upset me? Or maybe he didn't know, and if he didn't, that didn't bode well either.

I watched him talk animatedly with Stanis and another Consortium member named Luka—another big, strapping male with a buzz cut so short I wasn't sure of his actual hair color. These three seemed to share a closeness that spoke of growing up together. I didn't know a lot about Alexei's childhood; he didn't like talking about it. But seeing him with Stanis and Luka made me wonder if all three were created in the same manner. Had the other two men also been given a chance to head the Consortium as well? It was something to think about, and I watched as they slipped between English and Russian so I could only follow half of what was said. If so, the Consortium certainly liked to breed their boys big and pretty. I decided I'd gotten the best of the three as I snuggled into Alexei, using his warmth to drive away the chill the rain had left behind.

Belikov was in another flight-limo—which I found strange. Why not ride with us? I assumed Alexei and Belikov communicated frequently via the CN-net, but now that they were face-to-face, wouldn't they want to speak in person? Granted, there were issues with accommodating the mobile-assist chair, the nursemaids, and the guards. Alexei had also made it clear I wasn't leaving his side. A single flight-limo couldn't take all of us.

I needed my cards. I need them so badly, my fingers started tapping on my knee. Alexei caught my hand, lacing his fingers through mine. I shot him a look and he arched an eyebrow in return, privately calling me out. He really did know me too well.

"I'm sure there will be time for that later," he said, then smoothed back strands of wet hair clinging to my cheek.

Naturally, this seemed to require mocking and catcalls from his friends, most of it in Russian, which I didn't understand since I was still at the "I left my red sweater at the restaurant" portion of my language classes, not the crude sexual innuendo part. And since neither of the men seemed eager to translate and Alexei looked like he wanted to throttle both of them, I figured I was probably never going to find out.

After getting everyone sorted and dropping them off at various locations around Elysium City—with far too many at Alexei's house in my opinion—they wanted to be entertained. After being cooped up on the *Martian Princess* for a month and a half, our visitors wanted to enjoy what Mars had to offer. Well, most of them did. Some, like Belikov, disappeared into their rooms to rest. Either that, or to plot; I wasn't sure which. I almost felt sorry for the unsuspecting citizens of Elysium City. A few of Alexei's people looked wild and rough around the edges. I could only imagine what they might get up to during Witching Time.

I was supposed to go to class tonight, but decided to skip it—my third in a row. I was never going to learn Russian at this rate. Yet instead of going out, I begged off, saying I was tired, that I didn't feel well, that I was still in shock from the bombing incident. Maybe it was rude, but I wouldn't be able to concentrate on anything if I couldn't figure out what I saw today. Alexei gave me a hard, inscrutable look, but eventually left without me, taking a horde of overexcited Russians with him.

Grabbing an apple, a glass of water, and as many crackers as I could carry from a kitchen that looked looted by savages, I squirreled myself away in my new office. Alexei said he'd made this part of the house off-limits—no one would be allowed near any of the private rooms we used on a regular basis. I pulled several different Tarot decks out of my cupboard because I was going to need them, woke up Eleat, finally gave in to my gut feeling, and submerged myself in the cards.

I wasn't sure how much time had passed when I heard a scratch at the door. A quick time-check showed me it was nearly Witching Time. I'd been at it almost six hours. No wonder I felt like crap—bleary-eyed, headachy, and my wrists and fingers ached from all the shuffling I'd done. I'd run through every question, every scenario, laid spreads for everyone I'd met today, made notes, compared one deck's reading against another, but I had an answer. Unfortunately, it was an answer that scared the shit out of me.

I opened the door to find Alexei, looking rumpled. Only two buttons of his shirt were fastened but they were in the wrong holes, exposing most of his chest and part of his abs, his tattoos on full display. He reeked of smoke, alcohol, and a cloying perfume that made my eyes water. And was that lipstick on the side of his neck, near the spider tattoo? Definitely not mine.

The way he walked unsteadily into the room, clutching the door frame as he passed it, left me gaping. Was he drunk? He'd claimed that was nearly impossible because he metabolized alcohol too quickly. Yet if he *was* drunk, what the hell had he been doing all night—which was basically what I blurted out as he slammed the door behind him and leaned against it.

"This is what happens when a bunch of fucking Russians are trapped together for over a month." His accent was so thick, I could have spread it on toast with a knife. The words were also slurred, taking me a moment to figure out what he'd said. "They wanted to see the Jewel Box, then they wouldn't leave!"

Prostitution was legal throughout the tri-system, but like anything else, no one was going to make any gold notes if they didn't have the most beautiful girls, the best floor show, or whatever gimmick ensured success. The Jewel Box was rumored to have that and more—one square block devoted to all pleasures of the flesh. Most visitors to Mars, and particularly Elysium City, wanted to visit the Jewel Box at least once. Even I'd wanted to see it, though I'd yet to have the opportunity.

"Is that why you smell like the inside of a whore's closet? For the record, Coral Sunset isn't your color," I said, gesturing to the lipstick.

He swiped at it with his hand, grimacing. Then he staggered from the door and fell on me. I ended up sprawled in my chair, his face in my lap. I heard him sigh, his breath gusting over my bare legs. "Hmmm...I could stay here all night. Fuck, I love how you smell."

"Get off me. You're heavy and you stink to high heaven." Instead, I felt a determined hand questing its way into my shorts and a mouth pressing hot, wet kisses into my thighs. I started to squirm, getting aroused despite myself. I needed to talk to him, damn it! Now wasn't the time for this. "Quit it, Alexei. I mean it. I don't want you groping me after you've been trolling brothels all night! Gods, how many women were hanging off you anyway?"

"Doesn't mean I wanted to be there," he protested, raising his head enough to look at my breasts. "If I want to see great tits, I've got yours. They're perfect and they're mine. I love how they bounce in my hands and fill up my mouth."

I slapped his hands away when he moved to illustrate his point. "Ass. Why the hell are you so drunk?"

"Because I was bored waiting for those *duraki*. After a while, I just left them. Only hope I don't need to bribe any MPLE officials to get them out of jail."

I had no idea why, but this whole conversation struck me as hilarious. Maybe because it served as a giddy outlet after what I'd read in the cards. "So you didn't have fun tonight with your friends?"

"*Nyet*, but I am now. Only want you. Want you naked. Under me. Or riding me. Or..."

He was off, describing all the things he planned to do to me in glorious, filthy detail. Unfortunately, I didn't catch most of it because his accent got thicker as he spoke. Also, most of the words were punctuated with kisses and licks, followed by hands I couldn't fend off. Soon he'd removed my shorts and panties while he held my legs up in the air and spread open wide. His tongue plunged into me and I was gasping for breath and clutching the arms of my chair to keep from tumbling out of it.

Several orgasms later, he looked a lot more sober while I was a limp, oozing puddle, nearly dripping out of my chair. He sat back and regarded me, looking smug.

"Looks like we both need cleaning up," he drawled. Then he finally took his attention off me and looked at the cards I'd spread everywhere. "I thought your cards were lost in the explosion."

That had me scrambling to get dressed. "Brody gave them to me this morning. He said he found them at the site."

"Interesting how he's making himself so indispensable."

I didn't want to deal with the dark undercurrents in his tone, so I just kept looking for my panties. He sighed and produced them from somewhere. Then he had me stand while he slid them up my legs, his hands moving over me with appreciative slowness.

"I'm usually tearing these off, not putting them on. I don't like it," he complained.

When he'd finished, he rested his forehead against my stomach and his hands cupped my ass in a possessive grip. He sighed again and I got the feeling he was exhausted, that whatever he worked on for the Consortium was wearing him out. Tonight's drunken episode was him finding his own outlet.

Though he smelled awful, especially there in my small office with the door closed, I ran my fingers through his hair and let him hold me.

"Are you okay?" I whispered.

"That's the second time you've asked me that today." He lifted the cami I wore and pressed a kiss to my bare stomach. "Just tell me you love me."

"I love you. You already know that."

Another kiss before his tongue dipped into my belly button and became a lick that ended in another kiss. "Did you find the answers you wanted?"

And that was it. Back to the scary stuff I had to face if we were going to make it through this in one piece. "A few things are still confusing, but yes, I did. It doesn't mean it's set in stone. Things can change. Variables can shift. There are some random factors I can't quite figure out, but I will. Now that I know what's coming, it's possible to work around it. I'm concerned, but I'm not giving up. I'm never giving up."

A beat of silence, then, "Konstantin's dying, isn't he? He doesn't have much time left and he wants me to restart the homunculus project. He wants a new body."

Of course he already knew. But did he know everything?

"Yes," I whispered, then tilted his head back so I could kiss him. I had to and couldn't help myself. He was mine, even if he'd spent the night getting drunk in a brothel. I wasn't letting him go.

When his tongue dipped into my mouth and his hands threatened to stray back into my panties, I pulled away. I reached over to the table and grabbed a card, letting him see it.

"Is this literal, or metaphorical?" he asked.

"This time, it's literal," I said, then turned enough so he

could see the other spreads on the table. All the results were the same. All ended in the Death card.

He looked back up at me, his eyes meeting mine. "What does it mean?"

I dropped the card and ran my fingers through his hair again, needing to reassure myself that he was there with me and, for the time being, he wasn't going anywhere. His hands tightened on me as if needing the same reassurance.

"What does it mean?" he repeated, whispering now.

"It means, if you give him a new body, he'll want it all back. The power. The wealth. Everything the Consortium represents. If that happens, you'll be in his way. Even if you step down, it won't be enough. Just the fact that you exist is a problem because he'll always see you as a threat. The Death card isn't predicting death for him. It's for you."

17

I spent the morning after breakfast staying out of everyone's way. I had no idea how long the house would be overrun by the Consortium, but ever since I'd made my announcement, Alexei seemed determined to keep everyone as close as possible. Something about keeping friends close, enemies closer—the usual clichés. I just hoped he cleaned up the enemy business as quickly as possible. There were too many people in my personal space, watching and judging my every move.

Luckily, I had Celeste's party to get ready for and a mess of potato salad to make. Normally I might not be so enthusiastic about the task, but hunting down the ingredients meant I could spend hours at the market instead of home, my chain-breakers chaperoning my every move, of course. While I was out, I also visited clients I considered friends who were concerned after what they'd witnessed on Mannette's live-feed—Mrs. Larken and her dog Puddles among them. I assured everyone that closing my shop was only temporary and I'd be happy to make house calls.

By the time I got home, it was late afternoon. I didn't see Alexei, though that didn't surprise me. He also wasn't at dinner, where I endured more Consortium scrutiny. I did get a shim saying not to expect him until sometime the next sol, but little else. So I went to bed alone, got up alone, lay low again, then took over the kitchen to make my potato salad.

I ended up wasting most of the sol; I wasn't familiar with the kitchen and it took forever to find what I needed. Everything was state-of-the-art with AI this and programmable that, beeping and chiming at me, questioning why I wanted to use the manual overrides and not the CN-net interface. I'd never used equipment this elaborate and found the experience so frustrating, I wanted to throw everything in the trash and tell Celeste she could make her own damn salad.

I supposed I could have asked the house staff to take care of it for me, but that would mean admitting the machines had beaten me. Plus, you didn't hand out secret family recipes to strangers. Absolutely not! So I peeled mountains of potatoes by hand, chopped onions, ground mustard seeds, and set about making enough salad to feed an army. At one point, I shimmed Celeste demanding to know why she wasn't having her party catered. Her answer? *It wasn't part of the deal.* Trust my cousin to work out some kind of scam on the side to get her event done on the cheap.

I'd been sweating in the kitchen for what seemed like years when I felt hands slide around my waist and a kiss pressed to my throat. I stiffened in surprise, not sure how to fight off an attacker with only a fork and a pot lid in my hands.

"You could try for a fork in the eye, but I'm certain I could stop you," Alexei said, pulling me back against him, going in for another kiss.

I relaxed. "I was thinking of jabbing you in the hand and a knee to the groin," I countered.

"That might be just as effective if you could make contact." His arms tightened almost uncomfortably around me, and he buried his face in the curve of my neck and shoulder. "You may want to try both after we talk."

I tried to pull away, nervous. I wanted to see his face, but he wouldn't let me go. "What's going on?"

"You're not wearing my ring," he said instead.

The way he said it sent guilt cascading over me, crushing me like a waterfall. It was like he'd implied I'd purposely decided not to wear it. Or was it me being hypersensitive because of this thing with Brody I didn't know how, or even want, to stop?

"I had it on earlier, but the potato skins kept getting stuck in it. Then I somehow caught one of the claws with the peeler and this happened." I held up my left hand where I'd scraped my knuckles raw—a cheap shot from karma reminding me of my betrayal, in case I'd forgotten. The bleeding had stopped, but I hadn't had time to slap any skin renewal patches on yet. "I'm not used to wearing something that big."

"I'm sorry," he said, lifting my hand and kissing it. "I didn't consider practicality when I had it made."

Gods, he'd had it made? I felt even worse. "I'll just be more careful in the future." I tried turning again, and still he wouldn't let me, almost as if he didn't want to face me. "Alexei, you're acting strange. There's barely been a word from you in two sols. Now you won't let me look at you and say we have to talk. Talk about what?"

He sighed into my neck. "Because I don't want to see your face when I tell you I can't go tomorrow. I promised I would and I know it means a great deal to you, but I can't. I'm sorry."

I felt a horrible, awful dread slash through me, so sharp I dropped what I was holding. The fork and the lid clattered on the countertop. Along with the fear came something I hadn't expected—relief. It was almost like I was...*glad* he couldn't go. What the hell? How could I feel both at once? Or was I afraid because I was relieved?

"Why not?" I asked, my voice a whisper.

"The readings you did—I need to stay on top of this situation with Konstantin. I don't think it's wise to be away even for a few hours. Not until I have the full measure of the situation."

"Has something happened?"

"Not yet, but Konstantin is making noises and some in the Consortium support him. Others have taken my side because they're tired of his influence and like the new direction we're exploring, but I need to solidify my position."

"I get that. I understand how important this is. Whatever Konstantin's doing, you need to figure it out so what I saw in the cards doesn't happen. But can I just say I really need you with me tomorrow? I feel panicky and scared, and I'm worried I might do something I'll regret. Please, Alexei. I need you."

He made a noise like a wounded animal. "I know you do. I know, but I can't. Konstantin's being here has fucked with everything. I wasn't even aware he was en route to Mars until a few sols ago, and that's not acceptable. He can't continue to hide things from me, not if I truly lead the Consortium. And now that I'm investigating for myself, I see discrepancies in all the records. He's funneling the Consortium's assets elsewhere. I should have known he would attempt something, but I missed it. Probably because I never believed he would risk fracturing the Consortium like this, so I overlooked what should have been obvious. Now I see he's locked away the details in his memory blocks, in places I'm unable to access."

"Like the homunculus project?"

"That and I've no idea what else. I should be able to access anything from anyone in the Consortium at any time, but I can't. And the fact that he's locked me out and taken pains to hide from me is all the proof I need."

"Can you snipe his memory blocks?"

"With time, yes. It may take up to a week at most, but I fully intend to find everything he's hidden. He's carried the homunculus program on in secret. I've seen his latest model and Karol thinks it can do what the last one couldn't: host a human mind without the need to return to a physical body. I'm not even certain Konstantin needs me to pilot it, but I don't think he realizes that. Regardless, it won't be long before even I become irrelevant to his plan."

"How? I thought you were the only one who could merge with the homunculus."

He sighed. "In the beginning, yes. However, the intent was for everyone to have that ability. In the code I wrote for the Consortium's neural interface, I created a subroutine to launch a direct link between the human mind and AI mind in the homunculus. It copied the human brainwave data into a series of codes the AI could integrate into its own programming. After Brazil, I deleted the subroutine, or so I thought. Konstantin apparently kept a copy. Once it's tested, anyone could pilot a homunculus. In theory, the human body would become disposable."

The idea of people—of everyone—downloading themselves

into machines and abandoning everything that made them human so repulsed me that for a moment, I couldn't speak. It wasn't that I was against the idea of living longer, or even of living indefinitely. What gave me nightmares was thinking about what we had to give up to achieve that dream. What would we lose in our quest to be immortal? "Can you stop him?"

"I think so. For now, he believes my skill set and t-mods make me the only one able to operate it. He wants me to run it through basic field testing but I've told him I want to see the specs first. If I stall him long enough, I'll have the time I need to snipe his memory blocks."

I knew what he was saying made sense, but I could feel a tiny seed of doubt creeping into my heart—doubt Brody had sown. "I thought you said I would always be first with you."

He swore softly but viciously in my ear. "You know it will always be you, but this...I have to do this or there is no future. If I can't stay ahead of Konstantin, there won't be any us. I may be leader of the Tsarist Consortium, but it's in name only. I need to understand what he's doing and this is the only way."

I hung in his grip, stupidly watching my potatoes boil. He was right, of course. He needed to deal with Belikov. But he was also wrong and I couldn't make him see that because I wasn't sure I wanted to. I didn't know why, but I didn't want him there with me, surrounded by my family. I thought I did, but now the case was otherwise, and that knowledge scared me.

"You're right. Dealing with Belikov takes priority," I said, letting my head fall back against his shoulder. "Don't worry about me. I'll manage. What does a picnic matter when everything else is hanging in the balance?"

He spun me around and pushed me back against the cupboards, kissing me with such heated intensity, I didn't even notice the AI monitoring the water temperature had allowed the potatoes to boil over until he broke away. He rested his forehead against mine, both of us panting, wanting, needing to touch each other.

"If I didn't think someone might walk in here any second, I'd already have you spread out on the counter, coming for me," he whispered, before backing away and not so discreetly adjusting himself.

I shivered at the idea and had a moment where I couldn't remember if we'd ever had sex in the kitchen or not and maybe we'd better just to make sure, before common sense took over. "What are you going to do when we can't solve every problem between us with sex?"

He looked at me like I'd lost my mind before he grinned. "I look forward to finding that out with you." Then he sighed, looking off into the distance, obviously getting a ping from the CN-net. "Konstantin already wants to know when I'm coming back to the test lab."

"You're leaving right now?"

He touched my cheek. "I have to. I'm sorry. I might not see you for a few sols. I'm sorry...Fuck. I'm so sick of not being here and telling you how sorry I am. This...It will get better. I promise."

He looked so miserable, I couldn't be angry at him. I'd never seen him torn like this, so at a loss and grasping for control. "It's fine. We'll get through this. Just do what you need to do and I'll be here waiting for you. I love you."

"The second this is over, we're getting married."

I smiled, humoring him. "Okay, we'll get married."

Then he kissed me again—hard enough to knock the breath out of me and leave me aching for him—turned on his heel, and left.

And to my horror, I could not have been more relieved to see him go.

⟫◆⟪

So it was just me, my cards, and a heaping bowl of potato salad that went to Celeste's event. While I knew most of my scattered family on Mars, I wasn't as close to them as I was to those on Earth. That was something I hoped to change.

The flight-limo dropped me and a pair of chain-breakers in front of the venue, Spirit Park, though it wasn't really a park. It was an enclosed nature and garden sanctuary that hosted private themed parties. It was for the sort of person who wanted a party outdoors, but didn't want bad weather ruining the event. It was also over-the-top and the last word in ostentatious, making me wonder what sort of con Celeste and her husband were running on the park owners. There was no way they could have afforded this otherwise. Lotus probably knew the score. She knew everything. Or if she didn't know, she was nosy enough to ask. I was glad I'd dressed up instead of down, wearing a coral-colored sleeveless dress that floated like a dream around my legs and matching coral flats.

According to the invitation, the event was in the Gardenia Room—one of the event spaces in Spirit Park. As I entered the hexagon-shaped building, the citizenship chip in my c-tex was scanned by an automated chip reader so the event numbers could be reported to One Gov. Then I crossed the threshold and paused, momentarily baffled. I knew I'd gone through a set of doors, yet it still felt and looked like I was outside. The breeze ruffled my hair and the sun warmed my skin. Gravel crunched underfoot when I walked. The grass and flowers all felt, looked, and even smelled real. The tactile holograms were powerful enough to fool even a spook like me—without t-mods an AI could lock on to and "trick."

Following the marked path and posted signs, I made my way to the Gardenia Room. The whole time, I was so positive I was outside, I gave up trying to figure out how it worked and accepted it for what it was. One of my chain-breakers—gods only knew if they'd registered with the One Gov chip reader or not—peeled off for parts unknown while the other stayed at my side. I turned as the path directed, saw a shimmer of light beside me, and I was in another room. It still felt like outdoors, except instead of following a gravel path through the woods, I was in a glade full of leafy green shrubs teeming with white-petaled flowers. The air smelled like heaven, filled with the scent of gardenias. In the center of the glade were several circular tables with enormous centerpieces and pristine table linens. Most were occupied; looked like I was among the last to arrive.

"Felicia! You made it!" Celeste called out, swooping down on me. She wore a silver gown that nearly brushed the grass and her hair was pulled into an elaborate updo with silver feathers woven into the strands. "She's here, everyone!"

A chorus of "hellos" and "welcomes" followed from the various tables. Then I found my "made with love" potato salad yanked out of my hands before I was enveloped in a hug that threatened to crush me.

Celeste's hazel eyes swept over me. "You survived what happened on Mannette Bleu's disaster theater? It's all anyone could talk about."

"I'm fine, and I brought the cards so there's nothing to worry about." *Thank you, Brody*, I added silently.

"No one cares about the cards. You're more important," Celeste assured me.

Spoken like someone who didn't have the luck gene. "Thanks, but we know that's not true. I could name at least twenty people who would disagree."

"Then they're idiots," she said in a tone indicating it was her final word on the subject. She handed my salad to a passing teenage boy, some cousin or other, who grunted and headed off in the direction of the food. I hoped I got my bowl back later.

"Where's the boyfriend?" Celeste asked. Seemed like my other chain-breaker had peeled off as well or she probably would have thought we were a couple.

"He wanted to be here, but a work situation popped up. I did say he was busy."

I'm not sure Celeste was actually listening to me since she was looking at my hand, eyes widening.

"Holy fuck," she said, a phrase I couldn't remember ever having heard come out of her mouth. She picked up my left hand to examine my ring. "Is that real? They can probably see it from Earth."

I laughed self-consciously. "Yes, it's real. I guess I'm getting married. It just sort of happened so I haven't really told anyone yet."

"Married to someone none of us have met," Celeste said, frowning as she played mother hen. "You know we need to meet him first. See how he fits in."

Oh boy, that would certainly be interesting. "Well, Lotus knows him."

Celeste made a sound that could only be described as disapproving before pulling me toward the group.

"Let me introduce you to everyone first. I know there are some you still haven't met. Then we'll talk about this no-show boyfriend." She brightened suddenly. "Oh, if you're getting married, you know what this means?"

I looked at her worriedly as she pulled me farther into the crowd, some of whom were rising out of chairs to make their way toward me. "No, what?"

"It means more babies!"

"More babies? But I'm not having a baby."

I stopped short, the rest of what I wanted to say abruptly forgotten.

As my family approached, that was when I saw it. Maybe I wasn't having a baby, but it looked like every single female in my family who was of childbearing years was. All of them were pregnant. Every damn last one. I stopped counting at ten, but I'm pretty sure there were more. Maybe it was as high as fifteen.

Now I could see why Lotus was so keen on having a baby, and why my own thoughts were straying in that direction. The luck gene looked for ways to change events in its favor and now that our blacklisted status was revoked, it was prodding us to begin reproducing like damned rabbits.

I had caused this to happen, I realized. If I hadn't suffered and lost and fought and been betrayed and used over and over again, none of these children would exist. I had paid the price for all this, and it had been expensive, nearly costing me everything. Yet instead of feeling vindicated, it made me angry. It reminded me how miserable and helpless I'd felt, and let me know I was a pawn once again. I would never have my own life because I would always be luck's fucking pawn, always pulled in the direction it wanted and doing its bidding.

"Celeste, what the hell?" I blurted out, looking at the assortment of pregnant bellies ambling toward me. "Why didn't someone warn me?"

"What's to warn? We're having babies, not breeding locusts."

"But..." I opened my mouth, closed it, not sure what to say. I was never going to be free, I realized bleakly. *Never.* "You said a few of them were pregnant, but not this many. Not all at once."

"I know. Isn't it amazing? These women eat like calorie consumption points are a suggestion, not a law. You really should have brought more potato salad."

All I could do was nod because it was better than freaking out and running away.

"Yeah," I said helplessly. "More salad."

18

It was 8:00 a.m. sharp, and Lotus was late. Big surprise.

I stood outside the Stone Fertility Clinic security check-point, glancing at my c-tex and waiting for a shim to explain her delay while I sipped my coffee. It was all I could do to keep from tapping my toe on the sidewalk as I watched other couples sign in with the One Gov hooahs before entering the clinic. The building itself was squat, square, ugly, and very government-looking. It stood out from the rest of the buildings, refusing to fit in with the architectural flow of the neighborhood. It was like it had gone out of its way to be hideous. Well, at least there wasn't a protest blocking the entrance. No chance of a firebombing today.

After yesterday's blindside at the picnic, Lotus had asked if I wanted to go with her and Buckley to their appointment to have their fertility inhibitors removed. That way, I could see how the process worked. Then she winked and nudged me while gesturing to my ring, making me want to slap her. So now I waited, feeling an anxious, fluttering sensation in my chest. Why, I didn't know. There was no good reason for it. It was just there, kind of like the sun in the sky. Probably because I was excited for Lotus, I decided.

I'd gotten a shim from Alexei asking how the picnic had been and what my plans were for today. My answers were vague: "Good" and "Hanging out with Lotus." I hadn't known what else to say, and thankfully I could get away with brief answers on my c-tex; he knew typing replies took me so long, I usually kept them short. How could I explain yesterday and the confusing jumble of emotions swamping me? How could I tell him where I was now? I couldn't even explain it to myself. My state of mind was tangled and chaotic. Everything felt unpredictable and up in the air.

I sipped my coffee, waiting and getting more annoyed with Lotus—honestly, how had she ever made it to work on time—when I noticed a familiar figure coming toward me. Well, three actually, but only one that made me swear out loud. There were Buckley, Lotus, and beside her, Brody. Fuck. Why was he everywhere I was? What was he trying to do to me? And didn't the man ever work? I was tempted to shim Alexei and demand to know what was up with Brody, but didn't. It would mean having to explain a host of things I wasn't ready to tell him. I'd just upset him and gods knew he didn't need anything else on his plate. No need to create more problems, or so I justified it to myself.

Still, it was an awful realization to know I wanted to see Brody. The anxious fluttering grew as he came nearer. I was reacting like some stupid lovesick teenager. Gods, I was probably going to start giggling and twirling my hair next.

"Hey, Felicia. Look who we ran into," Lotus said as they approached me.

"Wow, what a coincidence," I said, scowling.

"Isn't it?" Brody agreed. "Such a small world."

I scowled deeper. "Don't you ever work?"

"Actually, I seem to find myself at loose ends this morning. Private Consortium meeting and I wasn't invited. Seems to be happening quite a bit lately."

"Maybe you're about to find yourself unemployed," I replied scathingly.

Brody kept grinning at me, as if the more unpleasant I was, the more he enjoyed it. "Unlikely, but thanks for your concern."

"You sure you want him here?" I directed the question to Lotus and Buckley. Buckley shrugged as if he were indifferent to the whole process and was just happy to have time off work. Lotus had a different approach.

"When we ran into him, it seemed like a good idea to ask him to come along." Which was code for "my gut wanted him there," so I couldn't argue with that.

I threw my empty coffee cup into the closest molecule scattering unit, where the cup would be broken down into its base elements and made into some other product. Then we all trooped inside once Lotus had the citizenship chip in her c-tex scanned, with it showing the details of her appointment. Next we went through security, endured a weapons scan, and eventually entered the building. A guide met us at the door—female, tall, slender, with striking blue eyes and light blond hair. Pretty in a way that was almost forgettable because it was so generic. She was a "type," fitting so well into the landscape of the genetic blueprint One Gov set for humanity, her prettiness didn't even rate.

Well, that wasn't necessarily true. Buckley was having a great time checking out her ass while she led the way, taking us down an industrial-looking gray corridor complete with bars on the windows. If he'd been my boyfriend, I would have killed him. Lotus rolled her eyes and gave me a long-suffering look.

"You sure you want to do this with him?" I whispered to her. "Eighteen years is a long time to be tied to someone."

Her expression was grim. "No, it's decided. We want to do this."

"But you could do so much better. You don't have to settle for..." I waved vaguely in Buckley's direction.

"At least I know what I'm getting and there'll be no surprises," she said, her voice just as hushed as mine. "We can't all have Russian gods falling into our laps. We also don't have whatever's going on here either." There, a subtle tilt of her head toward Brody. "I prefer to keep my problems uncomplicated."

Ouch. I kept my mouth shut after that and concentrated on the destination, not the journey.

Eventually we were taken to a small room at the end of the hall. Inside were a few uncomfortable-looking black fabric chairs, a data portal, and an examination table. The institutional gray theme continued, except without windows. That was the thing about One Gov—equality for all meant you couldn't please everyone. The basics were provided because every full citizen had the same rights and deserved the same treatment, but that was all. If you wanted more, you paid for it. And when you were paying, you were entitled to whatever you could afford.

"Someone will attend to you shortly," the woman said, leaving us all in the small room and closing the door behind her.

Luckily we didn't wait long. Otherwise, I had a feeling someone would start fighting—either Lotus and Buckley or myself
and Brody. Another female tech entered dressed in a white uniform: short skirt, short-sleeved top, and knee-high boots. Like
the other woman, she had One Gov's logo over her left breast—
yellow sun, three white dots representing the planets, all on a
black background. She looked similar to the first woman except her hair wasn't quite as blond. She cast confused glances
between Lotus and me.

"Lotus Sevigny?" she asked. "You and the father-elect—
Buckley Maslin—are here to have your fertility inhibitors removed?"

"That's us!" Lotus jumped up from her chair and dragged
Buckley after her.

"Your citizenship chips show your reproduction approval
permits are in order. It looks like today you're both here for
inhibitor removal and specimen harvesting. Then next week,
you'll be back for your fertilized implant," she said pleasantly,
then looked around the room again. "Would you like your
friends to remain, or do you just want the father-elect?"

"My cousin is here because I want her to see what the procedure is like," Lotus said. "He's moral support." The last was
said with a wave toward Brody, who leaned against the wall and
looked a damn sight more attentive than the father-elect, who was
clearly browsing the CN-net given the vacant look on his face.

"All right," the tech said, her smile brightening. "Let's get
started."

"I have a question," Brody said, hitting the tech with that
flirty smile he could do without even trying. "Could you check
to see if Felicia Sevigny is on the list for inhibitor removal?"

I stared at him. "Brody, no. Not now."

He shrugged and met my eyes, arching an eyebrow. "But aren't you curious? Don't you want to know if he was telling the truth?"

"I…" He was right. I'd refused to acknowledge it before because part of me just couldn't believe this might be my new reality, but I *was* curious.

I turned back to the tech. "Could you check, please?"

"This is highly irregular—"

"Please, I just want to know if I'm on the list, that's all."

"If she wants to you check, then check," Lotus ordered. Then she shot me a look. "You didn't say anything about filing for a permit at the picnic. Celeste even asked you about babies and you lied to her face. You are so busted when I tell her."

I smiled wanly. "You and Celeste together can be a little much. She went crazy when she saw the ring, and with every eligible woman in the family about to give birth, I didn't want to get into it."

"Hold on," Brody interrupted. "Every woman in your family is pregnant?"

"Not every woman," I said defensively. "Lotus isn't. I'm not."

"Minor technicality. This time next week, I expect to be one of *them*, so that leaves you and the old ladies." Lotus sounded smug, then looked amused. "Can you imagine the Russian as a father? I'm trying to picture it, but I can't."

"Found it," the tech announced, finishing whatever search she'd been conducting through the fertility clinic's data. "I located your name on the applicants list. It says…Oh…" The woman sounded surprised, then gave Lotus and Buckley an apologetic look. "Felicia Sevigny's appointment takes precedence over all others. I'm sorry, but I'll have to escort Ms. Sevigny to the primary care wing where the priority appointments are handled."

Then the tech turned to me, addressing her comments to both me and Brody. "You and the father-elect can provide your specimens today. Then we can finalize your list of preferences. A fertilized embryo can be prepared and implanted as early as this evening. I'm sorry it can't be done more quickly, but our geneticists need time to program your requested DNA sequences. However, rest assured this facility will provide you with the best of service and care."

"Felicia, what the hell's going on?" Lotus screeched at me. "Are you steamrolling my appointment? What the fuck did the Russian do? Is he fucking with my appointment for my baby?"

I think my jaw may have dropped to the floor. "No, of course not! This is a misunderstanding. It's your appointment, not mine."

"It doesn't need to be done today, if you're not certain. You can go home and think about it. I can summon another clinic representative for you to discuss your options," the tech offered.

I looked at the tech, stupefied. Vieira hadn't lied. Not only was I on the list to have my fertility inhibitor removed, I was at the top of it. All I needed to do was say the word and the inhibitor was gone. The enormity was so staggering, I couldn't take it all in.

"Ms. Sevigny, would you like to have your fertility inhibitor removed today?" the tech asked pointedly.

I blinked. Took a breath. Tried to think of something to do with my arms other than hug myself. Did I want it gone? Was it really this easy? "Yes. Yes, I want it out right now."

"Excellent. If you'll wait out in the hall, someone will be with you shortly."

"Right. Good. We'll do that. We'll wait in the hall," I babbled, then pushed my way through the door.

In the hall, I felt even less rational. This was happening so fast and my gut was positively giddy. I slapped my hands over my mouth, willing myself to calm down and think, to really *think* for once in my damned life, and not leap in like a crazy person the way I normally did.

I uncovered my mouth and announced: "I'm going to have my fertility inhibitor removed."

I said it as if it was big news and we hadn't just spent the last few minutes discussing it. But it was big news and I needed to say it out loud to someone, if only to make it seem more real. Brody was there and smiling down at me. He tucked a strand of hair behind my ear and because I suddenly wanted him to touch me almost as much as I wanted my inhibitor gone, I let him.

"You're sure?"

I thought about it, working it through in my mind, feeling excitement take hold. All these years of struggling, the countless disappointments as I went through one appeal after another to the Shared Hope program applying to have my reproduction approval permit granted, how I'd hated myself and thought I was a failure and no one could ever possibly want me because I wasn't good enough...

I nodded. Then I nodded again, just in case. "Yes. I want to do this. I want it so badly, it hurts."

"And the specimen harvest? Do you want to do that now too?"

Specimen harvest? I'd been so focused on getting my black-listed status revoked, I hadn't let myself dream that far ahead. It had been easier to deal with the devastation of constant rejection by only thinking about the process one tiny step at a time. Now I felt faint, overwhelmed by the possibilities.

"I could do that. I should do it. It would be easier, wouldn't it? I'm here and they can do it all at once," I said, the words coming out of me in a rush. "No, wait. I should probably think about this first. I should have a plan. Do you think I should have a plan?"

Brody laughed softly, amused as he watched me. "A plan sounds good."

"I'll get the inhibitor removed today, and do the specimen harvest later. For now, I can use the clinic's fertility suppressing treatments until I work out the rest of the details. I have a year to decide before the inhibitor goes back in." Then in my next breath, because gods knew I had to pause for air sometime, I asked, "You don't think I'm making a mistake, do you?"

"No, I don't. I think you should do this."

I could feel myself practically vibrating with excitement. I grinned at Brody, squeezing his hands, bouncing on my feet. "Okay. I'm going to do this. It's coming out." Then I faltered a little. "I should tell Alexei."

"Probably, but whatever he says, don't let him stop you. If he really wants you to be happy, he knows better than to try."

That deflated my excitement. "Why would you say something like that?"

He touched my cheek. "You're forgetting—I'm the only person on this entire planet who knew you in Nairobi. Not Alexei. Not your family on Mars. Just me. You were so unhappy then.

You tried not to show it, but sometimes it broke through the cracks in the façade you'd spackled over yourself. You didn't want the world to see how much pain you were in or how much you were hurting, but it was there. I'd hoped you would tell me, but when you didn't, I decided to find out for myself. I asked Charlie Zero, but he said it wasn't his story to tell so I paid Dante a visit and found out about your blacklisted status."

I gaped at him, shocked. "Why would you do that?"

"Because not knowing was killing me! I had to know what was breaking your heart, if only for my own sanity. You weren't telling me anything so what else was I supposed to do? I was falling in love with you."

I flushed and looked down at the ground, feeling like my heart would beat its way right out of my chest. I felt excited, hot, scared, and like I needed to put as much space between the two of us as possible. Instead, I stood there in front of him and let him touch my hair. "You never said anything," I whispered.

"Even if I had, I don't think you would have heard it. You never would have believed anyone could want you if you were blacklisted. I tried to make you feel otherwise, and when I thought you were coming around, I asked you to go to Mars. I didn't care if you were blacklisted and I thought we could start a new life together."

"Why didn't you tell me?"

"Because I wanted you to confide in me. I wanted you to open up and give me everything, but you wouldn't. Believe me, looking back now, I wish I'd done it all differently. I wish I'd forced you to see what you were doing and look at what we could have been. But I didn't, and now here we are."

I took a deep breath, fighting for calm even though everything in me felt entitled to being irrational. I blinked back tears and wondered if I was the stupidest woman in the entire tri-system. Gods, had I been that oblivious?

"I'm sorry if I hurt you. I didn't know."

He shrugged. "You read Tarot cards, not minds. It looks like we both had problems expressing how we felt about things back then."

Another fertility clinic tech appeared around the corner, wearing an outfit identical to the tech we'd met earlier. She looked between us. "Felicia Sevigny? If you'll follow me, I have a room prepped for you and the father-elect."

"No father-elect today, and no specimens are getting collected," I blurted out. "I just want my fertility inhibitor removed. That's it."

"It's your decision. We can reschedule the rest for another time. Please, follow me."

I thought we would be going to another room in the same hall. Instead, we passed through a set of doors around the corner, leaving the industrial gray walls behind us. Now the walls were a pleasant shade of blue with pictures everywhere, and the floor was a cream-colored tile instead of cement. We were eventually led to an examination room that was more like a hotel suite, with its own waiting room, toilet facilities, and plush, comfortable furniture. Even the guest chairs were a dream when I sat down in one. I exchanged a baffled look with Brody.

"Guess it doesn't hurt to be the Under-Secretary's grand-daughter," he said.

My citizenship chip in my c-tex bracelet was scanned to confirm my identity, then the tech ran a series of medical history checks, including when I'd had my last Renew treatment. That had been six months ago in late September, right after my birthday and shortly before I'd left for Mars. You couldn't have Renew treatments while pregnant, so I'd either have to miss my next treatment or hold off on a baby until six months from now. I told the tech I'd figure it out later.

"Since the father-elect isn't here and you're waiting on embryo collection and fertilization, you'll take your first dose of fertilization suppressant before you leave today and I'll provide enough for the next three months. You need to take it every week until you're implanted. Otherwise, you risk unplanned pregnancy and the potential for a One Gov–sanctioned disposal of an unapproved fetus."

I looked at her, confused. "I'm sorry—what did you say?"

"The chances are slight, but suppose you have relations with a male whose fertility inhibitor has been removed and he's impregnated another woman? The Shared Hope program only allows one child for every two people. Your fetus would be unapproved and require termination. Or should you decide to conceive naturally, there is always the risk of birth defects. This would also lead to termination."

I held up a hand to stop her, feeling sick as she described all the ways to kill the child I didn't even have yet. "Just give me the drugs."

The tech beamed. "Perfect. Now I need to prep you for the removal procedure." She looked to Brody. "Sir, kindly step into the waiting room, and Ms. Sevigny and I can get started."

Brody rose from his chair, brushing a hand over mine. "I'll see you when it's over."

I felt a moment of panic. "You're not leaving, are you?"

"Wouldn't dream of it. I'll be right next door if you need me."

Funny how that made me feel better, like I was a child needing reassurance I wouldn't be left behind.

The removal wasn't particularly difficult. I lay on the examination table and the tech inserted an IV into my arm. Then a machine pumped a solution into my bloodstream, killing off the nanos that regulated my hormone levels, prevented an egg from implanting in my uterus, or attacked and eliminated a fertilized egg should the first two measures fail. In a male's body, the nanos essentially sterilized the sperm, rendering it incapable of fertilizing an egg. Once the nanos were gone, there was nothing preventing pregnancy except me taking the weekly fertility suppressant.

The whole process would take no more than an hour. One hour, and everything would be different. I lay on the table, hearing my heartbeat through the cardio-monitor and feeling a tingling in my arm as the solution dripped into my bloodstream. I breathed in through my nose, out through my mouth, trying to calm the fluttering sensation in my stomach. Nerves. It was only nerves. I was scared and excited, and taking a step so monumental, it made moving to Mars seem like a trip to the market to pick up dinner.

Was I doing the right thing? I didn't know, but I was in too far to stop now. I should have told Alexei. Even if this was happening so fast I could barely process it, I should have shimmed him. I felt a pang—as much as I wanted Brody there, I knew it should have been Alexei out in the waiting room. He was the one I should have been talking to about specimen collection and DNA sequences. I wondered how our baby would look.

Definitely blue eyes, like his. And dark hair obviously, and...I didn't even know if he wanted a boy or a girl. A boy maybe, so they could bond? They could play catch together and...Had Alexei played catch as a child? I wasn't sure. Well, we'd figure it out later.

He might not be pleased at first, but he'd understand. I knew I could convince him. Everyone else in my family was having a baby, so why couldn't I? After all, I was the one who'd fought to have the blacklisted status revoked. Why shouldn't it be my turn? Maybe it wasn't an ideal time to have a baby, given what might be happening with Belikov, but Alexei would take care of it. I had a damned luck gene, after all. How could things *not* work out?

Either I fell asleep or there was some drug cocktail in my IV to put me under because the next thing I knew, the tech was telling me everything was done and helped me sit up. Then she handed me the fertility suppressing treatment—a tiny disk-shaped pill I placed under my tongue until it melted. She gave me a packet of tablets that made up a three months' supply, then led me from the exam room.

Brody was still waiting for me. "All done?" he asked, standing up.

"Looks that way." I felt my c-tex bracelet vibrate on my wrist. I checked the shim, surprised, but also feeling a little sick. "Word gets around fast. It's Vieira, congratulating me. He wants to see me again."

"When?"

"He says he'll leave it up to me." I bit my lip, anxious. "Is he going to try to control my life now?"

"No," Brody said forcefully. "He has no control over you.

Maybe he moved you up the list to get your inhibitor removed, but you don't owe him anything for that, okay?"

I nodded, but the sick feeling didn't go away. "Okay. Let's get out of here."

He nodded and put an arm around my shoulders, pulling me with him. We found Lotus and Buckley waiting for us at the clinic's main entrance. Lotus was practically glowing when she saw me. Buckley looked dazed, as if he wasn't entirely sure what he was in for.

"Did you do it?" Lotus burst out when she saw us.

"My inhibitor's gone if that's what you mean," I said as she rushed up to hug me.

"We can be pregnant together!"

"I'm not really sure when that's going to happen for me," I cautioned. "I need to tell Alexei and—"

But she wasn't listening, prattling on and pulling us after her through the security checkpoints and outside into the sunshine. Complaining she couldn't have sex for a week because she didn't want to risk a fate-baby and maybe she should have taken the fertility suppressant. Then again, maybe a week without sex wasn't so bad. The look on Buckley's face said otherwise, but no one could interrupt Lotus during her speech about the wonders of motherhood. Brody rolled his eyes and grinned at me. And me…

The sick feeling I thought was nerves continued growing until I thought I might puke on the sidewalk. I felt hot and clammy, my body perspiring. Dizziness washed over me and I clutched at Brody's arm.

"I don't feel well," I whispered, swallowing.

Brody caught me when my knees buckled. "What is it? What's wrong?"

"I think I'm going to be sick."

He swore. "Your body must be reacting to the fertility suppressant."

"But it's the same nano stuff she had in her before. Why would it make her sick?" That, from Buckley.

Logically it made sense, but my body wasn't interested in logic as I started to dry heave. Brody dragged me over to a bench. He'd barely stepped aside before I threw up over a small group of shrubs.

"And there goes breakfast," I mumbled, puking again.

I'm not sure what happened next. I heard Lotus say something about going back to the clinic. Then my stomach churned and I vomited again. Chills followed and I hugged myself, my teeth chattering as dizziness returned. I heard arguing. Voices I recognized, some I didn't. Then I felt myself picked up even though my stomach protested it didn't want to be moved. I saw something that looked like a flight-limo, then I lay on a bench seat. Hands rubbed my back and I moaned restlessly because the hands made me uncomfortable and nauseated again. I coughed and dry heaved, but there was nothing left in me. All I could do was close my eyes and pray to any deities listening to make it all stop.

I felt myself lifted and put somewhere cool and dark. No one touched me, or spoke to me, and it was sheer, perfect bliss. For about two seconds. Then I felt hands on me again and a series of sharp, painful pinpricks in my stomach. I couldn't stop them—not the hands or the jabs. I tried to scream, but my throat felt stripped raw.

Then finally they went away. In fact, everything went away and I couldn't have been more thrilled. And then, even that was gone.

19

I sat up in a rush, taking a shuddering breath as if I'd been struggling underwater and just burst to the surface. Then I fell back, dizzy by the move. My head hit a pillow and I realized I lay in bed. The room was in semidarkness, a faint light off to my right. When I squinted, I saw outlines of familiar things—a bedside table, a lamp, a potted plant in the corner.

There was movement beside me, someone reaching to brush hair from my face. "Felicia, relax. You're not at the clinic anymore."

I recognized that voice and I turned my head to see Alexei lying to my left, his face in partial shadow and expression unreadable. I looked back to the darkened ceiling, trying to breathe in and out, to calm myself. I couldn't. All I felt was this gnawing, terrifying fear. Why was Alexei there? How did he know about the clinic? What was going on?

"Am I dead?" I asked, just to be sure. It couldn't hurt to check.

"You put considerable effort into making it happen, but no. You had an allergic reaction to the fertility suppressant."

I felt a tear slide out of my left eye and I swiped at it with the back of my hand. "I don't remember much except being really sick."

"Brody contacted me. I had you brought home. It's late. Almost Witching Time."

I lay there, absorbing this news. "I'm sorry. I'm not really sure what I'm doing. I think I may have made a mistake."

He said nothing to that. Instead he got out of bed, stepped around to my side, and helped me sit. Then he held out a glass.

"It's water, and you're dehydrated."

I drank it, the cool water wonderfully refreshing as it slid down my throat. When the glass was empty, he set it on the bedside table.

"Any more dizziness or nausea?"

"No. I feel better, but my stomach hurts."

He nodded. "From the nano-trace needles. Once they countered the suppressant in your system, you stabilized. Apparently in the time between your inhibitor being removed and the suppressant readministered, you spontaneously developed an allergy to the nanos. The tech said the time elapse was approximately half an hour. There's no recorded case of that happening before."

"I'm sorry," I said again because I couldn't think of anything else to say.

"Can you shower yourself, or do you need my help?" he asked instead, ignoring my apology.

I frowned, confused. "I can do it myself."

He nodded. "Shower, then we'll talk."

That sounded ominous and the fear came back like a blow to my chest. I swung my legs over the side of the bed, stumbling a little. Alexei caught me, then let me go once I was upright. I made it to the bathroom under my own steam, wincing at the lights while my eyes adjusted. When I caught myself in the mirror, I saw I wore the same clothes from earlier, except now they were wrinkled and splattered with vomit. I looked pale and bruised around the eyes, while my eyes themselves were bloodshot and the whites discolored. My throat hurt, probably from all the throwing up I'd done earlier.

Stripping, I left my clothes where they lay. I also took off any jewelry, including my bracelet. That rarely came off unless I was doing a reading. *Or I lost my mind because I was doing drugs*, I amended silently, remembering my Euphoria incident. I was not an irrational person. I always saw myself as the sanest person in a family chock-full of crazy. Yet as I stood under the hot water spray, I saw my life as one episode of erratic behavior after another, culminating with me ditching my fertility inhibitor. Gods, who operated at this level of crazy on a regular basis? How could Alexei stand it? Maybe he couldn't. Maybe I was too much trouble on top of everything else he had to deal with.

I hurried through my shower. When I got out, I found my discarded clothing gone and a clean outfit on the counter. I dried off and dressed in what had been left—leggings and a long-sleeved tunic top both in green and my ballet flats. A pair of unremarkable-looking underwear I didn't even know I owned was in the pile. The same went for the plain but serviceable bra. It certainly wasn't going to incite lust in anyone. I pulled my hair into a loose ponytail before slapping my c-tex bracelet back on my wrist but the ring...I left it on the counter, not sure I was entitled to wear it after what I'd done.

The lights were on when I shuffled back into the bedroom. Alexei sat on the edge of the bed, looking like he'd paused while removing one of his many suits: He'd taken off the jacket and unbuttoned his shirt. His expression was vacant as he presumably scanned the CN-net—though I'd never really know where his thoughts wandered when he was like this. His eyes slid to me, but his face remained unchanged, as if he didn't see me. Maybe he didn't. Maybe in his mind, I was already gone, although that was too frightening a possibility to consider.

I stood on the other side of the room, crossing my arms and leaning against the wall. For long moments, we looked at each other. I couldn't think of what to say. I hadn't planned that far ahead. Or rather, hadn't planned at all. The longer I said nothing, the greater my need to confess, like I was a sinner who needed to be absolved of my guilt.

"When I got up this morning, I didn't expect things would end like this," I said finally.

"I believe you. I've never been able to determine how you do what you do, or why." He sounded frustrated when normally he might have been amused. I'd always suspected part of his initial attraction to me had been because he couldn't read me via the CN-net the way he could the rest of the world. Now it felt like a liability.

"I'm sorry," I said, yet again. "I shouldn't have removed my inhibitor. It made sense at the time, but now I see I didn't have the right to do it without telling you. I wasn't thinking straight. I was afraid—"

"You don't have to apologize. You warned me this would happen. You said you needed me, and I wasn't there for you. If I'd been paying attention where it mattered, none of this would have occurred."

That wasn't the response I'd expected, nor did I think I'd hear such resignation in his voice. It was like he'd already accepted everything had fallen apart and talking about it was useless.

"But I didn't think I'd manage to convince myself removing my fertility inhibitor was a great idea."

"I should have realized this was the road events would take," he continued as if I hadn't spoken. "After all, luck always finds the best advantage and seeks to preserve itself, regardless of what's standing in its way. Wasn't that one of your mother's rules? You were only doing what comes naturally. How could you be faulted for that? It's like getting angry at the rain for being wet."

"When you say that, it makes me sound selfish and stupid."

"Does it? Maybe that makes two of us."

"Look, I said I was sorry. I never meant for this to happen."

"I know. The irony is, I'm the one who set events in motion and brought this down on us. Luck merely turned the situation into what it needed it to be."

"I don't see how that's possible. It's not like you were the one puking your guts out all over town."

He rose from the bed, advancing toward me as if he couldn't stay away. The neutral expression on his face gave way to fury. "Is there some reason why you're deliberately missing the point?"

"What point? That I'm stupid and selfish or you're tired of dealing with my constant screwups?"

"Can you not see what's right in front of you? I'm not what you want. Do you think I don't realize your luck gene is pushing you toward *him*? That I don't know how often you're alone with him?" His hand touched my face, cupping my cheek. His grip wasn't painful, but it wasn't gentle either as he ran his thumb over my lips. "I waited for you to tell me it meant nothing, but you didn't. Instead all I have are reports of the two of you together. Of you in his arms. You kissing him. You didn't even try to hide it. Even after you agreed to marry me, you still went back to him. And like a fool, I turned a blind eye because

295

I couldn't believe it might be true. After all, why would you be here if you didn't want to be with me? Except you were at the clinic today with him. Not me. *Him.*"

I looked up at him, horrified and unable to defend myself because it was all true. I'd hid behind lies or tried to pretend it would all just stop while at the same time doing everything to sabotage things with the man I loved.

"Maybe I should have said something, and asked you to make him go away," I whispered. "He always seemed to be there when I needed someone, and you... You weren't. I'm not saying that's an excuse, just... He was at my shop. At the gym. The clinic. He came to see me at our hotel room in Apolli, and he had my shoes. Then I asked him to go with me to see the Under-Secretary because I didn't think you would understand why I needed to go... It made me so confused. I don't love Brody, but I don't know how to stop the feelings I do have!"

"And that's what I brought into our lives," Alexei snarled. "I did this."

"But I only love you!"

Frustrated, he punched the wall near my head, making me jump. The whole wall shook and plaster crumbled where he connected. His hand should have been killing him, but he didn't even react. When I tried to reach for him, his other hand pushed me back by the shoulder and held me in place.

"Don't you get it?" he railed at me, shouting now. "It doesn't matter if you love me! I don't have what you need so you're looking for it elsewhere."

"What am I looking for? What does Brody have that you don't?" I yelled back. The words so closely mirrored what Brody had said in the air-hack—that he could give me what Alexei couldn't—I felt panic rise. My hands grabbed the edges of his open shirt, fisting in the material. "Tell me!"

"How can you not see the obvious when we both know you're drawn to him? Even your cards know it."

"That's not fair! I'm *not* luck's pawn! I'm not some tool pushed around by my DNA! I make my own decisions."

"If that's the case, did you purposely set out to humiliate me? Do you enjoy seeing me like this?"

"Of course not! I never wanted to hurt you."

"Isn't that kind of you? I've killed people for less. Many people, Felicia. So many, I can't even recall the exact number and I make it a point to remember everything." His hand on my shoulder flexed until I winced. "Is that what you want? Does someone need to die for this situation to go away, because that's how I feel—like someone needs to be punished. Sometimes I actually enjoy the killing, like it's the only thing I do that has any meaning."

I was too far gone to register what he was saying. Instead I threw back: "Then kill me if it makes you feel better! Maybe I deserve it for being weak. I knew this was hurting you, but I couldn't stop myself. At least I have enough control not to sleep with him. Well, not yet anyway."

His other hand was at my throat then, and for a moment, he looked so furious, I thought he might just do it. I thought he would actually kill me. Yet his hand never tightened and the grip remained loose, even as I could see his control fraying. Fear leaped inside me. Not of him, but of what was happening and how we'd even stumbled into this situation. We were supposed to be in love, damn it! How had it gotten so twisted?

I went limp in his hands, the fight going out of me in the face of his suffering. I'd caused this. I'd hurt him and this was the awful result.

"I shouldn't have said that," I whispered. "I would never do that to you. I couldn't betray you like that."

He made a noise that sounded more animal than man before pulling me to him, and dragging me down to the floor. Both of us fell on our knees, clinging to each other with an air of desperation. Just as quickly, he shoved me back as if he couldn't bear to touch me.

"What does it matter? I can't be what you want," he ground out. "I've tried, but I see now it's pointless. It's always been pointless."

"Why? Am I holding you back from being the powerful crime lord you always wanted to be? Would you rather be out on some murderous rampage, scheming to take control of the tri-system away from One Gov?" All the fear and self-doubt I'd kept bottled up inside broke free, and I swallowed convulsively over the lump forming in my throat, making it a fight to get the words out. "Or were you just pretending you wanted to be with me? Is this not fun anymore because you realized I'm not enough? Did you finally figure out what I've always known—that I could never be enough for you?"

He groaned as if he were in pain. Then he took a shuddering breath of his own and reached out to touch my hair, running his fingers over my damp ponytail before letting it slip free. "Why would you even think that? What did I do to make you believe you weren't enough when you were the only thing I wanted? It was never pretend with you. Never."

"Then why are you saying this? Is it that you're not interested in having a baby? Were you just humoring me when I brought it up because you don't want that with me?"

His hands were on my face, thumbs stroking my cheeks. "I watched as you all but sold yourself and turned your life upside down trying to make the impossible happen. Of course I knew it was important and eventually you'd want us to try. I just told you what you wanted to hear because I was afraid of what the truth would do to us."

"The truth? What truth?" I gasped out the words. I pushed away his hands but they merely dropped to my shoulders, still holding me. My eyes widened as I gazed up at him, his words finally sinking in. "Are you lying to me? *Again?* What shocking secret are you hiding now? Gods, after everything we've been through, am I *ever* going to get the whole truth from you?"

"It looks as if luck has forced both our hands. I would have told you whatever I thought would keep you with me. For the past five and a half months, our lives have been perfect. But now it's all caught up to me. The problem was never you. It was me. I'm the one who isn't enough, not you."

"Not enough how?"

He laughed but it was bitter and without humor. "We're not biologically compatible. Everything the Consortium did to create me, every upgrade and every advancement they did, has made me into this *thing* that puts me outside of what it means to be biologically human. It's unlikely we could have a baby together. We may not even be the same species anymore."

I stared up at him, stunned and momentarily speechless.

"Goddamn it, say something!" he yelled, shaking me.

I blinked, flinching at the command in his voice. "How long have you known?"

"Always. I've known since the beginning, and now I've paved the way for someone else to give you what you need. Had *him* specifically shipped here for you."

"But..." I couldn't get my head around it. What he was saying didn't make any sense. "Is it because I don't have any MH Factor? Would it be different if I had t-mods that could regulate my body? Is it because I'm a spook?"

"Aren't you listening? It isn't you. According to the Consortium's lab results, it wouldn't make a difference. That's why I ordered Karol here. He was involved in my creation so I asked him to look into the original research to see if I'd missed something. He says he can't find any errors in the data or a single case where the Consortium successfully produced viable offspring in their test labs."

"But..." My voice sputtered out and it was a struggle to find the words. "Why would I be drawn to you if this was never going to work?"

"Because luck needed me," he said harshly, pulling me in close until our eyes were level. "Luck needed my influence to get your blacklisted status revoked. It needed me to get your mother out of the way. And now that it's done, it seems luck needs something else, and that apparently isn't me. It's *him*. Whatever you need now, you'll get it from him. Presumably it will be what you've always wanted: a baby."

"No," I breathed, horrified, crushed by disappointment, disbelief, and an awful feeling that what he said might be true— that I was a pawn after all. Maybe that was all I'd ever be. I shrank away from him, feeling sick and so damn scared of him and myself, and who I was, I couldn't think. "You're wrong. I can't...It's not supposed to be like this."

"But it is, Felicia. Whether you want to believe it or not, it's true. Luck used both of us, and now it wants him to give you what I never will."

I shook him off then, pushing at his hands and trying to scramble away. He let me go and I crab-walked backward until I hit the wall, then used it to haul myself to my feet. I had to get out of there. It was the only thing that made any sense. Get away from him and all his lies that couldn't possibly be true. I couldn't breathe. The panic closed in like a vise around my throat, cutting off the air. I hugged myself, feeling cold and hot, wanting to throw up even though there was nothing in my stomach. And my gut... It couldn't get me away from him and this horrible, crushing reality fast enough.

Now I knew who the Fool card referred to in all my readings. It was me.

"I have to go," I murmured, looking to the door. "I need to leave. I have to..."

I couldn't finish the sentence as I hurled myself across the room, grabbing the door handle to yank it open. Just as quickly, Alexei's hand shot out and he held it closed.

"Where are you going? To *him*?"

"I don't know but I need to get away from this, from... myself," I said, starting to cry in earnest. "All I ever wanted was to be with you and for this to be real. Only now you're telling me I couldn't have had it anyway, and everything is lies. That luck thinks I should be with Brody and I'm living the wrong life. Let me go because I can't listen to this anymore. I can't. This can't be how it all ends. It can't."

And just like that, he removed his hand. I threw open the door without looking back, flying through the hallway and nearly tripping down the stairs in my rush. Then I was at the main door, fighting with the AI to get the seals unlocked.

"Leaving, Felicia? And in such a hurry too."

The voice stopped me in my tracks. Konstantin Belikov.

He was in his mobile-assist chair, flanked by chain-breakers. They were leaving the library, one of the many rooms off the hallway.

"I heard you had a difficult time at the clinic today. I must confess: If I'd known Alexei planned on leaving for Mars with you, I could have told you all this beforehand and saved you the trouble," he said, as if he were doing me a kindness.

I looked at him, incredulous he could be so calm while everything fell apart. "I can't imagine why. I'd think you'd like the spectacle."

"Perhaps, but Mars was a long way to travel to see it. Still, despite the distance, I think it was well worth the trip."

I blinked. "Were you setting him up to fail?"

Belikov's expression hardened. "The Consortium takes care of its own. Going forward, you needn't concern yourself with Alexei's emotional well-being."

From upstairs, I could hear the sound of furniture smashing. The crashes were thunderous and terrible, reverberating throughout the house. I actually felt the whole structure shake under my feet as if we'd been hit with an earthquake. Belikov winced, and rattled off an order to two of the chain-breakers, then sent them upstairs.

For a second, I was worried. In all the time I'd known Alexei, I'd never seen him so out of control. Then I reminded myself he was a lying, murderous bastard I couldn't be around for another second. It was time to leave.

"Good luck with that," I spat out.

"Luck? Isn't that your department?" he asked, chuckling with inappropriate humor. "Not to worry. Soon this unpleasant business will be over and you a forgotten memory in the Consortium's long history. With a little effort, I'll bring Alexei round to where I need him."

Gods, how could I have ever believed I belonged in this world? "You do that. I'm sure you'll all be very happy together with your secrets and your plots for world domination."

Finally I wrestled open the door and was outside, breathing the cool night air. I raced down the laneway. Not thinking. Only running. But it's hard to run from who you are. Impossible actually. By the time I'd made it to the road, I sank into despair. With it came a stabbing pain in my chest more intense than anything I'd ever endured.

I stood for a while on the road in the cold light of Vesta and Pallas, crying. I couldn't go back to Alexei, even if the calculating gleam in Belikov's eye made me anxious. I couldn't go forward to Brody because I wasn't sure that was where I was supposed to be. I couldn't go to Lotus or Celeste either. How could I explain when they didn't know about the luck gene? Plus, I suspected Alexei would come after me once he'd calmed down and I didn't want to drag them into this. I didn't know what to do. Every direction was equally wrong.

Until it hit me. There was one place where I could feel protected, though it had its own inherent dangers. Even if my tech was old and crappy, my shitty c-tex bracelet could still reach anyone if I'd contacted them previously.

So I did the only thing I could think to do: I shimmed my grandfather.

20

Under-Secretary Vieira sent a flight-limo to collect me. It brought me to the house he'd rented while on Mars, just outside Elysium City in a posh district where other One Gov officials lived. Elysium City was the capital of Mars, primarily due to its proximity to the space elevator. Mars didn't have countries per se. Each city was more of a city-state, governing the surrounding area. Countries might come eventually, but not during my lifetime.

Because it was dark, I couldn't get a sense of the house other than it was big and One Gov hooahs patrolled the grounds. If Alexei wanted in, he could still manage it, but he'd also have to take on One Gov. I doubted he was that irrational.

Hooahs escorted me inside, each dressed in their standard-issue black uniforms and carrying a variety of weapons as if expecting an immediate attack. If I'd been in a different frame of mind, I might have rolled my eyes. Instead, I shuffled where I was led, barely taking in my surroundings.

Vieira met me in a formal office where it looked like he

might meet with other world leaders who could kiss his ring. It also looked like he was working. Given the time—the tail end of Witching Time—I thought it odd. Then again, Alexei was often awake most of the night working. The Under-Secretary probably kept a similar schedule. It made me realize this man, who practically ran the tri-system and had power over billions of lives, had come all this way to see me. And I was running to him all teary-eyed and pathetic because I'd just broken up with my boyfriend. I might have laughed at the absurdity of the situation if I didn't feel like dying instead.

He got up from behind a desk that looked to have been carved from a solid slab of granite and approached me.

"May I hug you?" he asked, his Portuguese accent softening the words. "You look like you need it, and I believe it's what grandfathers do."

I smiled weakly. "It might be stiff and awkward, but I guess it would be okay."

He pulled me into his chest and patted my back. Just as quickly, he let me go, though his hands remained on my shoulders. He peered down at me with green eyes unnervingly like my own.

"What has he done that's brought you to my doorstep in the middle of the night?" he asked gently.

I sniffed and rubbed an eye with the palm of my hand. I sort of laugh-cried, as I swiped away the tears. "The long answer, it's complicated. The short answer, he lied. I shouldn't have come here but I didn't know where else to go."

"It's fine. I'm sure One Gov can stand against the Consortium a little while longer as you sort yourself out. Perhaps this will allow us an opportunity to learn about each other. Relationships can't be forced, but we are family so who can say? I've had a room prepared for you." Then he gestured behind me and turned me slowly. "Andreza will show you the way."

A young woman waited. She had dark olive-toned skin, and long brown hair styled into impossibly shiny waves that made me want to touch it. Her brown eyes were framed with lashes so long, I felt like I was being fanned every time she blinked. She was so fresh and pretty, especially given the late hour, I felt like a bag of crap beside her. I wondered if she was one of Vieira's three mistresses, then decided I had other nonsense I could occupy my thoughts with.

"Thank you for taking me in," I said. "I know it's late and this whole situation is awkward, so again, just...thank you."

He smiled again. "If family called in the middle of the night and asked for help, would you turn them away?"

The answer was automatic. "Of course not."

"There's your answer. You can thank me by letting Andreza take you to your room."

I gave him a watery smile. "Okay. No more thank-yous then."

"Exactly. I'll see you tomorrow. Good night, Felicia."

"Good night...What do I call you? Sir? Mr. Under-Secretary? Grandfather?"

He laughed. "Let's leave it at Felipe for now."

My bracelet vibrated on my wrist. Steeling myself, I looked at the screen. Alexei. I powered it down, leaving it dead on my wrist.

"You will need to speak to him eventually," Felipe said.

"I know, but not tonight."

"No," he agreed. "Not tonight."

I followed Andreza, swallowed up by One Gov and a family I didn't even know I had, resolving to deal with everything later. But first, I had to make it through tonight. And that, I knew, wouldn't be easy.

———※·◆·※———

Later turned out to be an entire week later because once I stepped inside the bedroom, I couldn't bring myself to leave. I didn't know what to do. Usually, I relied on my cards or my gut feeling to direct me. No matter how deeply I wallowed in my own misery, I could always come up with a plan.

This time, nothing. I had no ideas. No strategy. No cards. No gut feeling. No way to deal with the situation. All the tricks and tools I'd used in the past felt like they'd betrayed me. I saw myself as a stupid pawn who made bad decisions, picked the wrong men, and bumbled through life without learning anything from my mistakes. Where were the great lessons I should have learned these past twenty-six years? Oh yeah, don't trust liars. And definitely don't fall in love with them. Well, too late. I'd done both of those things with spectacular results.

I wanted Alexei and I hated him. I missed him with a pain that made me ache, a pain worse than anything I'd experienced a year ago because, then, I hadn't loved him. Now I did and that made the agony crippling. I hated myself because I'd fallen for his lies all over again. I hated Brody too because he'd brought this chaos into my world and showed me how the life I'd thought was perfect was really a sham.

And now I was stuck on Mars, jobless, homeless, and broke. I had nothing but the clothes on my back and my c-tex bracelet. I didn't even have Granny G's cards. I don't think I'd ever been in more of a mess in my life. It was actually astonishing to me how far I'd fallen—from everything to nothing in mere minutes.

These were the thoughts that chased themselves in my head as I lay in bed for a week and ignored the world. Throughout, Andreza brought me meals whether I wanted them or not, silently taking them away when I couldn't eat. My new grandfather made a few efforts to talk, but mainly left me alone. So long as I didn't die in my room, it seemed I could take whatever time I needed to recover.

Eventually, I got up. I felt too gross and sore to lie in bed any longer. Plus, I was bored of my own company. I took a shower in a bathroom as big as my entire condo back on Earth, and lathered up with expensive soaps and shampoos that probably cost more than I made in a month. When I was done, I discovered the ever-helpful Andreza had been in my room, opening the curtains, selecting clothes for me to wear, and leaving more food. I ate part of the sandwich, all of the dessert because I liked chocolate, most of the tea just because I was thirsty. Then I put on the pale cream-colored linen shift and wedge sandals. The shift was pretty, belted at the waist and dotted with pink and white flowers, though it made me feel like I was ten years old.

I glanced down at my c-tex bracelet. I had no desire to turn it on and deal with the real world. Instead, I went in search of my grandfather.

The house wasn't as big as I'd first thought. It was also sparsely decorated, giving the impression of a hotel, not a home. Perhaps that was the case—a residence to be used only when bigwig One Gov officials were in town. There were bouquets of flowers on fancy little tables, lots of marble and stonework and pictures on the walls, but no sense anyone lived there. In a few places, I found One Gov sentries keeping watch. Their eyes flicked over me, but they mostly ignored me—something that might have freaked me out if I hadn't lived these past few months with chain-breakers watching my every move.

I found Felipe outside, on the edge of a massive rose garden that encompassed half the property. The sky overhead was a gorgeous, cloudless blue and the sun was warm as it beat down on us. No Phobos in the sky, which was something of a relief. I don't think I could have handled the uneasy feeling I now had in my gut whenever I saw Phobos overhead. Roses bloomed in a variety of colors and a cobblestone footpath wended its way throughout the garden. From the look of it, I could probably walk for hours before I reached the end of the path.

Felipe was dressed in a faded blue shirt and beige pants with dirty knees, pruning roses. He wore a hat to shade him from the sun and gloves to protect his hands from the thorns. The sight of arguably the most powerful man in the tri-system cutting roses stopped me in my tracks. It was so unexpected and, quite frankly, normal, I wasn't sure what to make of it. And the thing was, he looked like he knew what he was doing. More surprising, he seemed to be enjoying himself.

He grinned as I approached. "Glad to see you've finally decided to join me."

"I needed a change of scenery," I admitted. I gestured to the roses. "Aren't there drones to do this?"

"There are, but I find it restful. We have roses at home, and I tend them when I have a chance. I like the idea of cutting away what's faded to make room for new growth. Something about it appeals to me. I had these roses transplanted from home, but truthfully, I've only ever enjoyed them a handful of times."

"Are you going to prune the whole garden?" I asked, my gaze taking in the roses in their entirety.

"I might. It depends on how long my trip here lasts."

I nodded as if I had thoughts on the matter. "As soon as you're finished, you'd probably have to start pruning the whole thing over again. It's probably easier to leave it to the drones."

"Yes, but not as satisfying." Then he looked me over as if considering. "Would you like to help?"

I shrugged. It wasn't like I had anything else going on. "I wouldn't want to kill them. I've never had a garden. I couldn't afford the space, and condos aren't really conducive to growing things. Granny G—that's my great-grandmother—sometimes had a vegetable garden back in Nairobi if we lived anywhere long enough. I helped when I was little, though I probably got in her way more than anything."

"I'm sure she appreciated your help," he said kindly. Then he directed my attention to the rosebush in front of me. "It's not as difficult as you think. Besides, these are hardier than what's back on Earth. Much tougher to kill. Let me show you how it's done."

So he showed me where to cut and what to trim, how to open up the plant to let in light and let air circulate, at what angle to cut and to never leave a ragged edge. I went back inside and changed into something more appropriate for gardening. I tied back my hair so it wouldn't get caught in the thorns, was given a pair of pruning shears and a basket for my clippings, then set to work in my grandfather's garden.

Pruning roses was a different sort of workout than the gym.

Lots of kneeling, crouching, and bending over. My back was aching within twenty minutes. Added to that bit of nastiness, I was jabbed by thorns at least half a dozen times. Those little bastards poked right through the gloves, getting their revenge on me without a care in the world. But it was mind-numbing and oddly satisfying to make a rosebush take shape. It was also pretty and smelled like heaven. Being surrounded by all those colors and having to do nothing but decide where and when to cut was soothing.

Time passed, and at one point, I realized I was alone. I looked around, unnerved by the utter stillness with nothing more than me, the roses, the breeze, and the sun. Oddly, I felt like I was on display even though I knew I was alone. Shaking off the feeling, I went back to work because I wanted to get to the end of the section I was pruning. It was really starting to take shape and actually looked like I knew what I was doing. I looked back at the pink roses with an enormous feeling of satisfaction. I could see why Felipe would find this enjoyable. Maybe I should think about growing roses when I got to... Well, when I got to wherever I was going to end up.

By the time I'd finished, Felipe returned and told me it was time for dinner, which shocked the hell out of me. I checked my c-tex before remembering it was off—no wonder I'd lost track of time. My back and legs were aching, but it was a pleasant ache. It probably wouldn't feel so pleasant later when my abused body demanded to know what the hell I'd been doing with it, but for now, it was nice.

"I'd like to do this again tomorrow if that's okay," I said, watching as the sun cast longer and longer shadows along the ground.

Felipe grinned. "I think that can be arranged."

I pruned roses with my grandfather, the Under-Secretary for One Gov, for the entire week. When I asked him if he had other things to do, he admitted he could still check on work via the CN-net. Besides, a little time off never hurt anyone. Sometimes he went away and left me on my own for stretches of time. Others, we worked companionably together. We didn't talk much, and when we did, it was about roses. Or he'd tell me about his childhood on Earth. He was actually very funny, with a sense of humor I could appreciate. And when I did think about Alexei, it was in the few minutes before I fell into an exhausted, dreamless sleep.

I was disappointed when we finished pruning, and it seemed that once you were done, you didn't need to start again. It would probably be another few weeks before the roses needed tending. But by the time we were done, I also knew I couldn't keep pretending the rest of my life didn't exist.

We were having dinner that night, just the two of us, when Felipe said, "There's a problem on Venus I'd like your help with."

I looked up from my re-molecularized pork tenderloin, which was a thousand times better than anything I'd ever cooked myself, and stared at him. "I'm not sure how I could help."

"Perhaps all I'm looking for is a second opinion," he said. "There's a village in Aphrodite Terra, settled before the region could be properly mapped. They're stubborn on Venus. Left too long to their own devices, the colonists tend to run wild. It's like the American Old West there sometimes."

"I'm sorry, but I'm not familiar with that period," I admitted.

"Suffice it to say that they're reckless, headstrong, and can take advantage of a situation when no one's watching. I've been focusing more on issues with the Consortium than Venus, so I'll admit I haven't been giving events there my full attention."

I stiffened at that. "What's going on with the Consortium?" Even if I was upset with Alexei, if something bad had happened, or if my reading had suddenly come true, I wasn't sure what I'd do.

"I'm not entirely sure," he admitted. "There are rumblings on the CN-net, and of course there are always spies and double agents, but it's difficult to be certain."

"Is Alexei…Do you know if he's okay?"

"So far as I know, yes. And he still heads the Consortium, but there are issues with the mines. The incidents are isolated, but messy. People are dying. Resources aren't in jeopardy yet but the violence is escalating and we think the problem stems from within the Consortium's ranks. Unfortunately, my sources are only so good."

"It's because that snake Belikov is here," I muttered, stabbing at my food, nearly knocking it off my plate.

"That's entirely possible. But I'd like to talk to you about Venus and my village on Aphrodite Terra."

I tried to refocus and not let myself worry about Alexei. His problems weren't my concern anymore. Yeah, right.

"So what about Venus?"

"As I said, they settled in an area before it was properly surveyed, and now it appears they're on a fault line. A very dangerous and potentially active one. Do we forcibly relocate them or let them take their chances? If we leave them, they could die if there's a shift in the tectonic plates. If we move them, we risk making an already troublesome group even more rebellious. It won't be easy to relocate them, but if a quake hits, then what? We've already weighed the costs of both scenarios, but we can't predict what might happen."

"But you think I could?"

He shrugged. "Merely asking a hypothetical question."

I eyed him warily. "I don't have my cards."

"If you did, could you determine the best outcome?"

"Probably."

"I only want to find the solution with the least number of causalities. But I also understand your reservations. I don't want to pressure you. I'm merely asking you to think about what the result could be."

I sighed. "I'm not opposed to using my luck to help others. That's what I do in my Tarot readings, after all. And it's what Monique did when she created…" I let the sentence fade, not sure how to finish it.

"I know what she did," he said gently. "Is that why you left Petriv? Was he using you to read for the Consortium?"

I hung my head. "No. He never asked me to read for him, though I did it anyway. He didn't want me to think that's why he was with me."

"Ah. Well, he's a better man than I imagined. Better than I am, and I'm your own flesh and blood. I shouldn't be taking advantage of you. I'm sorry for asking this of you."

"Don't worry. My family uses me all the time. It's what they do for kicks, I think."

"And I'm doubly sorry to hear that. It seems Petriv may have been the only one not using you."

That startled me, and made my heart jolt unexpectedly in

my chest. I sniffed, looking down at my plate. "I left Alexei because we can't have a baby. More specifically, he can't with me or with anyone apparently, and he lied about it. He let me think we had a future together and...and we didn't."

He reached across the table and took my hand in his. "If I may speak so boldly, you know he did it because he didn't want to lose you."

"He still lied," I said stubbornly. "That's the one thing I asked him never to do, but he did it anyway."

"But it must have been difficult for him knowing he couldn't give you what you wanted most. Perhaps he thought the lies were justified if it kept you with him. Fear can make even the smartest among us do very stupid things, and Petriv is more intelligent than most. It would be challenging for anyone in your situation. I doubt many relationships would pull through unscathed under that sort of pressure. It must have terrified him knowing he couldn't give you everything he thought you wanted."

I gasped at that, finally realizing what Felipe was saying and what I'd been too upset these past few weeks to see. I'd been so angry Alexei had lied to me, just like he was always lying, I couldn't see my own faults. I'd treated him the same way Dante had treated me when I'd told him about my blacklisted status. Instead of supporting Alexei, I'd left him just as I'd been left. I thought Dante and I would be together forever, yet when he'd learned the truth, he told me we were finished and smashed my heart into a million pieces. And now I'd done the same to Alexei.

At least my blacklisted status could be revoked. He had less control over his situation than I did. For Alexei, there was no changing who he was. He'd been afraid to tell me because he thought I couldn't accept it. And once again when I learned the truth, I'd run away. Even worse, I'd been turning to Brody this whole time, pushed by a gut feeling I had to fight to ignore, because he was the quickest route to securing whatever it was luck thought I needed. And Alexei had watched helplessly as it unfolded under his nose because he didn't know how to prevent it from happening.

"Oh gods, how could I do this to him?" I whispered, tears rising. I swiped at them with the napkin from my lap. "I'm a horrible person."

"Not horrible. Just confused and hurt." Then he was quiet, holding my hand while I reined in my emotions. "May I tell you something?" I shrugged, not trusting myself to speak. He must have taken that as a yes because he continued with, "My daughter was gifted. Extremely intelligent, perhaps to a fault. And yes, it may have driven her insane. I think she found it frustrating dealing with us mere mortals. While I've read her research, even I don't understand everything she wanted to accomplish. However, one thing she knew with certainty, and it bore out in all her research, was the luck gene always struck true wherever it was applied. And she believed with absolute conviction, as odd and as twisted as this may sound, that you and Petriv could have a child."

That brought my head up. "How can you be so sure? The Consortium's been studying this for years. Wouldn't they have considered this by now?"

"Unlikely, since they didn't have access to you or Monique's research. And if I may say it without sounding like a boastful father, I would trust my daughter's genius over any Consortium think tank."

It made sense, but none of it explained my gut reaction to Brody. How did he factor into this? If I could have the future I wanted with Alexei, why did I feel pushed in another direction?

"I can see you're skeptical. If I may offer one more piece of unsolicited information, I know Konstantin Belikov. I've tangled with him for decades and I hate that man as much as I respect him. If he thought it would give him an advantage, he would withhold information as he saw fit. How do you really know you and Petriv are incompatible if you only trust the Consortium's word? How do you know Belikov isn't lying?" Then he let go of my hand, retreating to his side of the table. "I'm not certain Alexei Petriv is the right man for you, but I do think he loves you, despite his many faults."

I was silent, staring at my dinner on my very fancy and probably very expensive plate with its One Gov emblem on it, thinking about nothing and everything. "Can I ask you how you know Brody Williams?"

Felipe looked surprised, as if I'd thrown him a curve he wasn't expecting. "Is there a reason you're asking?"

"Just curious why he seems to be involved in all of this."

He thought a moment. "Well, at one point he was up and coming in One Gov's ranks. I remember him being brought to my attention because he had potential and his name was associated with yours. Even though Monique forbade me to contact you and kept your grandmother and me at a distance, I still had reports about you. When he was reassigned to Mars, I lost track of him. Frankly, since he was out of your life, I stopped paying attention. I found it odd he was with you again when we met recently, and when I investigated, I saw he worked for the Consortium. When I looked further, I noticed a three-year gap in his personal history. Whatever he's done during that time, I couldn't say."

I think my jaw dropped at that. Brody had three years of time that couldn't be accounted for? What the hell was going on? I pushed my plate away, no longer hungry and more stumped than upset. "Please excuse me, but I think I'm done for the evening. I should check my bracelet. I haven't turned it on in weeks. It's probably going to crash the CN-net once I start going through my messages. And... I need to think about what I'm going to do next. I can't stay here forever."

"There's always Earth," he suggested gently.

Yes, Earth was an option but I wasn't ready to run that far yet. "I should probably figure out things here first before I give up entirely."

"The offer is always open. And I'll be staying on Mars for a while longer. It's been at least a decade since I was here last and it's more interesting than I recall previously. I don't plan on making the return trip for at least another year."

I'm sure my eyebrows reached my hairline. "A whole year away from Earth? What about Secretary Arkell? Or your wife?"

"They'll make do without me. I have no doubt of that." Then he shrugged and grinned at me when I continued to stare. "What can I say? Things are happening and I'd hate to miss them. Besides, it will give us time to get to know each other, and that isn't such a bad thing."

"I guess not," I said slowly. "I assume we're not going to spend all our time pruning rosebushes."

"We have over twenty years of ground to cover. The topics we could discuss are limitless." Again the grin, and again I could see how the man had three mistresses.

"If I had my cards, I could look into that Venus issue for you," I said finally.

"I'll see what I can do. I confess, I would be interested in the answer."

"Someday, I'll have to read your cards for you," I said, getting up from the table.

He laughed. "I'm actually afraid of what you might see." Then his expression grew thoughtful. "Before you go, I wondered if I could invite you to a charity gala being held tomorrow night—if you're feeling up to it. It's a One Gov–sponsored event and I'd like it if I could introduce you as my granddaughter."

I wondered how long he'd wanted to ask, but been afraid to broach the subject. It wasn't like galas sprung up overnight. I could think of a hundred reasons why going would be a terrible idea. Reasons I'm sure he already knew and probably some I hadn't even thought of yet. I decided to see him as a lonely man full of regrets who wanted to reach out to me rather than everything else he was. Maybe I'd feel differently in time, but right then, I couldn't bring myself to dwell on what his faults might be.

So I said, "I'd say yes, but I don't think I have anything in my closet that says 'charity gala.'"

He looked so relieved, I almost laughed. It loosened some of the tightness in my chest that my answer made him so happy.

"I could get you a dress."

"And it's only One Gov personnel attending?"

"Primarily One Gov, yes. It is still a charity event, sponsoring reef and coral seeding projects in the Utopian Ocean. Anyone with enough gold notes to donate would be invited."

But if it was a One Gov event, it was unlikely anyone from the Consortium would be there just on general principle alone.

"All right then," I said as I powered on my bracelet. As anticipated, it started vibrating so violently, I took it off, set it on the table, and watched it dance across the granite. "Looks like I'm going to the gala."

21

As soon as I saw the dress in my closet, I was breathless with excitement. It was white, strapless, flared at the knees, and embellished with sea foam green crystal flowers that started at the waist and grew more plentiful at the bottom until it resembled a sea foam green garden. It looked like something I'd once marked in a CN-net target ad—something I could never afford and only drool over from afar.

When I worked up the courage to examine the laser-stamp inside, I saw it was a House of Christien original—the most prestigious fashion house on Mars. I immediately jumped back from the dress, afraid my unworthy presence would contaminate the very air around it. Obviously being One Gov Under-Secretary had more perks than I realized. Then because I couldn't stay away, I approached carefully and gently petted the fabric, helplessly in love. To wear that dress, I would have gone anywhere and done anything Vieira asked. I sighed at how easily I was consoled by something so frivolous. Even as my world fell apart, show me a pretty dress and I was happy—at least for a little while.

I also found open-toed platforms, their heels cleverly constructed crystal flowers that echoed those on the dress. I put them on and spent more time than I cared to admit admiring them in my room's full-length mirror. At that point, I realized I'd need a complete physical overhaul. After two weeks of letting myself go, I was a mess. I found Andreza and explained my dilemma. Within an hour, she arranged for an army of professionals to whip me back into shape.

I spent the afternoon enjoying a spa day, all without leaving the comfort of my room. First an all-over skin renewal treatment to eliminate the redness and swelling from my two beesting welts and the numerous thorn scratches covering me. Next, a massage. Then a skin-softening bath using a trendy new glitter finish I'd never tried. After that came nails, hair, and makeup, until I couldn't keep track of the parade of people fawning over me. It was so over-the-top frivolous, I wished Lotus were there just so I had someone I could roll my eyes with. Somewhere between the laser touch-up to my bikini area—which had been unnecessary in my opinion—and the little sandwiches with their crust cut off that tasted like heaven, my Tarot cards were hand-delivered to me.

The last time I'd seen them was two weeks ago, spread out on Eleat after the family picnic, in the hopes I could air out the burnt smell. I'd had a vague fear I might never see them again. Yet there they were—in a brand-new travel case, no less. They'd been nano-dipped so the smell was gone and the colors were vibrant and crisp. Somebody, and it wasn't me, had made sure my cards were restored to pristine condition.

I let out the breath I'd been holding, trying not to burst into tears. I'd like to think Felipe had arranged it, but that was unlikely. Only Alexei knew how particular I was about Granny

G's cards. Only he would have done this. I had another unsettling thought: How had Felipe even gotten my cards? Were he and Alexei *talking* to each other? About me? Now there was an uncomfortable feeling.

When I had a free moment, I laid a spread to answer Felipe's Venus question. At first, the task seemed daunting. This issue was so important, I was terrified I might make a mistake. What variables should I consider? What card would be the Significator? Could any one card represent a whole town? The more I pondered how to tackle it, the most excited I became. I'd never done a reading like this before, and certainly nothing that could affect so many lives. When I finally worked out how I wanted to proceed, I dealt the cards. What I saw made me frown. Things didn't look good for the colony on Aphrodite Terra. They needed to be moved within the next few weeks to a month or people would die. I sent Felipe a shim with my results and told him I'd explain when I saw him.

Eventually, my spa army finished fussing, leaving me to marvel at myself in the mirror. I was afraid to move because, frankly, I worried I'd ruin something. I looked amazing and that was saying something, considering I had no genetic modifications except what I'd inherited from my mother. I knew I was pretty and fit within One Gov's genetic specifications, but I wasn't in the same league as women with actual beauty MH Factors. But right then, I could compete with the best of them.

The dress was perfect, clinging to all the right curves. It was surprisingly light, considering the crystals weighing it down and how it swept along the floor. You couldn't see my shoes, which was too bad since they were so cute. Aside from a few tendrils to frame my face, my hair had been pulled back at the base of my neck into a heavy knot, secured with a wreath of sea foam roses. One of the beauty army attendants had wanted to tint my eyebrows and eyelashes sea foam green—color matching was all the rage. I'd vetoed it and insisted my makeup be kept light and natural. The dress looked and felt like a summer's day, and I wanted the makeup to reflect that. Besides, the glitter bath had my olive-toned skin glowing enough already. I knew drama, but I also knew stupid. I was the Under-Secretary's granddaughter, and now wasn't the time for green eyebrows. Lastly, I wore a necklace and earrings that sparkled in the light—the perfect finishing touch. That, and my c-tex bracelet currently vibrating on my wrist.

When I'd turned it on last night, it had vibrated the whole evening as it struggled to load the shims I'd received over the past two weeks. Some were from family, especially Lotus, who sounded nearly rabid that she couldn't reach me. Others were from former clients wanting to book private appointments. There were some from Brody, wanting to know if I was okay. But the majority were from Alexei—more than I had time to read even if I dedicated several hours to the task. They were of various lengths, coming at all hours. Telling me he missed me. He loved me. He was sorry. He wanted to see me.

In some, he talked about his worries regarding Konstantin. Then, what he thought of the new homunculus. Or how he'd almost cracked Konstantin's memory blocks. I felt his growing sense of disillusionment with the Consortium's aims and how they had changed from what he'd always believed them to be. Some shims were about what he had for lunch, what he saw in front of him, or what he was doing in a particular moment— just random observations he wanted to share.

And lastly were the shims that were downright pornographic. In them, he described things we'd done together and things he still wanted to do to me in such graphic and explicit detail, I felt myself flush. But that was unsurprising, given his advanced t-mods and memory blocks. He could recall everything with a clarity I couldn't, and he'd filled up a significant portion of his memory blocks with thoughts about...me.

I had to stop reading because there were just too many, with more still incoming. I could have blocked him or told him to stop, but I didn't want to. I just wanted...I didn't know what I wanted. I was upset, confused, and still in love with him. Sorting my feelings for him in light of Felipe's revelations would be a problem for tomorrow.

It was nearly 6:00 p.m. when I declared myself ready. Tonight, I'd be Felipe Vieira's granddaughter and see what I thought of the role. For now, I had to get through the gala. It included a dinner, a dance, and a charity auction. The last time I'd been to something like this, it had been a year ago on Earth and ended in disaster. Hopefully this didn't go the same route.

Felipe stood at the bottom of the staircase, his hands behind his back as he paced. With him was an army of One Gov hooahs in their black dress uniforms rather than the more militant, shoot-'em-up ones I was familiar with.

He stopped pacing and smiled at me, holding out a hand for me to take. I caught more than one of the male One Gov hooahs staring at me before they resumed their perimeter sweep, or whatever it was they did. Yeah, that's right—I may not have had an MH Factor, but I could rock an amazing dress.

"You look beautiful," he said, kissing my cheek. "I can see I'll have my hands full keeping all the fools away from my granddaughter tonight."

I laughed. "Don't worry. I can handle fools so long as they're not too persistent. Then, I might ask you to have them arrested." I said the last bit gesturing to the hooahs.

He grinned and, in a conspiratorial tone, said, "I'm worried they might be part of the problem." Then in a more normal voice, he said, "Tonight my only interest is getting to know my granddaughter. This will be fun, I think."

I forced myself to return his grin. "I hope so. Today's been incredible so far and now I'm wearing the dress of a lifetime. I love it, by the way. Thank you."

"You're welcome, and I'm glad you liked both it and today. I admit to having help since I'm not entirely versed with what you might enjoy."

My grin faltered a little. There was only one person on Mars he could check with and that wasn't something I was ready to acknowledge yet. "Well, thank you for taking me in and giving me time these past two weeks. I'm not thanking you for the bee stings in the rose garden, though. I could have done without those."

He smiled down at me, his green eyes crinkling at the corners, as he tucked my arm around his. "You're welcome, bee stings excepted, of course. And I want to thank you for the card reading. I've already spoken to my staff. Evacuation will commence once word reaches the outpost in Ovda Regio. Probably within the next sol."

I blinked. "That fast?"

"You said we only had a few weeks to act."

"But what if I'm wrong and those people are uprooted for nothing?" I protested, flabbergasted. My readings had never actually impacted so many people, so quickly. This was a level of influence I couldn't even imagine.

He arched an eyebrow. "And are you often wrong?"

"Not really," I admitted.

"In that case, look at the lives you've saved. You're just thrown off by the scale. When it comes to dealing with the tri-system, you need to think big."

"But..." I couldn't think of a compelling argument to use against him, because I couldn't wrap my head around the scope of what he was saying.

"I know I said I was ashamed to ask you to use your gift this way, but consider what you could do for the tri-system. I think all of us, and One Gov in particular, could benefit from your skills. If you came to work for my office, you could influence billions of lives for the better."

I stared at him, not sure if I was horrified or amazed. "Are you offering me a job as part of One Gov?"

He paused, considering. "I suppose when you put it that way, yes, I am."

"Doing what exactly? I'm just a Tarot card reader. I don't have any MH Factor or t-mods. I barely fit into One Gov society as it is. I'm not qualified for whatever you're suggesting."

"I disagree. With your gifts looking out for the fate of humanity, I don't believe there's anyone in the tri-system more qualified than you to guide One Gov into the future. The ideas behind One Gov are sound, but there are many who believe it needs fixing. Perhaps you might be the one who could do it."

The idea was so staggering, I could only nod mutely.

"And if One Gov reached a compromise with Petriv and the Consortium over the future of the tri-system, it would be due to your influence. You would be what binds us together. You do realize that, don't you?"

"I never thought about it that way," I admitted, or maybe I had but on a level so vague and nebulous, it didn't count as a real thought. Yet now that he'd flung the idea out there, it seemed... exciting. Scary, but exciting. My gut seemed to agree.

"Well, take some time and think about it. Helping to settle the unrest in the tri-system might not be such a bad way to use your talents."

Wow. I felt like I stood on the cusp of something so potentially huge and life-changing, I didn't even know where to begin. Something that was so far beyond my current world of Tarot card readings for dogs and their idle-rich owners, it was like I was trying to look at the whole universe using only a magnifying glass. Could I do this? Did I even want to? Then again, how could I not? If there was a way to make things so that no one ever went through what I had because of One Gov, or ensure no one felt like a second-class citizen, I had to do it. If I could do more than tell people they were going to find love again or get that promotion at work... If I could actually, really help them...

So I nodded—hard enough that I worried I might shake the sea foam roses out of my hair.

My grandfather regarded me quizzically. "Is that a yes?"

I nodded again. Breathless. Excited. Not really caring about the details because I knew they'd work themselves out later. Only really knowing that I had to do this or I would regret missing this opportunity forever.

"Yes, it's a yes."

He grinned at me. "Good. Then let's celebrate and enjoy ourselves tonight."

With that, I was whisked away to the gala in much the same

way I'm sure Cinderella was taken to the ball, except I had a lot more to think about. And I was pretty sure I had nicer shoes.

⇒◆⇐

Our flight-limo was part of a multi-vehicle escort. When we arrived at Red Angel Center, hooahs surrounded us to the point where I barely saw where we were. I didn't even get a chance to see the famed Elysium light display bouncing out over the water, and only caught the signal lights of the space elevator in the distance. Vieira took my arm and kept me stepping along purposefully when I preferred to gawk.

Red Angel Center was *the* premier venue in Elysium City, hosting big money events for the Martian jet-setters, charity galas, some religious ceremonies, and Mars founding sol celebrations. I'd been there only once—when Mrs. Larken had thrown a "Welcome to Mars" party for her dog Puddles and cemented my unenviable status as the psychic dog whisperer. It was located on the edge of the Waterfront District, overlooking Isidis Bay, and surrounded by golf courses that boasted the longest fairways in the tri-system and numerous high-end hotels.

Inside the center, the hooahs kept a bubble of protection between us and the crowd. We were directed through a lobby with massive chandeliers dripping with ruby-colored crystals, in keeping with the red theme. The glossy-tiled floor alternated between red and white circular pattern blocks. Some of our hooahs dropped back, partially eliminating the wall between us and the rest of the world. I clung to Felipe's arm, afraid I'd be swept away by the crowd if I let go. I found myself with a glass of red wine in my hand courtesy of a glamorous woman in a skintight, floor-length red gown with what looked like angel's wings grafted to her back. She walked through the crush of people carrying a tray of glasses. I saw other such "angels" working the crowd, each carrying trays.

"Watch," Felipe murmured, his mouth close to my ear so he didn't have to raise his voice. "This is where things become interesting. Stay close. I don't want to lose you."

"Don't worry," I assured him, awed by the sheer number of people. "If I was any closer, I'd be in your pocket."

He laughed and I sipped my wine, which turned out to be the smoothest, most flavorful wine I'd ever tasted—so good, I knew there would be trouble if I didn't eat something.

"If anyone proposes marriage to you, tell them they must go through me first. I have to approve all potential suitors," he said.

I nearly choked on my wine. "No one's going to ask me to marry them. You can't be serious."

But there was no chance to say more because at that point, the crowd descended on us and I realized I was with the most powerful man in the room, if not the entire planet.

I lost track of how many people I was introduced to or how many men kissed my poor right hand. Wisely, I gripped my wineglass firmly in the other hand, preventing anyone from kissing it as well. Some slobbered. Some licked. Some had dry lips. Some were sweaty. After a while, all I wanted to do was wash my hand. I was examined like prized livestock. My breasts were ogled, the color of my eyes commented on, and my beauty praised until I think I threw up a little in my mouth. And I had no doubt they were all over my CN-net flat-file avatar, tagging it so they could harass me at their leisure. I received no fewer than six offers of marriage, and couldn't even count the offers to "date" me and show me the sights of Mars.

And while everyone I met had the same basic level of physical attractiveness thanks to One Gov's genetic standards, most of them repulsed me. I hated how they fawned over me or sidled up to Felipe, clearly hoping to gain his attention. They were so obvious, it was nauseating. I knew few were interested in me. I was just a means to gaining access to the Under-Secretary. Actually, the same happened with Alexei, but to a lesser degree. He'd made it clear from the outset I was off-limits and no one was to approach me. I had to make the first move. This smarmy group were so obvious, my intelligence felt insulted and I wanted to scream.

I didn't, which should have earned me karmic brownie points. Instead I smiled, made sympathetic noises, asked polite questions, and laughed when it was appropriate. Some were One Gov ministers of one department or another. Some owned industries that manufactured either agricultural goods or medical materials; it was hard to keep track of who owned what. However, what I did see was the influence and power Felipe wielded. I saw how he worked a crowd and turned on the charisma. The world rotated around him. No, three worlds actually, and this was the man Alexei needed to replace: my grandfather.

In that moment, I understood how caught in the middle I really was and how true Felipe's words were. My boyfriend needed my grandfather out of the way in order to take power. But I didn't want my grandfather out of the way, and I didn't want my boyfriend to be the one who did it. And now that I'd agreed to work for Felipe, I had been maneuvered into a position so confusing, I'd need an AI flowchart to decipher it.

I gulped my wine, my second glass of the evening. Not smart, and I could already feel it. I had two al-effect tablets in my clutch purse I could take to neutralize the alcohol. Maybe it was time I used them.

I set my glass down on a passing tray, plucked my other hand away from whoever's lips were kissing it, and announced I needed to refresh myself because, damn it, I needed to pee! That last bit I cleverly kept to myself.

"Forgive me, Felicia," Felipe said, looking amused as I cut the latest hand-kisser off mid-compliment. "We haven't even found our places. Some of my people will escort you and bring you back once you've finished. After, we can look over the auction items." He leaned in, kissed my cheek, and in my ear murmured, "Your grandmother would be thrilled to see you here, almost as thrilled as I am."

He then patted my cheek in the most paternal touch I'd ever received before sending me on my way. I turned, dazed, my hand going to my cheek as if I could somehow hold on to that touch. Wow. How the hell had I been affected by him so quickly? But the feeling was unlike anything else I'd experienced since saying good-bye to everyone I had ever known and coming to Mars. This was finding a grounded center in the middle of all the whirling chaos around me. In its own way, being with Felipe Vieira felt like I was with Granny G again. Different obviously, but so similar it made my heart ache. This was family. And family lasted. It mattered. I couldn't walk away from him. Whatever happened, this was one relationship I couldn't leave behind.

Three One Gov hooahs took positions around me—one in front, one in back, one on my left. The one to my left was a woman. I hoped she wasn't going stand watch over me while I peed. My shy bladder wasn't down with that level of closeness.

From previous experience, I knew the facilities were down a floor, close to the banquet hall. We headed in that direction, my hooahs effectively pushing back the crowd. No one stepped on my foot or jammed an elbow into my ribs. I also had enough space that even though I was weaving a little, I wasn't tripping over anyone.

We finally reached the top of the massive escalator that led down to the actual banquet hall. It was wide and quite long, with multiple handrails spaced throughout depending on where you stood. I paused, catching myself so I didn't plunge headlong to the bottom. My hooahs paused with me, waiting until I pulled myself together.

And that was when I saw him, in a place he had absolutely no business being—a One Gov–sponsored charity event— waiting for me at the bottom of the escalator. Alexei Petriv.

He wore a suit, but more fitted and formal than anything I'd ever seen him in before. It showcased his utter physical perfection from the broad shoulders, deep chest, and lean waist. The jacket was longer, hitting just above his knees, but couldn't hide the muscular thighs or the hint that there might be something else spectacular going on down there. But while everyone else wore light colors, he wore black. It made him looked predatory and dangerous, like a wolf standing in the midst of a flock of sheep. With his thick black hair slicked back from his face and his head tilted to watch me, I couldn't help but admire those sculpted cheekbones or the eyes a blue so vivid, I felt pinned in place.

Women walked by him, staring as they passed. He paid no attention, his eyes fixed on me, his hands behind his back.

Time stopped and I shivered under the intensity and the weight in that gaze. I knew he could track my every movement through my c-tex once I turned it on, but how had he known I would be at the gala? Felipe must have told him. It was the only explanation that made sense.

And after two weeks apart, he'd come for me at the first opportunity—right in the middle of a One Gov event. He wasn't stupid, but he was arrogant. Maybe he wanted to prove he could get to me whenever he wanted. Yet I could also see how he stood at the bottom of the escalator, making no move to approach.

It took a minute for my drunken thoughts to process it as I watched him, waiting. If I still wanted him, I had to go to him. He wanted me, but it couldn't be all him. No doubt that was why he'd let me run in the first place. I'd asked him to let me go, so he had. Now I had to decide if I wanted this. I had to make a move too, even if it was a single step in his direction.

He was a liar, a killer, and probably worse. But seeing him there, waiting for me to come to him...Gods, he was beautiful. He took my breath away and made me ache with longing. Had he really lied, or had he held back the truth because he'd been afraid to tell me, as Felipe suggested. Had his fear of losing me brought us to this? And was Felipe right? Could I have everything I wanted with Alexei? I used to be so certain of that. Certain he could give me everything I would ever want or need, despite who he was. How had I veered so far off course? How could my gut so willfully lead me away from what it had once wanted so badly? Was it possible to get that feeling back?

I reached out a steadying hand to the railing, using it so I could get my drunk and uncoordinated legs to cooperate with my brain. Tentatively, I put one foot on the moving step, afraid I'd lose my balance if I went too quickly but also worried I'd miss the second step if I took too long. I bit my lip and put my other hand on the railing until I clung to it like it was the only stable thing in the tri-system. Then miracle of miracles, my feet caught up to each other. Both were on the same step at the same time, moving in the same direction—down to Alexei. My eyes met his and I shrugged, embarrassed at my predicament. His expression softened and he took a step forward, no doubt to save me from falling on my face when I reached the bottom.

Except I didn't. A second later, the One Gov hooahs shifted around me. The rear hooah grabbed my arm and plucked me off the steps. I stumbled backward and nearly fell. One of the other hooahs set me back on my feet away from the escalator.

"Ms. Sevigny, we have reports of violence outside the Center. We need to move you and Under-Secretary Vieira to a secure location," the female hooah informed me.

I gawked at her. "What's happening?"

The hooah looked momentarily blank, presumably receiving intel of some kind. "Militants," she said. "We believe it's dissatisfied miners protesting the Consortium and One Gov crackdown after the bombing a few weeks ago."

I looked at her, confused. Crackdown? What was going on?

Before I could puzzle it out, I heard someone calling for me. My eyes flew to Alexei, but he was gone. My name was shouted again, more insistent this time. I turned to see Brody striding toward me, a determined look on his face.

He moved quickly, not quite at a jog, but something close to it. He also wasn't dressed for a charity gala. In fact, he looked like he was there for a straight-up break-and-enter. As he strode closer, I saw something in his right hand. Now I regretted my two glasses of wine; I had trouble following his movements.

When he was almost on top of me, I saw the stun wand. He caught two of my hooahs in the chest, hitting them with the wand. The woman and one of the men went down immediately as a bolt of electricity zapped through them, frying their t-mods along with most of their brains.

He spared the wand a brief glance before dropping it. Instead he took out my third hooah with a handful of punches to the stomach, too fast for me to see. The man crumpled, moaning in pain. Brody moved past, grabbed my wrist, and yanked me after him. When I stumbled in my platform heels, he jerked me mercilessly upright.

"Brody, what are you doing?"

"Don't fight me on this, Felicia," he threw over his shoulder. "Resist and you're a dead woman. Come with me and maybe you'll live."

"My shoes!" I protested. "I can't run in these things!"

But he said nothing, just dragged me after him and hauled me up when I fell. In seconds, my arm was on fire and felt like he might wrench it from its socket. He pulled us through the crowd, shoving aside anyone in his way. I tried to keep up, but my shoes and dress made it impossible. And it was all happening so fast, my brain couldn't process it. At least I was sobering up now that fear had adrenaline pumping through me. But I wanted him to stop and I wanted Alexei. And I wanted to know what the hell was going on.

We cleared the hall, veering down one empty corridor after another. Brody picked up speed, but it was too much. He sent me tripping over the hem of my dress to land hard on my knees and I heard fabric tear. I cried out in surprised pain, my eyes watering. He yanked me up again, looking like he might rip the offending dress right off me and throw me over his shoulder. His grip eased. The second it did, I yanked my wrist free and backpedaled away.

"Stop dragging me around like a sack of potatoes!" I screamed at him. "What the hell is wrong with you? Why are you even here?"

"I'm here because you need to get away from this place before it's too late and I'm the only one who can keep you safe," he snarled, grabbing for me again. "Not Petriv, not Vieira. I mean it, Felicia. Only me."

"I'm not going anywhere until you tell me what's happening! Safe from what?"

"Take another step with her, you die. Touch her again, you die. I've had enough of you. This ends now."

Alexei. He appeared behind Brody, less than ten feet away, so calm and cold, it would have terrified me if I didn't know him. Brody let out a frustrated sigh, looking like he wanted to be anywhere than where he was.

He turned to Alexei. "I don't have time to deal with you, especially not when it's your fault this shit-storm is even happening. You've put Felicia right in the middle of your goddamn mess, and you don't have a clue how to get her out of it. Get the fuck out of my way and let me clean up this disaster before she winds up dead. She's coming with me because at least I know how to keep her safe. It's more than I can say for what's happened to her on your watch."

Alexei's eyes narrowed. "I think I finally see what Konstantin wanted to achieve in bringing you here. I should have realized what you were when I couldn't access your memory blocks, and left you to rot in your cell. My mistake. One I won't repeat once I permanently remove you from her life."

"You can try, but I doubt you'll succeed. You'll lose her the same way you seem to be losing everything else."

"Brody, what are you talking about?" I demanded.

He ignored me, eyes fixed solely on Alexei. I had a feeling they were fighting over me, but not. That the antagonism ran deeper than jealousy, descending to a rivalry so basic and primitive, I didn't fully understand it. I may have been the catalyst and the spark that started this, but there was much more at stake than I could see.

In that moment, I don't think I existed for either of them. Everything else dropped away except for the two of them facing off against each other. I merely served as the audience, watching the conflict unfold. Then they were charging toward each other down the hallway. Alexei was on Brody first, landing a series of solid punches I couldn't follow. Surprisingly, Brody absorbed the blows and followed with his own hits. It sent the two of them sprawling and grunting down the corridor as they fought, exchanging punch after punch. Neither man went down, both giving as good as they got. There was nothing I could do. I couldn't stop them or make this insanity go away. I could only witness as the disaster unraveled.

Then I heard a familiar female voice behind me. One I couldn't immediately place, but recognized nonetheless.

"How predictably boring. Men are such stupid creatures," the voice said.

I turned and saw her. Novi Pazidor. Who'd come into my shop for a reading. Who'd tried unsuccessfully to kill me. I saw a syringe in her hand, barely registering it before I felt the pinch of pain in my neck. A few seconds later, dizziness hit and I swayed.

"You won't need this where we're going," she said, pulling off my c-tex bracelet. Then she snapped it in half and dropped it. She gestured to someone with her, a man I hadn't seen before. "Quickly. Take her."

I felt him grab me, and couldn't stop him. Couldn't do much of anything really. But I could get dizzier. So I did. And apparently, I could pass out, so I did that too. Seemed like I was doing that all the time lately—getting drugged and passing out. Must be my new thing. How lucky for me. I wanted to tell Novi that—that I was lucky, and she'd better watch out. Too bad she didn't seem to care. And frankly neither did I as I felt myself float away into nothingness.

―――◆―◆―――

I woke up in jail. Honestly, in fucking jail. *Again.* How many damned times in a person's life could she be drugged and have the awesome displeasure of waking up in jail?

I sat up on my dingy cot, feeling like my mouth was stuffed with cotton. There was one dim overhead light in my cell, showcasing its three gray cement walls. The other wall was bars, and through it was another cement wall. The air felt cool, stale, damp, and smelled vaguely of mold. I wasn't in my dress anymore. Instead, I wore a shapeless gray tunic and baggy pants. My feet were bare, but I found canvas slip-ons waiting for me. A quick check showed I wasn't wearing a bra or panties. Someone had stripped me naked and changed my clothes. Fan-fucking-tastic. There was a toilet in the corner, but I noticed I didn't have to go anymore, so obviously I'd pissed myself at some point. Even better. Worst of all, my c-tex bracelet was gone. I'd worn it every day since I turned twelve, and without it, I felt naked. Now I was basically a nonperson, less than no one. A true spook.

I couldn't decide if I was scared, mad, or a blending of the two. I eased off my cot with its lumpy mattress and stood carefully. A check of the bars showed the lock was secure. No escape there. My cell had a window of thick, scratched-looking glass, woven through with mesh to making climbing out impossible. Still if I stood on my cot, I could see outside. Maybe I could get an idea where I was. So I stood and looked and realized I had just slid from anger into sheer terror.

Out my window, I saw a blue-green orb, so close it filled the entire view except the topmost left corner. There I saw the blackness of space. For a moment, I didn't realize what I was seeing until Olympus Mons slid into view, its flattened caldera poking through the cloud cover and rising high enough to be seen from space. And as my head turned to watch until it sailed out of sight, that was when I screamed.

I wasn't on Mars anymore. I was on Phobos.

22

If I thought my screams would bring someone, I was wrong. Time passed, nothing happened, and I calmed down because I had no choice. I sat with my back to the window, arms looped around my legs, resolutely determined to avoid looking outside. I could only take so much. No need to kick-start a freak-out all over again.

So what did I know? Novi had kidnapped me. Her husband, or whoever, worked in the off-world mines and had a grudge against Alexei. The miners were rioting, so I'd probably been taken as a hostage to negotiate a compromise; otherwise I'd be dead. However, this assumed Alexei wanted me back and that wasn't a certainty. Not after the look I saw on his face when he'd launched himself at Brody. No, best not to dwell on that part.

Back to Novi. Obviously she had access to significant resources if she could crash One Gov's charity gala, grab me, and stash me in a cell on Phobos. Somehow Brody knew about it and had attempted to save me. The end result—me on Phobos in jail. Why hadn't he just told Alexei what he knew? Why couldn't they have worked together to prevent this? And what kind of angle was Brody working for him to know I was in danger? Did he have some connection to Novi and the miners? I had too many question and absolutely no answers.

I swore and resettled on my cot. None of this made sense. Worse, I hadn't run my cards in ages so I was completely in the dark. Maybe I wasn't a hostage. Maybe I'd just been removed from the picture and I'd never leave this cell. No, I couldn't think like that. Alexei would find me. I had to believe that or I'd go crazy. But did he know where I was? With my bracelet smashed, I was completely off the grid. All I could do was wait.

So I waited. And I dozed, stretched, paced, shook the cell bars just to be sure they were still locked, used the toilet, paced more, braided my hair, finger-combed it loose, rebraided it, and started the circuit over again. Out of sheer boredom, I looked out the window and could see Space Station *Destiny* anchored above the space elevator. I wondered how much time had passed since my abduction. Phobos circled Mars three times a sol, but also had its own rotation. How many times had Phobos orbited Mars so far? There was no way to know.

My first visitor came soon after that. Male, tall, and built like a brick, with short, dark hair and deeply tanned skin. It could have been Tru-Tan, meaning his skin had been artificially pigmented to protect it against the sun, but I didn't think so. He carried a tray of food, and when he bent to push it through an opening between the bars and the floor, I noticed tan lines on his muscular arms. Whoever this guy was, he wasn't a miner. He didn't have the pale, lanky look that came from spending a lifetime in low- to zero-g and no time in the sun. This was guy was hired muscle.

Dinner was watery stew with sketchy-looking meat, a plastic cup of water, and a moldy bun. Disgusting, but I was hungry and who knew when I'd get my next meal? I picked off the mold and dug the carrots out of my stew because I'd never been a fan of anything orange. The water I gulped greedily, wishing I had more.

My guard watched me eat, following my movements. He was recording me—something I wouldn't have realized if not for hanging out with Mannette Bleu's human PVRs. Either someone was watching me via live feed, or I was being recorded and the images would be downloaded from his memory blocks later. I wished I had something clever to say, but my mind was blank. Whoever the intended audience was, I was determined not to give them the show they wanted. Instead, I ate my food with all the poise I could muster. When I finished, I kicked the tray back through the slot. Then I lay down and studied the wall, running my finger along its cracks.

I knew my visitor was still there. Moments passed until finally he spoke. "They want you to say something."

Oh, did they? Funny how I couldn't feel much more than tired apathy. Too bad they'd caught me in between panic attacks. I rolled over, raised myself on an elbow, and said, "My fiancé will probably kill all of you for this."

Granted, I wouldn't be so cocky later if they tortured me or cut off body parts, but in that moment, it completely summed up my disdain. Then deciding it was the ultimate insult, I lay down, rolled to my side, and drifted off to sleep.

I woke to hands dragging me from the cot. That, and an annoyed male voice I didn't recognize.

"She really is a piece of work. Nothing but a spook but she's got the whole planet in an uproar. Rise and shine, princess. Time for her majesty to present herself."

Any other time, I would have dazzled my captors with a smart-assed comment for their enjoyment. However, I found that waking from a terrifying dream where I was locked in prison then rediscovering it was my new reality robbed me of the most basic comebacks.

I was placed on my feet in the ugly canvas slip-ons with my hands secured by unbreakable carbon ties. I shook my hair off my face so I could see what was happening. There were three other people with me—the asshole binding my hands who'd brought my dinner, the man who abducted me from the gala, and Novi. All wore black stealth gear and were decked out with a variety of weapons. They were clearly some kind of military unit, even Novi, who I'd once thought so young and naïve. Not anymore. She looked tough and merciless, making me wonder how I'd been so wrong about her. My cards could never lead me this far astray. I had to be missing something.

"Let me guess. The miners are hiring mercenaries to do their dirty work now?" I threw out, just to see what I'd hit. "They must be really desperate to get back at the Consortium if kidnapping me is their big plan."

The asshole who'd bound my hands snorted a laugh. "As if they could afford us."

What? I shot a look to Novi. "You're not connected to the off-world mines?"

"Nice to see you're follow along, princess," said the asshole.

He tapped the side of my head. "Was wondering if there was anything up in there."

Novi smirked at me. "We're connected. Just not the way you think."

That shook me. "But your husband…"

Another smirk. "So much for being a big-deal fortune-teller. Guess you don't know as much as you think you do."

I knew I should have been worried about whatever was happening next, but having Novi smirk at me just pissed me off. I tried to remember the reading I'd done for her all those weeks ago. "Okay, so not your husband. But I know there's a man controlling you, and you do whatever he tells you."

"We're all controlled by somebody, princess. Our somebody just happens to have access to a lot of gold notes."

I blinked. Mercenaries? Someone had hired mercenaries to abduct me and stash me on Phobos? And Brody had somehow known and tried to prevent it. What the hell was going on?

"Who do you work for? Who's paying you?"

Novi rolled her eyes like I was an idiot, then looked at the other two men. "Bring her. Let's go."

"At least tell me what happened to the baby," I blurted out before she could turn away.

That seemed to catch her off guard. "Not really something you need to concern yourself with, is it?"

No it wasn't, but her response did make me hate her. Well, I hadn't liked her after she'd tried to kill me; this was just icing on the cake.

I was jarred from my thoughts as my captors jerked me down the hall by my carbon ties and past a row of cells, all empty. Then we went through a series of locked doors and the cells were full.

It was here where the reality of my situation staggered me: The Phobos penal colony housed the most violent and reviled criminals in the tri-system. Their lives were regulated by a special branch of One Gov's AI queenmind that dictated all aspects of their pitiful existence. It was completely automated with little human interaction from the outside, because once you were on Phobos, the human race was meant to forget you existed.

The overhead lights were dimmed and the cells darkened to simulate night. I could hear light snores and heavy breathing as our little parade passed. However, some cell occupants were awake and watched us with interest. Explicit sexual suggestions were shouted, so crude they made me cringe. I tried to keep my eyes forward, back straight, and not look as scared as I felt, but I don't think I succeeded. Based on the catcalls, if I somehow ended up in one of those cells, it was unlikely I'd be heard from again.

"Why am I here?" I asked, tugging on my arms and digging in my heels. "How long are you planning on keeping me prisoner?"

No answer. Instead, I was yanked forward. My already aching arms screamed in protest and it took everything in me not to cry. Gods knew it wouldn't help and I wasn't letting these assholes know they were getting to me. Maybe it was time for false bravado to show up.

"I may not know what's going on, but I know you're going to fail. Whoever's paying you and whatever your plan is, you won't succeed. Everyone involved will die. I remember the final card now: the Tower. Everything you value in your life is shaking apart right now whether you acknowledge that or not."

From the asshole: "Shut it."

And to think he'd actually wanted me to talk earlier. Some people were never satisfied. For good measure, I threw in, "By the way, I'd like to add my predictions are *never* wrong."

That earned me a punch in the face. Not a hard one, more like a close-fisted slap, but enough that my head snapped back, I tasted blood in my mouth, and felt pain—stinging and sharp—spread across my upper lip, nose, and cheek. I saw stars when I went down. Wow, if my gut could warn me about exploding bombs, you'd think I could get a heads-up about a punch in the face. Apparently not.

"You weren't supposed to touch her," one of the men said. I couldn't tell who since my ears were ringing. "They wanted her unmarked."

"Amateurs. That's not how you get attention. You send back body parts and blood splatters, not pictures of her eating soup."

"I'm going to edit it out."

"No, leave it. Besides, she had it coming. I've wanted to do that for the past month," Novi said, sounding angry. "Slap a web-compress on her and she'll be fine. The orders were to subdue her. What does it matter how I did it? It's not like she'll leave here alive anyway." A pause, then, "Someone pick her up. Make sure you record that part too."

I was hoisted to my feet and thrown over someone's arm. Novi made a disgusted noise as if this was somehow special treatment. All it did was make my head hurt and spike the awful throbbing pain in my cheek.

The rest of the trip passed in a blur of pain and shock. Whoever these people were, I was nothing to them, and when this was all over, I would be dead. They were going to kill me. I couldn't get my brain to overcome the hurdle of that realization. Couldn't even figure out how to come up with a plan. And my gut...Forget it. No help whatsoever. Where the hell was my luck gene now?

I was dropped in a pathetic heap on the floor, and that upset me too. I always thought I was tougher. After all I'd been through, I really thought I could handle myself better. In fact, it annoyed me I couldn't. I tried consoling myself with a reminder that I was having a bad couple of weeks, but that didn't help. Well, maybe being annoyed at myself was better than nothing. Maybe it was better than crying.

I looked up, wiping blood from my lip with the sleeve of my prison uniform, wincing at the tender feeling on the left side of my face. Directly in front of me, at eye level, were bent knees. Someone was sitting and I'd been dropped at their feet. I pulled back and refocused. A floating chair. Then as I thought about it for a bit because apparently I wasn't at my most brilliant, I realized I was looking at a mobile-assist chair.

I tipped my head back to see Konstantin Belikov seated in front of me: my real life King of Swords. Gods, how could I have forgotten? That card had figured significantly in Novi's reading. At the time, I assumed it meant something else and now...I almost laughed, but didn't since the joke would have been on no one but me. The answer had been staring at me the whole time. I just hadn't realized it until now. It had always been Belikov pulling the strings and controlling the game. Always that fucking Russian kingpin.

With him were a couple of chain-breakers, two male members of the Consortium I vaguely recognized as having arrived on the *Martian Princess*, another handful of black leather military types, and Brody—who took looking furious to a level I'd rarely witnessed. Betrayal lanced through me. He'd said only he could save me, but now he was there working for the enemy. There could be no doubt of his connection to Belikov, even if I didn't know how it all fit together.

"She was supposed to be intact," Belikov said, throwing an annoyed look to one of the mercenaries—dark-skinned, close-cropped black hair, imposing build, lots of weapons.

"We know our job. We get results. If she's hurt, she brought it on herself," came the answer in a rough, gravelly voice.

"She was mouthy." This from Novi.

"You haven't even heard mouthy yet," I muttered, wiping at my face with my sleeve again. Still bloody, though it seemed to be just a trickle from my upper lip.

"You should have tortured her. Torture recordings have a guaranteed success rate," the man in black advised. "I don't care who they are or how many t-mods they have, there isn't a person alive who can stand by when they see a loved one being hurt."

"While I don't disagree, I need her intact," Belikov repeated. "That was my only stipulation. If this damages the negotiations and the experiments fail, your people will pay for it."

"Someone should pay," Brody said, staring daggers at Belikov.

"That's enough from you, Brody," Belikov said. "Your actions are becoming a hindrance. It would be a shame if everything fell apart when you're so close to achieving what you wanted." I didn't like the sound of that. I hauled myself to my feet. Now wasn't the time for lying on the floor when I needed to get ahold of my fear and get out of this mess.

"What does he get out of this? What the hell is even going

on?" I demanded. "You kidnap me and bring me to Phobos and...Whoa."

I stopped talking. Now that I stood, the view had suddenly become much more interesting.

We were in a large industrial space, full of machinery. I could see robotics and what looked like an assembly line, filled with thin metal frames hanging upright on a relay track, being fed into a series of machines. The frames looked human sized, but from my vantage point, I couldn't see what happened once they disappeared into the machines. Whatever the Consortium was building, they were making a lot of them. A lot of people-sized lightweight metal frames that needed nothing more than a coating of skin and hair to make them more...human. I gasped, putting the pieces together. A factory on Phobos where the rest of the tri-system couldn't see, with a pool of unmonitored labor—or raw material, depending on how you looked at it—to draw from. Human-sized machines. And since I was summing up the equation, for good measure I added in Alexei's programming subroutine that could connect a human mind to an AI and download it into another body.

I was looking at a damned homunculus assembly line.

Then I saw the black box, the one I'd watched the chain-breakers unload from the space elevator. Except now, the lid was off.

To be honest, I expected to see Mr. Pennyworth with his bowl-shaped haircut, sexless features, gray-black hair, and the all-purpose pantsuit. Not so. This homunculus was quite obviously male, naked with genitals fully intact, a muscular build, and short blond hair. Apparently some significant upgrades had been made, but it was no less horrifying.

I shot a look to Belikov. "I'm guessing you decided to reno-vate your new home."

"The homunculus you interacted with was a prototype," he said stiffly. "This is closer to the ideal we originally envisioned."

"Good enough for you to dump the dying human body you have now and live in it full-time?" I asked.

He gave a sharp, angry bark of a laugh. "Didn't your cards show you that?"

"They show me a lot of interesting things. You think I got this bloody lip from telling her everything would work out all sunshine and rainbows in the end?" I jerked my head in Novi's direction.

Belikov laughed again, a real one this time that ended in a cough before he settled. "It's such a shame Brody wasn't able to recruit you for the Consortium when he was given the task. As for occupying the homunculus on a full-time basis, we'll know better once Alexei conducts the appropriate field tests. I've grown tired of his delaying tactics. With you here on Pho-bos, I think he'll be properly motivated to perform."

He floated away on his mobile-assist chair while I stood rooted to the spot. I had no idea whether I was meant to follow. Instead, my mind kept looping back to what he'd said, trying to reconcile the words in a way that made sense. Brody was sup-posed to recruit me for the Consortium? *Recruit me?* My eyes flew to Brody, who was looking at me so hard, it was a wonder his words didn't project actual thoughts into my head.

Brody was a member of the Consortium? Had *always* been a member? But Felipe had said he was a rising star in One Gov.

"Is it sinking in yet?" Belikov asked in a tone of long-suffering patience from where he floated by the homunculus. "Do you understand what I'm saying, Felicia?"

The anticipatory look on his face sickened me, like he was enjoying smashing his favorite toy. The meaning in his words was clear, even if Brody's eyes said otherwise.

"Brody tried to recruit me for the Consortium in Nairobi?" I asked. But there had never been any mention of that between us.

"Yes, Nairobi. Don't forget: Your mother came to us first. She wanted the Consortium to support her research. We turned her away, but when the time was right, one of our operatives approached you. It was thought your luck gene might prove useful. Obviously he failed. In fact, it seems everyone I send after you fails. It's also shown me the luck gene can't be trusted. Its inherent selfishness and desire for self-preservation override everything else. And that's why, when this is done, you need to die. It infuriates me to no end that a woman as insignificant as you constantly ruins plans that have taken centuries to implement and finalize."

He waved one of the men forward and said something in Russian, too fast for me to catch. The man nodded, looked in my direction, and snapped his fingers. I was pushed to my knees in an unshakable grip.

"Years of bioengineering and genetic research all wasted because of you," Belikov continued, warming to his theme. "First Brody. Then Alexei. Then the homunculus project. The quantum teleporting. Everything that came near you was sucked into your orbit until it failed. It was as if you were One Gov's greatest weapon against us and they didn't even know it."

I looked at Brody, stricken. I'd always thought he'd been the one to help me get over Dante's rejection. And now to learn he'd been using me? That recruiting me had been his test to assuming the Consortium leadership just as Alexei's had been to win the Mars transit bid? Was it once again all lies? Gods, was there a man in the tri-system who *wasn't* lying to me?

"When he failed with you, he thought he could leave this behind. What he forgot is no one walks away from the Consortium," Belikov chided, throwing a glance in Brody's direction. "He may call himself Brody Williams and not bear the Consortium's markings as Alexei does, but inside, he's the same. He just happens to come from an earlier genetic stock."

I gasped softly. How was this even possible? Brody and Alexei were both experiments bred by the Consortium? And I'd been thrown into each of their paths. Suddenly I had to ask even if I dreaded the answer: "Vieira said Brody had three years of time unaccounted for. Where has he been?"

Brody's lips pressed together in a thin, hard line and he said nothing. Not that it mattered because Belikov was more than willing to share. "Why, here on Phobos, locked in a cell. As I said, no one walks away from the Consortium. Punishment was required for his failure. Since Siberia disappeared under the waters on Earth, we don't have gulags anymore. This penal colony was the best I could arrange under the circumstances. With a few tweaks to One Gov's queenmind, it was easy enough to have him arrested. Of course, getting him out wasn't as simple. I had Alexei break him out when I needed him again."

And now I had the answer to the question I'd forgotten I asked: Alexei had been on Phobos the night I'd witnessed the explosion in the sky. He'd been breaking Brody out of prison at Belikov's request.

"Why would Alexei agree to that?"

"Even I concede I created a tangled web for myself," Belikov lamented. "Sometimes my ideas don't always bear the fruit I anticipate, so I thought it best to revert to the original plan. Alexei was taking the Consortium down a path I didn't want it to travel. I couldn't control him any longer nor stop where all this was heading. Brody convinced me he regretted his past failures, so I decided a second chance was in order and brought back the only credible threat to Alexei's hold." He gestured to Brody. "Alexei may have suspected there were others out there like him, but he couldn't know for certain. I worked hard to keep them unaware of each other."

"So you told him some bullshit story that the Consortium needed Brody and Alexei broke him out of prison for you?"

Belikov looked impressed. "Yes, it wasn't as difficult as I thought to convince Alexei he needed help managing his Consortium responsibilities. Despite your uselessness, you really do have flashes of surprising insight. You must get that from your mother."

"Except with less crazy," I said between gritted teeth.

"But more annoyance," he added, laughing as if he'd just told the most hilarious joke. "Of course, Alexei mightn't have been so willing if he'd known he was freeing his rival. But after it was done, it was easy to keep him occupied. The threats to you, the unrest with the mining unions, and off-world tunnels collapsing—all carried out by mercenaries Alexei couldn't link back to the Consortium." He gestured to Novi and all the others dressed in their black leather and loaded down with more weapons than seemed necessary. Then he made another gesture to the factory and the machines with the half-assembled homunculi. "I couldn't have put this together if he was watching, could I?"

"And if Alexei is out of the way, does Brody know he's only holding the reins until you get your robot body and can take over the Consortium?" I asked, loading the statement with all the sarcasm I could muster.

Belikov looked thoughtful. "You're better at this game than I gave you credit. There may be something salvageable in you after all. We'll see in the next round of breeding templates." Then he sighed and murmured, "I'm tired of explaining myself to children. Someone silence her before her nattering kills me."

My nattering? I was immediately gagged by either Novi or one of the two men with her. My gold notes were on Novi.

With the bloody lip, pain throbbing through my cheek, and my fear cresting hard, it was nearly impossible not to hyperventilate. Looking at Brody hurt. I thought our time together had meant something. And now to realize how big and twisted this game was and how high the stakes were—it was frightening.

"Why isn't this working? Does Alexei need more incentive, or was I wrong about her importance to him?" Belikov mused, sounding frustrated.

"We could try it my way." That, from the dark-skinned man I guessed was leader of the mercenaries.

"Fine. See what your people can do."

A hand grabbed my hair, using it to yank my head up. My pained scream was muffled by the gag, but it didn't stop the hot, prickly tears from rolling down my cheeks. I was dragged face-to-face with the asshole who'd recorded me earlier. Only now, I understood the purpose: I was being recorded in all my pitiful misery as a personal invitation to the only person in the entire tri-system who could pilot the homunculus but, so far, much to Belikov's annoyance, had refused to do so.

The other two Consortium members were muttering softly

with Belikov while they stood over the black box. Abruptly, they jumped back. It didn't take long to figure out why.

The homunculus had opened its eyes and was slowly rising out of the box.

Everyone watched with a muted awe as the thing rose from its coffin. I know I was mesmerized as it pulled itself up on two feet. It stretched, as if its muscles were cramped from lying in the same position too long. Then it shook itself the way I'd seen dogs do when they were wet, before settling to stare passively at all of us.

It…He? I wasn't sure what to call it. I knew Alexei piloted the body and the body was obviously male, but it was still an *it* to me. It was tall—not as tall as the chain-breakers, but certainly tall enough. The skin was a smooth, golden color, and I could see the eyes were deep blue. It was decently muscled throughout and almost too well endowed. Definitely a step up from the Pennyworth model; Belikov had certainly gone for flashy the second time around.

"You took your time," Belikov murmured.

"There were issues with the connectors," was the answer, said in a low, deep voice.

"How do you feel?"

"Tolerable."

"Does it feel as if you could pass for human?"

It looked down at its hands, legs, and whatever else it could see of itself. "Perhaps. I can't be certain yet."

Belikov nodded with approval. "The key at this stage is to make the homunculus as human as possible, or the mind won't accept the transition. That was the problem with the previous model—it wasn't human enough. And of course, the toxin buildup from the energy source," he said, giving us all a science lecture nobody wanted. "Both are overcome this time. The energy source is self-contained and rechargeable, with built-in power nodes that link directly to the Consortium's net-interface. This model also has biological imperatives that give the pilot a sense of its own humanity. It will still feel hungry, though there is no need to eat. Food will be consumed and the by-products voided. Some energy will be gained, but it won't be the primary source."

As he spoke, the homunculus examined its surrounding. I couldn't take my eyes off it, unable to reconcile that this...thing was Alexei. I was having Pennyworth flashbacks, sickened by the wrongness of it. If I lived through this, I was going to put myself into the best therapy I could afford.

When it spotted me, it fixed me with a look so penetrating, I felt it creep along my skin. It made its way toward me, the gait unsteady, then moving with increasing confidence and speed until it stood in front of me. I shrank back into the hands holding me captive, going to my knees when my legs gave out. The fist in my hair tightened and I felt a metal tube pressed to the base of my skull. Great, if I moved another inch, Novi would blow my brains out.

I tried not to flinch as the thing touched me, moving a hand over my hair, along my skin, carefully grazing the tender area around my cheek. Fingers went under my chin, lifting my face. Its own face was expressionless, as if it hadn't figured out how to move the muscles. Even though the hand didn't feel like Alexei's, the way it tilted my head and the tenderness as the fingers trailed over me were the same.

I heard rather than saw Belikov float up beside us. "Do you want her?" he asked. "Physically? Emotionally?"

"Yes," it said honestly. "I want her very much." And it seemed to be the case too because at my eye level, I caught twitching in the genitals. Wonderful. I was giving it a hard-on.

Belikov clapped his hands, thrilled. "Then we were successful in replicating the human sex drive. This is excellent news," he said to anyone who cared to listen. I personally wasn't one of them and would have said so if I wasn't gagged.

As if reading my mind, the homunculus removed my gag, carefully lowering the cloth until it fell around my neck. When the hand pulled away, I saw my blood on its fingertips. The homunculus looked at it too, staring hard.

"I said she was to be unharmed," it said.

"So you did, but you can't anticipate every detail."

"No, you can't," it agreed.

As it spoke, it brought its other hand up to touch me, as if it couldn't leave me alone. This was familiar behavior—these constant touches and little strokes along my skin. Alexei did that when we were in public, silently communicating that he wanted me and planned on having me at the soonest opportunity. That the homunculus did it now freaked me out, yet it also reassured me Alexei was in there somewhere.

"Don't touch me like that," I whispered, trying not to flinch from its fingers as I gazed up at it.

"I'm sorry. The synthetic hormones running through this body amplify its responses so they're stronger than anticipated. Every urge and emotion feels magnified."

I nodded as if that actually made sense. "Don't let them turn what we have into a field test they can analyze after they kill me."

That stopped the touching. It nodded, then caught my

hands and scowled, the facial muscles finally working as it gazed down at the carbon ties binding my wrists.

It turned to Belikov. "So this is the direction you've chosen?"

"I will do whatever is necessary to ensure this project succeeds. *Prosti*, but it means using whatever resources are available."

"Then we have a problem, Konstantin. I was unanimously appointed head of the Tsarist Consortium. That means all issues are brought to me first. All projects come to me for approval. You have input, as do all members, but the final decision is mine."

The homunculus snapped my carbon ties as if they were nothing. Circulation resumed as blood rushed back into my hands, the tingling almost painful. I flexed my numb fingers, trying to shake off the sharp, itchy ache.

"Do you believe your decisions outweigh the wisdom of nearly five centuries?" Belikov scoffed. "An organization as old as ours shouldn't be led by one so easily manipulated by a pretty face. There are billions of others like her who would willingly spread their legs for you. When you realize where your real responsibilities lie, maybe you'll be ready to truly lead the Consortium."

The homunculus shook its head, a scolding look on its face. "You may not be aware of this, but I cracked your memory blocks a week ago. I also spent considerable time sifting through the data."

I was pulled to my feet in one swift movement. The tube pressing against my neck and the fist clutching my hair disappeared, and I heard shouts around me. Next I heard the sounds of a weapon being discharged dangerously close to my head. A second later, the homunculus held a plasma disrupter in its hand, looking at it in annoyance. Had the homunculus just shot everyone with Novi's weapon? From the sound of the groans behind me, the answer was yes.

"Seems like overkill," it said.

"How did you move so quickly?" Belikov asked. "The limiter should have prevented it."

"Did you miss the part where I said I cracked your memory blocks? I've disengaged the limiter. This homunculus has some impressive features I'm interested in using. Allow me to give you the field test you wanted. Brody, take her," it said, letting me go.

I felt arms around me, dragging me out of the way. I struggled against them, twisting enough to see Brody.

"Stop fighting me, Felicia!" he barked. "We need to get out of here!"

"I'm not going anywhere with you, you lying scumbag!"

"We're leaving, even if I have to knock you out and carry you. Who do you think will rescue you while Alexei deals with everybody else?"

"Drop her!" shouted Novi, rounding on us and pulling something from her belt. Probably another plasma discharger.

Before she could fire, the homunculus was already there, knocking it out of her hand. Everybody scattered. At the same time, I saw movement on the other side of the warehouse space. The lightweight frames on the assembly line were climbing down from their racks. If they had legs, they walked. If not, they dragged themselves across the floor using their arms and tugging their torsos behind them. It was a terrifying sight watching all that machinery creep toward us on its own, like some robotic army intent on humanity's destruction.

"What's happening?" I asked, eyes widening as the crawling frames slinked closer.

"Alexei's got this," Brody murmured. "He's sniped into the override protocols and activated the homunculi with motion capability. They'll subdue anyone he can't."

"Leave, Brody," it said over its shoulder. "And if you lose her in the penal maze, you'll answer to both myself and the Under-Secretary. It will not go well for you."

"Don't worry: I don't plan on losing her again," Brody said, hauling me after him.

I kicked at Brody's shin, trying to free myself. "Let go, ass-hole! I'm not your property!"

"Go with him, Felicia." This from the homunculus as it cast a final look at me. "I need you to leave."

I met the thing's eyes, and in that moment, I realized it...he...Alexei didn't want me to see what was coming next. Whatever his plan, it would be horrific and he would do things that couldn't be unseen. Things that would keep us safe, but would scar me if I witnessed them. Things I might not under-stand or forgive. He tried to be human for me, but to save us now, he needed to be a monster. So I gave up fighting Brody and went limp in his arms.

"Frankly, I don't want to see him in action either," he said in my ear.

"It shouldn't have to be like this. This is bullshit."

"If it gets us out of here, I'm not complaining," Brody said. "Now hold on, sweetheart, and save some of that earlier energy for later."

Sweetheart? "Why should I do anything you say?"

"Because the next few hours will be crazy what with our dar-ing prison break and the trip back to Mars."

Finally something that made sense! So I shut up, and let him lead me out.

23

Behind us, I heard horrific screams I wasn't sure I'd ever live to forget. I clung to Brody's hand and let him pull me after him. We ran headlong down badly lit concrete hallways that forked in multiple directions. The lower gravity on Phobos made it difficult to control where I ran, with my steps launching me in directions I didn't want to go. Brody was constantly yanking me after him, and pulling me back into place. To me, it felt like he chose pathways at random, darting down each with little warning. I jump-ran until my body ached as much as my bruised cheek. Eventually I stumbled and fell, tripped by the stupid canvas slip-ons.

Brody caught me before I could face-plant on the concrete. He pulled me up and against him, holding me hard to his chest.

"This place is a shifting maze," he explained as he stroked my back. "In the event of a prison break, the AI queenmind shifts the pieces to control prisoner movements. There's no such thing as a perfect jailing system so breakouts do happen, no matter what One Gov tells you."

"Then how do we get out?" I panted into his chest.

"Vieira gave me the access override codes to hack the queen-mind and the floor plan to the maze. I've essentially shut down the whole prison and we have ten minutes before the queen-mind automatically reboots it. In that time, we need to get to the launch area where the prisoner transfer jet is docked. Then I fly us out of here. Easy."

"And if it takes more than ten minutes?"

"Then we're crushed when the maze shifts and repositions it-self."

"Why not just create a system to put everyone back in their cells instead of killing them?"

"Because if you can escape Phobos, you don't get a second chance to redeem yourself. Death is the only option," he said, pushing me back onto my feet. "Can you run? I estimate we've just lost a minute on this informative chat."

I nodded grimly. "Can you really fly a jet?"

He grinned, apparently high on adrenaline. "Babe, I can fly anything."

We resumed running down more hallways, Brody leading us unerringly. At last, the screams behind us faded, either because we were too far away or Alexei had finished whatever he was doing. But then I could hear other sounds: the grinding of cement sliding against cement. In the distance at first, then much closer. Brody swept me up over his shoulder since I wasn't fast enough and kept bouncing everywhere in the awful low grav-ity. He put on a burst of speed that made me gasp and cling to him. I heard more walls shifting, sounding like it came from behind, beside, then on top of us. The floor beneath us began to tremble, then buck like a wild animal.

Abruptly we spilled out into another cavernous space. I saw yellow, red, blue, and black lines painted on the floor from my upside-down vantage point over Brody's shoulder. Then it felt like we were running up steps and into a darkened, confined corridor. Along the way, Brody smashed into every wall and conceivable piece of furniture in the universe, bumping me with him, both of us swearing like sailors. Eventually he dropped me then pushed me hard enough that I fell. I shrieked until my fall was abruptly halted by a cushioned chair under my butt.

"Strap yourself in. This is a one-way trip to Mars, taking us directly to the Under-Secretary's backyard. If we're lucky, no one will shoot us down."

"I'm not sure my luck's holding anymore," I muttered, searching for my shoulder strap then securing it in its buckle. I was in the cockpit of a jet, sitting in a high-backed black leather pilot's chair, surrounded by dials, buttons, and levers. In front of me was a pressurized window. Outside, I saw a launch bay door beginning to open. Beyond, the blackness of space and the blue-tinged Martian horizon.

"I was kind of hoping you'd be lucky enough for both of us." He flicked some switches and I could feel the jet rumble to life around us.

"Don't AI units do the flying?" I asked as he punched buttons.

"I want to be ready in case the weapons system outside the launch bay doors isn't offline and they start firing."

Great. "Just when I think I can stop worrying, up pops another disaster."

He grinned at me. "Hold on. It might get bumpy."

And he launched us into blackness.

I passed out from the g-forces pressing down on me. Not that Phobos had a huge escape velocity, but Brody wanted the speed to evade any automated weapons. Made sense, but it was damned uncomfortable with all that pressure squeezing me into my seat. Passing out had been a lovely blessing. I came to when I felt something being smoothed across my throbbing cheek. The pain faded to a dull ache until even that disappeared. I opened my eyes in time to see Brody plunk back in his seat.

"Web-compress and skin renewal patches," he said, scanning my face with a critical eye. "I found some on board and figured you could use them on that hit you took."

I touched my face self-consciously. "Thanks," I said. I looked out through the window to see Mars looming ahead of us. "How soon until we land?"

"Two or three hours. Doesn't seem like anyone's giving pursuit. I'm not picking up any chatter either, so we're clear." He tossed a hair band at me, both of us watching it float by in the zero-g. "You might want this. Your hair's all over the place."

"Oh, sorry." I took a few minutes to braid and secure my out-of-control hair. Then I tucked the braid into the back of my shirt. "Lotus keeps telling me to cut it."

"She doesn't know what she's talking about. I've always liked your hair," he said, eyes on me.

I looked away, watching Mars get closer, uncomfortable and not sure what to say. I checked with my gut, surprised to find no reaction. There we were, utterly alone together, with at least two hours before we landed, and nothing. Not one twinge, pull, tug, or kick. Absolutely nothing. Apparently now that I didn't need a knight in shining armor anymore, the pull had faded. The intense attraction was gone, tucked back into whatever box inside me it had escaped from. I was embarrassed by my own feelings and the fickleness of the luck gene.

"Do you want to talk about what happened?" he asked, tone deceptively neutral.

"I can guess. Belikov took me to coerce Alexei into testing the homunculus. Then he planned to transfer himself into his new body using Alexei's brain-transferring code. We'd all be dead and Consortium would have gone on to take over the tri-system, with everyone living in their new 'Built on Phobos' homunculus. Except you, Alexei, and my grandfather worked out a truce and got me back. Now we're safe, with the tri-system none the wiser. Does that sum it up?" I asked, studying my fingernails. My lovely sea foam green manicure hadn't survived all the excitement.

"No, I figured that stuff was obvious. I meant about what happened with us," he said patiently. "You and me."

No, I didn't want to talk about it. I felt too brittle and confused. "You're like Alexei. They engineered you with some off-the-charts MH Factor and t-mods, and hoped you'd be the next stage in human evolution. You were supposed to lead the Consortium to greatness, but that didn't work out. Did I guess right?"

He sighed. "Close enough."

"Can you pilot the homunculus too?"

"No. I was part of a different program, with altered physiological specs. Unlike Alexei, I'm closer to the base DNA."

"So you're more...human than he is?"

He shrugged. "I guess that's one way to look at it. With me, you wouldn't have the incompatibility issues that exist with Alexei."

"Meaning we could have a baby?"

"Meaning we could have everything, if you wanted it." And now I could see why my gut had reacted to Brody the way it had. As far as the luck gene was concerned, Brody was perfect. He could be everything I'd ever need.

"Why is there a difference between you?" I asked instead.

"My program was meant to infiltrate One Gov and take it down from the inside. Consortium who didn't seem like Consortium—that's what I was supposed to be. I can snipe into One Gov's queenmind like there's no tomorrow. With a little effort, I could probably dismantle the queenmind and cripple One Gov."

"Was that the plan for you?"

"Who knows? Konstantin scrapped the project. I do know I had no desire to run the Consortium. I didn't really want anything, just sort of coasted half-asleep through life until I met you. Then I woke up and realized there was something in the tri-system I wanted. Belikov wanted you too, mostly so he could splice your luck gene into the Consortium breeding pool. However, there was no way I was letting that happen. Belikov may have pointed me in your direction but from the first moment I saw you, I had no intention of letting him get his hands on you."

"And you ended up serving three years on Phobos for your trouble," I said, finally looking at him. "I'm sorry for that. I didn't know. If I had, I would have done something."

He chuckled softly. "I actually believe you. And you know,

I'm not angry about it. Well, I am, but not like I was. When Belikov approached me, I agreed to everything he wanted just to get off Phobos. I lived a miserable, hellish existence there. I lost time, my life, and part of myself. But when I saw you again, I just wanted to be near you. Maybe it's because I hated Belikov and his casual cruelty more. Or maybe not killing Alexei and taking over the Consortium makes me the biggest fool in the tri-system."

"I want to be mad at you, but I can't," I admitted. "You may have created this façade in Nairobi, but you didn't try to influence me or make me do anything I didn't want to do. You didn't try to recruit me for the Consortium or haul me into some secret scheme. You were there for me when I needed someone and made me want to start living again. That meant a lot to me. I don't want to tarnish that by hating you now."

He sighed. "You were never some task the Consortium assigned me. Being with you was one of the bright spots in my life." He reached up and pushed a few buttons on the dashboard, shutting off some of the blinking lights. "Vieira's offered me a position in One Gov. Maybe he did it out of pity, or maybe he has a use for me. I think I'll take him up on it since I'm pretty sure there isn't a place for me in the Consortium now." I felt him look at me. "Vieira said you agreed to work for him as well."

I shrugged. "The exotic Tarot card reader thing isn't doing it for me anymore."

"It means we'll be working together then. Probably seeing a lot of each other. We could be what we were before, if you wanted," he said softly. "In fact, it could start right now."

"I don't think that's a good idea."

"Why not? Is it as good with Alexei as it was with us, because what we had was amazing. It was simple, uncomplicated, and perfect. You know it was, Felicia. And it would be the easiest thing in the world to have that again."

I met his eyes because I couldn't say what I needed to say while looking down into my lap, afraid. "Maybe that's because we were both hiding who we really were. We didn't let ourselves worry about the big issues. Maybe if we had, it wouldn't have worked."

"You don't know that. How can you say that when we never even tried?"

I shook my head. "Maybe, but I can't do this with you. I love him."

"And you don't love me," he said flatly.

"Not the way I love him. I'm sorry."

He swore, his knuckles white as his hand gripped the throttle, as if he might snap it off the control panel. "How many times has he broken your heart already? How many more times will he smash it before you wake up and realize you're making a mistake?"

"Brody—"

"If that's the life you want, maybe you deserve it. All I know is I walked away when I shouldn't have and now I've lost four years with you because of that mistake. I can wait awhile longer because I know Alexei can't help but fuck things up with you again, but I can't wait forever."

I could think of absolutely no response to that, and because there was nowhere else to go in the tiny jet, we both sat in the cockpit, neither looking at the other. The rest of the trip passed in uncomfortable silence laced with my own guilt over being such a fickle, silly creature, which I decided was probably better than I deserved.

24

We landed in the Under-Secretary's backyard, beside the rosebushes, and nobody arrested us—which had to be a personal best for me.

Brody lowered the loading ramp and opened the hatch once we landed. Despite the tension, he helped me from my seat, checked the progress of the web-compress and skin renewal patch, and removed them when he said my bruise was gone. Then he escorted me out when my legs felt like rubber and wouldn't support me. He didn't have to do any of that, which proved his feelings went deeper than I realized and made me feel even worse. Then we were outside, with the autumn sun shining down on us from a cloudless sky. The lawn was torn up from the landing, but at least the roses were okay. Considering the week I'd spent pruning, I probably would have started crying if they'd been ruined.

I saw him then, standing beside Felipe and some others I couldn't take the time to recognize. He looked tense, anxious, and so rumpled, I wanted to tell him to comb his hair and put on another shirt. Then again how he looked didn't matter, only that he was there. I wanted to go to him, but walking felt impossible on my shaky legs. It became easier the longer I stood on solid ground, until I found I could creep toward him. He did the same, except he moved much more purposefully.

Alexei caught me in a hug that lifted me clear off the ground, holding me so tight, it almost hurt. I threw my arms around his neck, enjoying the feeling of his solidness, and the fact that he was *there*. If I was mad at him, I couldn't remember why. I couldn't recall what we'd fought about last or why it mattered or if it was going to matter in the future. All I wanted was his arms holding me as if I was the most important thing in his universe like he was in mine.

I started crying into his shirt—just awful, gasping sobs where I could barely catch my breath. I knew I looked terrible and probably smelled worse. I wanted to tell him to put me down because I was sweaty and gross, but I couldn't. All I could do was cling to him, afraid that if I let go, this might not be real and I'd be back in my jail cell.

"I want to go home," I whispered. "Please take me home."

"I am," he promised, cradling me against him.

This seemed like the best thing I'd heard in ages. I merely held on and trusted he would take me wherever I needed to be.

At one point I murmured, "I need to tell Felipe I'm okay."

"He knows. For now, only we matter."

I felt rather than saw him slide us into the flight-limo, marveling that he managed it without jarring me. Darkness closed around us, then I felt the tug in my stomach as we took off. I burrowed into him, my hands tucked between us, and my face pressed into the curve of his neck and shoulder while I huddled in his lap. I couldn't stop shivering, my body feeling like a tightly wound spring. One of his hands stroked my back in soothing circles. The other held my right foot, then my left, rubbing his thumb along the arch. Minutes passed as he massaged the feeling back into me and I'd thawed enough to relax against him.

Finally, I felt safe. Though I'd technically been rescued hours ago, it wasn't until I was in Alexei's arms that I could relax. Alexei—the cause of, and solution to, all my problems. He had the ability to make me feel worse and better all at once.

I raised my head so I could see the line of his jaw and a hint of stubble. I reached up to gently scrape a nail along it, enjoying the scratchy feeling I sometimes complained about, sighing and letting myself sink into him.

"What happened with Belikov?" I asked, my voice a whisper.

"I took care of him in the only way that would give us peace." As he spoke, he pulled my hair out from where I'd tucked it and unwound the strands until they flowed loosely down my back.

"Do I want to know what that means?"

"It means you're safe and I've dealt with any remaining leadership issues in the Consortium," he said, his lips brushing my temple.

"Is he dead?" I pressed.

"Yes. They are all dead."

I let out the breath I'd been holding, worrying a little that the only thing I felt was relief. "I know you didn't want me to see it. Are you okay with what you had to do?"

For a moment, the hand stopped moving on my back before the slow circles resumed. His voice was very bland and neutral when he said, "He betrayed my trust and ultimately wanted both of us dead. In the end, I did what was necessary to ensure we survived. Does knowing that bother you?"

"It should, but he wouldn't have stopped until he'd killed us. I'd rather we lived, not him," I decided as I absently ran my hand over his chest and smoothed the wrinkles in his shirt. "Is it all right to say I've had enough life-threatening situations and I'd like to pass on them in the future?"

I felt his chest move with a quiet chuckle. "Perfectly all right." His lips brushed my hair. "I talked to the Under-Secretary about what the Consortium's next move will be."

That made me blink. "I can't imagine you working together, never mind talking to each other."

"You'd be surprised. After all, I had to go through him to get to you; said he would arrest me if I approached you. I wasn't sure he could, but I didn't want to risk it. I spent all last week watching you prune roses."

"You watched me with the roses?" I asked, both mesmerized and shocked.

"I had to see you," he said, his nose running along my throat. "You looked so pretty and content. All I wanted was to go to you but he wouldn't allow it, so we talked. He told me some things, made some suggestions, and I've been sorting through Konstantin's memory blocks. It's been...illuminating. Things aren't quite as I believed them to be. I want Karol to run tests on my DNA, and yours, and see what he discovers."

I nodded, not sure what to say. All I knew was I felt this tiny burst of happiness in my chest that pushed out any remaining fear. It hurt and made my throat ache like I wanted to start crying. I didn't—gods knew I'd ugly cried enough over him already.

"I need to ask you something and I need you to tell me the truth," Alexei said, his hand stilling on my back. He turned my face to his, running his fingers gently over my cheek where the web-compress had been. "Do you want him? Is your gut still pulling you to him, because if it is, I need to know."

"No I don't, and that upsets me because I feel like a horrible person. Luck used him to force a particular set of events to occur then cut him loose. And if I did wonder 'what if,' it never had any substance because you were always what I wanted. I've never felt for anyone what I feel for you regardless of how I'm pulled in another direction."

"Did you ever think you were subverting your own luck, forcing it onto the path you wanted instead of the other way round? Wasn't that one of your mother's rules—that you could short-circuit your luck on another's behalf? If this was what you really wanted, you wouldn't accept any other options because, for you, this was your only choice."

"You know you make my head hurt when you get like this," I murmured.

Again he laughed softly, the sound rumbling in his chest. "It means I'm the one you want. The *only* one," he said, moving me so I straddled his thighs. Our eyes were level, locked on each other's. My hands curved around his shoulders so I could pull myself closer. His own hands slid under my hideous gray top, trailing over my ribs. Then he stopped, frowning. "What if I can't give you everything you want?"

I ran my fingers over his face, smoothing away his frown and the lines that came with it. "I don't need you to give me everything. I just need you to be by my side while we figure this all out."

Alexei gazed at me, his expression serious. "If that's what you believe, then we can try."

"Nothing like two science experiments conducting their own research," I agreed, running my fingers through his hair, loving that he was mine. "We can be...lab partners, working on a science project together."

He laughed out loud at that, his hands moving over my skin again. "When you put it like that, I don't see how this plan could fail. Maybe we should get a dog first," he suggested, arching an eyebrow. "For practice."

"Okay, we'll get a dog. A cute puff ball I can carry in my purse. You can take it for walkies."

He looked at me like I'd lost my mind. "I'm not walking a puff ball."

"Sure you are. It will be adorable. I'm enjoying visualizing this already."

He jerked me more securely into his lap and might have done more if the flight-limo hadn't begun its descent. Soon we were on the ground and we entered the house together.

I noticed the house was quiet, and clean. "I've moved everyone to other locations," he said as we climbed the stairs. "For those who'll be staying on Mars permanently, we needed more space."

In the bedroom, there was new furniture and the walls were white and bare. I didn't ask and he didn't explain. When I left that awful night and heard furniture smashing, I knew Alexei had been so upset and out of control, he didn't know what to do with the anger he'd felt. I couldn't fault him when it really had seemed like everything was falling apart.

While I looked, he lifted my arm and clicked something

onto my wrist. My c-tex bracelet, except not the one Novi destroyed. This was sleeker and more beautiful, with extra jeweled outlets. It had a shiny silver finish, but both the silver and the jewels changed color to match what I wore. Amazing, even if the outfit I wore happened to be prison grays.

"I had Karol make it," he said. "He transferred your data and your citizenship chip."

"Thank you," I breathed. "I wasn't sure what I would have done without it."

Rather than let me go, he pulled me closer until his arms were around me. Even as I leaned in and looped my arms about his waist, I murmured, "I need a shower. I feel disgusting."

"No," he said, and backed me up until my legs hit the edge of the bed. "You're perfect and I need you more than the shower does. Besides, I can't let you go."

"Then don't," I whispered, sliding my hands over his body, loving the feel of him. "I'm sorry I ran or made you feel like you like you couldn't be honest with me. I've never belonged to anyone the way I belong to you, and whatever the Consortium made you, I don't care. I love you and that isn't going to change."

"And I belong to you entirely. Nothing will come between us again. I love you too much to lose another second with you." He brought me flush against him, letting me know exactly how much I affected him. "And now we need to make up for lost time."

My eyes flew up to his. "I don't have a fertility inhibitor anymore."

"I know."

With that, he kissed me. It was so sweet and gentle, I sank into him, not resisting when he lowered me to the edge of the bed or carefully peeled off my clothes and kicked the offending things away.

"Burn those," I murmured.

"Consider them burned."

He removed his own clothing, then eased me back until we were both on the bed, lying on our sides atop the sheets. For long moments, we just looked at each other as if memorizing everything we might have forgotten about the other. We'd been apart before, but not like this, not when it seemed like events would break us forever. His hands traced my face, then moved over my body, caressing with slow, feathery touches and kisses. I sighed and arched against him, lost in the intimacy of the moment. I mirrored his touches, loving his groans when I took him in my hands and felt the throbbing heat of him, knowing no other woman could ever make him feel the way I did.

As if he could sense how much I needed to possess him, he rolled us so I was on top of him, straddling his hips. I gasped and put my hands on the hard muscles of his chest to catch my balance.

"I want to watch you," he whispered, his hands stroking my thighs and along my sides. "I want to feel you moving over me and see your face when you come. I would take anything you wanted to give just to be with you."

"Alexei—"

Rolling his hips skillfully under me, he made me gasp when he pressed a thumb against my clit. "Take what you want. I'm yours. Own me."

Maybe it was strange, but him giving the power to me when I'd recently been so powerless felt like the most erotic thing in the world. My body clenched with anticipation.

Taking his wrists—though the idea that I could ever hold him down was laughable—I pinned his arms over his head. His eyes narrowed but he let me, the muscles in his biceps flexing enticingly. Then I leaned down to kiss him, parting his lips with mine and dipping my tongue into his mouth. I pulled away when he thrust back or when I felt his hands open and close restlessly as if he couldn't help wanting to grab me.

"Don't or I'll stop," I threatened, running my tongue along the edge of his ear.

Immediately he settled, but I could feel the frustration in him. Flipping me onto my back and driving into me would be as easy as breathing for him. The fact that he didn't made me want to reward him.

I resumed kissing him, letting my breasts brush against his chest. As I did, my nipples tightened, aching for his touch. I scooted up until they hung over his mouth, brushing his lips. He took the obvious invitation, sucking one then the other. His tongue circled my nipple, his teeth gently scraping until I gasped and floundered against him, barely able to hold myself up as pleasure washed through me. That was when I noticed he'd freed a hand and stroked between my legs. He toyed with my clit, rubbing in a way that sent shocks of heat through me.

I gave him a stern look. "Keep it up and this stops," I warned, although gods knew I was so far gone, the threat had no bite.

With superhuman effort, he pulled his hands away and let them drift to my thighs, kneading the skin lightly. I leaned back, sliding down his body until I was over his hips. My hands flowed over him at the same time, loving the feel of him, all the power and strength under my palms. All of him, mine.

"I get off just looking at you," I whispered. "Sometimes I look at you and it's all I can do not to jump you. Anywhere. Anytime. That's how much I want you."

His hands tightened on my thighs. "Now, Felicia. I need to be in you *now*."

I arched away. "Not yet. I'm not ready."

"I can make you ready," he assured me.

"I don't doubt it. I've enjoyed your work before," I said, adjusting my position until my hips hovered over his. I placed a line of kisses down his chest and abs. "But until I'm ready, you'll have to wait."

He swore and stilled himself under me. I don't know why, but watching him struggle was so hot, I thought I might catch fire. Suddenly I was the one who couldn't wait. I raised myself up and took his straining erection in my hand until his tip brushed my opening. Taking a breath, I lowered myself onto him. This angle made him feel larger, making it a struggle. I could feel myself stretching to accommodate him and the bite of pleasure-pain was too much, making me doubt I could do this. He was almost too big like this, too deep. I whimpered, caught in that limbo of wanting him more than my own life and being afraid I couldn't handle him.

I felt his hands on my hips, pulling me down as he worked himself into me. My breath caught and I threw my head back as shudders racked my body. My arms flew behind me and I braced myself on his thighs, my back arching as I took all of him. I cried out at the feeling of being so full, the pain turning to pleasure as I held him inside me. I didn't want to move and have the sensation end, despite knowing what followed would be even better.

"You feel so good inside me," I whispered raggedly. "So good I can't even think."

I felt his hands tighten and spasm on my hips. "You are so fucking beautiful like this," he murmured. Then his hands began to stroke me, urging me onward. "Move for me. Let me see you come."

Slowly at first, with his hands guiding me up and easing me down, I rose and fell on him. Each move left me breathless, the rhythm uneven at first, until I was able to glide over him. Alexei told me how beautiful I was, how sexy, how he wanted no one but me, how much he loved me. His hands stroked me, the touches growing more heated. His hands had gone from my thighs to one bracing my back, the other stimulating my clit, caressing in steady circles my hips couldn't help but chase. The friction increased, my breathing growing unsteady.

He began to thrust, his hips rising to meet my downstrokes. The feel of him driving up to meet me while I came down on him was too much. It pushed me over an invisible ledge I didn't even realize I'd been standing on. I fell into a shattering climax that had my back bowing so deeply, it was a wonder I didn't fall over. It shook my entire body, making me clench helplessly around him and lose all sense of self. All I could do was feel as the orgasm whipped its way through me, turning me into a quivering mass atop him.

He flipped me onto my back, never missing a stroke while he continued his thrusts. As he controlled the speed and movements, they became more forceful, more powerful, and so, so deep. My orgasm had barely ended when another started to build. I clung to him, arms around his neck and legs at his waist. My heels dug into the backs of his thighs, arching my body up to his. His tempo increased, the thrusts so overwhelming, I knew I wouldn't be able to endure much more. Even as my orgasm built and threatened to crush me under a tidal wave of pleasure, I was sure I would drown.

When it broke over me, I screamed. My pleasure brought his, making him shout my name, clutching me so tightly to him, I thought he'd shatter me. It went on as both of us strained against each other, fighting to make it last. And even when it finished, we lay together, breathing each other's breath, sweat-soaked bodies locked together, neither wanting to separate from the other.

An eternity later, he eased off me, trailing kisses across my lips, cheek, and shoulder. I heard movement beside me, then he was back, turning us until we were on our sides. He brushed the hair from my face, looking at me so intensely, it hurt. In his other hand, he held the ring he'd given me, the one I hadn't seen since the night I'd stormed out.

"I'd like to give this back to you, if you want it. If it scares you, I can put it away and we forget it ever existed," he said.

I looked from the ring to his carefully neutral expression. It was the only clue I had to how anxious he was. In many ways, he knew me better than I knew myself, just like I could say about him. I smiled and brought my left hand between us.

"I want it. I never stopped wanting it even when I ran away," I said, and was rewarded with a smile that had me melting inside as he slipped the ring on my finger. Then he kissed the knuckles of my hand before looping my arm around his neck.

"Vieira said something similar. That your family had a tendency to run, and if I wanted you, I had to chase you. Little does he know I've already chased you halfway across the tri-system."

"Very funny!" I punched him in the shoulder, or tried to. He caught my arm and pinned it over my head the way I'd pinned his earlier. "Am I going to hear more of these pearls of wisdom in the future?"

"You might. You spent a week with the roses. It forced Vieira and me to talk about things we would never have discussed otherwise and decide how we wanted to shape the future."

"I see," I said, hoping I sounded unconcerned when I was anything but. "Were you dividing the tri-system up between you?"

Alexei made a noncommittal noise in his throat. Then he ran his lips over the curve of my shoulder, rolled me, and pinned my other arm over my head.

"He wanted to know when we were getting married and if he would be invited," he said instead. "I told him this week, and we'd think about it."

"What?" I tried to sit up, shocked. I couldn't with the way he pinned me, as if he'd planned it. "Are you out of your mind?"

"That's what he said, so we both agreed the following week would be better."

"What?" I shrieked again. "That isn't enough time!"

"Actually if the bride is willing, it should be more than enough," he said, placing hot, openmouthed kisses along my throat.

"But..." Two weeks to arrange a wedding? I couldn't do everything I needed to do in two weeks. Then again, what did I really need except him? "I'd want my family there—Lotus, Celeste, as many as you can round up," I heard myself say as if from a million miles away. My gut perked up with interest.

"Done."

"And I want a nice dress," I added, just so it was clear.

"Of course." He kicked my legs apart and settled himself

between them. "I've already arranged for that. And food, and a venue. And shoes."

Shoes, huh? "What about flowers?" I asked, testing him.

"Roses." He secured my wrists one-handed and lifted my leg until it was hitched around his waist. "Lots of roses."

He seemed so sure of me and so in control of everything, a small part of me couldn't help wanting to throw him. "So while you two were making plans for the foreseeable future, did it come up that I have a new job? What if I'm busy and can't get time off?"

The comment didn't even faze him, as if he'd anticipated that too. He merely lifted my other leg and raised my hips enough to open me to him. "Vieira told me about Venus. Told me he offered you a position in One Gov. Said you agreed to working with him."

"I want to do this, Alexei," I murmured against his shoulder. "Maybe I can fix what's broken in One Gov. Or maybe that's impossible and the Consortium should keep challenging it. I know you don't agree with One Gov, but I need you to be okay with my decision."

He pulled back enough so that our eyes met. "It may seem otherwise, but I don't know the future. That's your specialty. However, I have no doubt· you will turn the entire tri-system on its head and mesmerize all of them. I intend to be there to watch it happen."

I arched an eyebrow. "We're all working together now?"

"Did you imagine it would happen any other way?" he asked, sounding anything but innocent. "Once we start making Consortium-style changes to long-standing One Gov policies, I'm curious to see how we'll influence the tri-system. Personally, I'm looking forward to the reactions once we break down the heart of One Gov's bureaucracy."

"It sounds like you have it all worked out."

"Not everything. Some things will always be beyond my ability to control. You, for example. You are the one thing I can't predict but never want to be without." His hands tightened on me—the one around my wrists and the one now on my hip. The pressure was enough to let me know that, for now at least, he'd caught me and wasn't letting go. "Tell me this is what you want. That this is the life you want," he whispered.

"It is," I promised. "I want this. I want you. I want us."

"And I know you read the shims I sent. You know everything I am, everything I want, everything I think. I've given you all I have to give. There are no secrets left between us."

"And you need to keep doing that. So do I. We can't let anything drive us apart like this again."

"I swear to you we won't." His serious expression changed then, becoming a grin so wicked and hot, my breath caught. "Now focus, Felicia. In the spirit of sharing, I want us to try something I've been thinking about doing with you for some time. Pay attention, as I'd hate for you to miss what's happening next."

Breathless, I asked, "You sure I'm going to like it?"

The look he gave me was one full of dark promise. "You've read the shims. We both will. Ready?"

I could only nod and give myself over to him as his grip on me changed. I felt myself lifted before his lips slanted across mine. I wasn't sure what we were even talking about anymore—now, tomorrow, or the future in general. Maybe it was all three, and I could always check with my cards later. For now, I would just focus as I'd been advised and hold on to him for the ride of my life.

The story continues in...

THE GAME OF LUCK

BOOK THREE OF THE FELICIA SEVIGNY NOVELS

Coming in SEPTEMBER 2018

ACKNOWLEDGMENTS

Thanks to everyone who read the first book, liked it, and encouraged me with their support. Hopefully you'll like this one just as much. A special shout-out to my husband, Steve, who was smart enough to realize he had to give up announcing things like tub time and bedtime because he knew he couldn't enforce any of the rules.

No one ever really expects to write a sequel to their first novel, so another big thanks to my agent, Rena Rossner, for her support when I started doubting myself and wasn't sure I could do this. And an extra special thanks to my editor, Lindsey Hall, who helped me polish out all the rough patches and kept me on track when I was sure everything was going to go off the rails.

extras

orbit

meet the author

CATHERINE CERVENY was born in Peterborough, Ontario. She'd always planned to move away to the big city but the small-town life got its hooks in her and that's where she still resides today. Catherine is a huge fan of romance and science fiction and wishes the two genres would cross paths more often. *The Rule of Luck* was her first novel.

if you enjoyed
THE CHAOS OF LUCK

look out for

SIX WAKES

by

Mur Lafferty

A spaceship far from Earth. A murdered crew. And a clone who must find her own killer—before they strike again.

Maria Arena awakens in a cloning vat streaked with drying blood. She has no memory of how she died. This is new; before, when she had awakened as a new clone, her first memory was of how she died.

Maria's vat is one of six, each one holding the clone of a crew member of the starship Dormire, *each clone waiting for its previous incarnation to die so it can awaken. And Maria isn't the only one to die recently...*

THIS IS NOT A PIPE

Sound struggled to make its way through the thick synth-amneo fluid. Once it reached Maria Arena's ears, it sounded like a chain saw: loud, insistent, and unending. She couldn't make out the words, but it didn't sound like a situation she wanted to be involved in.

Her reluctance at her own rebirth reminded her where she was, and who she was. She grasped for her last backup. The crew had just moved into their quarters on the *Dormire*, and the cloning bay had been the last room they'd visited on their tour. There they had done their first backup on the ship.

Maria must have been in an accident or something soon after, killing her and requiring her next clone to wake. Sloppy use of a life wouldn't make a good impression on the captain, who likely was the source of the angry chain-saw noise.

Maria finally opened her eyes. She tried to make sense of the dark round globules floating in front of her vat, but it was difficult with the freshly cloned brain being put to work for the first time. There were too many things wrong with such a mess.

With the smears on the outside of the vat and the purple color through the bluish fluid Maria floated in, she figured the orbs were blood drops. Blood shouldn't float. That was the first problem. If blood was floating, that meant the grav drive that spun the ship had failed. That was probably another reason someone was yelling. The blood and the grav drive.

Blood in a cloning bay, that was different too. Cloning bays were pristine, clean places, where humans were downloaded into newly cloned bodies when the previous ones had died. It was much cleaner and less painful than human birth, with all its screaming and blood.

Again with the blood.

The cloning bay had six vats in two neat rows, filled with blue-tinted synth-amneo fluid and the waiting clones of the rest of the crew. Blood belonged in the medbay, down the hall. The unlikely occurrence of a drop of blood originating in the medbay, floating down the hall, and entering the cloning bay to float in front of Maria's vat would be extraordinary. But that's not what happened; a body floated above the blood drops. A number of bodies, actually.

Finally, if the grav drive *had* failed, and if someone *had* been injured in the cloning bay, another member of the crew would have cleaned up the blood. Someone was always on call to ensure a new clone made the transition from death into their new body smoothly.

No. A perfect purple sphere of blood shouldn't be floating in front of her face.

Maria had now been awake for a good minute or so. No one worked the computer to drain the synth-amneo fluid to free her.

A small part of her brain began to scream at her that she should be more concerned about the bodies, but only a small part.

She'd never had occasion to use the emergency release valve inside the cloning vats. Scientists had implemented them after some techs had decided to play a prank on a clone, and woke her up only to leave her in the vat alone for hours. When she had gotten free, stories said, the result was messy and violent, resulting in the fresh cloning of some of the techs. After that, engineers added an interior release switch for clones to let themselves out of the tank if they were trapped for whatever reason.

Maria pushed the button and heard a *clunk* as the release triggered, but the synth-amneo fluid stayed where it was.

A drain relied on gravity to help the fluid along its way. Plumbing 101 there. The valve was opened but the fluid remained a stubborn womb around Maria.

She tried to find the source of the yelling. One of the crew floated near the computer bank, naked, with wet hair stuck out in a frightening, spiky corona. Another clone woke. Two of them had died?

Behind her, crewmates floated in four vats. All of their eyes were open, and each was searching for the emergency release. Three *clunk*s sounded, but they remained in the same position Maria was in.

Maria used the other emergency switch to open the vat door. Ideally it would have been used after the fluid had drained away, but there was little ideal about this situation. She and a good quantity of the synth-amneo fluid floated out of her vat, only to collide gently with the orb of blood floating in front of her. The surface tension of both fluids held, and the drop bounced away.

Maria hadn't encountered the problem of how to get out of a liquid prison in zero-grav. She experimented by flailing about, but only made some fluid break off the main bubble and go floating away. In her many lives, she'd been in more than one undignified situation, but this was new.

Action and reaction, she thought, and inhaled as much of the oxygen-rich fluid as she could, then forced everything out of her lungs as if she were sneezing. She didn't go as fast as she would have if it had been air, because she was still inside viscous fluid, but it helped push her backward and out of the bubble. She inhaled air and then coughed and vomited the rest of the fluid in a spray in front of her, banging her head on the computer console as her body's involuntary movements propelled her farther.

Finally out of the fluid, and gasping for air, she looked up.

"Oh shit."

Three dead crewmates floated around the room amid the blood and other fluids. Two corpses sprouted a number of gory tentacles, bloody bubbles that refused to break away from the deadly wounds. A fourth was strapped to a chair at the terminal.

Gallons of synth-amneo fluid joined the gory detritus as the newly cloned crew fought to exit their vats. They looked with as much shock as she felt at their surroundings.

Captain Katrina de la Cruz moved to float beside her, still focused on the computer. "Maria, stop staring and make yourself useful. Check on the others."

Maria scrambled for a handhold on the wall to pull herself away from the captain's attempt to access the terminal.

Katrina pounded on a keyboard and poked at the console screen. "IAN, what the hell happened?"

"My speech functions are inaccessible," the computer's male, slightly robotic voice said.

"*Ceci n'est pas une pipe,*" muttered a voice above Maria. It broke her shock and reminded her of the captain's order to check on the crew.

The speaker was Akihiro Sato, pilot and navigator. She had met him a few hours ago at the cocktail party before the launch of the *Dormire*.

"Hiro, why are you speaking French?" Maria said, confused. "Are you all right?"

"Someone saying aloud that they can't talk is like that old picture of a pipe that says, 'This is not a pipe.' It's supposed to give art students deep thoughts. Never mind." He waved his hand around the cloning bay. "What happened, anyway?"

"I have no idea," she said. "But—God, what a mess. I have to go check on the others."

"Goddammit, you just spoke," the captain said to the computer, dragging some icons around the screen. "Something's working inside there. Talk to me, IAN."

"My speech functions are inaccessible," the AI said again, and de la Cruz slammed her hand down on the keyboard, grabbing it to keep herself from floating away from it.

Hiro followed Maria as she maneuvered around the room using the handholds on the wall. Maria found herself face-to-face with the gruesome body of Wolfgang, their second in command. She gently pushed him aside, trying not to dislodge the gory bloody tentacles sprouting from punctures on his body.

She and Hiro floated toward the living Wolfgang, who was doubled over coughing the synth-amneo out of his lungs. "What the hell is going on?" he asked in a ragged voice.

"You know as much as we do," Maria said. "Are you all right?"

He nodded and waved her off. He straightened his back, gaining at least another foot on his tall frame. Wolfgang was born on the moon colony, Luna, several generations of his family developing the long bones of living their whole lives in low gravity. He took a handhold and propelled himself toward the captain.

"What do you remember?" Maria asked Hiro as they approached another crewmember.

"My last backup was right after we boarded the ship. We haven't even left yet," Hiro said.

Maria nodded. "Same for me. We should still be docked, or only a few weeks from Earth."

"I think we have more immediate problems, like our current status," Hiro said.

"True. Our current status is four of us are dead," Maria said, pointing at the bodies. "And I'm guessing the other two are as well."

"What could kill us all?" Hiro asked, looking a bit green as he dodged a bit of bloody skin. "And what happened to me and the captain?"

He referred to the "other two" bodies that were not floating in the cloning bay. Wolfgang, their engineer, Paul Seurat, and Dr. Joanna Glass all were dead, floating around the room, gently bumping off vats or one another.

Another cough sounded from the last row of vats, then a soft voice. "Something rather violent, I'd say."

"Welcome back, Doctor, you all right?" Maria asked, pulling herself toward the woman.

The new clone of Joanna nodded, her tight curls glistening with the synth-amneo. Her upper body was thin and strong, like all new clones, but her legs were small and twisted. She glanced up at the bodies and pursed her lips. "What happened?" She didn't wait for them to answer, but grasped a handhold and pulled herself toward the ceiling where a body floated.

"Check on Paul," Maria said to Hiro, and followed Joanna.

The doctor turned her own corpse to where she could see it, and her eyes grew wide. She swore quietly. Maria came up behind her and swore much louder.

Her throat had a stab wound, with great waving gouts of blood reaching from her neck. If the doctor's advanced age was any indication, they were well past the beginning of the mission. Maria remembered her as a woman who looked to be in her thirties, with smooth dark skin and black hair. Now wrinkles lined the skin around her eyes and the corners of her mouth, and gray shot through her tightly braided hair. Maria looked at the other bodies; from her vantage point she could now see each also showed their age.

"I didn't even notice," she said, breathless. "I—I only noticed the blood and gore. We've been on this ship for *decades*. Do you remember anything?"

"No." Joanna's voice was flat and grim. "We need to tell the captain."

* * *

"No one touch anything! This whole room is a crime scene!" Wolfgang shouted up to them. "Get away from that body!"

"Wolfgang, the crime scene, if this is a crime scene, is already contaminated by about twenty-five hundred gallons of synth-amneo," Hiro said from outside Paul's vat. "With blood spattering everywhere."

"What do you mean *if* it's a crime scene?" Maria asked. "Do you think that the grav drive died and stopped the ship from spinning and then knives just floated into us?"

Speaking of the knife, it drifted near the ceiling. Maria propelled herself toward it and snatched it before it got pulled against the air intake filter, which was already getting clogged with bodily fluids she didn't even want to think about.

The doctor did as Wolfgang had commanded, moving away from her old body to join him and the captain. "This is murder," she said. "But Hiro's right, Wolfgang, there is a reason zero-g forensics never took off as a science. The air filters are sucking up the evidence as we speak. By now everyone is covered in everyone else's blood. And now we have six new people and vats of synth-amneo floating around the bay messing up whatever's left."

Wolfgang set his jaw and glared at her. His tall, thin frame shone with the bluish amneo fluid. He opened his mouth to counter the doctor, but Hiro interrupted them.

"Five," interrupted Hiro. He coughed and expelled more synth-amneo, which Maria narrowly dodged. He grimaced in apology. "Five new people. Paul's still inside." He pointed to their engineer, who remained in his vat, eyes closed.

Maria remembered seeing his eyes open when she was in her own vat. But now Paul floated, eyes closed, hands covering his genitals, looking like a child who was playing hide-and-seek and whoever was "It" was going to devour him. He too was pale, naturally stocky, lightly muscled instead of the heavier man Maria remembered.

"Get him out of there," Katrina said. Wolfgang obliged, going to another terminal and pressing the button to open the vat.

Hiro reached in and grabbed Paul by the wrist and pulled him and his fluid cage free.

"Okay, only five of us were out," Maria said, floating down. "That cuts the synth-amneo down by around four hundred gallons. Not a huge improvement. There's still a lot of crap flying around. You're not likely to get evidence from anything except the bodies themselves." She held the knife out to Wolfgang, gripping the edge of the handle with her thumb and forefinger. "And possibly the murder weapon."

He looked around, and Maria realized he was searching for something with which to take the knife. "I've already contaminated it with my hands, Wolfgang. It's been floating among blood and dead bodies. The only thing we'll get out of it is that it probably killed us all."

"We need to get IAN back online," Katrina said. "Get the grav drive back on. Find the other two bodies. Check on the cargo. Then we will fully know our situation."

Hiro whacked Paul smartly on the back, and the man doubled over and retched, sobbing. Wolfgang watched with disdain as Paul bounced off the wall with no obvious awareness of his surroundings.

"Once we get IAN back online, we'll have him secure a channel to Earth," Katrina said.

"My speech functions are inaccessible," the computer repeated. The captain gritted her teeth.

"That's going to be tough, Captain," Joanna said. "These bodies show considerable age, indicating we've been in space for much longer than our mindmaps are telling us."

Katrina rubbed her forehead, closing her eyes. She was silent, then opened her eyes and began typing things into the terminal. "Get Paul moving, we need him."

Hiro stared helplessly as Paul continued to sob, curled into a little drifting ball, still trying to hide his privates.

A ball of vomit—not the synth-amneo expelled from the bodies, but actual stomach contents—floated toward the air intake vent and was sucked into the filter. Maria knew that after they took care of all of the captain's priorities, she would still be stuck with the job of changing the air filters, and probably crawling through the ship's vents to clean all of the bodily fluids out before they started to become a biohazard. Suddenly a maintenance-slash-junior-engineer position on an important starship didn't seem so glamorous.

"I think Paul will feel better with some clothes," Joanna said, looking at him with pity.

"Yeah, clothes sound good," Hiro said. They were all naked, their skin rising in goose bumps. "Possibly a shower while we're at it."

"I will need my crutches or a chair," Joanna said. "Unless we want to keep the grav drive off."

"Stop it," Katrina said. "The murderer could still be on the ship and you're talking about clothes and showers?"

Wolfgang waved a hand to dismiss her concern. "No,

clearly the murderer died in the fight. We are the only six aboard the ship."

"You can't know that," de la Cruz said. "What's happened in the past several decades? We need to be cautious. No one goes anywhere alone. Everyone in twos. Maria, you and Hiro get the doctor's crutches from the medbay. She'll want them when the grav drive gets turned back on."

"I can just take the prosthetics off that body," Joanna said, pointing upward. "It won't need them anymore."

"That's evidence," Wolfgang said, steadying his own floating corpse to study the stab wounds. He fixated on the bubbles of gore still attached to his chest. "Captain?"

"Fine, get jumpsuits, get the doctor a chair or something, and check on the grav drive," Katrina said. "The rest of us will work. Wolfgang, you and I will get the bodies tethered together. We don't want them to sustain more damage when the grav drive comes back online."

On the way out, Maria paused to check on her own body, which she hadn't really examined before. It seemed too gruesome to look into your own dead face. The body was strapped to a seat at one of the terminals, drifting gently against the tether. A large bubble of blood drifted from the back of her neck, where she had clearly been stabbed. Her lips were white and her skin was a sickly shade of green. She now knew where the floating vomit had come from.

"It looks like I was the one who hit the resurrection switch," she said to Hiro, pointing to her body.

"Good thing too," Hiro said. He looked at the captain, conversing closely with Wolfgang. "I wouldn't expect a medal anytime soon, though. She's not looking like she's in the mood."

The resurrection switch was a fail-safe button. If all of the clones on the ship died at once, a statistical improbability, then the AI should have been able to wake up the next clones. If the ship failed to do so, an even higher statistical improbability, then a physical switch in the cloning bay could carry out the job, provided there was someone alive enough to push it.

Like the others, Maria's body showed age. Her middle had softened and her hands floating above the terminal were thin and spotted. She had been the physical age of thirty-nine when they had boarded.

"I gave you an order," Katrina said. "And Dr. Glass, it looks like talking our engineer down will fall to you. Do it quickly, or else he's going to need another new body when I'm through with him."

Hiro and Maria got moving before the captain could detail what she was going to do to them. Although, Maria reflected, it would be hard to top what they had just apparently been through.

Maria remembered the ship as shinier and brighter: metallic and smooth, with handholds along the wall for low-gravity situations and thin metal grates making up the floor, revealing a subfloor of storage compartments and vents. Now it was duller, another indication that decades of spaceflight had changed the ship as it had changed the crew. It was darker, a few lights missing, illuminated by the yellow lights of an alert. Someone—probably the captain—had commanded an alert.

Some of the previous times, Maria had died in a controlled environment. She had been in bed after illness, age, or, once, injury. The helpful techs had created a final mindmap of her brain, and she had been euthanized after signing a form permitting it. A doctor had approved it, the body was disposed of neatly, and she had woken up young, pain-free, with all her memories of all her lives thus far.

Some other times hadn't been as gentle, but still were a better experience than this.

Having her body still hanging around, blood and vomit everywhere, offended her on a level she hadn't thought possible. Once you were gone, the body meant nothing, had no sentimental value. The future body was all that mattered. The past shouldn't be there, staring you in the face with dead eyes. She shuddered.

"When the engines get running again, it'll warm up," Hiro said helpfully, mistaking the reason for her shiver.

They reached a junction, and she led the way left. "Decades, Hiro. We've been out here for decades. What happened to our mindmaps?"

"What's the last thing you remember?" he asked.

"We had the cocktail party in Luna station as the final passengers were entering cryo and getting loaded. We came aboard. We were given some hours to move into our quarters. Then we had the tour, which ended in the cloning bay, getting our updated mindmaps."

"Same here," he said.

"Are you scared?" Maria said, stopping and looking at him.

She hadn't scrutinized him since waking up in the cloning bay. She was used to the way that clones with the experience of hundreds of years could look like they had just stepped out of university. Their bodies woke up at peak age, twenty years old, designed to be built with muscle. What the clones did with that muscle once they woke up was their challenge.

Akihiro Sato was a thin Pan Pacific United man of Japanese descent with short black hair that was drying in stiff cowlicks. He had lean muscles, and high cheekbones. His eyes were black, and they met hers with a level gaze. She didn't look too closely at the rest of him; she wasn't rude.

He pulled at a cowlick, then tried to smooth it down. "I've woken up in worse places."

"Like where?" she asked, pointing down the hall from where they had come. "What's worse than that horror movie scene?"

He raised his hands in supplication. "I don't mean literally. I mean I've lost time before. You have to learn to adapt sometimes. Fast. I wake up. I assess the immediate threat. I try to figure out where I was last time I uploaded a mindmap. This time I woke up in the middle of a bunch of dead bodies, but there was no threat that I could tell." He cocked his head, curious. "Haven't you ever lost time before? Not even a week? Surely you've died between backups."

"Yes," she admitted. "But I've never woken up in danger, or in the wake of danger."

"You're still not in danger," he said. "That we know of."
She stared at him.

if you enjoyed
THE CHAOS OF LUCK
look out for
THE IMMORTALS
by
Jordanna Max Brodsky

*Manhattan has many secrets. Some are older than
the city itself.*

*The city sleeps. Selene DiSilva walks her dog along the
banks of the Hudson. She is alone—just the way she likes it.
She doesn't believe in friends, and she doesn't speak to her
family. Most of them are simply too dangerous.*

*In the predawn calm, Selene finds the body of a young
woman washed ashore, gruesomely mutilated and wreathed
in laurel. Her ancient rage returns. And so does the memory
of a promise she made long ago—when her name
was Artemis.*

PUNISHER

Selene DiSilva crouched in a narrow alley between two run-down apartment buildings, watching the street. When she'd begun her vigil hours before, the smells of roasting chicken and frying plantains had wafted from the surrounding apartments. Families laughed and bickered, doors slammed, cars honked. But in the small hours of the morning, the only scents were those from the trashcans overflowing nearby, and the street before her lay nearly deserted. Even in the city that never slept, there were quiet corners like this: a forgotten neighborhood perched at Manhattan's northernmost tip. Here, most people obeyed the ancient human instinct to seek refuge from the dark. But not Selene—and not the man she'd been sent to hunt.

A single dark SUV rolled by, a wave of Caribbean hip-hop pouring through the open window to briefly shatter the silence. From her hiding place, Selene peered at the driver, but let him pass unmolested.

Later, a group of swaggering young men strolled along the street, laughing and shoving as they claimed the sidewalk for themselves. Selene watched them carefully but didn't move. Then two women passed her alley, speaking in slurred Spanish, their eyes purple with fatigue. She felt no empathy—as usual, she'd slept all day and only awoken with the moonrise.

Finally, a solitary figure appeared at the far end of the block. Long before she could see his face, Selene knew him by his stride. *Chin forward and shoulders high like he's looking for a fight,* she thought, *but only with someone he's sure he can beat.*

She glanced at the apartment building across the street—a wide 1920s façade, its art deco grandeur long since gone. A window on the third floor flickered blue behind thin curtains. Jackie Ortiz was awake and watching TV, just as Selene had instructed.

She stood up slowly as the man approached the building. Mario Velasquez. Medium height—shorter than her own six feet—but broad across the shoulders, his muscles bulkier than hers. He wore a rhinestone-studded cross on a thick gold chain around his neck and kept his hands shoved into the front pocket of his sweatshirt. She couldn't be sure if he was armed or not, but she'd find out soon enough.

She could see his face now, the same one she'd been stalking for a week: high cheekbones and a neat goatee, dark skin that made his light blue stare all the more alluring. *Once again,* she thought, *a woman falls for a pair of pretty eyes and never bothers to find out what's behind them.*

Mario stopped opposite Jackie's building. Looking up at her window, he pulled a cell phone from his pocket. Selene couldn't make out his murmured conversation, but she recognized the aggravation in the rising pitch of his voice. It wouldn't be long before he started throwing punches.

She let the tiniest of smiles cross her lips. She was, after all, going to enjoy this.

Mario stepped into the building's small vestibule. Through the cloudy glass of the front door, Selene watched him jab repeatedly at the buzzer for Jackie's apartment. Next to him stood a doorman's podium. *Just for show,* Selene knew. No lobby guard would appear to protect Jackie from her boyfriend. Her only defense was a weak lock on the building's inner door and the woman she'd hired to strike Mario down.

Selene crossed the street and waited just out of Mario's sight. *Come on, Jackie,* she urged silently. *Be brave.* The young woman appeared in the vestibule, closing the inner door behind her so that Mario couldn't get upstairs. Selene tensed, ready to spring forward. *But not yet, not yet.*

Jackie, short and skinny, looked even younger than her twenty-two years. She'd made a vain attempt to cover her swollen black eye with a smear of turquoise shadow. One hand nervously twirled a lock of dyed blond hair. She held her other arm across her body like a shield. Mario flashed her a smile and sneaked a quick kiss on her neck. Jackie shuddered—whether with delight or fear, Selene couldn't tell. Then he took a step closer, and the woman put a hand on his chest, pushing him away. He kept coming, backing her into a corner, still smiling despite Jackie's protests. He rested one hand possessively on her neck and hooked the other around the white leather belt at her waist, pulling her against him. Jackie struggled in his grip, her eyes darting back and forth, searching for Selene.

Just a moment more, Selene thought, *so the police have evidence.* Then it happened, quick as a snake bite: Mario slapped Jackie across the face.

Selene yanked open the outer door and put a light hand on Mario's shoulder. Still holding on to Jackie's belt, he turned to the intruder.

"Hey, Mario," Selene said with her best attempt at casual courtesy. She didn't want to antagonize him until Jackie was safe.

"Who the fuck are you?"

"You don't recognize me?" Selene gave him what she hoped was an alluring smile.

His defensiveness dissolved as quickly as it had appeared. He made a low sound of pleasure, like a man savoring some succulent morsel. Jackie slipped from his loosened grip as he turned all of his attention toward Selene. His eyes traveled appreciatively over her body, seeing past her loose cargo pants to the long, lean legs underneath. "If I'd nailed you, I think I'd remember." Unnoticed, Jackie scurried back through the inner door and pulled it shut behind her.

"Perhaps." Selene nodded with exaggerated thoughtfulness. "But considering the number of women you're currently sleeping with, perhaps not."

"What do you know about—"

"Lyla? Miriam? Fatima?" She ticked them off one by one on her fingers. "Raquel? Yolanda? And, of course, Jackie. Although you don't sleep with Jackie so much as beat her up, so I'm not sure I should count her."

Mario put his hand in his sweatshirt pocket and didn't draw it back out. *A knife,* Selene decided. *Hopefully not a gun.*

"You a cop?" he asked. "Not at the moment."

"Then back away, lady. Mind your own business."

"It's my business to keep you away from her."

He smirked. "And how you going to do that?"

Selene drilled a right hook into his face, spinning him away, then a left into his kidney. With great satisfaction, she watched a line of bloody spittle drip from his mouth onto the floor as he doubled over. But Mario recovered quickly, coming upright with a long, serrated hunting knife in his hand. He barreled toward her. She sidestepped him easily, thrusting out a foot to send him stumbling forward into the opposite wall. Before he could regain his balance, she jabbed an elbow into his spine, bringing all her superior height to bear. Mario grunted and dropped the knife but stayed on his feet. Faster than she'd anticipated, he spun toward her and kicked her hard in the knee.

Biting back a yelp of pain, she fell, slamming the injured knee into the ground. He kicked again, striking her in the jaw. Her teeth sliced the inside of her cheek; she tasted blood. Cold panic rushed through her veins as a third kick smashed into her ribs, knocking the breath from her body. Vision wavering, she reached across the floor toward the fallen knife—Mario beat her to it, bringing the blade down in a slicing arc toward her face. She moved her head just in time to prevent losing her nose; the knife whistled through the air beside her ear and struck the tiled wall with a sharp ping.

"You're going to wish you hadn't gotten in my way, *puta*." He kicked her backward and kneeled over her body, pinning her in place. For decades, she'd been dreading this moment—the fight she couldn't win, the woman she couldn't protect. *Have I finally grown so weak that a mere man can defeat me?*

"Who do you think you are?" he demanded, raising the knife once more.

Selene grabbed his upraised wrist. "You wouldn't believe me if I told you," she gasped, her arm shaking with the effort of holding him off.

"Try me."

A hundred names came to mind, whispered in long-forgotten tongues, but she couldn't lay claim to a single one. Not any longer.

Mario laughed at her silence and waved the knife just out of her reach. "Don't even know your own name, huh? Guess it's true—the hot ones *are* dumb."

One look at his grinning face burned away Selene's self-pity. As he leaned forward, ready to strike, his rhinestone cross swayed above her. The symbol of everything she'd lost, everything she despised. She allowed herself a quick second to imagine grabbing it and punching it through his pretty blue eye. Then she hooked the base of the doorman's podium with her foot and brought it crashing down on Mario's head instead.

He collapsed, unconscious, on top of her.

Jackie rushed back into the vestibule. She stopped a few feet away from Mario, her hand to her mouth. "Did you kill him?"

"Unfortunately, no," Selene wheezed from beneath his bulk. To her dismay, it took Jackie's help to free her from the dead weight.

She slipped a length of wire from her pocket and tied Mario's wrists together.

Jackie stared at Selene's face, wincing. "Damn, you okay?"

Selene raised a hand to her throbbing jaw, wondering just how bad it looked.

"I already called the cops," Jackie went on, as if that would make Selene feel better.

"I told you to wait until I was gone," she said, more angrily than she'd intended.

"I saw him kicking you. Then I saw him holding that knife over you like he was going to slice off your eyebrows." Jackie put her hands on her hips. "Was I supposed to just let him carve you up?"

"Yes, that's exactly what you're supposed to do. I make myself the target so you don't have to." She looked at the red handprint on Jackie's cheek. "At least . . . not anymore."

"The cops will be here in five minutes. They're bringing an ambulance. You sure you shouldn't get your face looked at?"

"Don't worry about me. Just make sure to tell the cops that this time you're pressing charges. And tell Mario that if he ever threatens you again, the police are going to be the least of his worries."

Jackie looked down at her boyfriend. "He's not going to be a vegetable when he wakes up, is he?"

Selene just shrugged.

"I mean, I didn't think about that before, but the podium made this sound when it hit his head. . . like a *thunk*, like a wet *thunk*."

Selene stared at the young woman for a moment, a scowl creasing her forehead. "What're you doing?"

Jackie looked up. "I just—"

"You're worried about him."

"He's not just a—"

"Have you already forgotten our agreement?" Selene couldn't keep the acid from her voice. "I protect you, just like I protect all the women who come to me. And all I ask in return is two promises: You won't tell the cops about me, and you won't hook up with assholes again." Jackie opened her mouth to protest but Selene cut her off. "You want to get down on your knees and tell him you're sorry. I can see it in your face."

Jackie huffed indignantly. "I asked you to get him away from me, not to tell me what to feel."

Selene tried to summon the fury that had once defined her life. Instead, she just felt tired. She'd heard it all before—thousands of times over thousands of years. "If you go near

Mario again, you're on your own," she said wearily, opening the door.

Limping down the sidewalk with her head down and shoulders hunched, she listened to the approaching sirens. She ran her fingers along the swollen bruise on her jaw and the tender spot on her ribs where she'd been kicked. The pain in her knee flared with every step she took. In the moment before she knocked the podium into Mario's head, she'd been in real danger, as vulnerable and helpless as the women it was her duty to protect. If he'd had a gun instead of a knife, Selene would be the one waiting for an ambulance.

And what would happen then? she wondered. *If a man put a bullet through my skull, would my tenuous hold on immortality finally rip free?*

She looked up at the moon, a hazy crescent just discernable between the buildings, heading toward its daily oblivion beneath the horizon. *And if I die—so what? The goddess Artemis vanished a long time ago. What's left of her is nothing but shadows and memories. Both disappear with time.*

Maybe I should, too.

Then, despite the balmy air, a sudden shiver crawled along her arms, as if from a distant shriek more felt than heard.

In another age, she might have recognized the sensation as a summons. She might have listened more closely to the prayer upon the wind. She might have heard the anguished cry of a woman in mortal danger, far away on the other side of the city, calling out for the goddess who might save her.

Now, Selene merely grimaced and zipped her leather jacket a little higher beneath her chin.